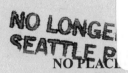
"I don't know what's right for the first time in my life. I really don't know what's right," Adam said.

"I'm sorry. I just can't wrap my head around this. Is it horrible of me not to want to lose my home?" Georgia asked.

"No. Of course not."

"And I'm going to blame you for it. No matter how well-intended, how do I not blame you?"

"Do we have to do this right here, right now?"

"Why? Are you going somewhere? What else do we have to do?"

"This." He placed a hand on the back of her head and pulled her into him. With the other hand, he softly cradled her face. She couldn't resist this kiss if she wanted to. And God help her, she did not want to. . . .

Books by Mary Carter

SHE'LL TAKE IT
ACCIDENTALLY ENGAGED
SUNNYSIDE BLUES
MY SISTER'S VOICE
THE PUB ACROSS THE POND
THE THINGS I DO FOR YOU
THREE MONTHS IN FLORENCE

Books by Laura Florand

THE CHOCOLATE THIEF
THE CHOCOLATE KISS
THE CHOCOLATE TOUCH
THE CHOCOLATE HEART

Books by Kat Martin

DEEP BLUE
DESERT HEAT
THE DREAM
HOT RAIN
MIDNIGHT SUN
THE SECRET
THE SILENT ROSE

Published by Kensington Publishing Corporation

No Place Like Home

LINDA LAEL MILLER

KAT MARTIN

MARY CARTER
LAURA FLORAND

ZEBRA BOOKS
KENSINGTON PUBLISHING CORP.
http://www.kensingtonbooks.com

ZEBRA BOOKS are published by

Kensington Publishing Corp.
119 West 40th Street
New York, NY 10018

All Kensington titles, imprints, and distributed lines are available at
special quantity discounts for bulk purchases for sales promotion,
premiums, fund-raising, educational, or institutional use.

Special book excerpts or customized printings can also be created
to fit specific needs. For details, write or phone the office of the
Kensington Special Sales Manager: Attn. Special Sales Department. Kensington Publishing Corp., 119 West 40th Street, New
York, NY 10018. Phone: 1-800-221-2647.

Zebra and the Z logo Reg. U.S. Pat. & TM Off.

ISBN-13: 978-1-4201-3253-3
ISBN-10: 1-4201-3253-9
First Printing: December 2013

eISBN-13: 978-1-4201-3257-1
eISBN-10: 1-4201-3257-1
First Electronic Edition: December 2013

10 9 8 7 6 5 4 3 2 1

Printed in the United States of America

CONTENTS

THE CHRISTMAS CAROUSEL

Mary Carter

CHAPTER ONE

Holiday traditions are as unique and varied as the families who celebrate them. Especially Christmas traditions. Some families allow their little munchkins to open one present each on Christmas Eve, others have to wait until after church Christmas Day. Some people carve into golden-brown turkeys, others succulent hams. Some stockings are hung with care, others carelessly slung over chairs. Some folks send out newsletters braying about their achievements, others Twitter their tragedies. Some real trees look fake, some fake trees look real. Some people's lawns erupt in a carnival-like display of lights and animation that promptly comes down the second of January, others throw up a single strand of bulbs that choke the house until July.

Some things are the same for all revelers. Televisions up and down the block cascade through *It's a Wonderful Life*, *A Christmas Story*, *Rudolph*, and *Frosty*. Mailboxes overflow with Christmas cards. Christmas carols blare from department store speakers, and Santa Claus and his elves hit the mall. Everyone's bank account takes a bit of a hit. Children flock to their windows, clasp their tiny hands underneath their chins, and pray for snow. Once, one of those sets of clasped hands belonged to Georgia Marie Bradley. Christmas was her favorite time of year. And not just because of the carols, and candy canes, and lights, and toy trains, and snow, and Frosty. Oh, she loved all those things, still did, but really it was her father, and their special yearly tradition that lifted the season to the realm of the sacred. She cherished those times with her father more than a miser cherished his piles of gold.

Every year, the week before Christmas, her mother would take her older sister, Virginia, shopping, while Georgia and her father visited the carousel by the ocean. Georgia was in love with it. It was situated in an abandoned warehouse, which had been refurbished to house the carousel year-round. There was something so magical about looking out on the ocean, while they twirled around like snow-flakes. The music, the lights, the tented top striped in blue and gold, the glorious, painted horses bobbing up and down on their regal golden poles. Georgia picked a different horse every time; that was part of the game. As she glided up and down, she eagerly waited to spot her father in the crowd, who in turn would be trying to guess which horse she was on, often pretending not to see her until the third time around. After that, each time she went by, he would make a funny face, or put on a Santa hat, even hold up a bouquet of candy canes. Georgia could hardly wait to come around again, to see what in the world he would do next. Sometimes people gave her father funny looks, but that just made the father-daughter duo laugh even harder. By the time the carousel stopped, Georgia would be gig-gling so hard, tears would be streaming down her face. Afterward they would stroll on the beach, hand-in-hand, looking for shells to hang on their Christmas tree.

The last year she and her father went to the carousel, she met a friend. A girl about her age, but much thinner, and strange, it looked as if she didn't have any hair, just a few wispy strands peeking out of her knitted, pink cap. The first time Georgia noticed her, she wasn't on the carousel. She was standing a few feet away from Georgia's father, clinging onto the hand of a boy just a few years older. The boy looked very serious for a child; he stared at Georgia with somber sky-blue eyes that burned a hole into her. Why was he so sad? It was only because of the brightness of the girl that she was able to look away. Because the girl certainly didn't look sad. She looked as if the carousel was the most amazing thing she had ever seen. Georgia felt like that too, so the moment she saw that little girl's delighted face, her shining eyes, she felt an instant bond.

When the ride was over, Georgia went over to introduce herself. "Hi," she said. "What's your name?"

"Cindy."

"I'm Georgia. Aren't you going to ride?" Cindy shook her head. "Why not?" Cindy shrugged.

"She wants to," the boy said. He nodded to his sister and nudged her forward. Then he turned those blue eyes on Georgia and once again she felt as if she'd been struck. But it wasn't polite to stare, so she tore her gaze away, and glanced at her father. He nodded. Georgia was thrilled. Normally she only went around once.

"I'll ride with you," Georgia said. "It's the most fun ever." Georgia held out her hand. With a little encouragement from her brother, Cindy clasped Georgia's hand, and together they hopped on side-by-side horses. Georgia helped Cindy onto a magnificent black inside-jumper, then swung onto a regal, white outside-stander. This time, instead of making funny faces, her father smiled at them as they went around. Soon, a woman and a man appeared next to the boy with the striking blue eyes. They clung to each other and waved and smiled at Cindy. With a little encouragement from Georgia, her father finally made one of his famous funny faces. Cindy got it right away. She threw her head back and giggled. A rush of warmth and pride welled up in Georgia. She made sure to give her father an extra big smile, and as their horses galloped around and around, their laughter rang out like ringing bells. And suddenly, it began to snow.

Georgia didn't know what that little girl was going to get for Christmas, but she couldn't imagine a bigger or brighter smile on her face, a smile that was captured forever on their last turn around, by the little boy and his instant camera. Georgia and Cindy parted by waving their mittens at each other, and catching a few stolen glances as they were each led away from the carousel by the ocean. Georgia couldn't wait to see her friend again. And the next time, she would ask her. How did her brother get eyes so blue? And why did he look so sad?

Georgia's second-most favorite place in the whole world was her father's enormous white barn, out of which he ran the family business: Trash and Treasures. They sold pre-owned items, everything from tools to toys. The only thing Georgia loved more than the carousel at Christmas was helping her father sell his wares. Each season offered something special, but everybody in the small Rhode Island town knew it was the place to come for a holiday treat. The barn was covered in twinkling multi-colored lights, while the pair of tall spruces outside glittered with red bows and white bulbs. Plastic reindeer stood on the roof guiding Santa on his sleigh, and Bing Crosby sang from the old-fashioned record player behind the counter.

Out would come the space heaters, and gloves, and scarves, and free hot cider, and powdered donuts, and winter items for sale: sleds, Christmas ornaments, tree stands, lights, and presents. They would gift wrap items for free, oh the hours Georgia spent curling the ribbon on the packages just right, handing them over, wishing she could be there when the recipient opened them on Christmas morning. If they were lucky enough to get a snowfall, the property would fill with kids making snowmen and throwing snowballs. If you bought a pair of ice skates, you could often try them out on the frozen pond. Sleds could be tested on the hill out back. The inside of the barn was stacked with shelves and tables, and crates, and every single space was stuffed full with every item imaginable. And even though the vast array of things you could find inside were varied and complex, the sign that hung out front was simple:

TRASH AND TREASURES
ONE MAN'S TRASH IS ANOTHER MAN'S TREASURE

It was there, underneath the sign, that she next saw the boy with the blue eyes. Suddenly, there he was, standing in the middle of the barn, staring up at it. Georgia didn't recognize him right away, not until she said, "Hello," to his back. Then, he turned around and she saw those eyes. Up until now, Georgia had only been obsessed by things. Colored marbles in glass jars. Dainty hand-painted teacups. Carousels. Licking frosting from the bottom of the bowl after making cookies. This was the first time that another person had gripped her as much as her favorite *things* and it made her feel all funny inside. She wondered if it was okay to feel this way about another person, a boy. She wondered if this was what they called a "crush." She wondered where Cindy was, eager to see her new friend again.

"Are you looking for toys?" Georgia asked. He simply

stared at her. Oh, what had she done? He was a few years older than her, too old for toys. Why didn't she say, "sleds," "Are you looking for sleds?" As she stared at him, she was instantly back on the carousel, going around and around, listening to the snap and whine of his instant camera. Maybe he would be interested in all of their old cameras. There were some really cool ones. She liked the ones with the fancy cases and lenses you twisted on and off. One case actually had a red velvet lining. Georgia liked to run her fingertips over it when no one was watching. She wondered if someone royal used to own it, like a queen. She did this with objects that came in, imagined who owned them, and what their lives were like. But suddenly she was too afraid to suggest anything else in case he thought her too young and annoying.

"Where's Cindy?" she asked. The boy's mouth dropped open. Instead of answering her, he reached into his pocket, pulled out an instant picture, and shoved it at her. It was the shot of her and Cindy, riding the carousel. Cindy had such a big smile on her face. "Cool," Georgia said. She looked over his shoulder. "Is she here?" He didn't answer. After a minute she held the picture out to the boy, but he didn't make a move to take it back.

"Let's go," a man's voice called to the boy. She recognized him as the man who had joined the boy at the carousel to wave at Cindy. The father didn't even say hello to her. So strange that the little girl was the only happy one in the family. The boy turned away from Georgia, head down, and began to follow his dad.

"Wait," she said. "Your picture." He acted as if he didn't hear her. She knew he did. Everything echoed in the big barn, and the Christmas music was barely turned up. For some reason, she felt panicked. As if he mustn't walk off without the picture of Cindy and her beautiful smile. "Hey," she yelled. Just then, the boy's father looked at her.

He glanced down and saw the picture in her outstretched hand. Then, he looked at his son for a long moment, and, as if something had been decided, gave a curt nod.

"He wants you to have it," the father said. He put his arm around the boy and they were gone. Georgia ran to the entrance, and stood staring after them. Long after their white station wagon kicked up dirt and disappeared down the driveway, Georgia still stood and stared.

"Georgia. Please come here." Obediently, she walked up to her father, who stood behind the table that constituted their "counter." On top of the table was a large box labeled CHRISTMAS.

"What's that?"

"The gentleman just dropped it off."

"Do you remember him?" Georgia asked.

"Should I?" her father asked. Georgia handed him the picture. He studied it for a moment. "That explains a lot," he said.

"What?" Georgia asked. "What does it explain?" She reached for the box. Her father gently placed his hand on hers.

"We're not going to open it," he said.

"Why not?"

"In case they come back for it someday."

"Why would they come back for it? And why don't they want it?" Her father took her hand and held it. He told her that Cindy had been very sick. Something called "leukemia." She passed away shortly after that ride.

"Is that why she didn't have any hair?"

"Yes," her father said. His voice sounded choked. Georgia didn't know what to say. She felt hot in the face. She felt like crying. She remembered her little head, with no hair. And her big smile. "I'm so proud of you, Peaches," her father said.

"Why?"

"Because of you, that little girl had one last ride. One last, wonderful ride." Georgia had never seen tears roll down her father's cheeks before.

"Don't cry, Dad," she said.

"Your mother and I love your sister and you more than anything in the world," he said. "Do you know that?" He stared at her, expecting an answer, so she nodded. And she did know that too. But she didn't like to see her father so serious or so sad. Luckily, he wiped his tears and presented her with a familiar wink. "Speaking of which— she's expecting you in the kitchen, isn't she?"

"We're making cookies."

"Call me when they're done. I'll pretend I'm Santa Claus."

"You're not fat enough," Georgia said. Her father laughed and winked at her. "I want to lick the bowl, too!"

"Virginia and I get to lick the bowl!" Georgia said as she headed for the house.

"We should put the picture in the box," her dad said. Georgia stopped.

She looked at the picture, then at her father. She didn't really want to give it back. She knew it wasn't logical, but somehow she felt if she kept the picture, she'd be keeping Cindy alive. "In case they come back for it?"

"Yes."

"I want to keep it."

Her father tapped his head. "You'll keep it in here," he said. Then he touched his heart. "And here." Georgia still wanted the picture.

"I won't lose it, or rip it or anything," Georgia said.

"Please, Peaches. Let's put it in the box for them." Georgia nodded, handed her father the photo, and watched as he slipped it in the box. And even though Georgia often went up to the box and put her hand on it, she never opened it. The following year, when the time came to visit the carousel, Georgia asked her father if they could go sledding instead. She still loved the carousel, but from now on they would only visit it during the warmer months. To Georgia, it was just like when their cat, Sammy, curled into a sleeping ball by the fireplace. No matter how much she wanted to go up and pet him, there was just something so soft and sweet about it, she didn't dare disturb the moment. Christmas and the carousel were one of those sleeping moments now. Forever linked with little Cindy, and her last, wonderful ride.

CHAPTER TWO

Twenty years later

Georgia was fast asleep when the fire alarm shrieked through her bedroom. She was upright in an instant, swinging her feet over the side of the bed, smelling for smoke. Before she even hit the floor, she called out for her seven-year-old.

"Ranger!"

"Mom?" He came pounding into her room, his soft brown hair sticking up, his *Star Wars* pajamas way too small. Even amidst the blaring beeps, Georgia couldn't help but make a mental note to herself to buy him new pajamas for Christmas. Georgia grabbed Ranger's hand, and together they approached the hall outside her bedroom.

"Did you see or smell any smoke?" she asked.

"No." Thank goodness, neither did she. They stood overlooking the railing that looked down onto the auction floor. They technically lived in a giant warehouse, although Georgia liked to think of it as a hip loft. Below she ran her business, Rhode Island's premier auction house, The Treasure Chest. If there was a fire, she would stand to lose everything. She headed for the stairs, still clinging to Ranger's hand, while mentally trying to remember how much her insurance would cover if worse came to worst. She grabbed the fire extinguisher off its hook at the top of the steps, then together they headed down at a brisk pace.

"Maybe the alarm is broken," Ranger said.

"Let's hope," Georgia said.

"Dad's watch," Ranger said. He stopped in the middle of the steps. "I forgot Dad's watch."

"No things, honey, remember?" It was hard for Georgia to spit this out, for she, more than anyone, knew how one could come to love objects, especially those that once belonged to a cherished loved one.

"Please?"

"Here, and here," Georgia said, touching her head and her heart.

"But—"

"I'm sorry. Let's go." They navigated the rest of the stairs and were soon on the main floor. The control panel for the fire alarm was at the front of the auction floor by the office. They ducked past rows of stacked oriental rugs, statues, swords, crystal bowls, and a plethora of other treasures awaiting future auctions. The floor was cold underneath their bare feet, and by the time they reached the office, the alarm suddenly stopped.

"It's off," Ranger said.

"We're going outside anyway," Georgia said. "I just have to grab my cell."

"No things."

"We need to call the fire department. Wait for me right outside the door." Georgia grabbed the phone off her desk, knocking a pile of blue envelopes onto the floor. Georgia resisted the urge to spit on them. Instead, she hurried to Ranger, who was working the numerous locks on the enormous steel door. Georgia joined him and together they opened it and stepped out into the cold, morning air. It was only now that she realized she was only wearing a nightgown. There was no sign of fire anywhere. It must be a false alarm. Still, she wasn't going to take chances, not with her son. Georgia was about to call the fire department when a figure approached from the shadows. Georgia let out a scream.

"It's Mrs. Weaver," Ranger said. Sure enough, Georgia saw her elderly neighbor standing in front of them in a ratty peach house robe, her long gray hair frizzing out above her shoulders, her eyes bright beneath her heavily wrinkled face.

"Three minutes and forty-five seconds," Mrs. Weaver said, thrusting up a stopwatch.

"What?" Georgia asked.

"Not bad, but you need to get it down to two minutes."

"You set our fire alarm? How? Why?"

"I rigged mine to yours," Mrs. Weaver said. Mrs. Weaver had a bakery next door. This stretch of Cranberry Street was where all the shops were located, all owned and run by locals. Mrs. Weaver, at eighty-four, had been here the longest. Her baked goods were the best in town, and during the holiday season, Georgia and Ranger were spoiled with whatever was left at the end of the day. It was sad to see that Mrs. Weaver was becoming slightly crazy and forgetful.

"Come inside," Georgia said. "It's freezing."

Georgia made tea for herself and Mrs. Weaver, and hot chocolate for Ranger. Only after they were warmed up did Georgia speak up.

"What do you mean you rigged your fire alarm to ours?"

"My father was an electrician. He never had a son. So he taught me a few tricks."

"Can you get free cable?" Ranger asked.

"You betya."

"Mom?"

"No." Georgia turned back to Mrs. Weaver. "Okay. So why did you rig your fire alarm to mine?"

"So that when my place burns down, you'll have plenty of warning." Georgia glanced at Ranger. His cup was frozen halfway to his mouth, his eyes as large as saucers.

"Why don't you take that upstairs. You can read a little if you can't fall asleep right away," Georgia said.

"Your place is going to burn down?" Ranger asked.

"No," Georgia said.

"Yes," Mrs. Weaver said. Georgia tried to give her a look but the old lady was too demented or just too stubborn to pick up on it.

"Ranger, bed."

"Mom."

"Bed." Ranger sighed, and pushed away from the table, jostling hot chocolate out of his cup. He leaned down. Georgia thought she was going to get a kiss on the cheek, but instead he whispered in her ear. "Tell me everything," he said.

"Night, kiddo."

"Night, Mom. Night, Mrs. Weaver." Georgia waited until she could hear his footsteps crossing the length of the warehouse floor and heading up the stairs.

"I know what you're thinking. I've lost it. I'm bananas." Mrs. Weaver raised her hands high in the air.

"You can't seriously tell me you're thinking of burning down the bakery."

"It's better than selling to those Scrooges!"

"What Scrooges?"

"Have they not come knocking on your door yet?"

"The developers?"

"Who else would I be talking about?" An image of the

blue envelopes in her office, well, now on her office floor, rose to Georgia's mind. Once she knew what they were after, she hadn't opened a single one. "I'd rather burn her down and collect the insurance than let them turn this block into a mini-mall, or monumental-mall, or whatever the hell they have in mind," Mrs. Weaver concluded.

"They're just trying to scare you. They need the whole block to build their mall, and none of us are going to sell." There were eight businesses on the street, all locally owned. But the land itself was leased. Technically, if the city wanted these developers to have the lot, they could let all of their contracts expire. Which was due to happen at the end of the year, barely a month away. But the city officials, some up for re-election, would never want to be cast as Grinches responsible for closing down a succession of family- and minority-owned businesses. The developers knew this. Which is why they were trying to seduce them into selling.

Big buyouts, quick closings, playing on their fears that the city would eventually look at the bottom line and not renew their contracts at all. Times were tough, and these predators were using it to their full advantage. Georgia wasn't going to sit back and let them be bullied, or lured in just to crash on the rocks.

"Strength in numbers," Georgia said holding up her teacup as if making a toast.

"Joe is thinking of selling," Mrs. Weaver said.

"No," Georgia said. Oh, no. She wished it were more of a shock, but everyone knew Circle Books wasn't doing so hot. Georgia bought from him at least once a month, an antiques guide or mystery paperback for her, and a children's book for Ranger, but that was hardly enough to keep it going. He had a lot of traffic during the touristy summer months, but he said most of them just browsed, and wrote down titles that they were later going to download.

"I'll talk to Joe," Georgia said. "But even if he does sell, they can hardly do much with his little section."

"Three others are thinking of jumping ship, too."

Georgia clanked her teacup down on its saucer. "Who?"

"Jess, Roger, and Sue." The butcher, the hardware store owner, and the florist.

"You've got to be kidding me."

"This new mini-mall is going to have a meat section, a hardware section, a florist, a baker, discount books—"

"Don't say 'is.' It isn't. It's never going to happen." Georgia looked around at her brick walls covered in oil paintings, her ceiling from which a hundred chandeliers shone, her shelves stacked with treasures. Stories, actually, for each item carried with it the lives of the previous owners. She couldn't fathom seeing discount detergent in place of crystal goblets and oriental vases. How could people let go of the past so easily? Didn't they recognize the quality, the history, the stories? Didn't they want to stay connected to those who lived, and toiled, and learned before? Everything was being tossed aside to make room for progress.

What progress? How many families spent dinnertime engrossed in their own little smartphones or tablets? Auctions brought people together. There was always an excitement in the room like opening night at the theater. Treasures from the past brought people together. Even bidding wars were friendly. The investors didn't care about any of it. Instead, they wanted people to come in here and crush each other over Black Friday sales. Over Georgia's dead body. They would have to make her into a wax figurine if they wanted her to leave this place.

"They are offering really good money. I mean really good. What have they offered you?"

"I don't know."

"What do you mean you don't know?"

"I haven't opened the letters or answered their phone calls."

"Rebel. Good for you. Let the rest of them sell. We'll go down with the ship. Up in a blaze!"

"Hold up there, Pyro Patty. I won't have you messing with fire. I have a kid to protect, remember? If you pull any more stunts, I'm going to have to report you."

"And the rebel falls." Mrs. Weaver pushed her tea away and slumped in her seat.

"I'm serious. How can you even think of messing with a fire with my business and my seven-year-old son next door? I'm shocked at you, Mrs. Weaver."

"Oh, I wasn't going to do it. I just hate the thought of everything changing. I always thought the bakery would be my legacy. Twenty, even thirty years after I was gone, people would come in, look at a photo of me hanging prominently on the wall as you enter, and say, 'There's Mrs. Weaver. She's the reason we have such heavenly treats.' "

Or big thighs. Georgia tried not to imagine the picture of Mrs. Weaver looking like she did right now in a pink ratty robe and science hair. Besides, she understood her point. We all wanted to be remembered, honored even. Which is what Georgia strove to do every day of her life. Honor the past.

Mrs. Weaver was in her eighties. She didn't have children and her husband died many years ago. The bakery should be her legacy. And she should be enjoying retirement instead of literally working herself to the bone. In fact, Georgia was the youngest owner on the block. The others could sell and retire with ease. Georgia would not only be out of a job, she'd be out of a home. If her father were still here, he would tell her to fight. She couldn't believe they were going to have to celebrate this Christmas without him. Before tears could well in her eyes, Georgia stood and picked up her teacup. Mrs. Weaver got the hint and stood up.

"Don't worry," Georgia said. "I'm going to do something about this."

"You're a fighter. Like James." Georgia always suspected Mrs. Weaver had a little crush on her dad. They certainly got a lot more free sweets when he was alive. And Georgia didn't blame her. Her father remained handsome and charming until he died last year at the too-young age of sixty-eight. But James Bradley showed no interest in women after her mother passed away five years prior. Just antiques, and family. Yet another thing she and her father had in common. Georgia hadn't had a single date since Paul died. Four years.

Who had time? Life was hard enough without inviting heartache in the door. Paul had been a good man, a loving man. He loved her. He would've been a great father. It seemed impractical, greedy even, to expect to find that kind of a match again. Yes, Georgia knew there were probably any number of men she could love as much as she loved Paul, and vice versa, but actually finding them was another matter entirely. Someone who loved her love of collectibles and auctions, and most importantly, Ranger. That was certainly a rare find. And she didn't want to take the risk that some man would swoop in and then abandon or hurt Ranger. Not even a tiny bit. Not even unintentionally. He'd had his share of hurt and loss.

"We need to have an emergency meeting with all the owners," Georgia said. "I'll get on it."

"I don't think it will do any good."

"It's the holiday season," Georgia said. "Sales should

be picking up soon." Oh how she hoped it was true. But so many people were pinching pennies these days, and shopping for sales online. People might buy more cookies this time of year, but not fourteenth-century silver candlesticks. Although she did have a pair fit for a king's cupboard.

"Nobody wants to celebrate Christmas this year," Mrs. Weaver said. "That man! He's Scrooge! A good-looking Scrooge, but a Scrooge nonetheless." A good-looking Scrooge? This was news to Georgia. It shouldn't be, but it was funny to hear something like that come out of the old lady's mouth. We aged on the outside, but stayed the same on the inside. Mrs. Weaver, boy-crazy in her eighties. How marvelous life could be. *Better her than me,* Georgia thought. She didn't realize she was smiling until Mrs. Weaver snapped at her. "What? I can't say a man's good-looking? Why? Because I'm an old hag?"

"Absolutely not. I'm just sleepy is all, and when I'm sleepy everything seems funny."

"Well this isn't a bit funny."

"I know. I'm going to do something. I promise. Now go home, and the next time you get the urge to wire something, steal a car. Preferably not mine."

CHAPTER THREE

Georgia began the next morning by putting on Bing Crosby's Christmas CD and opening the little storage unit where she kept the decorations. She waited for Ranger to hear the music and come bouncing down the steps to help her decorate. He took after his mother: it was his favorite time of year, too. Oh how her father loved joining in the festivities. It was so hard not to have him around this year. What would she do if she lost this place? It was the only thing she knew. She wouldn't even be qualified for a minimum-wage job. Who was going to hire someone who put *Antiques Roadshow* under the Special Skills section of a resume?

"Ranger?" she called up to the second floor. When there was no answer, Georgia headed up. She found him on his bed with his head buried in the pillow. "Honey. What's wrong? Are you sick?"

"Turn it off," Ranger said. "Turn it off." He was clutching a picture of her father, one they took last Christmas.

"Hey," she said, sitting on the bed. "Come here." Ranger allowed her to fold him into her arms. She knew this wouldn't last, the phase where it was still okay to let your mother hold you. "He's with us. In spirit. And I know he would want us to celebrate, and decorate, and enjoy."

"How can we? I miss him."

"I miss him, too. But that's why we have to do it. Grandpa loved Christmas. And he loved us."

"Mrs. Weaver said nobody in the whole town wants to celebrate Christmas this year!"

"I thought you were in bed."

"This place echoes."

"It sure does. What else did you hear?"

"Something about Scrooge. Was she talking about *A Christmas Carol*?"

"I think she sees it every year and it gets her worked up," Georgia said. She didn't want to out and out lie, but now was not the time to worry him about the investors.

"But he turns out nice in the end. He helps Tiny Tim and buys them a goose, and gives pennies to the poor."

"I know."

"Grandpa watched it with me once."

"Come on. Let's just get the decorations out. We don't have to put them up today."

"All right." Ranger wiped his nose on his sleeve. Georgia ruffled his hair. Ranger raced in front of her, and was already tearing into boxes before she even reached the bottom step. *That's my boy*. She was on her way to help when the office phone rang. "Be right there," Georgia called as she passed Ranger. He barely looked up. She was humming along to "It's Beginning to Look A Lot Like Christmas" when she finally reached the phone.

"Finally," her sister said when she answered. "Aren't you ever in the office?"

"Hello to you too, sis. We're decorating."

"God, remember how much of a fuss Dad used to make?"

"I loved it."

"Of course you did." There was a sigh and then a baby crying.

"How's my niece?"

"Teething."

"Ouch. Give her a kiss for me."

"Will do. Listen. We need to talk." Uh, oh. Georgia knew this tone of voice. Virginia was upset with her over something. What was it this time?

"About?"

"Why didn't you tell me someone made an offer to buy out The Treasure Chest?"

"How could you possibly know that?" Had someone from the town called her? No, her neighbors didn't have her sister's number.

"I had a visit from a pair of investors, that's how." Georgia rose from the edge of the desk where she had planted herself.

"They came to *your* house? In California?"

"I am part-owner, you know."

In name only. Because when Georgia opened up the auction house, part of the money was their father's. Virginia didn't need it. Her husband made a gazillion dollars a year as a consultant. "What exactly did they say?"

"I'll get to that. First, I want to know why you didn't tell me."

"Because I wouldn't sell to them in a million years. That's why."

"It's not your decision. It's ours."

"They're just bullies, Gin. They want to buy out this entire street and turn it into a mini-mall." She realized as she railed against it that her sister wouldn't really care. She was in California now, and didn't even seem to miss their little New England town. Virginia had never been a Trash and Treasures girl.

"They weren't bullies. One was incredibly good-looking. A bit moody maybe, but hot."

"So I've heard. I'm telling you—they're predators. Mrs. Weaver almost burned her bakery down because of them."

"She's still alive?"

"Yes."

"She's got to be as nutty as her fruitcakes by now."

"She is. But that's not the point."

"Look. There are a few things I haven't told you either."

"Like what?" Georgia listened to Virginia sigh. She loved to draw out the drama.

"Devon lost his job."

That was a shock. Devon was all about consulting and sales. Georgia could only imagine how he was dealing with it. Or Virginia for that matter. That was the other thing about having a man around. You had to put up with them. "Oh, my God. I'm so sorry. When?"

"Four months ago."

Georgia glanced out at the floor. Ranger was barely visible, hunkered down with Christmas decorations all around him. It gave her a rush of joy to know he was still capable of experiencing the simple pleasures. She hoped Devon would get a job soon. If Virginia wasn't happy, nobody was happy. Four months was a long time. Virginia had probably told everyone else about this already. Especially her girlfriends. It was all because Georgia followed in their dad's footsteps. She always suspected Virginia was jealous, felt left out. Guess it was payback time. "And you're just telling me now?" Georgia couldn't help but let some of the hurt seep out.

"Well, what were you going to do about it?"

Her sister sounded harsh and matter of fact. Virginia, always the practical one. It never occurred to her that leaning on your sister in times of trouble could be a good thing. "Listen. Support. Empathize."

"What you could have done was tell me about the offer."

A cold chill ran through Georgia. Oh, no. "Don't you guys have a lot of savings, though?"

"Not as much as you think. Having a baby is like having an ATM machine that constantly throws up money and mushy peas."

"Thanks for that image."

"I told them we'd consider the offer. I'm going to have Devon fax it over to you. Is your fax machine on?"

Georgia glanced at the machine. It was blinking, set to go. "I don't think it's working," she said. Just then she heard the telltale ring and then sound of a fax coming through.

"Liar. I can hear it."

"Virginia, I'm not selling."

"I thought you'd say that. And I'm sorry. I really am. But if you aren't going to sell, then Devon and I are going to need our share."

"And how much is that?"

"It will be covered in the second fax."

"I see."

"Don't be that way. It sucks. The economy sucks. Losing a job sucks. Progress sucks."

"A mini-mall on this block is not progress!"

"Business is terrible. You said so yourself."

"Tell me you did not say that to the investors." There was a telltale silence on the other end. "Ginny!"

"We've escalated to 'Ginny' already? Look. In a small town—it's just not sustainable. Maybe you could start again, in Manhattan."

"If I can't even afford it here, what makes you think I could be successful in Manhattan?"

"They have more people with nothing better to spend their money on than 'antiques.'" Georgia could hear the sarcasm in her sister's voice. She'd never seen the magic side of selling all these wonderful items. Once in a while she even joked that Georgia was in the OPC Business. Other People's Crap. Except for licking the icing from the bottom of the bowl, she and her sister never did have much in common.

"I could never afford this much space in Manhattan. And I certainly can't compete with Sotheby's and Christie's."

"Don't bite my head off. I have a baby and husband for that."

"Don't you miss how we grew up? The barn at Christmas? Making cookies with Mom?"

"Of course. What's your point?"

"That's what I'm trying to give Ranger."

"You don't live on a farm. It's a warehouse. To be perfectly frank, I think it's a terrible environment for a child."

"It's a cozy small town, and this place is over six thousand square feet. He's the only kid I know allowed to skateboard in the house."

"And don't even get me started on your dating life," Virginia said, ignoring Georgia's defense of the warehouse.

"I don't have a dating life."

"Exactly. And you never will living on that geriatric block. Who are you going to date? That butcher, the baker—"

"There's no candlestick maker—"

"What?"

"Just saving you some time. Look. I don't want to date. I had Paul."

"He's been gone for four years."

"I had my turn. I'm done."

"Don't be ridiculous. You're too young to be done. As long as Santa puts a little Botox in our stockings, we'll be young for another fifty years."

"I have to go." Georgia wanted to decorate with her son, not get lectured by her sister.

"We're broke, Georgia. There. I said it. We're broke. And I'm scared."

"I'll get you your share. If I have to beg, borrow, or steal, I will get you your share."

"Okay. There's a deadline, though. I'm sorry, sis. It's just business."

"Fine. What? How long?"

"The end of the year." Virginia whispered it.

"That's impossible."

"That's when the investors said we'd get our money by."

"They're liars! Don't you see? They are the worst of the worst. Preying on desperate people." Although it was still hard to see her sister as desperate. Devon was probably the one pushing her to sell. He liked the antique business even less than Virginia.

"I'm sorry. I'm really, really sorry. Devon is too. Tell Ranger we love him, okay? And if you decide to sell, just pack things up and come here for Christmas."

Georgia mumbled good-bye and hung up the phone before Virginia could hear her crying. *No, Virginia, there isn't a Santa Claus*. She wiped her eyes, took a deep breath, and returned to Ranger. He'd pulled down all of the Christmas lights, boxes, and train sets. Georgia loved setting the miniature trains up around the warehouse. She had a couple of rare ones to auction off this year. God, she loved the holidays! She didn't care what anybody said. This was a magical time of year. She was going to keep it alive if it killed her. Ranger was humming and running the engine of a toy train along the floor. She didn't blame him. Decorating was actually a lot of work. What was she thinking starting it on a Sunday—

Wait. Her sister never called her on a Sunday. That was family day. She usually called her on—

"Ranger. What day is today?"

"Monday."

"Why aren't you in school?"

Ranger looked at her, shrugged. "I thought I was sick," he said. Georgia glanced at the wall. The cool thing about living in an auction house was that you didn't just have one of everything, you had about twenty. Most of the clocks read nine-thirty. He was over an hour late.

"Get dressed as fast as you can."

"But I want to decorate for Christmas."

"I made a mistake. I thought it was Sunday. Up, up, up." To her son's credit, he was ready in fifteen minutes, and five minutes after that he had an apple and a yogurt in his hand, lunch money, and they were out the door. The minute they stepped onto the sidewalk, they nearly rammed into a deliveryman wheeling a huge crate toward them. He wasn't looking where he was going, and Georgia didn't want to be run off the sidewalk.

"Watch it," she said.

"Oh." The crate stopped. "Sorry, sorry," the man said. He peeked around the crate and smiled. He was much younger than their usual delivery guy, about her age. Handsome too, from what she could see under his base-ball cap. See, she wanted to call Virginia and say, "This isn't just a geriatric block." Not that she wanted to date the delivery guy. Not that there was anything wrong with being a delivery guy at their age. Per se—

"Is that for us?" Ranger asked. "Is it an elephant?"

"An elephant?" Georgia said. The man laughed. For some reason, the sound completely startled Georgia. It had just been so long since she'd heard an attractive man laugh. She hated to admit it, but maybe her sister was right. Maybe she did want to go on a date. Just one. A nice dinner. Some dancing?

"It's certainly heavy enough," the man said.

"See. It could be an elephant," Ranger said.

"Better not be," Georgia said. Once in a while people would just ship them their items with a letter begging them to put it up for auction. If Georgia accepted it, she was legally bound to ship it back to them if it was something she couldn't sell. Nine times out of ten, it was something she couldn't sell. Once a man sent her a dozen mannequin torsos. She still had nightmares. "Maybe it's not for me."

"Georgia Bradley?" the deliveryman said. He had a deep and almost melodic voice.

"Shit," Georgia said.

"Awwww," Ranger said. "Bad word."

"Sorry, sorry," Georgia said to both Ranger and the deliveryman. "I'm taking my son to school. I can't open the warehouse for you right now. We're already late."

"I don't mind," Ranger said.

"I do," Georgia said.

The deliveryman glanced at Mrs. Weaver's bakery. "I'm due for a break," he said. "When could you be back?"

He lifted his face, giving her the opportunity to confirm that he was very good-looking. Besides being tall and muscular, it was a handsome face, with wicked blue eyes. It made her think of all sorts of delivery jokes along the lines of "I've got a package for you." Thank God nobody could read her mind. She hoped nothing showed on her face.

"Fifteen minutes," Ranger said. Ranger stuck out his hand and shook on it with the deliveryman as if he had just brokered a deal. The kid never stopped surprising her.

If he secretly wanted an elephant for Christmas, he was going to be sorely disappointed.

"I'll wait," the deliveryman said. Georgia wanted to argue, ask where the heck the giant crate was from, but she wasn't going to waste any more time.

"Fine," she said. "I'll pop in as soon as I'm back."

"Get an éclair," Ranger shouted as they headed for the car. "And steer clear of the fruitcake."

He was sitting by the window in the bakery when she returned. The huge crate was on the sidewalk, on the other side of the wall from where he sat. *Pretty confident no one would steal it*, she thought. Then again, he had the dolly inside with him, and the crate was elephant-size, not exactly something someone could sling over his shoulder and make off with.

She glanced at the crate before entering. It was postmarked from right here in Rhode Island. Not helpful. "You'd better not be an elephant," she whispered. A bell tinkled as she entered the bakery, and the aroma of sugar and melting chocolate hit her right between the eyes. It wasn't until she glanced at the deliveryman's table that she saw he wasn't alone. Hidden in the corner was a second man, a big stocky fellow. He had a near-full slice of fruitcake in front of him while the deliveryman she met was taking the last bite of an éclair.

"Georgia," Mrs. Weaver called from behind the counter. "You came." Oh, no. She didn't have time for another go-round.

"Hi, Mrs. Weaver. I'm actually just here to sign a delivery slip."

"Nonsense. Cup of coffee and an éclair coming right up." There was nothing more heavenly than Weaver's chocolate and crème-filled éclairs. During the holiday season she painted a mistletoe on top with red and green icing. It was the little things that mattered in life. Something those investors would never understand. The deliveryman glanced up at her and waved.

"Your son was right about the éclair," he said.

"And the fruitcake," the other man said with a sigh.

"I got him good," the first one said. God. Blue eyes and dimples. Dimples on a grown man. It was extremely endearing. Almost made you want to smile against your will. And a really nice jawline with stubble. A memory of running her hands over Paul's stubble hit her in the solar plexus. She hadn't thought of Paul that way in a long time. Grief had a funny way of clobbering you just when you thought you'd finished mourning. She'd only been blessed with Paul for four years. But he couldn't have left a better legacy. Ranger. The fact that this deliveryman was making her relive her private pain, stirring up feelings in her, suddenly infuriated her. And what deliveryman had ever taken a fifteen-minute break to deliver a package? She'd been in too much of a hurry earlier to put two and two together. And now here they were. One, two.

"Who are you?" she asked. Although part of her already knew. She heard Mrs. Weaver in her head. *He's a Scrooge, even if he is good-looking.* And then her sister. *One of them was incredibly good-looking.*

"Scrooges," she said under her breath. So what was the crate—a Trojan horse?

"Please, join us," the good-looking one answered with a smile that brought out his damn dimples. "All will be answered."

CHAPTER FOUR

Knowing Mrs. Weaver was staring at her, Georgia took her coffee and éclair, and reluctantly sat down. He pushed the delivery slip in front of her.

"This was being delivered as I came up to your door," he said. "I signed for it."

"Excuse me?"

"I'm not with the delivery company."

"I know." She glanced at her coffee and considered spilling it into his lap while making a run for it. It wasn't fair that he was so handsome. He was instantly likeable. Not how she wanted to feel about the man threatening her very existence. And he smelled good, too. Clean, and something manly and musky. Probably an expensive cologne given to him by his girlfriend. He wasn't wearing a wedding ring. That didn't mean anything. And of course, it made no difference to her. "Where do you get off signing for something for me?"

"Oh. Sorry. The delivery guy was leaving. Said no one answered the door. I didn't want you to miss your package."

"And if I hadn't come out the door when I did? Were you going to drag that crate around with you all day?"

"Couldn't abandon a possible elephant, now could I?"

Georgia turned and gave him the dirtiest look she could summon, and afterward was even a little surprised with herself. She wasn't usually hostile to strangers. But the man didn't seem to notice, he just stared at her in an open, expectant way. She had the strongest feeling of déjà vu. *Santa, I want him for Christmas.*

"That's what it is?" the burly man asked, glancing at the crate. "An elephant?"

Georgia took her time putting cream and sugar into her coffee, then slowly bit into her éclair. "My God, is this good," she said, glancing at the man and his fruitcake. He looked at her éclair like it was a scantily clad model on the beach. Then he glanced at his fruitcake, sighed, patted his stomach.

"On a diet."

"You're supposed to do that after the holidays," the good-looking one said. Nobody had ever mentioned their names. She would make up her own names. Scrooge One and Scrooge Two.

"There are a lot of things that should wait until after the holidays," Georgia said. "Diets. Bad news. Foreclosures. Knocks on the door from peddlers, and scum-sucking investors eager to tear down the quaintest street in New England to slap up a hideous mini-mall." She dropped her éclair onto the plate. Now her appetite really was ruined. Why did he have to be an investor? Surely he could make some money doing underwear catalogues, or flashing those dimples for Folgers Coffee or whatnot.

The burly man let out a gruff, "Hey!" but the handsome one laughed. It was a nice laugh. Georgia wanted it to stop. She wanted to smear the éclair in his face. Then lick it off. This was insane. She had to get out of here. Just as she slid back her chair, Mr. Gorgeous held out his hand for Georgia to shake.

"I'm Adam," he said when she didn't take it. "And this is Ben." Georgia grabbed her packing slip, and stood up.

"I'm never signing. And neither are the others."

"That's funny," Ben said. "We just got Joe to sign about an hour ago, didn't we Adam?"

"Damn it," Georgia said.

"Look," Adam said. "We just want to talk."

"I don't care if you get all of them to sign. My warehouse is six thousand square feet. You can't build without my space, can you?" Their looks said it all. "That's what I thought. Give everyone their money back, pack your bags, and get out of town. Because I'm not going anywhere. Guess you would have saved yourselves a lot of time if you had approached me first."

"We've sent you at least twenty letters, and many more voice mails," Adam said. His laughter was long gone.

"Guess you didn't get the hint," Georgia said. "I'm just not that into you." Although she could be. In another life. Georgia started for the door. "Mrs. Weaver. Would you keep your eye on my giant crate while I fetch my dolly?"

"You can use mine," Adam said. "It actually belongs to the deliveryman. I told him I would leave it at your place."

"You thought of everything, didn't you?" Georgia said. She headed for the door.

"Your sister wants to sell," Adam called after her. Georgia whirled around. She wanted to leap across the tables and strangle his beautiful neck. Georgia wished she had a winning comeback that would slice him to the core. Since she didn't, she simply walked out the door with as much attitude as she could.

* * *

On her fifth attempt to maneuver the giant crate, Georgia looked up to find Adam standing in front of her. His baseball cap was off. In addition to his beautiful face, he had a thick head of dark hair. He seemed so familiar. Just that type. The type of man a normally sane girl could fall in-love-at-first-sight with.

"I'd like to help," he said quietly.

"Not necessary. I'm sure you have puppies to kick or old ladies to drag out of their homes."

"You sound hostile. I come in peace."

She could not believe him. She raised her hands in frustration. "There is nothing peaceful about some evil corporation bulldozing over an entire street of family-owned businesses to slap up a shoddy discount mall!"

"Georgia." Startled, she looked up. Something in the way he said her name. Familiar. Intimate. "That's not the whole picture."

"You can stop. Mrs. Weaver might find you charming. But I don't."

"Mrs. Weaver finds me charming?"

"I've got to go."

"I'm not a bad guy. And the corporation isn't evil. Do you have any idea how many people they help?"

"Spare me. You're not getting my warehouse. Case closed." She jerked on the crate and it almost toppled over. Adam lunged in and steadied it before it could crush her foot. Secretly, she was grateful: She appreciated her foot, but she wasn't going to thank him.

"You're going to kill yourself or break whatever is inside. Is that what you want?" He was right. She usually wasn't so careless with items. She just wanted it inside and she wanted to be away from that man. Those men. She wasn't bothered one way or the other by Adam, or Scrooge One as she preferred to call him.

"Fine. But let me be clear. You bringing this inside the door of my warehouse does not mean I'm going to sell you my warehouse. *Capisce?*"

"Yep." She watched him tip the crate back onto the dolly like it was as light as a feather. Jerk. "Lead the way." Georgia opened the steel doors, and Adam maneuvered the crate inside.

"You can just leave it here by the office," she said.

"Are you sure? I can put it wherever you need it."

"Depending on what it is, it may not even make it to the floor," Georgia said. "Here is perfect." Adam set the crate down where she asked. He looked out to the floor.

"I'd love a tour," he said. He sounded sincere. Georgia felt the familiar rush of pride. Her place. Her business. Her life's work.

"Happy to," she said. "You should see why I would never sell." She showed him all there was to see, conscious of him directly behind her every single step. She'd given this tour numerous times to numerous men but had never once fantasized about taking them behind the shelves. She had better speed this up before she lost her mind. Besides, he wasn't here to buy, he was here to take. So she zipped through the sections. Antique furniture. Persian rugs. Sword collections. Paintings. Crystal chandeliers. Circus toys. When he reached out to touch something, he froze as if he expected her to reprimand him, and when she didn't, his expression was almost one of wonderment. Interesting. Scrooge might have a heart after all. If she were a devious person, she might think about using that to her advantage. When they were finished they ended up back at the office by the crates.

"You're amazing," he said. "I mean. This place is amazing." Their eyes locked. *You're amazing.* But he didn't mean it. He took it back, didn't he? Then why was he blushing? Staring at her in a way that made her weak in the knees? This wasn't happening. She wasn't some naïve schoolgirl.

"I'm never going to sell," she said.

"I understand. But it's not that simple. Life never is, is it?" He sounded sad for a moment, and Georgia had an urge to know him, all of his private pain. She'd never had a thought like that about a total stranger before and it bothered her. The sooner he was out of her sight, the better.

"Oh I think it is that simple, Mister—" She saw him looking at the office floor. She turned to see all of the blue envelopes spread out. She snatched one up and looked at the return address. "Mr. Thrift," she said.

"Cavalier."

"Pardon?" Was he talking about her attitude?

"Ben's last name is Thrift. Mine is Cavalier."

Adam Cavalier. It made her think of him on top of a horse, galloping toward her with a sword in one hand, and an offer of love in the other. "Whatever."

"I see why it's been so easy for you to turn down our offer," he said. "Given that you have no idea what it is."

"I don't care if it's a million dollars."

"I admire that. I really do. But it's not just you that stands to lose everything if you don't sell." Was he talking about her sister? Her neighbors? How dare he. He didn't know her. Or them. Oh, why did the rest of them have to be near retirement? Here these developers were offering a nice fat stack of cash; of course many of them were going to want to take it. She was going to be the stubborn woman who kept them from retiring in Florida and becoming a parrot-head, or whatever it was those Jimmy Buffet lovers called themselves.

"Get out," she said.

He pointed at the office floor where the blue envelopes skated the surface of the tiles. "At least look at our offer!"

"Are you implying I can be bought?" Georgia asked.

"I. I. No. No. I just—"

"Get out."

"This investment. It isn't just about the money."

"Oh, no? What's it about then?"

"I should have told you this up front," he said quietly, intensely. "I know you."

"You *know* me?"

"I just—mean. I know about you. This place."

"How?"

"I live the next town over. Everyone knows of this place."

"I've never seen you here." *I would remember*.

"I always meant to come," he said. He was so serious. So intense. "I never wanted to meet like this," he added. "Never."

He liked her. He wanted her. The thoughts struck her like a one-two punch. Almost took her breath away. This beautiful man wanted to throw her up against the wall and take her. At the least, he wanted to kiss her, right here, and right now. Or was she just hoping he did? Projecting her outrageous thoughts onto him? It was terrifying. Because most of the time, the men who wanted her weren't men who she wanted back.

"Please go," she said, immediately angry with herself that it came out in almost a strangled whisper.

"What time does your son get home from school?" The minute he said it, she imagined taking him up to her bed. Could she do such a thing? Would she ever do such a thing?

"How dare—"

He put his hands up, then actually blushed when it dawned on him what it sounded like. "Because of that," he said, pointing to the crate. "I figured you were waiting for him to get home to open that."

"Oh." Now Georgia was the one mortified. To think, she almost slapped him. And worse, she thought about it. She thought about taking him up to her bedroom. She didn't even want to think about how long it had been since she'd been with a man. She would never do it in a million years, take this blue-eyed monster to bed just after meeting him, but she did take a few minutes to fantasize about it. She wouldn't clean up after either. She'd leave the sheets messy all day just so she could relive the moment, sleep in the sheets again at night. A loud, and quite unladylike, laugh escaped her. Once she started laughing, she was like a snowball rolling downhill, gathering strength. To her surprise, he started laughing too. Within seconds the two of them were bent over, tears streaming down their cheeks, laughing. When she finally got it under control, and was wiping her eyes, she felt winded, and even a little tired. And that's when she started to cry.

Pent-up stress came pouring out of her in half-broken sobs. She missed her father. She couldn't believe he was no longer here. Bing Crosby didn't sound the same without him. He would know what to do about this takeover. He would handle her sister. He would make Ranger feel like he had a father figure. She expected some kind of sarcastic remark out of Adam Cavalier, or worse, some kind of patronizing "There, there." To her surprise, he did none of these. Most surprising of all, he seemed at ease with her pain. He reached into his pocket and handed her a tissue. A clean tissue! From a strange man. With dimples and the body of a strong warrior. She needed Xanax.

Scrooge, she reminded herself. And not the end-of-the-story reformed one. This was the pre-goose-giving Scrooge. It woke her up, instantly dried her tears. Now he would really think he could take advantage of her. Well it wasn't going to work. She was on to him.

"Thanks," she said. "I'm sorry."

"There's no need."

"I don't mean about the tears. I'm afraid you're not going to find out what's in this crate. At least not today." Why did she say not today? Was she implying there would be tomorrow?

"Well," he said in that low voice that made her thrum from her toes, all the way up. "A guy can dream, can't he?" There was no mistaking his gaze this time. It was pure lust. Damn him. Georgia walked to the steel door, imagining a curt and swift opening. Instead she fumbled with lock after lock, as she wondered if he was looking at her body, as she even hoped a little that he was. Despite practically becoming a born-again virgin she had taken very good care of her body, and it was nice to think a man was appreciating her if only for a few stolen seconds.

"It's a lot to worry about, isn't it? Living here alone with all these valuable things."

Finally, Georgia got the door open. "Trying to scare me now, are you?" She turned around to face him, look him in the eye, hoping her anger would disguise all the other feelings racing through her. Once again, looking into his eyes was akin to being zapped. Her urge to touch him, throw herself into his arms, was overwhelming. This was no way for a grown woman to behave. She didn't even know grown women *had* these feelings. Stop it! She wanted to scream at him. Stop doing this to me.

He, on the other hand, looked stricken. Why? She couldn't even remember what she just said. "Scare you? No. God, no. I was just. Never mind. I'm sorry." He seemed sincere, and totally flustered. Maybe she was coming down a little hard on him. She could hear Mrs. Weaver sitting in her kitchen, as clear as day.

Don't fall for him.
Scrooge.

"Good day, Mr. Thrift." He was Mr. Cavalier. She hoped if she said the wrong name he would think she couldn't care less about him.

"It's Adam," he said. He didn't take his eyes off her. Finally, she raised hers and allowed another moment of prolonged eye contact. How was she supposed to not fall for him when for the first time in years, everything inside her was going *Zing, Zing, Zing?!* It wasn't fair. It wasn't fair at all.

"Adam," she said.

"Can I—say something? Just for a second? Something I shouldn't say? And then you can go back to hating my guts?"

Something he shouldn't say? Who could say no to that? Not trusting herself to speak, Georgia nodded.

"I know you," he said. "And you have turned into the most beautiful woman I have ever seen." And then with a nod to her astonished face, he was gone.

CHAPTER FIVE

They decided to hold the business owner's meeting in Roberto's Italian restaurant. First, people were more likely to be agreeable on a full stomach. Second, if that failed, there was plenty of wine. Georgia and Ranger walked in ten minutes early. Roberto came out of the kitchen's swinging door, wearing an apron smothered in flour and marinara sauce. It didn't stop him from enveloping Ranger in a bear hug.

"Spaghetti and meatballs?"

"Yes, please."

Roberto glanced at Georgia. "Make it two?"

"I'll probably take mine to go," Georgia said. She was too nervous to eat. If it was true and four of them were on the verge of selling, or had sold, Georgia definitely wouldn't be able to eat.

"They're in the back," Roberto said. "Why don't you let Ranger sit up here and watch the television? Marta will keep an eye on him." Marta, Roberto's wife, was a round, smiling woman who always remembered everyone's names but watched the cash register like a hawk. She'd do the same with Ranger. Georgia glanced at her son.

"Can I have Sprite?"

Georgia ruffled his hair. "Just one," she said. "And don't fill up on bread." She headed for the back table, her spirits already better from the enticing smells emanating from the kitchen. What would Cranberry Street be like without Roberto's? Without any of them? She was halfway to the back table when she looked up and saw that it was filled. Jess, Joe, Roger, Sue, Daniel, Mrs. Weaver—they were all sitting down already. And she was early! Georgia felt her stomach twist. The minute she reached the table, they all stopped talking and looked up.

"Hello, Georgia," Joe said. "Have a seat."

"Am I late? I thought we said six-thirty," Georgia said. It was the latest they could all get the early-bird special. Once again, Georgia was reminded that they were all nearing retirement. Roger was wearing a shirt with a parrot on it. And they all had little umbrellas in their drinks. She could practically see visions of golf courses and bingo halls hanging above their heads. They weren't here for a meeting, they were here to pounce on her.

"You're right on time, dear," Mrs. Weaver said. "Is Roberto getting you a plate?"

"No. I'm taking it to go."

"Hurry," Sue said. "Pour her some wine." Hurry? Georgia sat and watched as the decanter of red wine was passed up the table like life-saving equipment.

"You guys are scaring me," Georgia said.

"Just have a drink," Daniel said. "Relax."

"How did you make out with that hunk?" Mrs. Weaver asked.

"Excuse me?"

"I saw him follow you into your place. I told you he was gorgeous, didn't I?"

Georgia took what she meant to be a tiny sip of the

wine, but the comment from Mrs. Weaver flustered her so that instead she drank almost all of it in one go.

"Thatta girl," Roger said. "That should soften the blow."

"Wait," Georgia said. She stood up and tried to look tall. "You have to let me speak first."

"Darling," Sue said. "We've made up our—"

"Oh, let her speak," Jess said.

"Thank you." Georgia plastered a smile to her face. "I have ideas for all of us." She pulled her e-reader out of her purse. "Joe. E-readers."

"E-readers?"

"You could partner with a company and offer them in your store."

"I want to sell the books. The actual books!"

"Or—maybe you could design your own e-reader."

"I can't even program my coffeemaker."

"Or maybe for every actual book they buy, they get credits to download a book."

"Doll, you're a nice woman. Great kid, too. You've auctioned off a couple of my rare books. I'm grateful. But I've been done for a long time. You know that."

Georgia swallowed. She gave a quick nod and turned to Jess, their local, chubby butcher. "Jess. What if you go organic?"

"Organic?" Jess sounded horrified.

"Grass-fed beef only. That goes for chicken and every-thing else. From humane farms. Your customers will pay extra to feel as good as they can about what they're eat-ing. It's healthier and—"

"It's not cost-effective," Jess said.

"Winter barbeques," Georgia said. "We'll have block barbeques during the winter. We'll buy all the meat from you."

"How much have you had to drink?" Mrs. Weaver asked.

"It's either too much or not enough," Daniel said.

"And Sue. I can order more flower arrangements from you for my auctions."

"I don't really think—"

"And Roger? What if you kept the pharmacy open twenty-four hours?"

"Twenty-four hours? What am I? A frat boy?"

"I know it's not going to be easy. But we need to change a little with the times," Georgia said.

"We're too old," Sue said.

"Mrs. Weaver. You can reduce some of your inventory—"

"Reduce my inventory?"

"Does anyone really eat fruitcake anymore?" Georgia asked. There was a gasp at the table, followed by a giggle and a couple of coughs.

"What are you saying about my fruitcake?"

"It's just—compared to all your other goodies—"

"She's saying you can use it as a doorstop," Daniel said.

"You're just jealous because you're losing sales in that hoarder's paradise you call a hardware store," Mrs. Weaver said.

"Speaking of which, Daniel," Georgia said. "I thought you could offer DIY projects."

"Die?" Sue asked.

"D-I-Y," Jess corrected. "Do-it-yourself."

"If I'm going to do it myself, why do I need Daniel?" Sue persisted.

"Let's all calm down," Jess said. "We should tell her the good news."

"Yes," Georgia said. "Please. Tell me the good news."

"We want you to auction off all of our inventory," Roger said. "How's that for good news?"

Were they kidding? They called dumping all their crap on her good news? Then again, it would draw plenty of interest at auction. Watching all their lives go up in flames.

"We could try and get on a reality show," Georgia said, using up the last of her big ideas.

"Like *Pawn Stars*?" Sue asked.

"Porn?" Mrs. Weaver asked. "I'm not doing porn. Although back in the day I had the body for it, believe you me."

"And you could finally carry *Fifty Shades of Grey*," Sue said to Joe.

"I am not selling that smut in my bookstore! I draw the line at *Lady Chatterley's Lover*."

Daniel stood up. "It's been decided. We've all signed. We're just waiting on you."

"No," Georgia said. "All of you?" One by one they nodded their heads. Georgia slumped back in her seat. Daniel sat. They all watched her for a few minutes.

"It's a really good offer," Sue said. "More than I would make at the flower shop for the next five years."

"You know I can't keep my doors open," Joe said. "Books are dinosaurs."

"I'm thinking of becoming a vegetarian and taking up yoga," Jess said. "Forty years of being around raw meat will do that to a man."

"Daniel? Roger? The town can't live without a pharmacy or hardware store."

"They've given us options," Daniel said. "If we'd like, they're offering us space in the megastore. At greatly reduced rent, I might add."

"Or we could take their buyout," Roger said.

"Mrs. Weaver. You swore you weren't going to sell."

Mrs. Weaver threw her hands up. "That was before they went snooping around. They say I owe so much back taxes that I don't have a choice!"

"Oh, no," Georgia said. "And Roberto?"

"They're letting me stay, doll." Georgia didn't realize he was behind her until he spoke. She turned to him. "I'm on the end of the street here. They said they don't really need my portion. And if the mega-mall goes up, so does my business." Georgia felt everyone staring at her. The message was clear. She was the only one holding them up. From vegetarianism, and yoga, and wealth, and parrot-heads with margaritas.

"It's Christmas," Georgia said. "We can't decide this now. Not before the big celebration." Unlike most towns, which boasted a town square, their little slice of Rhode Island had a town circle. Every year residents gathered in the circle to celebrate Christmas. They had crafts and Santa, and food tents, and fake snow during the years when they couldn't get the sky to supply them with the real stuff.

"We're canceling the celebration this year," Sue said gently. "It just doesn't feel right."

She must be joking. Georgia's eyes scanned the table as she waited for someone to admit she was joking. "You've canceled Christmas?" It brought her to her feet. "But the business. The kids!"

"We have to start clearing out our shops," Sue said. "If we don't take this deal now, it disappears."

But I'm not taking the deal, Georgia thought. *And if I don't—yours won't stay on the table.* She didn't say it; she was outnumbered. What a mistake she'd made. She should have drunk the entire decanter of wine. "I have to go," Georgia said.

"Your sister wants to sell," Roger said.

Virginia! She'd been talking to them behind her back. She took a deep breath. She felt a hand on her shoulder. Roberto.

"We can't stop progress, darling," he said. Easy for him to say. He didn't have to give up his restaurant.

"I have to go," Georgia said.

"But you'll take the deal?" Daniel asked. "Won't you?"

"Right now I don't have anything to say," Georgia said. "Except Merry Christmas to all, and to all a good night."

Long after she'd read to Ranger and tucked him into bed, she couldn't sleep. Couldn't eat, couldn't sleep, couldn't think. She entered the office, and stared at the papers piled on top of the fax machine. Her sister's ultimatum. Pay up or sell. Just like Dad eventually had to sell Trash and Treasures, and their land, and their house. Georgia didn't know much about the family who bought it, except that the white barn was going to be turned into a mother-in-law apartment. Even though they were only twelve miles from the house, she'd never been able to go back. You can't go back. You can't stop progress. Georgia gathered the blue envelopes off the floor, grabbed the faxes from the machine, and headed for her bed.

On her way past the shelf of vintage wines, she stopped. They had some really good ones, just waiting for auction. *Well, now we have one less,* she thought, swiping one off the shelf. These bedtime stories definitely needed it.

An hour later, after reading through every single letter from the investors and the two faxes from her sister, everything was crystal clear. There was no way she would be able to come up with the money to pay her sister and Devon. And, as everyone said, the offer was good. Five years good. And she'd make a little off auctioning her neighbors' goods. But what then? Georgia wouldn't be anywhere near retirement. Ranger would only be twelve years old. This offer was good for retirees. Not her! She supposed she could look for somewhere else to set up shop. And home. But where? It had taken over a year for her Realtor to find her this space. Maybe she could get a loan for the money she owed her sister. She owed it to Ranger to try. And to her father. She still couldn't help feeling that none of this would be happening if he were still here. He'd have helped her.

It killed him to sell Trash and Treasures. The only time a little bit of light came into his eyes was when she announced she was opening this auction house. He even lived with them in the end. It was amazing to see her father happy again. He was in the front seat of every auction, and he was great help when they received tools or farm equipment. For pretty much everything else, Georgia brought experts in to help her appraise. She couldn't imagine a more exciting job. Once again, she was left with a hollow ache, and increasing panic. If she couldn't find a new space, what on earth would she do?

The next morning, after dropping Ranger off to school, she dressed in a suit, bought a dozen éclairs, and went to her local bank. She'd had her personal and business accounts here for years. And she was debt free! That had to count for something.

"It doesn't," the banker told her. "No debt means less of a repayment history."

"Because I pay for everything as I go."

"Too risky," the bank told her.

"And I bet you're just thrilled to death that a mega-discount store might take our place," Georgia couldn't help but say.

"This isn't personal, Georgia," he said. At least he knew her name. Would he learn the names of the mega-discount people? Probably. They would probably even get Christmas presents. She stood to go.

"Were those for me?" the banker asked.

"No," Georgia said. "Sorry."

"Try online," the banker said. "You might get a loan that way." Georgia nodded, then gave him one éclair, and walked out the door.

They all turned her down. Every single online bank. Too risky, they said. Not in today's economy. Not with the loss your company took the last year. Yes, business had been down. But it would pick back up again. Everything went in cycles, everybody knew that! But nobody else was acting like they knew it. It was just gloom and doom.

Georgia needed a break. She bundled up and headed outside. She walked Cranberry Street, trying to memorize everything the way it was. She ended up in the town circle. Where they should have been decorating for Christmas. Instead, nada. Not a single twig of holly could be seen. Maybe she would come out here with Ranger and decorate it herself. Although until she signed away her lease, her efforts wouldn't be appreciated.

Why couldn't all of this wait until the New Year? Not that it would hurt any less, but at least she would have enjoyed Christmas. She always enjoyed Christmas. Not this year. Not only was her father not here, but they were going to lose everything. Even the town celebration was squashed. For the first time in her life, Georgia understood that some years, due to death, or tragedies, were just too painful to celebrate. And real life wasn't like *It's a Wonderful Life*. No happy ending coming in two hours. Santa Claus wasn't real.

But that didn't mean she wanted to ruin things for Ranger. This was his childhood. The only one he would ever get. Wasn't it bad enough he'd lost his father and his grandfather? Was she really going to take away even one precious Christmas memory? That's when she knew exactly what she was going to do. She had no choice but to sell, but at least they were going to have one last Christmas party in the town circle. And not just any party. An all-out spectacle. Paid for by Scrooge One and Scrooge Two. She picked up the phone and called the business owners, and when that was done she called her sister, and when that battle was finally won, she called the blue-eyed Scrooge. There was no reason she called him instead of Ben. Either one would have done. It was simply his number she dialed first. Nothing special about that.

Georgia set aside the entire next Saturday for decorating the auction floor with Ranger. The best of the best came out. She hired photographers to come and take pictures of all of her inventory. It would all go up for bid in a series of final auctions beginning just after the New Year. The contract, once signed, would allow for ninety days to sell everything and relocate. Georgia had to argue hard for that as well, but in the end she won out. It wasn't ideal, but by the time she had to close everything should be sold. Of course she didn't break that part to Ranger yet. Not until Christmas was over. Not until she could tell him without bursting into tears. She'd already seen to it that this was going to be the best Christmas ever, the rest of the business owners agreed to the party in the town circle. All that was left to do was sign on the dotted line. She scheduled a face-to-face meeting bright and early the next morning with Scrooge One and Scrooge Two.

By the time the decorating was done, The Treasure Chest had never looked so magical. Colored lights hung all around the space and their best trains ran on the special tracks that were laid on the shelving that circled the entire warehouse. No matter where you walked, there would soon be a train passing overhead, blowing real smoke and sounding its whistle. They had standing reindeer, and Santa, Nativity scenes, and entire Victorian villages set up on tables and bookshelves that instantly became display centers. They hung ribbons, and holly, and garland. The only project left was to get their Christmas tree. Georgia was prepared to go out and get the biggest and best they'd ever had. The sky would be the limit. Heck, maybe they would get several trees so they could deck each one out with its own special design. Even without the tree, Ranger's eyes were wide with excitement. Georgia saved the best for last.

"Guess who's coming for Christmas?"

"Santa?"

"That's a given. Also—coming in a close second—Aunt Virginia."

"She's coming here?"

"Yep. With your cousins. And Devon."

"Yes!" Ranger jumped about the place while Georgia looked on with a smile. Adam and Ben weren't the only ones she made demands upon. Virginia would rather pull out her hair and paint antlers on her bald head than fly here for Christmas. But with Adam and Ben paying for it, how could she say no? Besides, she needed her sister here for her last hurrah.

A few minutes later, she found Ranger staring at the crate. "When are we going to open it?"

"Oh," Georgia said. "I totally forgot." Talk about the elephant in the room.

"Let's do it now."

"It's been a full day."

"Please, please with a star on top?" Her father's favorite saying.

"Honey, this thing is sealed to high heaven. We're going to need to hire some muscle to help us pry it open."

Ranger made a bicep. "I have muscles."

"You're going to need them to build snowmen and

throw snowballs." They were due for snow in a few days. A blizzard if the weatherman was correct.

"Tomorrow?"

"We'll see."

"Why are you having pictures taken of everything?" The photographers were still at it. There was no choice, she had a ton of inventory.

"We're going to have several post-holiday auctions," Georgia said. Every half-truth she told him carved her up inside. But this definitely wasn't the time to break the news.

"Cool."

"TV, book, game, or bed?"

"Game."

"Clue or Monopoly?"

"Clue." Thank goodness. Monopoly always took too long and Ranger always ended up with Park Place. And as fate would have it, she always got stuck with Virginia.

"You grab the game. I'll make popcorn and hot chocolate." Ranger raced off to get the game and Georgia headed into the kitchen. She stood at the stove, making the popcorn, and biting back tears. This is what life was all about. Popcorn. Games with your kid. Hot chocolate. *We can do this anywhere,* she thought. *I will miss this place like my right leg. But wherever we go, we will have games, and popcorn, and each other.* But try as she might to cheer herself up, she was still left with an endless hollow ache in her center, and a rising crest of fear. This was home. This was her dream. This was where her heart was. What did they say about the Grinch? His was the size of a pea? *Sounds about right,* she thought, ignoring the part of her that argued she wasn't being fair to Adam. *Sounds about right.*

CHAPTER SIX

The next morning Georgia was awake at five A.M. She loved the warehouse in the early morning. Before the phone started ringing, before paperwork appeared on her desk, before the computer screen was ready to research items, before inventory was taken for upcoming auctions, before appraisers came to consult about items. It was just her, the slight whine of the heater, and her shelves of sleepy treasures. Some women liked mani-pedis and shopping. Georgia's "me time" was simply being alone in her space with a cup of coffee. She would wrap her hands around the warm mug and walk among her treasures. It was like strolling through her own personal flower garden. Sometimes she picked things up. Sometimes she talked to them. Often she imagined the people who had sat in a chair, or lifted a crystal goblet in a toast, or brandished a sword. She felt as if her space were filled with unseen friends; ghosts of things past.

She padded into the kitchen, eager to get to her routine. If only she could do it without counting down the days in her head. Focus. She headed for the cupboard where she kept the coffee beans in a terrific old tin she kept out of auction a few years ago, along with an old-fashioned grinder. Set just off the office, it was a simple galley kitchen, but it was stocked with the essentials. Georgia prepared the coffeepot and leaned against the counter as it started to brew. The gurgle, the smell, the first couple of drips. Adam and Ben would be here in two hours. She scheduled the meeting this early on a Sunday for two reasons. One, Ranger was sure to be asleep. Especially after all the decorating and playing from yesterday. Second, she predicted the early hour would annoy the Scrooges.

I know you. And you've turned into the most beautiful woman I've ever seen.

She'd spun that phrase around a thousand times in her head, and couldn't come up with an explanation. Other than—he was a liar. But he'd sounded so sincere. So intense, and she believed him. But just what did he mean by that? It made absolutely no sense. She'd never seen him before in her life. She would definitely remember him. And now look. Here she was spending stolen moments thinking about him. Actually thinking about him. Imagining him standing beside her bed, taking off his clothes, reaching for her. That's where it should have stayed—after all, she was a woman, she had desires, having amorous fantasies about him she could handle. But she just had to take it a step further, didn't she? And so it didn't stop with picturing him in bed. She actually allowed herself to imagine Adam spending the day. Decorating with them, running toy trains along the floor with Ranger, playing Clue with them. Ridiculous. It was the old guilt raising its ugly head. Ranger with no father. Her father had been his only remaining male guide. And now he was gone. How could she rip his home from him too?

They would find another. She would make sure of it. But the man responsible for taking it all away from them would not be sitting at their dinner table, picking Mr. Plum with the candlestick in the library, or placing the star at the top of the tree. It wasn't Adam she wanted, it was just a man. Any man. Well, not any man. The thought of dating again was truly horrid. Blind dates. Men who didn't like children. Married men who lied and said they were single. Men who preferred much younger women. Men she wasn't attracted to. The list of obstacles was daunting. She'd stick to fantasizing.

But not about Adam Cavalier. Or his handsome face, muscular tall frame, deep, low voice.

She took her coffee to the fireplace section. None of them were actually working fireplaces, not currently anyway, but they could easily be made to work in the right homes. She loved the collection of ornate wood mantels, all from older Victorian homes, when care was put into everything they built. When things were built to last. She lit the candles in each fireplace, and sat in one of the comfy chairs positioned facing them. The effect was divine. It really felt as if there were a roaring fire. She would have to make a list of places she was going to donate items that didn't sell. Families in need, and grass-roots organizations. Even as she tried to think of business, she was imagining Adam standing over her, leaning in, and kissing her neck.

Damn him. In a little while, she would be signing papers selling him her lease in the New Year. That would stop the fantasies in their tracks. And even if they continued for a little while, she wouldn't ever see him again after this morning. Adam and Ben weren't invited to the Christmas party in the circle. She would have to make sure to remind them of that. By the time the doorbell rang, Georgia had done a quick workout, showered, and changed into jeans and a cashmere sweater, the indigo one that so many people had complimented her on. And so what if she took time with her layered black hair, and applied make-up even though the sun was barely out. And the perfume? It was all for her. Let Adam be just as tortured thinking about her. And she would spend all of her time looking and talking to Ben. Childish, maybe, but she had to do something to keep from throwing her arms around Adam and kissing him on the mouth. Hard.

She glanced at the wall of clocks as she headed for the door. They were fifteen minutes early! How dare they be so eager? She should just let them stand out there until it was seven on the dot. Maybe the blizzard would come early and bury them alive. *Here stand two Scrooges, frozen in time. Yes, one is a hunk. Don't let him fool you.* Then again, she didn't want a repeated doorbell to wake Ranger. *You put on make-up, you put on the indigo sweater, you like him!* She undid the locks and threw open the door, determined to look only at Ben. But Ben wasn't in front of her. Adam was. And he was alone.

"Hello, Georgia," he said. Why did he have to say it as if she had just rolled over in bed and he was greeting her from the next pillow?

"You're early." She sounded snappy. She had to. He was not going to get under her skin this time.

"May I come in, or do you want all your neighbors to hear you shouting at me?"

Like lovers, having a quarrel. "I'm not shouting." Georgia stepped back. "Come in." Adam gave a half-bow, which she would have found charming had she not been purposely concentrating on hating him. "Where is Ben?" she asked when he was just inside the door. He stomped his feet on the rug and shook out his head.

"It's snowing? This soon?" That was the downside to the warehouse. There were only a few windows. One in the kitchen, one in the bathroom, and one in Ranger's bedroom. Georgia opened the door again and peeked out. Sure enough, under the dim streetlamps, she could see a light curtain of snow, falling sideways.

"They're saying we could get up to three feet," Adam said.

"Ranger is going to be thrilled."

"Especially if school is canceled tomorrow." For a second Adam had a glint in his eye as if he were a child getting off for a snow day. Georgia shut and locked the door.

"Would you like coffee?" she asked, heading for the kitchen.

"You bet." He was right behind her, following her. She didn't so much hear him as feel him at her back. Why did it feel so normal to have him so close? Ordinarily she was very stiff around strangers, but with Adam she had to keep reminding herself that he wasn't a stranger at all— and then she had to remind herself that she couldn't stand him. For some reason, it was taking an awful lot of reminding.

When she was at the coffeepot she turned to ask him if he wanted cream and sugar. "How do you take it?" The minute she said it a thousand dirty thoughts ran through her mind. He was right there. Barely an inch away. Why was he so close? Why did he smell so good? Why did he make her feel as if she was getting a snow day? And now he was looking deep and long into her eyes, and she was staring back.

"Any way you want to give it to me."

"What?"

"That's how I'll take it." Georgia turned back, moved away from him, grabbed mugs out of the cupboard.

"You're a comedian. But I would really like to know if you prefer cream and sugar or—"

"Just sugar," he said. Everything out of his mouth

sounded sexual. Maybe it wasn't him, maybe it was her. She was reading into everything he said. Soon they were seated next to the fireplaces. Uh-oh. Now this really *was* romantic. She leapt up and started blowing out the candles.

"Oh," he said. "I thought they were cozy."

"We're not on a date," she said as she blew the last one out. She headed for the dimmer switch for the bank of lights nearest them. She turned it up higher than she normally would.

"Let's sit over here," she said. She moved them away from the comfy chairs to the dining table. She waited until he sat down and then she sat all the way at the other end. Since it was a table that could seat twelve, it put plenty of distance between them.

"Much better," Adam said. "We look very professional." Was he mocking her? He was studying her, and smiling. Did he think she was attracted to him? Was she overcompensating? Then again, he was the one here a half an hour ahead of time. Alone.

"Why are you here so early?" she asked.

"Why are you selling?"

"Excuse me?"

"The last time I was here, you said you wouldn't sell to us if we were the last investors on earth and zombies were eating what was left of your warehouse."

"I did not."

Adam grinned. "It was certainly the sentiment," he said.

"You're that surprised, are you?" She laid it on thick so that there was no way he could miss the sarcasm.

"You were pretty resolute."

"Why does this matter? This is what you wanted, isn't it?"

"Not like this."

"How then? You want me to hand my life's work, my life's dream over to you with a smile? Is that it?"

"You're totally misunderstanding me. I just want you to know—my intentions are good."

"Seriously?"

"Did you read the literature I gave you?"

"No. Why? Was it homework? Part of my contract?"

"I just think if you knew how I plan to invest the money—"

"I don't care. You win. Is that what you want to hear?"

"No."

"You're afraid I'm going to back out, is that it?"

"No."

"Of course you're not. Because you've left me no choice, have you? God forbid I make my sister go bankrupt and keep the neighbors from yoga, parrots, and veganism."

"What?"

"Never mind. Why are you so early? Did you come to gloat?"

"Absolutely not. I take no pleasure in your pain. I'm sorry. Georgia, I'm really sorry."

"Whatever. Do you have the paperwork?"

"Ben's bringing it. I came early to see—I was hoping maybe you'd changed your mind because you liked our offer. I was hoping you read up about my plans for—"

Georgia stood and planted her hands on the table. "I can't believe you. The arrogance. You're actually looking for my approval for kicking me out of my home and my life's work in one fell swoop—"

"I just thought if you knew—"

"You aren't going to get it. Whatever it is you want to tell me—I don't care."

"You don't even want to—"

"I don't care! I don't care! Are you deaf?" She was

ashamed of herself, for sounding so childish, but he was pushing all her buttons and really, wasn't it enough that she was giving in? She didn't want to care. He didn't get to take everything away from her and force her to *like* it.

"No. Well, maybe a little. Because of all your shouting."

"I will stop shouting if you will stop trying to recruit me to see this deal through discount-mall rose-colored glasses."

"Fair enough," he said finally. "But you can at least admit it's a good offer." He still looked as if he wanted to say more but at least he knew better this time.

"If you're in your seventies and looking to retire. Not for me. Not with another forty years ahead of me."

"But surely you can find another place—"

Georgia slammed her hands down again. "Why do you care?"

"Because. I know you—"

"Stop saying that. You don't know me."

"I—"

"We're not friends. We're not dating—"

Adam stood too, and raised his voice. "That's the second time you've mentioned us dating." Was it? She couldn't remember. Or maybe he could read her every thought. How dare he. How dare he come in here and call her out like this before she signed away all rights to this warehouse. Her future. She hated him. She backed from the table. But he was coming straight for her.

"Leave the paperwork. I'll have it messengered after I've signed it." She headed for the door. Once again, Adam was right behind her. He touched her arm and she whirled around. Having him so close stripped all coherent thoughts from her mind. She knew she was staring at his lips and she couldn't stop.

"I like you," he said in a soft, low voice. "I want to go on a date."

"You're kidding, right?" she asked quietly. He actually thought she was going to be putty in his hands. Arrogant. Probably came with being so damn gorgeous.

"I know it's a little awkward—"

"A little awkward?" This time, she advanced on him. He didn't move an inch, like someone not wanting to scare off a wild animal, he stood very still. If she wasn't mistaken, he was holding his breath.

"I'd rather cut off my arm than leave this place. This is home. This is work. This is the last place my father ever lived. And every time I think of what I lost—it's going to be your face I see. You, I blame. We are never. Ever. Ever. Ever. Going on a date." Their long stare was broken by the harsh ringing of the doorbell.

"Get out," she said, opening the door and gesturing. But Ben was already barging in.

CHAPTER SEVEN

"What did I miss?" Ben asked. Georgia and Adam stood opposite each other, like boxers squared off at a match. Soon little footsteps came pounding down the stairs and across the floor.

"Great," Georgia said. "You woke my kid."

"Is she talking to me?" Ben asked. "Because she's looking at you. What's going on? Lovers' spat?"

Lovers' spat? Did he actually just say that? People could tell. She knew it. People could tell. Even her private thoughts weren't private anymore. Her lust for Adam was coming out her pores. How could this be happening? Georgia glared at Ben. He slightly bowed in apology.

"Sorry, ma'am. Just that Adam here hasn't quite been himself since he laid eyes on you." He wasn't talking about Georgia after all. He was talking about Adam. He hasn't been the same since he laid eyes on her. That was worse. This was making the zing start all over again. She was not going to have zing right now. Not him and not now.

"You're not helping," Adam said.

"Not at all," Georgia said.

"I'm not trying to," Ben said. "What are you doing here? We were supposed to arrive together."

His words were a jolt to her system. Adam came early to be alone with her. Because he felt it too. She wanted to scream. This wasn't fair. Of all the times she imagined this happening, falling in love again, it was with someone who could be there for her and Ranger. Be on their team. Adam was on the opposite team. You don't fall in love with somebody from the opposite team. She turned to her son, grateful for the interruption.

"They were just leaving," Georgia said.

"No," Ranger said. "We need muscle, Mom. Remember?" Georgia glanced at him. She loved him just out of bed. The *Star Wars* pajamas skewed. The hair sticking up. His breath was probably atrocious but she loved him anyway.

"Muscle?" Adam said with a raised eyebrow. Georgia tried not to look at his biceps. Ranger bounded up to the crate and placed his hand on it.

"Let's get cracking," he said.

Adam's eyes lit up when he understood the reference. Georgia knew he'd been dying to find out what was in that crate, and Ranger had just handed him the key. "Now you're talking," Adam said.

"No," Ben said. "We're not her handymen. We're here to sign a contract."

"What contract?" Ranger asked.

"Not now," Georgia said to Ben. "Not here and not now. Understand?" She slid her eyes to Ranger, and then pointedly back to Ben. She'd clobber him if he didn't understand.

"But—" Ben started.

"It'll get done," Adam said. "We'll leave it with her."

"Leave what with us?" Ranger asked.

Adam stepped up and placed his hand on Ranger's

shoulder. It looked so natural there. Seeing a man pay attention to Ranger was physically painful. Knowing all that he was missing, that no matter how good of a mother she was, a boy needed a father figure. Georgia turned away before Ranger could see tears in her eyes. Adam must have noticed this, for when he spoke again, he sounded much more upbeat. "It's just a contract to protect workers. Us muscle just can't be too careful these days. We might get a splinter opening this baby."

"We've got gloves. Don't we, Mom?"

"Workers usually bring their own gloves," Georgia said. "Don't they?"

"I've got muscle, too," Ranger said. He held out his skinny little arm and tried to make a muscle.

Adam let out a whistle and felt Ranger's bicep. "You are amazing," he said. Georgia felt the tears, hot and stinging, rise in her eyes. You are amazing, Ranger, she wanted to say. But his eyes were alight not only with what was said, but who had just said it.

"I help Mom all the time, don't I, Mom?"

"I couldn't do it without him," Georgia said. "He's the best."

"I help the auctioneers, too," Ranger said.

"That must be fun," Adam said.

"It is. Except when they try to tell bedtime stories. They end too fast."

Adam let out a genuine laugh, one that made Ranger laugh along with him. Adam stopped laughing when he caught Georgia staring at him. He turned back to Ranger, winked, and then rubbed his hands together. "Who has a crowbar?" he asked.

"I'm going to go out this door, and when I come back in, I want to be in the right universe this time," Ben said. Adam began to whistle. Paul used to whistle. God, she missed that. When a man whistled you felt as if everything was going to be all right. Like they could handle whatever came their way. Adam could hold a tune too. She wondered if he sang. Or played an instrument. He would look incredible playing the saxophone without a shirt. It didn't matter. All she needed to know was that he wanted a mini-mall right where they were standing. Ranger wouldn't remember. He was only a few years old when Paul died.

"My Dad used to whistle," Ranger said.

Georgia's hand flew to her mouth. "How did you know that?" It came out in a strangled whisper.

"Grandpa told me," Ranger said. Oh. Of course. She hadn't realized her father had ever talked to Ranger about Paul, but it made perfect sense. And now she could see it was true. Ranger didn't merely want to be around men, he craved it. Case in point, he was following Adam around like a baby duck. What was she going to do? She didn't want him to get close to Adam, especially not Adam, but she didn't want to crush this moment either.

"You can put your coat here," Ranger said, pointing to an iron coatrack just outside the office. "Do you want me to show you where to find the crowbars?" He sounded like an old man in a Bloomingdale's elevator. Fourth floor, crowbars.

"Absolutely," Adam said. "Any chance of getting a cup of coffee? Muscles flex better with a little caffeine."

"Sure. Mom? Would you throw on a pot?"

"Ranger, you're in your bare feet and you haven't had breakfast. We can't open this crate right this very moment." She would make Ranger something to eat, get rid of these guys, and later get one of the auctioneers to help open the crate.

"How about it," Ranger said to Adam. "Are you hungry?"

"No," Georgia said. "Ranger I'm sure he can't—"

"Starved," Adam said. He flashed a huge grin.

"I could eat," Ben said.

This time they sat at an even larger dining table, one Georgia usually reserved for big celebrations. Like Christmas dinner. It was made of thick, dark wood and it stretched forever. Georgia could imagine it sitting in a medieval castle somewhere. She hadn't planned on making them her famous French toast, but Ranger insisted on it. It had been her father's favorite, too. She made a little strawberry cream filling for the middle.

"Is this from the bakery?" Adam asked. "These are better than the éclairs."

"And the fruitcake," Ben said with his mouth full.

"From the bakery," Ranger said. He laughed like it was a good joke. "Mom made them," he said.

Georgia could feel Adam staring at her from the far end of the table. Okay, maybe she'd picked this table so she could set the men as far down as possible. She didn't anticipate Ranger sitting across from Adam. So now it just looked ridiculous, the three of them bonding over powdered sugar and syrup, she stewing in her own zip code.

"My dad was a park ranger," Georgia heard her son say. "That's why they named me Ranger. He died when I was three."

Once again, Georgia felt as if she could feel Adam staring at her from the other end of the table, even though she hadn't lifted her head to his.

"I'm very sorry to hear that," Adam said. "I know what it's like to lose someone you love."

"Who?" Ranger asked.

"Ranger," Georgia said. "Please help me clear the plates."

Adam leaned over and whispered something to Ranger, who nodded his head seriously. She felt flushed with irrational anger. Was he usurping her authority? The minute she and Ranger placed dishes in the sink, she turned.

"What did he say to you?"

"Who?"

"Adam. What did he whisper to you just now?"

"He said I was very lucky."

"What? Why?"

"To have you as a mom."

"Oh."

"Are you mad at him?"

"What?"

Ranger shrugged. "You seem mad at him about something." For a second she wanted to tell him. He was a smart kid. If he knew who Adam really was, he'd show him to the door himself. But she had to put Ranger first. This was supposed to be his best Christmas ever.

"Go get dressed, and I'll show the muscle where the crowbars are."

"Sounds like a plan." Georgia whirled around to see Adam enter the kitchen, his hands full with the rest of the dishes, and that interminable grin on his stupid, beautiful face.

After breakfast, Ben looked at his watch.

"Why don't you take off?" Adam said. "I can help them with the crate." Ben stared at Adam for a long time, then glanced at Georgia. She looked away. Finally, Ben took his leave, but not before turning to Georgia.

"We'll need those papers signed right away," he said.

Luckily, Ranger was too busy hopping around the crate to hear. Georgia simply nodded. After he was gone, Adam wheeled the crate to the center of the auction floor.

Adam looked around, glanced at the folded seats. As usual, Ranger was studying him.

"You should totally come to one of our auctions," Ranger said. "They're awesome."

"I bet they are," Adam said.

"Adam doesn't care about such things," Georgia said. "Isn't that right?" She was going to have to be careful not to let her venom spill everywhere, but she also wasn't going to stand by and let her son get attached to a Scrooge. Ranger would resent her even more once he found out the truth.

"I do care about such things," Adam said. "I care about a lot of things. I've been trying to tell you how much I care." For a second he looked ashamed. They tilted the crate off the dolly and Adam picked up the crowbar. Georgia went over and indicated which side he should start with.

"Stand back," she told Ranger. Adam placed the tip of the crowbar at the upper-right-hand corner of the crate, and once again she couldn't help but notice his muscles flex as he pulled. The sounds of splintering wood and grunts echoed through the warehouse. Adam moved around the giant crate, applying equal pressure to each side. Soon, it broke open, revealing a large shape covered in a heavy red blanket. Adam gestured for her to do the honors. Georgia stepped up and whisked it off. There, leaping in mid-air as if it had just burst through the wood itself, was the most magnificent carousel horse Georgia had ever seen.

Still on its golden pole, rising out of a circular mounting attachment, a majestic, black jumper horse. Its front legs were curled under in a gallop, its back left leg stretched forward, its right arched back in full gallop. Crowning its head was a silver windblown mane, paired with a luscious black tail made of real horsehair. Its shiny black saddle rested upon a jeweled blanket that wrapped around the horse's wooden body. The blanket was fringed in red but populated with every colored jewel in the rainbow. Even the bit around the horse's neighing mouth was littered with multicolored jewels. The three of them literally stood in front of this artistic marvel with their own mouths hanging wide-open. Tears immediately welled in Georgia's eyes.

"It's from Grandpa," she said. "It has to be."

"You mean it's ours?" Ranger asked. "Not for auction?" Georgia noted that Adam seemed to stumble back from the horse as if struck by a blow, but she was too preoccupied to ask him what was the matter. She stepped forward and reached out her hand as if the horse were made of flesh and blood. Sure enough there was a little note wedged above the saddle's knob. Georgia's hand shook as she picked it up. She began to read aloud.

> *Dear Peaches and Ranger,*
> *Merry Christmas! I know this is a bit over the top,*
> *but it was something I just had to do. No happier*
> *memory exists for me than you flying on your horse.*
> *If anyone can find a place for children to ride again,*
> *it's you, Peaches. I will stand forever, just outside,*
> *watching you soar.*
>
> *Love, Dad (and Gramps)*

An unexpected sob tore out of Georgia as she finished the note. She threw her arms around the mane of the horse, and hugged it.

"Mom?" Ranger said. He was worried. She wiped her eyes and turned to him.

"These are happy tears," she said. She swooped Ranger up and placed him on the back of the horse. His eyes lit up as he held on to the pole.

"I wish I could really make it go," Ranger said.

"I know," Georgia said. Why did the note sound as if he'd sent the entire carousel? Maybe it was just age, or maybe he was just fantasizing. Either way, the horse was the best present she had ever received. She turned and looked at Adam. He had moved even farther away, and he was staring at the horse with what could only be described as a look of horror.

"Are you all right?" Georgia asked.

"Did you do this on purpose?" Adam asked.

Georgia had no idea what he was talking about. "Do what?"

"You still don't remember me?" he said, choked. "This is just a coincidence?"

"Remember you?"

"Trash and Treasures," Adam said. "Just off Tremont Road."

"You've been there," Georgia said. It wasn't surprising. They were only forty-five minutes from the home where she grew up. She hadn't been back since the last time her father asked her to take him there. Too many memories. It was just wrong to see anyone else living there. Wrong to see Trash and Treasures gone. Like The Treasure Chest would soon be gone.

"When I was a kid," Adam said.

"That's where you know me from?" Was he one of the many boys sledding down their hill, making snowmen, and throwing snowballs at Christmastime? Was he one of the ones who stomped around and threw fits if they didn't get to buy marbles, or toy guns, or baseball cards? Was he the kid who stole her ruby ring? It would figure, he was still trying to steal from her.

"The horse," Adam said. He walked around the horse, muttering to himself. When he looked up at Georgia, she felt a strange shock of recognition as his blue eyes held hers. Suddenly, she was on the horse, flying around with her new friend, then meeting the eyes of the very serious brother who waited on the ground.

And again, she saw him, in the barn, staring up at the sign, TRASH AND TREASURES, and then his arm outstretched, as he handed her the instant picture.

"My God," Georgia said. "You're Cindy's brother."

Adam met her eyes and nodded.

"And you knew? All this time you knew who I was?"

"I wanted to tell you—"

"And you still came here to—" She glanced at Ranger, then let the sentence drop.

"It's not like that. I thought once you let me explain, you'd understand. I didn't mean to keep it a secret. You were so angry." He, too, was aware of Ranger hanging on to every word. "I have more to tell you. But this. This horse. This is the *exact* horse Cindy rode." Georgia looked at the horse again, and immediately saw Cindy atop it, smile wide.

"Oh, my God," Georgia said. "You're right."

"Why?" Adam asked. "How?"

Georgia didn't have the answers. It was as if her father were speaking to her from heaven, sending the strongest signal he could that it would be a mistake to sell. Thank God she didn't sign the contract. Thank God. "Sit down," Georgia said. "Before you faint."

"I'm not going to faint," Adam said. But he stumbled back to the dining table and sat. Every once in a while he looked at the horse as if it were alive and about to charge him. Ranger sat across from him, not daring to take his eyes off him. He didn't know what was going on, but he wasn't going to miss a second of it.

"I thought I was doing the right thing," Adam said.

"How? Tell me how."

"The money. I tried to tell you." He stopped mid-sentence. "No. You were right. The reasons don't matter. You're still losing your place." He was still just as haunted all these years later. "When I found out you were one of the owners of the lots we were trying to take over—I—I'm sorry if this sounds insensitive but I thought it was meant to be. I know these guys. No matter how long you stalled this deal was going to go through. So I thought if you knew—"

"Knew what? That it was you?"

"It was a mistake. I see that now. I'm not a Scrooge. I'm just a guy who tries his best and tries his best. It's just not always enough. In fact I don't think it's ever been enough."

Georgia stared into his eyes as he stared back. He meant it. She nodded, and then disappeared into the side storage closet where she kept the box.

CHAPTER EIGHT

It didn't take her long to find it, she knew exactly where it was. Every year she would open it and spend a few minutes looking at the picture of her long-lost friend, filling her in on her life in whispers, wishing her well wherever she was on her journey. She brought the box to Adam and set it in front of him.

"Dad always thought you'd come back," she said. "And here you are." Adam opened the box as if he was slightly afraid of it. He lifted the picture of Cindy out and stared at it as if it were a miracle.

"You saved it," he said. His voice was torn and ragged.

"Come on, kiddo," Georgia said to Ranger. "Let's get you dressed." As angry as she was with Adam Cavalier for swooping in to take her auction house, she wasn't going to gloat about his most private pain. He'd been telling the truth when he said he knew her. She couldn't believe she didn't see it earlier. In a lot of ways he still resembled that serious little boy watching over his little sister. Although he'd grown up to be much better looking than she could have ever imagined. And what on earth did all of this mean? When did her father buy Cindy's horse, and why? She felt as if none of this was accidental. What goes around come around, she thought. Like a carousel. She was convinced. Her father and Cindy were reaching out to help her. Although Cindy might be trying to reach Adam. To tell her something. To tell him something. To tell them something? No, Georgia wasn't going to turn this into some match made in heaven. Literally. Although it felt a little bit like that. She liked the idea of winding up with a man her father had already met. She'd been so disappointed he didn't let her keep that picture. *In case he comes back someday.* Well, here he was. So what was she supposed to do now?

Don't sell. The words slammed into her as she and Ranger climbed the steps to the second floor. *Don't sell.* Somehow, the carousel horse, Adam, Cindy, her father. It was all connected. At the very least she was going to postpone signing the contract. Yes, ignoring her sister's wishes wasn't going to be easy. Not to mention the eager soon-to-be retirees. But one thing was for sure. Something was happening here, she could feel it. And if anyone doubted her, she could say she got it straight from the horse's mouth.

When she came down, Adam and his box were gone. Georgia walked over to the horse, wrapped her arms around its wooden neck, and leaned against it. For some reason, Adam's departure made her sad. And there was something else. The contract was gone as well. But she didn't have time to figure out what it all meant. Soon enough her sister would be calling, and the townsfolk would come knocking. She had precious little time to find out exactly who had shipped the horse.

"This is where it stood." Georgia, Ranger, and Adam got out of the car, and took in the parking lot and the enormous pharmacy. Where once upon a time, there stood a carousel. "Paved paradise," Georgia whispered. It was so strange, so out of place with the background of the ocean. The drive to the spot of her childhood carousel had been ripe with silence. Even though Georgia knew it was gone, her father had mentioned it one year—

Georgia gasped.

"What is it?" Adam asked. He had insisted on coming. And she could hardly say no. After all, Cindy was trying to reach him too. Probably trying to tell him not to put her out of house and home. She knew it. They had been fast friends since the moment they met.

"Dad tried to tell me about it when the carousel was taken down."

"What can you remember?"

"I was in the middle of getting ready for an auction. My God. I think I barely commented on it. He must have been so hurt."

"I'm sure he understood."

"I acted like it meant nothing to me. How could I have been so horrid?"

"Grandpa liked how you got," Ranger said. "Absorbed in your work." Georgia glanced at her son, his nose was starting to run in the wind and the cold. She dug a tissue out of her pocket. He accepted it, but instead of blowing his nose, he simply shoved it in his coat pocket.

"What?"

"Look at her," Ranger said. "A meteorite could crash through the ceiling and she probably wouldn't even turn to look."

Georgia laughed. Ranger sounded just like him. She put her arms around him. "I'm sorry it's no longer here," she said.

"Where?"

"Here," Georgia said. She gestured around the parked cars. "It used to sit right here."

"In the middle of the pharmacy?"

"There was no pharmacy back then. Just grass and the ocean, and flying horses."

"That's sad," Ranger said.

"What's sad?" Georgia asked.

"That there was no pharmacy back then. What happened to all the kids with sore throats?"

Georgia didn't dare look at Adam. "Their mothers probably made them tea with honey," she said.

"What about baby aspirin?" Ranger asked.

"I'm sure there was a local pharmacy," Georgia said.

"This says twenty-four hours," Ranger said, pointing to the sign. "Was the local pharmacy twenty-four hours?"

"If you plan ahead, you don't need a store to be open twenty-four hours," Georgia said.

"Still. It's kind of lucky that it is, isn't it?" Ranger said.

"Yes, it is," Adam said. "It certainly can be."

"Greed always wins out," Georgia said under her breath.

Adam looked at her. "You can't possibly think it's that simple."

"Can't I?"

"This pharmacy may have saved lives. Did you ever think of that?"

"Or had a sore throat in the middle of the night," Ranger said. Georgia glanced at him. She was starting to wonder if he got a lot of sore throats in the middle of the night.

"Exactly. And it employs people." Just then an elderly man in a red apron came out to sweep the sidewalk. Adam looked at her. *See?*

Maybe he'd rather be running the carousel. Although it was bitterly cold. Still. There had to be a balance. What

price could you put on making memories? She didn't
have a single warm and gooey memory about a pharmacy.
Did he? *Your sister's last great moment was on this
carousel.* Georgia wouldn't dare say it. She'd already
touched such a nerve.

"I wish it were still here, too. Don't you know that?"
Adam was talking to her, and he sounded very intense. As
if he urgently needed her to believe him. Ranger sniffed.
She handed him another tissue. Instead of using it, he
stuffed it in his pocket like a squirrel who was saving up
for a bout of the flu.

"Let's get out of the cold and find someone who remembers what happened to the carousel."

"Good idea," Adam said, rubbing his hands. "There
has to be a diner nearby."

"Ah. Always the center of local gossip."

"And pancakes," Ranger said. Adam and Georgia burst
into laughter at the same time. Their eyes caught for a
moment, mouths open in smiles. And then they stopped,
like opposing football players suddenly realizing they
weren't on the same team.

Georgia took Ranger's hand. "I'd give anything if the
carousel were still here," she said. *And Dad. I'd give anything to have the two of us stand out here and make funny
faces as you go by. Anything.* Georgia closed her eyes for
a moment and instead imagined the memory. When she
opened her eyes, she kneeled down and put her hands on
Ranger's shoulders. "Grandpa would have been so proud
of you," she said.

"And Dad?"

Georgia was taken by surprise. Ranger had been mentioning Paul a lot more since her father passed. And since
Adam arrived. "Of course. They're looking out for us.
Which is why he sent us that horse. Now let's go get pancakes."

They started to walk away. It took Georgia a few minutes to realize Adam was still standing in the parking lot, staring at the space where his sister once rode the carousel. Suddenly, she felt his hand in hers and he whirled her around. Her heart thudded in her chest, and she could hear the ocean churning in the background.

"There's not a single day that's gone by that I haven't thought about that moment. Not a single day."

"I'm sorry. To be honest. Me too. I only met her that day. But your sister was someone special. I know that. And again. I'm sorry." Georgia started to walk away.

"Not just her." She stopped.

"What?"

"That memory. The one I replay every day. I don't just see Cindy. You're there too. On the carousel. In the barn. Every day since that day, I've thought of you too."

They held eyes. And of course, the same was true for her. How could she not see the serious little boy going around and around in her head? "I'm not a bad guy," he whispered. "I'm not a Scrooge."

I know, she wanted to say. Instead she glanced at the carousel, and then at the empty lot, and she didn't have to say a word, it was as loud as day. *Tell me then, if you had to choose right now. Which would it be? The pharmacy or the carousel?*

"Of course you aren't," Ranger shouted from ahead. Georgia couldn't believe what hearing he had. "If you were *that bad,* Mom would have never made you French toast."

Georgia had never seen anyone eat so many chocolate-chip pancakes in her life. Even Ranger, who had been told he could only choose between blueberries and strawberries, was in awe. Georgia glanced at her egg-white omelet and felt sorry for herself. Adam *was* a Scrooge. She'd been staring at his plate for ten minutes and he hadn't even offered her a bite. At least the waitress was helpful when she came to refill their coffees and Georgia asked about the carousel.

"I have to say. I don't miss it," the sixty-something with dyed orange hair said. "I used to get dizzy every time I looked out the window. And that music. Nonstop. Used to give me headaches something awful."

"And there was no pharmacy to get aspirin!" Ranger said.

"Right you are, young man," the waitress said.

One man's trash is another man's treasure, Georgia thought. Who knew her son would be on the side of the evil corporation? He would have changed his tune if he had ridden that carousel. "Do you know what happened to it?" Georgia asked.

"They turned it into a pharmacy," the waitress said.

Adam laughed. Georgia glared at him, but he continued to grin as he shoveled in more chocolate-chip pancakes.

"No. I mean. What happened to the carousel itself? Did they move it to another park or something?"

"I have no idea," the waitress said. So much for that.

"Some blockhead from Block Island bought it," an old man sitting at the counter yelled.

"Block Island?" Ranger said. "That's my island!"

Adam raised an eyebrow. "Book report," Georgia said.

"Located in the great state of Rhode Island, Block Island is located on the Atlantic Ocean, thirteen miles south off the coast of the great state of Rhode Island." Georgia mouthed the quote along with him.

"Mom said I shouldn't say great state of Rhode Island twice in the same sentence," Ranger told Adam. "But I told her. That's what makes it so great."

Adam nodded and pointed a syrupy fork at Ranger. "Genius," he said. Ranger beamed.

"Separated from Rhode Island by Block Island Sound," Ranger continued. "Named by The Nature Conservatory as 'One of the last great places.' "

"Do you know the name of this blockhead?" Georgia called to the old man.

"Nope. But there can't be too many horse carvers out that way."

"Horse carvers?"

"He's a carousel maker and restorer," the old man said. "On Block Island. That's all I got."

"I got more," Ranger said. "Forty percent of the island is set aside for conservation."

"Wow," Adam said.

"That means no discount stores," Georgia said. Adam gave her a look, but she didn't respond.

"Presidents Bill Clinton, Dwight Eisenhower, Franklin Delano Roosevelt, and Ulysses S. Grant have visited Rhode Island."

"Not at the same time I hope," Adam said.

"They weren't all alive at the same time." Ranger gave a look to Georgia that clearly lamented Adam's lack of education. It was all she could do to keep from laughing. Adam was feeling the exact same way for she could see his shoulders shaking. Although to his credit, he played along.

"Good point."

"Also Amelia Earhart and Charles Lindbergh—both alive in 1929 but not at the same time."

"You are a really smart kid," Adam said.

"Because I live with objects from all different times in history. History is really just stories about people. Right, Mom?"

Now a tear came to her eye. If she couldn't figure out how to save it, they would lose their things. Their history.

Their stories. "Right, kiddo," she said. Adam stared at her intensely. She hated that he seemed to be able to home in on exactly what she was feeling. His hand even stretched across the table as if he wanted to hold hers.

"I love stories," Ranger said.

"Except when the auctioneers tell them," Adam piped in. "They end too fast." Together, Adam and Ranger laughed. *Great,* Georgia thought. *Male bonding.* "Are we ready?" Adam asked, holding up the keys to his Jeep.

"For what?" Georgia asked.

"Block Island," Adam said.

"Yes!" Ranger said. "Yes, yes, yes! Can you believe I've never been?"

"A travesty," Adam said. "One we will rectify immediately." He threw money on the table.

"We can't go to Block Island and home in a day," Georgia said.

"We'll spend the night," Adam said.

"Yes!" Ranger said. "Yes, yes, yes!"

"But." She stopped. But what? The final auction wasn't until after Christmas. Her sister wouldn't be arriving for another four days. And she wanted to know everything she could about her father buying that horse. Cindy's horse. "We'll need toothbrushes and contact lens solution, and—"

Ranger's hand shot out. "There's a pharmacy right there!" he said. Adam didn't dare look at her, but once again his shoulders were shaking with laughter.

"I'll meet you two over there," Georgia said.

"What's up?" Adam asked. "I paid the bill."

"Never you mind," she said. He gave her a funny look but soon left with Ranger, his arm looped over his shoulder like they were father and son. Georgia made a beeline for the waitress, and ordered a stack of chocolate-chip pancakes to go.

Chapter Nine

It wasn't hard to get information on the local carousel man. He was a character, they were told by several locals, in his eighties, and reclusive. "You'll be damn lucky if old Sherman even opens the door for you," a local man warned. But he gave them directions anyway, and soon Adam was pulling up to the gray cape house, set above the ocean.

"It looks old," Ranger said.

"Around 1760," Georgia said.

"How do you know that?" Adam asked.

"It's her job," Ranger said. Georgia smiled, aware that Adam was once again staring at her with an intensity that made her shut off the myriad of thoughts pinballing around her brain. In addition to the house, two enormous white barns sat on the three-acre lot. Georgia felt a pang, as an instant picture of Trash and Treasures rose to mind. Sometimes, she was just suddenly there again. She could see and feel it all. The lighting, the chill, the smell, her father's smile. The tall green spruces with white lights and red bows. Here, not a single Christmas decoration was in sight.

"Are we going in?" Ranger asked.

"Do you think he has large dogs?" Adam asked, surveying the house. Every single window was sealed with a heavy curtain. Several old cars were parked alongside the house, but otherwise there was no sign of life. The sky was gray, and as they sat, snow began to fall. "He looks like the type of man who has large dogs."

"I love dogs," Ranger said. Before they could stop him, he popped out of the car and headed for the house.

"Wait," Georgia said. Ranger stopped. "He wasn't talking about cute, fluffy dogs. Mean dogs, Ranger. Wait for us." Georgia looked pointedly at Adam, and did not budge until he nodded and took the lead. Seconds later, they stood on the porch looking at the front door.

"No doorbell," Adam said. He rapped on the door.

"Snow!" Ranger said as if he'd just noticed it. Georgia stepped up and knocked on the door herself.

"Much better," Adam said. "Mine was such a lousy knock. I'm sure yours will do the trick." Ranger laughed. Georgia wanted to slap Adam, but she didn't like driving in the snow so she refrained.

"We can find a place to stay and drive back in the morning," Adam said.

"Maybe he's in one of the barns," Ranger said, once again taking off ahead of them.

"Ranger," Georgia called after him. "What did I tell you?" She took off after her son, following him to the closest barn. It was sealed tight as a drum. *Pah-rum-pa-pa-pum.* Ranger was already trying to peek into one window over a side door when Georgia caught up.

"I can't see anything," he said. He started to put his hand on the doorknob.

"Don't," Georgia said. "You know better."

"It could be unlocked."

"We're not here to trespass," Georgia said.

"How much snow do you think we're going to get?" Ranger asked. He twirled around with his arms outstretched. How quickly kids could change tracks. Georgia was dying to try the door, but she certainly couldn't get away with it now. She knocked on this one as well, and waited.

"Let's try the second barn," Adam said. He and Ranger plowed ahead. Georgia glanced back at the house. It wasn't more than a feeling, but she knew, she just knew the old man was home. What if he came out with a shotgun? They would have called first, but the man in town said that Sherman shut off his phone last year. Definitely not the type of guy who wanted to receive Christmas carolers or the three not-so-wise men. By the time she caught up with them at the second barn, she caught sight of its door swinging open. Adam and Ranger stepped inside.

"Wait," she shouted. She watched as Adam and her son entered the barn. It was smaller than the first barn, but still standard size. Georgia began to run. She was breathless by the time she reached the door, which was still open about half an inch. She pushed it open and slammed into Adam.

"Sorry," she said. She rubbed her temple that had made severe contact with his shoulder. He immediately turned.

"Are you okay?" He saw her rubbing her forehead and instantly his hand was on her face, feeling for a bump. For a minute all she could see was his shape in the dark, and she imagined him kissing her.

"Who opened the door?" she asked.

"No one," Ranger said. "It swung open all by itself." Georgia turned to open the door again for they couldn't see a thing. The door squeaked and the wind rushed in along with the light. The barn was one big open space. There were no stalls, or animals, or John Deere tractors.

Instead, in the middle of the floor, covered in numerous tarps, but not enough to completely disguise it, was a full-sized carousel. And not just any carousel. It was the carousel by the ocean. Georgia would know the tented blue and gold top anywhere.

"Cool!" Ranger said. Suddenly the door slammed shut, hurling them once again into pitch black.

"Must be the wind," Adam said. He turned and Georgia heard him trying to open the door. Just then came the sound of a board sliding across it and the definite snap of a lock. Someone had just locked them in.

"Hey," Georgia said. "Hello? Hello?"

"I've got you now," the voice of an old man yelled.

"We come in peace," Adam said as if he were trying to negotiate with an extraterrestrial.

"Are you Sherman?" Georgia asked.

"Who wants to know?"

"I'm Georgia. And I'm here with my son, Ranger, and our friend Adam." It slipped so easily off her tongue. Our friend Adam.

"Breaking and entering," Sherman shouted. He definitely sounded like the type who had a shotgun.

"Open this door right now," Georgia said. "I have a seven-year-old boy and he's scared to death."

"No, I'm not," Ranger said.

"Take one for the team," Adam whispered.

"One what?" Ranger asked. "What team?"

"As I said. My name is Georgia Bradley, and we've come here about a horse." She was surprised to hear Adam laugh beside her. "What?"

"We came to see a man about a horse," Adam repeated, barely getting the words out between laughs.

"Great. I'm stuck here with a couple of comedians," Georgia said.

"I'm calling the police," Sherman said.

"You don't have a phone," Georgia said.

"How do you know?" he barked.

"Because if you did, we would have called first," Georgia said.

There was a moment of silence. When he spoke again, he was a little bit calmer. "What horse?" he asked.

"From a carousel. A beautiful black jumper," Georgia said. "I think my father must have bought it from you."

"Trash and Treasures?" Sherman asked.

"That's it."

"Then you must be 'Treasure,' " Sherman said. Was he calling her father "Trash?" It would have infuriated her had her father not made the same joke several times.

"Sounds like you knew my father pretty well," Georgia said. "Now can you please open this door?"

"How do I know you are who you say you are?"

"We have cell phones," Adam said. "Open this door or we'll call the police."

"My cell phone is in the Jeep," Georgia whispered. Adam pawed his pockets.

"Mine too," he whispered back.

"I can hear you. You just said your cell phones are in the Jeep." Wow. He had incredible hearing for an old man. "Which is parked in my driveway."

"Do you have the picture?" Georgia asked Adam. Her eyes were beginning to adjust to the dark, and she could see him nod. He removed the instant photo from his pocket.

"Slide it under the door," Georgia said.

"No," Adam said. "I don't want to ruin it."

"I have to go to the bathroom," Ranger said.

"Hold on, hold on," Sherman said. They heard the sound of the door being unlocked and the board sliding again. Soon the door was thrown open and an old man with a white beard stood in front of them. He could have been Santa except for the fact that he was skinny as a rail, and from the scowl on his face, Georgia couldn't imagine a single "Ho" coming out of him let alone three. Georgia, Adam, and Ranger stepped cautiously outside. The snow was really coming down.

"Show him," Georgia said. Tentatively, Adam showed Sherman the picture of Cindy on the horse. The old man nodded, then stared hard at Georgia. Seconds later he whirled around, heading back to the house.

"Follow me," he said. "Before the lad has an accident."

The interior of the house was surprisingly sparse and clean. Old wood floors and stone tiles, and rustic wood furniture. Every surface polished to a shine. A fire was roaring in the living room. He pointed down a hall.

"Restroom is that-a-way, young man." Ranger nodded and hurried off. Sherman pointed to a leather sofa.

"Make yourselves comfortable," he said. "Would you like some tea?" Georgia and Adam shared a look.

"Love some," Georgia said. "My God," she mouthed as Sherman disappeared into what she assumed was the kitchen. She gestured around the lovely home.

"Never judge a book by its cover," Adam whispered back.

As they sat and drank their tea, Sherman flipped through photographs of all the carousel horses he'd restored over the years. Outside standers, and inside prancers, and jumpers. Bidirectional manes, and armored horses covered in jewels, to more whimsical rides of horses with top hats. The colors and styles and details were astounding. Rhode Island, Sherman told them, has 150 original American wooden carousels. The oldest in the United States, the Flying Horse Carousel, was situated at Watch Hill in Westerly. Instead of mounted to poles, the horses were attached by ceiling chains.

"The faster they turn that beauty up, the farther out the horses fly," he said.

"Like reindeer," Ranger said.

The old man let out a series of laughs, that did sound to Georgia like ho, ho, ho. Never judge a book by its cover was right.

"Like reindeer," he confirmed. "And then you have the Crescent Park Carousel made by Charles I. D. Looff. All but one hand-carved and original. If you ever get a chance to ride it, see if you can pick out the lead. Once you do, you'll see all the other horses fall in behind. Like Rudolph," he added to Ranger with a wink.

"Do you carve horses too?" Georgia asked.

"I've done a few in my day," Sherman said. "Mostly I just restored them."

"And what about the carousel in your barn?" Adam asked.

"It's a hodgepodge. Made from horses from all different manufacturers. Dentzel, Spillman, Looff, Herschell, Armitage, you name it. I've got lions, zebras, even a Dentzel deer."

"I used to ride that very carousel when I was a little girl," Georgia explained. "That's why my father was interested in it."

Sherman suddenly became very animated, agitated almost. His teacup shook in his hand and he violently slammed it down and then shot straight up. "And you can't have it! I gave you one and that's all you're going to get. The rest is mine. Now get out!"

Georgia stood, put her hands up. He changed so suddenly. He seemed normal, but he was obviously mentally unbalanced. Or his memory was going and he'd already forgotten their "We come in peace" speech.

"We don't want to take your carousel," Georgia said.

"I want to see it," Ranger said. "Can I ride it?"

"No," Sherman said. He was so upset, he literally looked as if he was shaking head-to-toe.

"I just want to ask you about my father," Georgia said. "James Bradley? How did he come to buy the horse off you?" Sherman didn't sit back down, but he did take a deep breath, and some of the shaking seemed to ease.

"James Bradley," he said.

"Trash and Treasures," Georgia repeated. "And the black jumper—it belonged on a carousel I used to ride as a child."

"Yes, yes. By the ocean."

"Yes. It's a pharmacy now," Georgia said. She looked at Adam. "I guess some people are fine with that."

"It's open twenty-four hours," Ranger said.

"Some people just grasp that everything in this world isn't black and white," Adam said.

"I like colors," Ranger said. "Lots of colors."

"Me too," Georgia said.

"But it is pretty cool in *The Wizard of Oz* when it starts in black and white. Then you're really amazed by all the colors." Ranger again.

"Exactly," Adam said. "Exactly."

"Sorry," Georgia said, turning to Sherman. "We've digressed. When did my father buy the horse from you?"

"The horse," Sherman repeated slowly. "When did he buy *the horse* from me?"

"Yes," Georgia said. She spoke louder and clearer. "When did he buy the horse from you?" Sherman folded his arms and studied her as if she had just asked him to figure out a riddle.

"What did he tell you?"

"My father passed away last year," Georgia said.

"That explains a lot," Sherman said. He fell back into the couch as if all the air had been taken out from under him. Georgia sat back down too, but kept on the edge of the sofa.

"What does it explain?"

Sherman looked as if he'd been caught saying something he wished he hadn't. "He wanted it delivered this Christmas," he said. "I could have sent it along sooner, but he was very adamant."

"Our first Christmas without him," Georgia said.

"You've got your horse, so will you go?" Sherman said. "We're going to get a heck of a storm."

"You bought the entire carousel when they sold it off?" Georgia asked. "And somehow my father traced it back to you?" Adam removed the picture again and pointed to Cindy's black jumper.

"Did he ask for this horse in particular?" he asked.

"His instructions were very clear," Sherman said. "I waited, but I never heard from him again. That's not my fault. I sent that horse by Christmas!"

Once again, he wasn't making sense. He ushered them to the front door. Georgia glanced out the window. The snow was really coming down. The yard was already coated.

"We just wanted to meet you," Georgia said. "And thank you. The horse is beautiful."

"I take pride in my work. They can accumulate a lot of damage from the salt and wind and water."

"I bet."

"Can we see the rest of it?" Ranger asked again. Once again, Sherman looked alarmed.

"Oh, come on," Georgia said. "What do you think— we'll just carry it off?"

"You'll be wanting to get a move on with this blizzard," Sherman said.

"Do you know of any motels in town?" Adam asked.

"Or hotels," Georgia said. The day had been strange enough; she certainly didn't want to do any *Psycho* recreations.

"Can't we just see the carousel before we go?" Ranger pleaded.

See, Georgia wanted to say. *You wouldn't beg to see a pharmacy one more time.* "We could come back," Georgia said.

"No, you can't," Sherman said. "But I suppose you can see it. But that's it! No touching. No riding. No pictures." He stood again, opened a cabinet, and came out holding a kerosene lamp. When he turned it on, Ranger was mesmerized by the little flame.

"Cool," he said.

Sherman nodded, then turned the flame off again. "Follow me," Sherman said.

Georgia wasn't sure what the whole charade about the kerosene lamp was about, for the barn certainly had lights. In fact, she felt as if they were standing in the middle of a circus tent as Sherman clicked them on one at a time. It was still covered in tarps, but even just the shapes of the animals was enough to take Georgia's breath away.

"Does it work?" Ranger asked.

"Of course she works," Sherman barked. "What kind of man do you think I am?"

"Don't mind him," Georgia whispered in Ranger's ear.

"I don't," Ranger said. "I like him."

Sherman glanced at Ranger and the two stood staring at each other. "You can help me take the tarps off, but that's it," Sherman said. "Then one ride and you're gone."

Ranger's head snapped to Georgia and a huge grin covered his face. Georgia couldn't help but laugh. Suddenly she felt Adam right behind her, his breath on her neck, his low voice in her ear. "That's one great kid," he said.

"Finally," Georgia whispered back. "Something we agree on."

CHAPTER TEN

One by one they pulled the tarps from the animals. As Sherman mentioned, each one was unique, made by a different manufacturer, and it was obvious when you took them in individually. Some were whimsical, others menacing. In addition to horses, there were zebras, and tigers, and as promised a reindeer. They were all magnificently restored, the paint was bright and bold. "Who wants a ride?" Sherman shouted. "Pick an animal, let's go, let's go." Georgia glanced at Adam. Was this guy for real? Ranger was already on his: a magnificent tan jumper.

"Come on," Adam said. He grabbed Georgia's hand and together they stepped onto the carousel. The lights came on. Georgia felt a rush of joy, just like opening a window and having childhood rush in. She chose the tiger next to Ranger, an outside-stander, mainly because she had never ridden a tiger before. Adam chose a white prancer slightly behind the two of them. *He's protecting us, keeping an eye on us,* Georgia thought. She had to admit, it gave her a rush of warmth. As soon as they were all seated, the carousel began to turn, and the carnival-like music began to pipe through the barn. Up and down, just like galloping. Georgia and Ranger looked at each other at the exact same time, joy stamped on each of their faces. And then she turned back to Adam. He grinned at her, and held her eyes for a long, long time. She smiled back, although bittersweet. She couldn't help but think of little Cindy. Still, this was the happiest she felt in a long time.

What was she doing? How could she be so happy with this man? How could she forget that he had come into her life to take it all away? In fact, all this romancing he was doing, if that's what you called the lingering looks, and protective nature, and driving them around—it was probably just an act—

But this wasn't a stranger. He was Cindy's brother. That changed things, didn't it? He hadn't once asked her to sign the contract since he found out who she was. But what did she think was going to happen? He'd turn down all that money—for what? A ride through memories past?

It's over, Georgia realized as the ride started slowing down. I wasted every second of it. But Ranger hadn't. He still looked overjoyed. That's what she was doing, living through her son. Sherman watched them get off the carousel, standing just by the opening of the barn.

"Thank you," Georgia said. "We loved it."

"Can we ride again?" Ranger asked.

"You'd best get going," Sherman said. "I said one ride."

"My father," Georgia said. "How did he come to buy the horse?"

"And why just that horse?" Adam asked. "Did he say why?" Georgia glanced at Adam. He was just as intense as she was. His feelings for her may have been an act, but he was definitely shaken by seeing Cindy's horse. Georgia suspected Adam was wondering if Cindy was somehow trying to contact him. Georgia had been wondering the same thing about her father.

"I already explained everything. He wanted his horse and he got it. Just what are you accusing me of?"

"We're not accusing you of anything," Georgia said. "We just . . ." She stopped, not knowing how to explain.

"We just miss him," Ranger said. Georgia wanted to grab him and hug him. And so of course, she did.

"It's just such an amazing coincidence," Adam said.

"What are you accusing me of?" This time Sherman shouted it. He was crazy. The old man was downright unstable. Nice one minute, almost snapping their heads off the next. They weren't going to get any answers here, it was time to leave before he worked himself into a heart attack. Her father was always searching for items to buy; it wasn't unusual that he'd want a horse from this carousel. It was their Christmas surprise. As Georgia looked back at the carousel, she found it. The one empty spot where the black jumper used to be.

"I'm sorry you're missing one now," Georgia said. "I really am." It wasn't like her father to rip a horse from its carousel. His desire to give it to her must have won out.

"Get out!" Sherman said. "Get out, get out, get out." He slid open the barn door and a gust of white wind slammed into them like a wall. The snow was now so thick that she couldn't see anything but a wall of white parading toward them. And it was so cold! Frostbite probably only took seconds in this frigid weather.

"You've got to be kidding me," Adam said. Georgia held on to Ranger, and she felt Adam's hand on her shoulder.

"We can't go anywhere in this," he said.

"Sherman?" Georgia said. She could no longer see the old man, but then again, she couldn't see anything. "Sherman?"

"He's already heading for the house," Adam said.

"Well, we'd better catch him before he locks us out," Georgia said. She clamped on to Ranger's hand, and then as a second thought grabbed Adam's too. *How is it,* Georgia thought as they bared the snow and whipping wind, *that the best possible scenario has just become having a sleepover at the home of a cranky, old man? Scrooge Three.*

"He can't just leave us out here," Georgia said as they trudged the last few steps to the house.

"I don't think we're dealing with a stable guy."

"Can we make it to a hotel?"

"I don't even know if we can make it to the front porch."

"First he gives us tea, then he yells at us, then he gives us a ride on his carousel, then he yells at us. We're due for Mr. Nice again," Georgia said. Adam laughed. "What's so funny?" she demanded.

"Naughty and nice," Adam said.

"Right. Santa must be confused," Ranger said. Georgia wished she could see his little face; she was getting the feeling this year that he didn't believe in Santa. He hadn't come out and said that or even asked her, but there were a lot of little comments thrown here and there. "It's freezing," he added. Georgia hugged him tighter. She was going to get him inside and warm if she had to huff and puff and blow Sherman down.

"We're almost there." Ranger broke from her and began to run.

"At the least we can crawl into the Jeep, get a little heat," Adam said.

"Oh, no. That old man is going to open up." Georgia's foot rammed into a step. "Found the porch," she said.

"That's a tree, darling," Adam said. "Ranger and I are on the porch." Darling. How long had it been since a man called her darling? Wait. No man had ever called her darling. Sweetie or sweetheart was her father. Paul called her "babe" once in a while. Darling was a first. Old-fashioned yet strangely edgy. Slightly cocky of him. Was she wrong for liking it?

Tree. Liar. She was on the porch, and she was going to prove it by accidentally bumping into him. She headed for the back of him, but at the last minute, she slipped on a patch of ice and instead of a light, teasing bump, the force of her body slammed against his sending them both straight to the ground.

"OOF," Adam said. Georgia had never heard anyone outside of a cartoon say OOF, and if she had any breath left in her body she would have laughed.

"MOM," Ranger said. "MOM. Did he hurt you?"

"She landed on top of ME," Adam said as Georgia rolled off him. "But I admire your loyalty."

"He's looking," Ranger yelled.

"I can't see a thing," Adam said. Georgia lifted her head in time to see Sherman's head disappear from the curtains.

"Sherman," she yelled. "We can see you!"

"I have to pee," Ranger shouted.

"Again?" Georgia said.

"No. But it worked the last time."

Adam finally lifted himself off the ground. "Let's sing 'Jingle Bells,' " he said.

"Jingle Bells, Batman smells, Robin laid an egg," Ranger began.

"This is hardly the time," Georgia said.

"Sherman probably hates carolers," Adam said. "He'll open just to shut us up."

"Good plan. But we'll sing the real version," Georgia

said, giving Ranger a look. Adam and Ranger exchanged a look of their own.

"Girls," Adam said. Ranger laughed. It was a special kind of laugh, one she'd only heard him use with her father. Ranger liked Adam. That wasn't all good. Ranger had already suffered too many major male losses. She wanted him to enjoy himself, and laugh again, and have a man around—but Adam wasn't going to stick around. Don't get too close, she wanted to tell Ranger. Or was she really trying to warn herself?

She was so lost in thought she hadn't realized that Adam and Ranger were already singing. She joined in. They sounded pretty good despite their teeth chattering. They finished two whole rounds of it.

"It's not working," Ranger said. He stepped up to the door and pummeled it with his little fists.

"We should break the window," Georgia said.

"That's the Christmas spirit," Adam said.

"Oh, so you're Mr. Christmas now, are you?"

"I have felt unusually jolly lately," he said. "Since I met you." It was said quickly, and quietly, almost under his breath, almost so fleeting she wasn't sure if he'd said it at all or if she'd imagined it. "Let's get in the Jeep," Adam said, resuming a normal tone of voice. "Get some heat. Figure this out."

"Sherman! You can't leave us out here. It's a blizzard." Just as she was about to agree with Adam that they needed to get to the Jeep, a mail slot in the door opened, and a piece of paper was shoved through.

"Sign this," Sherman said. My God, everyone wanted her to sign something. She looked at Adam. He looked just as confused, but shrugged, like, *What do you have to lose?* He would think that. Crazy old man. She snatched the paper up and read it.

THE CAROUSEL BELONGS TO SHERMAN

My God, he was paranoid. What did he think? They would all take a side and walk off with it? Nuttier than Mrs. Weaver's fruitcake.

"Sherman," Adam said, reading over his shoulder. "Like Madonna. Or Beyoncé."

"Do you have a pen?" Georgia asked.

"Yes. Just in case we got stranded, I wanted to write the great American novel," Adam said.

" 'No' would suffice."

"I really do have to pee now," Ranger said.

"Come on," Adam said. "We'll write our names in the snow."

"You will not," Georgia said. "You'll get frostbite." She slipped a tube of red lipstick out of her pocket. She did not bring it for Adam. She had a right to wear lipstick. And everyone always commented how good this shade looked on her. Perfectly normal. She scrawled on the paper and shoved it back through the mail slot. A second later, the door opened. Georgia didn't hesitate. She gently pushed Ranger inside, then even grabbed Adam's hand and yanked him in behind her. She shut and locked the front door as if it were her own, before Sherman could change his mind.

CHAPTER ELEVEN

They sat around the fireplace. Sherman sank into an easy chair and didn't move. Adam asked if he'd be allowed to rummage through the kitchen, and Sherman gave his assent with a simple nod of his head.

"Anything will do," Georgia called after Adam. She was starving, which meant Ranger must be nearly out of his mind. She ruffled his hair and pulled him closer. Even though the fire was generating plenty of warmth, they were still bundled under blankets. Ranger kept sneaking looks around the place, and Sherman.

"Why don't you have a Christmas tree?" he asked. Sherman squinted at Ranger.

"Trees are meant to be outdoors," he said.

"Mostly. Except for Christmas trees."

"Especially Christmas trees," Sherman said.

"What's that?" Ranger said. He pointed to the mantel above the fireplace where a beautifully gift-wrapped present sat.

"What does it look like?" Sherman said.

"Who's it from?"

"My daughter," he grumbled. Georgia wondered

where she lived and what their relationship was like, and like her son, wondered what the present was.

"It's an iPhone," Sherman said, as if reading her mind. "Now what on earth would I ever do with an iPhone?"

"How do you know?" Ranger said.

"Because before she sent it she said, 'Dad. Do you know what an iPhone is? I think you'd like it. We can call each other and see one another on camera. And you need something in case there's ever an emergency.' "

"That's nice," Georgia said.

"Nice?" Sherman said. "It's going to cost me a ridiculous amount of money. She's already got me signed up to some kind of plan. Imagine that. Set up the damn thing, charged it, and signed me right up. I don't even know why she bothered wrapping it."

"You have a working iPhone?" Adam said. "Can I use it?"

"No," Sherman said. "I'm not opening it until Christmas. Besides, who are you going to call? Santa? Make sure he's still on time?"

Ranger's eyes grew huge as saucers. Georgia smiled and gave him a reassuring nod.

"Depending on your plan, I might be able to get online, check out when this storm is going to end—maybe even see if it's possible to drive into town."

"It's my Christmas present and it's going back, and you're not opening it," Sherman said.

Adam looked at Georgia. She shrugged and waved it off. Who were they to open an old man's Christmas gift?

"Progress, progress, progress," Sherman said. "If you ask me, there was nothing wrong with the telegram. Short and sweet. Who needs all this technology stuffed down our throats?"

"Or discount stores," Georgia said.

"I'm hungry," Ranger said.

Adam poked his head out of the kitchen. "I'm making ham sandwiches," Adam said. "Coming right up." He carried out two plates, and presented them to Ranger and Georgia. Ham sandwiches and potato chips. Heaven. He stared at Georgia until she smiled and thanked him, and then he stayed some more until he saw her take the first bite. Georgia bit into her sandwich. God, how simple. Ham, white bread, cheese, and mayo. It was the best thing she'd ever tasted. This time, when Adam headed back to the kitchen, he was whistling "Jingle Bells." "I've got a sandwich for you too, Sherman," he said. Sherman slid his eyes over to Georgia.

"Is he always this jolly?"

"I don't know," Georgia said. *I don't think so*.

"Why are you two smiling so much?" Ranger asked.

"I just love ham sandwiches, don't you?" Georgia said.

"I like baloney a little bit better," Ranger said.

"Makes sense," Georgia said. "Because you're usually full of it." She laughed and ruffled Ranger's hair again, and he looked at her as if she had four heads. When Adam came out with the next two plates, his grin matched hers and they stared at each other for a few seconds before Georgia made a conscious decision to look away.

"You two are acting so weird," Ranger said.

Sherman shot out of his chair, almost knocking his ham sandwich over. Georgia shot up too, for if that ham sandwich hit the floor, she only had seconds to rescue it. "What are you up to? You plan on robbing me in my sleep?"

"My God, no," Georgia said.

"We're just . . . happy," Adam said. This time he only glanced at Georgia for a few seconds, but it was enough. Oh, my God. This was infatuation. Love. Whatever you wanted to call it. They'd been struck with it, hard, stuck here with a paranoid old man, and her son who she needed to protect, mostly, right now, from her.

Ranger was softly snoring, Sherman was asleep in his chair by the desk, and Georgia and Adam sat near the fire. She was so comfortable with him, practically a stranger, yet he didn't feel that way at all; in fact, if he were to put his arms around her right now, would she stop him? Could she? The fire crackled and radiated a soft glow between them. She'd forgotten how intimate this could be, simply staring into someone's eyes, someone who wanted you as much as you wanted him. Maybe more, considering the looks he gave her.

"Why are you here?" she asked. "Ben probably wouldn't approve."

"I don't care about Ben," he said.

"Are you telling me you no longer care if you get to put up your discount store?"

"I don't know what's best for the town anymore," he said. "There are a fair number of folks who are struggling and that money could do them a lot of good."

"So that's all you care about now? The greater good?"

"Is that really so hard to believe?"

"When you stand to make a lion's share. Yes. It is."

His face contorted, and he looked like he wanted to respond, instead he stared at the fire. She liked him. That was the truth. So why was she pushing him away like this? Because of what he planned on doing to her. Taking from her. For a profit.

"I don't know what's right. For the first time in my life. I really don't know what's right," Adam said.

"I'm sorry. I just can't wrap my head around this. Is it horrible of me not to want to lose my home?"

"No. Of course not."

"And I'm going to blame you for it. No matter how well-intended, how do I not blame you?"

"Do we have to do this right here, right now?"

"Why? Are you going somewhere? What else do we have to do?"

"This." He placed a hand on the back of her head and pulled her into him. With the other hand, he softly cradled her face. She couldn't resist this kiss if she wanted to. And God help her, she did not want to. His lips were soft but insistent and the kiss was passionate and deep, and all that pent-up longing she'd had the minute she saw his beautiful blue eyes, the serious brother when she was a child, to the grown-up gorgeous man just outside her door, with his cap, and his shy smile, and his—

Partner. Ben. She broke off the kiss, although what she really wanted to do was straddle him and work her lips up and down his face, and her hands up and down his body, and she wanted to feel him, every bit of him as he explored her, and she wanted to sneak out to the carousel and take two rides at once. But first she was going to kiss him again. And so, she did.

"Stop it," she said, breaking away, catching her breath. "Damn you. Stop it." She stood up and walked away.

"You initiated it the second time," Adam pointed out, following her. "Please. I want this. I want you." He was on her again, and okay, one more kiss, just one, just so she could feel them standing up, pressed up against one another, his strong body plastered to hers, just a few more seconds and then she would stop. She'd stop, and that would be it, he wouldn't do this to her ever, ever, again, but my God, he was so good at it, they would be so good together, she just wanted to feel like this forever. But nothing lasts forever, does it?

An investor. A discount mall. Don't fall for him. Here

she was ready to tear off both their clothes. She tore away for the third time.

"I can't," she said. She ran to the bathroom for that was the only place she could think to go. She splashed cold water on her face, although she could still feel her lips burning, or was it just intense tingling? In fact everywhere he had kissed, and touched, was on fire. Why hadn't she let him speak? Maybe he was ready to give up the discount mall for her. Now that would be a Christmas miracle! For some reason it struck her with fear. Was she afraid of what he was going to do, or afraid of what he was going to say? If he said he'd give it all up for her, wasn't this crazy? Wasn't it moving too fast? But how did they stop it now? "Get ahold of yourself," she said into the mirror.

The minute Georgia walked back into the room, Adam tried to talk. "I think we—"

"Shhh," she said, taking her index finger from her mouth and placing it on his. Before she could stop him, Adam kissed her finger, then his tongue darted out and ran over the tip. The tingling was back, tenfold. Damn him. She yanked her hand away. If he was Scrooge, he was the hottest Scrooge she had ever met. She snuggled up on the sofa where Ranger slept.

"Go away," she said when she could feel Adam standing over her. She squeezed her eyes shut. The next thing she felt was a blanket being gently placed over her. She listened to him move away and opened one eye. He was stretched out on the floor, hands behind his head, staring at the ceiling.

"Thank you," she said.

"Go to sleep," he said. "Or I'm carrying you out to the Jeep where I'll have my way with you."

When she finally did go to sleep, visions danced through her head, only they were anything but sugarplums.

Georgia was up early the next morning, and the first thing she did was peek over at Ranger. His spot on the sofa was empty. She bolted up, heart jack-hammering through her chest. She quickly ran to the bathroom. The door was open and it was empty. She checked the kitchen. Ditto. Georgia ran over to Adam, still laid out on the floor, arms flung over his head. God, he looked inviting. And he didn't snore. That was nice. She kicked his shoe. He stirred, but didn't open his eyes. She kicked it harder. He opened one eye, and fixed it on her.

"Morning, sunshine," he said after a minute.

"Ranger's missing." Adam was up in an instant.

"Missing?"

"He's not in this house, I've looked everywhere."

"Outside," Adam said. Together, they ran to the entryway where their boots and coats were stashed, and shortly thereafter they were trudging through the snow, which at this point appeared to be about three feet high. The Jeep was nothing more than a mound of white, and the wind stung their cheeks. Ranger was not in the front yard.

"Barn," Adam said.

"Carousel," Georgia agreed. They were halfway to their destination, when a scream rang out. "Ranger!" Georgia screamed back. Where was he? Had something fallen on him? Was someone or something out there with him? It came from the direction of the barn. Adam tore off ahead of her. Georgia tried to pick up her pace, but twice ended up facedown in the snow. Panic was not her friend, and she was relieved to have Adam. She reached the barn in time to see Ranger at the opening, Adam kneeling in front of him. Her heart squeezed. From what she could see, it didn't look like he was bleeding or anything was broken. Thank, you, Universe.

"What's wrong?" she called, reaching him and putting her hands on his shoulders.

"It bit me," Ranger said, pointing back to the carousel. "A horse bit me." Georgia was about to admonish him for saying such a crazy thing when she saw a little red circle on top of his left hand.

"He stuck his hand in one of the mouths," Adam said.

"The white one," Ranger said.

"Looks like a spider bite," Adam said.

"Oh boy," Georgia said. "Does it hurt?"

Ranger shrugged. Tears formed in his eyes. "A little," he mumbled. Georgia pulled her son into her. "We'll get some ice on it," she said. "And some breakfast into you."

"I'm sorry, Mom," Ranger said. "I thought it would be funny."

"You're in the great outdoors now. This carousel has been sitting out here for who knows how long. So think about that before you stick your hand anywhere else, okay? And where are your gloves?" Ranger shrugged again. Georgia took his frozen little hands in hers and rubbed. "It's very dangerous to be out in this cold without protection. You could get frostbite."

"I was only coming out for a minute."

"Let's get you inside." Georgia headed to the house, with Ranger's hands still in hers. When she glanced back, Adam was disappearing into the barn. What was he doing? Off to kill the spider? She wondered if he was showing off. It wasn't necessary. Then again, what woman didn't want a man who would hunt down the spider that bit her kid? She glanced at Ranger's hand again. It was red because of the cold, but not too swollen. You couldn't obsess over every little bump and scrape and bite, especially with boys. Adam would learn that when he was a father.

He would make a good father. And beautiful children. She was suddenly irrationally jealous of the woman who would want to bear them. Oh, what did it matter? If some random woman wanted a drop-dead gorgeous spider-killing Scrooge, what did she care?

Georgia was thrilled to see that Sherman had pancake mix. Nothing made a spider bite better than pancakes. She even made them into the shape of little snowflakes. Sherman joined them, and by the time Adam came back from the barn, they were all reeling from a syrup-induced high.

"I saw a few spiders out there," Adam said, "but I can't be sure what kind bit him."

"You were bit?" Sherman asked. He sounded concerned. Ranger held up his hand and showed him the bite, which by now looked like a little welt.

"He got it straight from the horse's mouth," Adam said. "Sorry," he added when Georgia just rolled her eyes, Ranger squinted, and Sherman frowned.

"I told you that carousel was mine!" Sherman began.

"Enough," Georgia said. "You will not make him feel any worse than he already does. He's a little boy. It's a carousel. Get over it."

"Are there any pancakes left?" Adam asked.

"Have a seat," Georgia said. "I'll bring them right out." From the kitchen she could hear Adam saying something to Sherman in a low voice.

"How should I know?" she heard Sherman say. "They're from all over the country."

"What's up?" she asked when she brought out Adam's stack of pancakes.

Adam glanced at Ranger. "Just asking Sherman if he's

sure he doesn't have a working radio. I'd like to hit the road today."

"That's not what you asked," Sherman said.

"Later," Adam said, in a tone that made even Sherman fall silent.

"What about our cell phones?" Georgia asked.

"I checked," Adam said. "They're dead. No charger." Georgia nodded and set down his pancakes. "Thank you," he said. Before she could pull her hand away, his fingertip gently caressed the inside of her wrist. It was the most intimate and erotic gesture she'd had in a long time. She snatched her hand away as if it were on fire, and then, fearing she'd overreacted and he would think she wanted him even more than she did, she patted his shoulder, before returning to her seat.

"Do you have any aspirin?" she asked Sherman, glancing again at Ranger's hand. He'd kept ice on it for a while, but then said it was too cold and he was fine.

"I'll check," Sherman said. "And I'll see if any of my radios are working. But I can tell just looking outside that you aren't going anywhere for at least another night."

CHAPTER TWELVE

The rest of the day was more fun that Georgia cared to admit. They drank hot chocolate, and surprise, surprise, Sherman had Monopoly and Clue. His daughter, she found out, had children of her own, two girls around Ranger's age. Georgia was so wrapped up in winning that it took her a while to notice Ranger was wearing one of his gloves on his left hand.

"What's with the glove, sweetie?" she asked.

Ranger shrugged. "Just feel like wearing it."

"Just one?"

"Yes." Georgia studied him. He gave her a Mom-please-don't-embarrass-me look. "Why don't you come into the kitchen with me? I spied a box of macaroni and I'm sure I'll need help."

"She always puts in too much milk," Ranger told Adam. He smiled, but he too looked concerned over the glove. "No cheating," she told Adam as they left the table. As soon as she got back she was going to bust Miss Scarlet in the library with the rope. She wasn't always this competitive, but she had to do something to get her mind off Adam, and the kisses, and all the sinful things she wanted to do. She couldn't stop imagining what might have happened if she had let him take her out to his Jeep and have his way with her.

Once in the kitchen, she took out the box of macaroni, and immediately turned to Ranger. "Let me see," she said. She knelt down and gently removed the glove. His welt was now the size of a quarter. Not completely alarming, but definitely swollen.

"Ranger. Why didn't you say anything?"

"It's not bad," he said. "It doesn't hurt."

"I want Adam to see it," Georgia said. "Okay?" He nodded. Bringing Adam into the fold was the last thing she should be doing, but she tended to over-panic when it came to Ranger and his health. Adam was at her side the minute she called. He gently took Ranger's hand.

"More ice?" Georgia asked. Adam smiled and nodded, but it wasn't his usual smile. Something was off.

"Hey—why don't you find Sherman for us?" Adam asked Ranger. Ranger nodded and started off.

"But don't open any closed doors," Georgia called after him.

"What?" she asked the minute Ranger was out of sight. "Do you think it's bad?"

"There aren't many dangerous spiders in Rhode Island. But those horses come from all over the country." So that's what he'd been whispering to Sherman about earlier. He was worried. Oh God, was this actually worse than she thought for once?

"Oh, my God," she said. "What are we talking here? A black widow?"

"Let's calm down. At the worst probably a brown recluse. I thought I saw one when I went back to the barn. But I wasn't able to catch it."

"That doesn't sound good!"

"Is this you calming down?"

"Is it deadly?"

Adam took her hands. "I don't want you to panic."

"Is it deadly?"

"In children. It can be. If left untreated."

"Oh, my God. Oh, my God."

"Georgia. Listen to me." He was still holding her hands. She gazed into his eyes, needing him to tell her it was nothing. "It's going to be fine. I just don't want to ignore it. Better safe than sorry, right?" Georgia nodded. A lump, along with her heart, was already in her throat. "We're going to see if Sherman has a thermometer. I'm going to find a shovel and start digging the Jeep out."

"Sherman's iPhone!" Georgia said.

"Good thinking," Adam said. "This is exactly why you need to stay calm." Sherman entered with Ranger in tow. Georgia expected him to say something nasty or sarcastic, but then she saw the look on his face. He met Adam's eyes first and didn't waver from them. Oh, no. He was worried too.

"I'd like to know if you have a shovel," Adam said, in an upbeat voice.

"And a thermometer," Georgia said quietly.

"Why a thermometer?" Ranger asked.

"We're just going to check your temperature," Georgia said calmly. "It's important whenever you have swelling." She ruffled his hair just to prove he was fine. "And Sherman. We're going to open your Christmas present."

The thrill of opening someone else's Christmas present was evident on Ranger's beaming face. He was going to be fine. They were simply acting like responsible adults preparing for the worst-case scenario. Sherman sat in his chair, opening the gift with long gnarled fingers. Ranger parked himself right on the edge, like Sherman's chair was a perch and he was the bird. Sherman didn't seem to mind the proximity. Georgia had even begun to suspect he was enjoying the company.

Georgia was prepared to give him only a nanosecond before she grabbed the iPhone out of his hands. Instead, he held up a box of cologne.

"Old Spice," he said. He glanced at Georgia. There was a note, stuck to the box. "Dear Dad. Love means not trying to change the Luddite. Enjoy!"

The Luddite. Just like her. And now, because of it, they had no way to dial 911. *At least I have a cell phone and a landline,* Georgia thought to herself. But the point still dangled in front of her, sharp and lethal.

"Let's smell it," Ranger said. Always happy.

"Can we find that thermometer now?" Georgia asked. As Sherman went off to look for it, Georgia went to the front door. Adam had half of the car unburied. *Please,* she thought. *Please start. And please let the roads be passable.* Nothing mattered in the world. Nothing but knowing that Ranger was going to be okay.

If Sherman's thermometer could be trusted, Ranger's temperature was normal. Adam came inside, stomping snow off his boots, just in time to hear.

"Great," he said. "What about the iPhone?"

"It was Old Spice," Georgia said. *Because he's a Luddite. Like me.* "What about the car?"

"It won't start. I think the battery is dead."

"What about one of Sherman's cars?"

"Both complete junkers," Adam said. "I checked."

"I have a snowmobile." Sherman stood in front of them.

"How close is your closest neighbor?"

"Ten miles."

"How fast does the snowmobile go?"

"Should get you there in about a half an hour."

The panic was back in Georgia, even though Ranger didn't have a fever. "What are you thinking?" she said.

"I don't know. We could go now."

"We?"

"If we're going to go, we should all go. Call nine-one-one from the neighbors."

"I don't even know if ambulances can drive through this," Sherman said.

"Why do we need an ambulance?" Ranger asked. The three turned to him. He stared at them while they all stared silently back.

"We don't," Adam said. "But Sherman has a snowmobile. We thought it might be fun to take a ride."

"Cool," Ranger said. He yawned and rubbed his eyes. "I'm tired. Can I take a nap before we go riding?"

Georgia looked at Adam.

"I think that would be okay," Adam said. "We'll wake you if anything exciting happens." He looked at Georgia. Meaning—if the swelling got worse, or Ranger developed a fever.

"Nap it is, then," Georgia said. But it wasn't right. Ranger hadn't napped since he was a toddler. Then again, it had been a long day. The snow falling outside and the fire crackling inside made her sleepy too. Ranger padded over to the sofa, and by the time she reached him, he was already lying down, eyes threatening to shut.

"Story," Ranger said. Georgia scooted closer to Ranger, tucked his blanket around him.

"One day, while I was working the auction floor," she started. Suddenly Adam was right next to her, on the floor, staring at her, like a second child. She was just about to tell him to give them some space when Ranger reached out and put his hand on Adam's shoulder.

"Mom tells really good stories," he said. "She picks different cool artifacts that come into our auction house and makes up stories about who owned them," he explained.

"That's really something special," Adam said. "Really something special," he repeated, staring at her in that way that made her insides loose all over and made her want to grin like an idiot.

"One day a carousel horse arrived. It had given pleasure to thousands and thousands of children all over the world, and it arrived in this sleepy town, just as Christmas was approaching. And the timing couldn't have been better, for you see, the town was very sad." Footsteps creaking along the floor interrupted her. They all looked up to find Sherman sneaking back into the room.

"Go on," he said with a wave of his ham sandwich as he settled back into his chair. Adam took the moment to retreat to the fireplace, and although he did poke the logs with a stoker, he remained by the hearth. Her story was hurting him already, and she was sorry, but she had to do it. She had to remind herself who he really was, and why he was really here. She could handle heartbreak, but seeing Ranger's hand so affectionately on Adam's shoulder was a wake-up call. She would not put her son through any more pain. Ranger deserved to know the truth.

"Why is the town sad?" Sherman barked.

"Because the town used to be thriving. Up and down Main Street there were lovely little shops. A bakery—"

"Like Mrs. Weaver's," Ranger said. He liked to chime in now and again and Georgia always let him.

"A bookstore, a butcher, a florist—"

"A pharmacy, an Italian restaurant," Ranger said.

"And an auction house," Adam finished quietly.

"The best place in the whole wide world, right, Mom?" Georgia could barely speak. A lump in her throat. My

God, what was she doing? Had she actually planned on telling Ranger he was losing his home via a bedtime story? What kind of mother was she? She had just been poised to introduce the two Scrooges who were hell-bent on ruining everything, including Christmas. But the story didn't have a happy ending. And one of the Scrooges was sitting right here. She needed her head examined. She was just as confused as Sherman, who, for the love of God, would he just finish that ham sandwich before she grabbed it out of his hands? Really. One was never enough. "Just when the town thought they were going to have to shut their doors forever, the carousel horse rode in and saved the day." There. It wasn't her finest story ever, but it didn't end with her stabbing her son in the heart with the truth.

"How?" Ranger asked.

"Yes, how?" Sherman asked. He sounded paranoid again.

"Yes. How?" Adam asked quietly. Intensely. As if he were actually trying to figure something out. She didn't dare look at him.

"The town had a circle in the center, the way others had a square."

"Like ours!" Ranger said.

"Exactly like ours. Every year this is where they would hold their big Christmas celebration. But this year, the circle was empty. Nobody had the money to celebrate Christmas."

"Wait," Ranger said. He sat up. "Ours is empty. Nobody is decorating. Mom?"

Oh, shit. She'd gone and done it now.

"I bet they are decorating as we speak," Adam said.

Ranger nodded, smiled, and settled back. He nudged Georgia with his dirty sock, a cue to keep going.

"So the owners of the auction house set out to find the

full carousel from which this horse belonged. Because the circle desperately needed something to fill it, and what fit better inside a town circle than—"

"A carousel!" Ranger shouted. He shot up again. "Mom! The carousel. We could bring the whole carousel to the town for Christmas!"

"I knew it!" A plate rattled to the floor, and Sherman was standing, shaking, raging. "You can't have it. Your father caught me at a bad time."

"What are you talking about?"

"I tried to take it back."

"Take what back?"

"You can't have it. You signed it away. I've got the paper right here." He stormed back to the writing desk and began whipping papers out of it, and piling them on top. Finally he came to what he was looking for. "See," he said, pounding back across the room and shoving it in Georgia's face. "This carousel belongs to Sherman."

Adam, who was standing closer than Georgia realized, took the paper out of his hand. "Signed, Mrs. Claus," he read. "Nice lipstick," he added, staring at the paper, then at her lips. Georgia stayed perfectly still although she was squirming inside.

"What?" Sherman roared. Adam looked at Georgia, who shrugged. He laughed. Wait until he saw how she planned to sign his contract. But now wasn't that time for that.

"You won't get away with this! I've done everything to keep him from getting his hands on that carousel—"

Georgia stood, just as quickly as Sherman had shot up previously. "Oh, my God," she said. She rushed over to the writing desk and began going through the papers piled on top. It didn't even take long to find it. A receipt. For the entire carousel. "Oh, Dad," she whispered. "You bought me the carousel." Now *that* was a Christmas gift. Imagine this versus an iPhone or some new gadget. Luddites unite! Their special time together at Christmas, year after year, his funny face in the crowd, just the two of them and horses galloping against the background of the ocean. The ride she pretended to outgrow the year after Cindy died; no matter how gently he tried, she would never go back. He had missed it, she realized. He hadn't pushed her, but he had missed his time with her and the flying horses. And now, he wanted her to have it, forever.

A sob tore from her as she closed her eyes and saw herself going around and around, up and down, hands planted firmly on the golden pole, carnival music wafting through the air, the taste of saltwater on her tongue. Only this time, as she looks out, searching for her father and his funny faces, she just can't find him in the crowd. From now on, no matter how often she rode, or how high the horses would fly, never, ever again, would she see his beautiful, smiling face, standing in the crowd, ready and waiting with his funny faces, and his never-ending love.

CHAPTER THIRTEEN

Everyone turned to stare at Sherman. He finally threw his arms up in the air. "All right, all right. And I've started shipping it to you, haven't I? It doesn't say anywhere that I had to send it all at once. So if you want it, you're going to get it one horse at a time!"

"That's definitely not the Christmas spirit, Mr. Sherman," Adam said.

"Look who's talking," Georgia muttered.

"Grandpa bought us that whole carousel?" Ranger asked.

"Never seen a man so desperate," Sherman said. "I upped my price four times and he just wouldn't quit. Although all I wanted was to restore it. So I agreed, and did a mighty fine job if I do say so myself."

"You did a wonderful job," Georgia said. "Dad would've been thrilled."

"But then I fell in love with it. Didn't want to let her go, I guess. But I didn't know it was for a town circle. I didn't know it was going to save a town!"

"That was just a story—" Georgia started.

Adam looked at her. "A carousel like this would attract a lot of people," he said. "Especially if you could build a structure that would allow it to operate year-round."

"If you're thinking of your discount store you can stop right there, Mister—"

"What discount store?" Ranger asked. "We don't have a discount store." Georgia was about to make something up when he hopped onto the couch, flopped down, and within seconds was snoring. Lights out, just like that.

"I think he's going to be just fine," Adam said.

Georgia couldn't wait to get out of here. She never meant to be away even one night let alone two. But what in the world was she going to do about the carousel? Sell it along with everything else? Now that they were leaving, there certainly wasn't going to be a place for it anymore. Yet more proof that even her father couldn't have seen this coming.

But again, nothing mattered but the fact that Ranger was going to be okay. Georgia hadn't taken her eyes off him for a minute. Adam was out messing with the snowmobile and Sherman stoked the fire. It was nice and cozy sitting on the end of the sofa, watching the flames, and her sleeping child. Soon they would be home, her sister would arrive, and they would have a blowout celebration in the circle. And then, Georgia had no idea where they would be. It wasn't fair. But she would still have the most important thing in the world. Her son.

Someone was shaking her. "Georgia, wake up." She opened her eyes to find Adam standing over her. She'd never seen such a panicked face.

"What?" She sat up, and immediately looked over at

Ranger. Beads of sweat were visible all over Ranger's little face. Georgia lunged forward, her eyes taking him in. His left hand was swollen the size of a golf ball. "Help," she cried to Adam. "Help."

"I've got the snowmobile. Let's go." Adam swooped Ranger up, blanket and all. Georgia threw on her coat, and followed him. She could not think. She would have to let Adam take charge; she was an absolute horrified blank slate. Adam had Georgia sit at the front of the snowmobile, then when she was steady, he handed her Ranger. He climbed on behind her, and had to wrap his arms around both of them to reach the handles. Georgia shut her eyes and began to pray. She felt the engine roar to life, and soon they were skidding across the snow. Still, it felt slow, way too slow. Ranger would have loved to be awake for this, she thought as they bounced up and down. She prayed to her father, she prayed to Paul, as the bitter cold stung her cheeks, instantly freezing the tears that were falling down her face. She didn't care about The Treasure Chest, or the discount store, or the carousel. Nothing in this world would matter if her son was taken from her.

By the time they could see the neighboring house, a solid brick structure, Georgia felt a tiny bit of relief, followed by more panic. What if they weren't home? Then they would break in and call 911. But the minute they neared the front yard, she saw a man standing on his porch, watching them. Adam maneuvered the snowmobile right up to the steps. The man, seeing Ranger in her arms, stepped forward, immediately offering his help. He had a cell phone in hand.

"Ambulance?" he said.

"No," Adam said.

"What?" Georgia was ready to take his head off.

"I have connections at Providence. We'll need a medevac." A helicopter. Yes, that's what they needed, especially with the roads. But would they actually send it? A few seconds later, as she was inside with Ranger, patting down his feverish face, she heard Adam on the phone. He had a very take-charge voice, and it offered some comfort. She almost didn't want to look at him when he hung up, in case it was bad news.

"They're coming," he said. "They're sending a helicopter." She had no idea how he had pulled it off, or what his connections were, and she didn't care. She simply nodded, closed her eyes, and gently rocked her son.

If Ranger was going to be sorry he missed a snowmobile ride, he was going to be doubly upset he missed the helicopter. Georgia was almost glad for the loud whir of the blades and the engine; it helped to drown out her worst fears. It landed more gracefully than Georgia could have imagined, a giant buzzing mosquito, here to save her son.

Immediately paramedics strapped him to a stretcher, and there was just enough room for Georgia and Adam to squeeze in alongside it. Ranger was still unconscious, and feverish. Georgia held his right hand, afraid to touch the left. She was relieved when the paramedics immediately injected him with something.

"Antivenom," Adam said. "He's going to be okay." Georgia couldn't speak, she was absolutely stuffed with tears. Adam had done it. Taken care of everything, saved his life. She wouldn't have known what to do. She wouldn't have had connections to a helicopter or even had the sense of mind to ask them to bring antivenom. She owed Adam her life. He could have the warehouse a hundred times over. And to imagine she called him a Scrooge. As the helicopter ascended and headed for the hospital, as the serum worked its way into Ranger's little body, she crumpled against Adam, and he held her tight as she sobbed.

* * *

Ranger was in a private room. He was awake, and the fever was gone, although they had him hooked up to an IV just to replace any lost fluids and make sure the infection was gone. He was back to his usual self, wanting to hear over and over again the story of the snowmobile and helicopter. Doctors who came in and out stopped to shake Adam's hand.

"May I speak to you?" Georgia said to Adam when Ranger had finally closed his eyes again after ice cream and endless cartoons. Adam nodded and together they stepped into the hall.

"How is all this happening?" she asked. "Why does everyone here act as if they know you?"

"I've made a few donations over the years," Adam said. "In Cindy's name."

"A few?" Georgia asked.

"A few." He kissed her on the cheek, then stepped back into Ranger's room before she could grill him some more. Georgia was about to follow him when a nurse stepped up.

"I couldn't help overhearing," she said. "Come with me." Georgia followed the nurse down the hall and through the entrance to the children's wing. The moment they stepped out, the nurse turned her around and pointed to a plaque just beside the entrance.

THIS WING WAS MADE POSSIBLE BY ADAM CAVALIER
IN MEMORY OF CINDY

"My God," she said. "How could he afford this?"

"Apparently he's a wicked investor," the nurse said. "His company builds—"

"Discount malls," Georgia said.

"And Adam pours almost every penny back into this."
As they walked back, Georgia was stunned to see the murals painted on the wall. Carousel horses. She'd been in such a panic before she'd never noticed them.

"Apparently his sister died when she was young."

"Leukemia," Georgia said.

"Her medical bills wiped his family out financially. That's why he's set up scholarships. Every child who gets treated in this wing has most of their medical bills taken care of."

"You're kidding me."

"Every one," she said. "He's Santa Claus all year round."

Progress. It's not all bad.

Technology saves lives.

You need to embrace some of the new—

She'd been so self-centered she hadn't listened to a word. The discount mall would not only allow her neighbors to retire comfortably, it would actually save children's lives. She could part with the past for that. And now she knew exactly what to do with the carousel.

It was the prettiest she had ever seen the town circle. Garlands and strung lights and animated reindeers and snowmen and Santas. Everyone in town was in attendance. Even Virginia and Devon looked as if they were having the time of their lives, although Georgia felt bad for her little niece, dressed up as an elf. But by far, the crown jewel of the evening was the carousel in the middle of the circle. Georgia had used a significant portion of her proceeds to have the carousel shipped, and it would only stay here a few weeks before being located close to the hospital where children who were well enough and siblings of the children in the hospital could forever ride it. When she told Adam of her intentions, it was the first time she had ever seen tears come into his eyes.

Then, he leaned forward and kissed her. It was a deep, slow kiss, and she yielded to it, no longer afraid of him, or the future, or anything else that may be in store. She simply took his hand, and then took Ranger's hand, and together, they stepped onto the carousel, finding three horses in close proximity. Ranger rode slightly in front of them, turning around, smiling at Georgia and Adam as they went around. And as Georgia looked out onto the town, and the Christmas lights, a gentle snow began to fall. And she could swear in the crowd, she could see them. Her father, and Cindy, and even Paul. Ghosts of Christmas past. Smiling, waving, and making funny faces with each turn of the ride.

Christmas morning was held in the auction house. Georgia and Ranger opened presents with Virginia and Devon, and Annabelle. They had just decorated their gorgeous Christmas tree on Christmas Eve. Georgia still hadn't told Ranger they were leaving; she would wait until after the New Year. There wasn't a single second to figure out her next move, but she knew whatever it was, they were going to be okay. They had just finished eating her famous pancakes, when the doorbell rang. Ranger was the first to the door.

"It's Adam!" he called. He couldn't hide the excitement in his voice. Georgia opened the door and invited him in.

"Actually," he said. "I was hoping you and Ranger could come out."

"Go on," Virginia said. The minute Georgia saw the look on her sister's face she knew something was up, and

Virginia knew exactly what. When they reached Adam's Jeep, he pulled out two red velvet strips of material.

"I have a surprise for you both. But I'm afraid there can be no peeking." A minute later she and Ranger were in the Jeep, blindfolded. If anyone knew she was allowing her son to be blindfolded on Christmas Day, they might have called the authorities. But Ranger laughing the whole way and trying to make guesses as to where they were going sealed the deal. The car was nice and toasty and Bing Crosby suddenly came on the radio.

It's beginning to look a lot like Christmas. . . .

"Grandpa!" Ranger shouted.

"Funny you should say that," Adam said. Soon the Jeep was slowing down and then it made a complete stop. "Keep them on a few more minutes," Adam said. Georgia and Ranger started to giggle the minute Adam stepped out of the car, tense with anticipation.

"This has been the best Christmas ever," Ranger said.

"It has," Georgia said. Soon their doors were opened and Adam helped each of them step out.

"Okay," he said. "You can take them off." Slowly, Georgia removed her blindfold. Stunned, she took in her childhood home, and her father's large white barn. Why had he brought her here?

"This is Grandpa's place," Ranger said. "Mom only brought me once." It was too painful to come again. Once again she couldn't believe how much Ranger remembered. Adam took Georgia's hand and he pointed in the direction of the house. That was when she noticed the FOR SALE sign. And just above it, another sign. SOLD.

"I know I'm being totally presumptuous," he started. Georgia threw her arms around him, and kissed him mid-sentence. Then, she grabbed Ranger's hand, and Adam's.

"Would you like to see your new home?" she asked Ranger.

"We're going to live here?" Ranger asked.

"What do you think?" Georgia asked.

"There's a yard. And a lot of windows."

"And trees. And a big barn for our treasures. And a hill out back for the most excellent sledding."

"Yes!" Ranger said. "I want to see everything." He took off at a run toward the house.

Georgia gently put her hand on Adam and stopped him. "I can't believe you did this," she said. "But I can't let you pay for it. I'm going to reimburse you."

"I won't argue for now," he said. "Because I'm hoping by next Christmas it won't matter. I'm hoping that what's yours will be mine and what's mine will be yours."

They stared into each other's eyes, and Georgia nodded as tears came to hers. He gently took his finger and touched one of the tears.

"I fell in love with you that day," he said. "When you reached a hand out to my sister. When you helped her on that horse. And when you came flying around and smiled at me."

"I love turning fairy tales on their heads," Georgia said. Adam raised an eyebrow. "This time it was the girl who rode in on a horse," she explained. Adam threw his head back and laughed.

"You certainly did," he said. "You certainly did. Now let's go inside and make a fire. And then it's time for my present." This time Georgia raised her eyebrow. Adam held up a plastic bag. Georgia hadn't even noticed it. She peeked inside. Bread, eggs, milk, strawberries, sugar, and chocolate chips.

"French toast," she said.

"With strawberries and chocolate chips," Adam said. Georgia laughed, then kissed Adam on the lips. Ranger was on the porch, peeking into the windows. He turned to look at her, and even from afar she could see excitement twinkling in his eyes. Adam slipped his hand into hers, then brought it up and kissed it. Snow gently began to fall. And even though it was just the three of them, it didn't feel like it. In fact, the place felt filled with unseen friends. Smiling, waving, celebrating.

"What are you thinking about?" Adam asked.

"That it's beginning to look a lot like Christmas," Georgia said. Adam grinned and squeezed her hand, and together they ran for the porch where Ranger waited with the biggest smile on his face Georgia had ever seen. Adam began to whistle, and when they reached the door he handed her the key. French toast with strawberries and chocolate chips. Christmas traditions were as unique and varied as the families who celebrated them. And as she stepped back into her childhood home, with Ranger and Adam close behind, Georgia had a feeling this was just the very start of theirs.

A ROSE IN
WINTER

Laura Florand

CHAPTER ONE

Never talk to strangers.

Kind of a silly rule. Allegra spun the little stack of business cards and phone numbers in her fingers, evening up one edge against the heavy wood of the bar, spinning it to the next. Her mother had tried to pound the tenet into her brain most of her life, but Allegra still didn't know who first came up with it.

Take this stranger right beside her, for example. He was standing far too close to be at the bar just to order a beer. But once she struck up a conversation, she could get him to treat her as a person and not his potential sex doll for the night.

Which might be a pity, given how hot he was. All big and muscled, with thick rust and charcoal hair that just begged her hands to sink into it and see what happened when she stroked his pelt. He was younger than the charcoal in his hair might suggest, early thirties tops.

And the mistral was blowing, that fierce, cold wind that roared down from the north without stopping and drove her indoors, into the little house that had so charmed her into a year's lease back in May but which made her frantic with isolation now that winter had set in. She had been baking cookies for two days to fight the wind. She understood now the stories of its driving people crazy.

Maybe this man was feeling just a little wild and crazy, too.

"So have you been helping someone set up a Christmas tree?" she asked her stranger with a friendly smile.

His head turned, and amber eyes sent a jolt right through her. *"Pardon,"* he said, in a low rumble, like a wolf waking to eye an intrepid mouse. "Were you talking to me?"

He had been leaning back against the bar, eyeing the rest of the space, letting his presence settle over her, clearly expecting to make his move before the mouse ever spoke. Prey didn't, in general, start the conversation with the predator. That was why it was such an effective maneuver in a bar. You just couldn't eat someone who was chatting with you as if you were her big brother.

"You smell like pine," she said. "Or fir. Something *Noël.*" Wait. That wasn't how you talked to your big brother.

Strong eyebrows went up a little. He shifted so that only one elbow was on the bar now, and his body was angled toward her, closing her in. "You're smelling me?" His voice rumbled over her skin.

All her nerve endings heated. "Good nose." She tapped hers. "It always knows."

It did, too. It was a good filter for someone who otherwise chatted with pretty much anyone.

Amber eyes drifted down her whole body and back up to her eyes, leaving a tingling everywhere. "I went for a hike up to the old village," he said.

"Ah." Allegra loved that piney trail, rising and rising above the world until she could look out over the valleys around, filled with flowers in the vales, vineyards and lavender on the slopes, occasional patches of olive trees. The beauty of the old village, with its quiet fountains and ancient stone and extraordinary view, had lured her into renting the little house up there. It had taken her two days to meet everyone in it, and five to fix several small problems in their lives for what *she* thought was the better, and then she had started getting a little stir-crazy and wished she hadn't taken a lease for her whole research stint. Especially given the plumbing issues. And the horrible draft she had discovered when the mistral started. Still, the walk through the pines was incredible. "Did you come in here to get warm, afterward?"

His eyes rested on her face with the astonished fascination of a lion watching a mouse nibble its cords free. *Are you* sure *you've thought this through?* "Perhaps," he said, and she gave him a cheerful smile and pretended to sip her full glass of beer. It tasted vile.

"What are those?" that rumbly voice asked.

She looked down at the cards she kept playing with. "Oh, phone numbers." Men were always giving them to her.

His eyes narrowed at the stack of them. "Did you give out yours?"

Why did men always think she looked like an idiot? She shook her head, with a wide smile and another pretend sip of her beer.

Now he smiled, too, a very slight curve of his mouth that brought every hair on her body to thrilled alert.

"Then allow me." He fisted that big hand over the pile of cards and paper, crushing them into something the size of a peanut. Then he stuffed them down the nearest beer bottle. As she stared, dumbfounded by his nerve, he gave her a small smile. "You smell like someone I want to eat up," he explained. "I have a good nose, too."

Heat flooded her. Her whole body surprised her by shivering in profound . . . hunger.

He shifted even *closer.* "And I don't like talking to strangers." His big hand enclosed hers in one warm clasp. "I'm Raoul. How about you?"

CHAPTER TWO

"A-Allegra." The sound of her own voice astonished her. When it came to strangers, she didn't have a falter in her. A firm handshake, a cheerful declaration of herself: *I am here, and aren't you lucky to know me? Don't even think about leaving me over there by myself, the only child watching the groups of kids have fun.*

His palm was firm, callused, so much bigger than hers that she felt entirely enveloped in it. When he started to release her, her hand clung for a second. *Oh, wait, don't go. That feels so—warm. Hot. Wrap me up.*

His eyes flared. He stiffened, his gaze going down to their hands and then tracking up her body in a sweep that seemed to probe straight through her winter clothes, to her face. Amber glittered in a rim around the black dilation of his pupils, hungry, incredulous. *Is the mouse* really *going to nibble those cords all the way through?*

"Allegra," he repeated, low and definite. He had turned his voice quiet. *They would, wouldn't they, predators? Go quiet when they were closing in on prey?*

The thought of being his prey made her heart beat so fast with excitement that she couldn't even recognize herself. Weird. She made friends with guys. If she wanted them to be something *other* than friends, she had to talk herself into it, force herself past sexual indifference to give them a try. Usually after a lecture from a college roommate: *You're not giving them a proper chance, Allegra. You make up your mind about a man in fifteen minutes, and it's always no.*

And hadn't that been a *crappy* experience, the resulting hook-up she had gotten herself into trying to override her own instincts after that little college roommate talk. What a lousy societal invention hook-ups were.

So now . . . what were her instincts *doing?*

"Allegra," he said again, as if he had to try the taste of the word on his tongue. He smiled a little, watching her. "That means happy, doesn't it?"

She nodded. The name had always seemed to suit her. She didn't brood much.

"And are you happy?" he asked. His hand covered hers and held it to the counter, like a prize he wasn't about to let any other predator get.

"I am now," she said honestly, gazing up at him in helpless fascination. *Really happy.* This was *glorious,* this sudden, crazy attraction. It felt so *fun.* What a nice Christmas present. *Seriously, Santa? Have I finally been good enough?*

He inhaled sharply, his hand flexing on hers. His body shifted, blocking her still farther from the room.

He's cutting me out of the pack. He's singling me out for him. Those predator eyes of his glanced around at his possible rivals, lingering on an empty table in a corner a moment, hesitating on the door. *He wants to cut me out from the herd entirely. Get me somewhere he doesn't have his back to anyone in order to keep me isolated. Somewhere it's just me and him.*

Attraction tightened her skin and softened her sex. She

wanted to slide off that bar stool into his arms and see what he would do with her.

Not in broad terms. In broad terms she had a very good idea. But specifically, touch by touch, what he would do with her. How rough or gentle he would be, how those big hands would handle her body.

Once her mother had yelled at her. Well, a few thousand times in her life—her mother was dramatic—but this was when she was home from college, Allegra's head slumped on the table, buried under her arms, as she mumbled about her failures at the college dating scene. *Your generation is so* stupid, her mother had yelled. *There might be irresistible temptations you have to resist. But you should* never *force yourself to do something you* can *resist, with no effort. I knew in fifteen minutes with your father. He knew in two with me. If it's resistible, you just haven't met the right man yet.*

Allegra's gaze tracked up his body, marveling. *You really exist? The man who makes me hungry? You're not just some myth my mother called on, so she didn't have to worry about me dating anymore?*

In his throat, the little pump of his pulse beat as hard as hers. Her fingers lifted to touch it wonderingly. So strong, so fast. If she could slip her hand under his shirt to his heart, it would be thundering.

His chest lifted and fell, heavily, and she met his eyes again. His glittered with famine and intent. And, in them, too, that hint of incredulous wonder.

She realized she was touching him quite intimately, for someone known less than ten minutes, and drew her hand from his skin reluctantly. "I'm sorry."

"No," he said. "No." He caught her hand and curled it back against the side of his neck. "Don't be." *You can touch me all you want,* his eyes said.

But he didn't say the words out loud because . . . *he*

doesn't want to scare me off, she realized suddenly. *Not until I get the cords all nibbled free.* He held both her hands now, one against the counter, one against his throat.

"Have you ever done anything crazy?" she asked him.

"Far too often."

She scowled a little. Meaning . . . this? He did this a lot?

His hand flexed, bringing her eyes back to his. "Not in a long time," he said quietly. "But I'm not the one acting crazy here."

Her heart beat still faster, as they both recognized the cliff she was about to jump off.

"Do you have any objection to a woman going with her instincts?" she asked very softly.

His hands tightened into a cage on hers. "Yes. Don't run. I'll behave. I promise."

That hot, hard body was so tautly focused on her. As if every cell was straining toward her. She drew a breath.

"It's all right," he said. "Even if you're teasing me. You're—all right. Don't worry."

She shook her head slowly. "I don't have any instinct to run."

Breath hissed through him.

"Or for you to behave," she confessed.

He shifted still closer; the rest of the room was shut off from her. She took a deep breath of his scent: warmth and pine and that hint of coming down from high, snowy hills. "What do you want me to do?" he asked very softly.

His pulse beat so fast, his skin so warm. And she didn't want to talk anymore, because she *knew* how good she was at changing men into friends. "This probably sounds crazy, but—will you walk me home?" she whispered.

CHAPTER THREE

She was crazy, Raoul decided, as the sounds of the lower town fell away from them, their footsteps on the path the only hint of human life. *Complètement tarée.* It must be the mistral. There was probably some unwritten male rule against taking advantage of a woman during the mistral—maybe even her first mistral, judging by her accent.

Pines embraced them, a wind-tossed scent that made homesickness ache like a wound he had to heal. He breathed past the ache, and the scent reached into the bundle of nerves at his nape and relaxed every one of them, sending the message out to the muscles in his body.

Then a wide-eyed, excited, wondering glance skated up his torso, coming from a very small woman who was trying her best to keep her eyes straight ahead, and every single muscle tightened again. Gloriously. Aroused and utterly full of himself. Insanely strong. Strong enough to pick a small woman up, and press her back against a pine trunk, and . . .

Yes, she had to be out of her mind. He and she were going to have a talk about her trust of strangers later.

When he wasn't one anymore and there was no chance he could be warning her off himself.

One of you single kids should go make friends with that little American researcher, Allegra Caldrone. She's spending a lot of time with the old woman. Who knows what Tante Colette might be telling her?

Raoul had been incredulous at his grandfather's suggestion. His homebound cousins got to flirt with pretty women as their *jobs*? When he was out negotiating with rebel warlords? He had a freaking bullet hole in him. So he had volunteered mostly out of sarcasm and because he felt like hanging out in a bar.

He was kind of hoping he would run into old friends, people who still recognized him from high school, people who would make him feel like he could come home. But no such luck.

So he had watched Allegra Caldrone, her friendly, welcoming ease with man after man who approached her. Watched her until he realized why he was growing more on edge with each approach: *I want that welcome and that ease for me. Only for me.*

And unlike all those other men, he knew how to take what he wanted. A thought that surged hot triumph through his veins.

He was afraid to grin his victory yet, even into the night. Even though with every yes he got out of her, it seemed less and less likely the last word would be a no. Surely she wasn't *that* insane, that she would let a strange man join her on this isolated hike up to her home, if she was still planning to say no.

Then again, she probably didn't have much of a plan going on in her head right now, because if she was thinking, she wouldn't be doing this at all.

He loved the fact that he had turned off her brain.

She tilted her face up to the brilliant winter stars, excited wonder in her attitude, as if, for all her friendly ease with every man who tried to hit on her, she wasn't at all in the habit of making this walk up the hill with one. He shrugged out of his coat, his blood so hot he needed the winter mistral biting through his knit cotton shirt. Her gaze skated up his exposed torso. Damn, it was erotic, to have her look at him like he was irresistible.

The beauty of the winter night silenced him and seemed to steal her voice, too. Or maybe it was the heat and hunger. He didn't touch her yet. Not yet.

Her gaze teased over him again, no fear in it, and every cell of his body swelled in hot, eager pride. The hike through the pines felt like a prowl toward home.

The little old village on the hilltop stood mostly empty, this close to Christmas, the artists and Provence-lovers and romantics who were drawn to live there all gone to grandmother's house for the holidays. They passed through a tiny *place* with an old, dry fountain, wind tossing the echo of her boot heels on the stones. His own feet prowled softly. The night-weakened mistral whined in the tiles, half-tamed by the lee of the hill.

Houses below sparkled in the dark until two small humans seemed to be lost among an infinity of stars. In the mistral-purified air, moonlight silvered the olive leaves on the far hills and cast squiggly shadows off the bare grapevines, turning vineyards into a pelt of short, dark curls.

He couldn't see the rich brown of her eyes, as she fished in her little purse for her key. He couldn't see the red of her coat. But he could see how tiny she was. Tiny enough for him to push her back against the door and kiss her, with no possibility of resistance.

Not that *she* seemed to realize that. In the bar, her cheerful handling of every man who approached her had put him so on edge that he had finally stationed himself right beside her and *that* had kept the other predators away. His teeth showed briefly. Yeah, one thing he was good at—scaring smaller predators.

She found her key. He had to risk touching her now or lose his chance.

So he touched . . . just the glossy hair caught in a clasp at the back of her head. And the shape of her ear, half hidden by the strands fallen from the clasp. "Allegra." Rough, predatory, his voice would make a woman who heard it through her window in the middle of the night shiver and hide under her bed.

Allegra peeked up at him, not hiding but maybe just a little shy and utterly fascinated. Eating him up. With a little wondering smile on her face. What a perfect name she had: Happy.

She made him happy. Hungry. Hopeful.

Creepy. He felt suddenly unutterably creepy, to have followed her home from a bar through the dark, to be looming over her against her door, his palm itching to grab her key. "Allegra." His hand slid carefully to cradle her head. He felt so awkward, as if the wrong move could crush her skull. "I want you to know—" His thumbs snagged on the corners of her lips. He was going to have to pick her up to kiss her properly. That was an all-or-nothing move. "I don't want you to say no. But if you do, I'll only groan and try to get your number. You're safe with me."

She drew a breath, pressing her body back against the door as she stared up at him. "I don't feel safe."

His thumb wanted to slip between her parted lips, but the words hit him in the gut. She *shouldn't* feel safe with a strange man she had let walk her home through the woods, but—

"I don't want to feel safe," she whispered, with that eager, starlit look. As if she wasn't at all familiar with what she was feeling, but she was going to throw herself off the cliff anyway.

"Oh, that makes everything so much easier on me," he groaned and lifted her off her feet, pressing her back against the door to kiss her.

Greed swamped him instantly, as soon as their lips met, as soon as he got his hands on her body, that urgent hunger to eat her up.

The scent of her overwhelmed him. He had the family nose, highly sensitive and highly trained, although he hadn't had the patience to become a *nez* or a perfumer himself. As much as he liked the natural production, fifteen minutes at a perfume organ, full of too many essences and oils at once, gave him a migraine.

But her scent . . . her scent made him drunk. Vanilla and butter and sugar, like coming home. He wanted to circle three times and bury himself in the bed of it, a damn dog. And he could swear he could smell under that scents of roses and jasmine and lavender and thyme and whispers of more exotic scents from Africa, scents of *him.* Of home. As if she had been marked for him. How could that be?

No, no questioning it. *Just take as much of her as she'll let you get.*

She gave a humming little gasp as he invaded her mouth, her hands sliding up his shoulders to grip in his hair. He kissed her deeper in reward for the way she pulled his hair till it stung, shaping his mouth to hers, loving the way she let him take her over. He kissed her tender and hot for the way her hands slowly loosened, all her muscles lost in him. Yielded to him.

"Allegra," he whispered, slipping his thigh between her legs so he could hold her up to his mouth and still stroke his hands over her body. "You are crazy."

Oops, he hadn't meant to tell her that yet. They could

have this conversation tomorrow. If he got that far. *Don't screw this up. Keep your mouth shut.*

Well . . . don't talk with it.

"You are hot," she retorted in a whisper, his concentration pricking to follow her drop into English. He had had to learn it, pronounced in all kinds of accents, to find a common language he could use in Africa. Making it out with an American accent after the plethora of other accents he had encountered was almost . . . easy. Just like her. So easy.

So welcoming.

"*Pardon,*" he whispered. He was indeed hot. Burning up. He had dropped his coat on her doorstep, but he wanted to rip off the rest of his clothes and let the winter bite at his naked body, glorying in the fact that it couldn't cool him off.

"No." She dragged her hands over his biceps. "I mean you're, you're—*sexe.*"

Merde, that was sexy. Her small hands kneaded his muscles like she couldn't get enough of them. Arousal punched him too hard, his hands dragging her up his thigh before he realized it, rocking her against him.

It was good to be *sexe.* Good to be the one man, out of all those she handled with such friendly ease, that she had let walk her home.

God, I'm so glad to be home. His brain fogged, as her hands slid over him and her mouth yielded to him, lost track of the fact that this wasn't his home but hers. *Let me in, let me in.*

His hands flexed into her ribs and dragged down to dig into her butt. She was so crazy, to say yes to him so easily. She couldn't even weigh half what he did. "Are you drunk?" he finally forced himself to ask, wrenching his mouth away from hers. It had to be done. At least if she was drunk, he knew where she lived and could come bring, what, *merde,* roses tomorrow and see if she still liked him sober.

"I don't drink in bars." She wrapped her arms around his shoulders, flexing her body into him. "A girl can get in real trouble that way."

What the hell was she in now?

"You shouldn't be going into bars alone at all," he groaned. With that cute little body and those warm brown eyes and that friendly smile. But he gloried in being the predator who had caught her. He pushed her coat off, spilling it on the ground, and she shivered in his arms. "It's too cold out here for you, *bébé.* Allegra. Please let me in."

She pressed her body into the heat of his, not answering, her mouth against his throat. He shivered all over, and he wasn't cold at all.

"You can still change your mind, if you let me in," he promised her, breathing too hard, hands stroking everywhere, sounding not trustworthy at all. "You can trust me. I promise you."

"You must think I'm out of my mind," she said. "I don't trust a man I just met in a bar."

Aïe. He winced. And slowly forced his hands off her.

She twisted off his thigh and pressed her forehead against her door, gasping. Her dark, sleek hair was tumbled down to mid-shoulder blades, her clip lost somewhere on the ground. He braced his own hands on the frame above her, breathing hard. Watching her fumble for her key. *Fuck.* He should have kept his mouth shut about the trusting. Bad time to bring that up, when a woman was just thinking about letting a man more than twice her size whose last name she didn't even know into her house.

Should he tell her his last name? It was a name that would stand in his favor with most women from around here, but then again, you never knew what Grand-Tante Colette might have told her about the Rosiers. He opened his mouth, hesitated, and his chance at happiness got the key in the lock and opened the door. *Merde.* He grimaced, pulling himself off the doorjamb and back a step as she went into the house.

She looked back at him, surprised. "I don't want to trust you," she said finally.

"Right," he said. "Right. *J'ai compris.*" He wouldn't want to have to trust someone twice as big as him, either. He breathed heavily, glad of the cold.

"Trust doesn't have anything to do with it," she said.

Yes, definitively out of her mind. He sure as hell was glad he was the man she had picked up in the bar. Because *he* certainly didn't trust the owner of every other phone number he had stuffed down that beer bottle to be standing as still as he could right now, trying to gulp in enough winter to calm down.

She bit her lip. "Are you having second thoughts?"

What? He took a step back, looming in the dark doorway. "You aren't?"

"I don't want to trust you," she said again. "That's what I keep trying to say."

Oh. *Oh.*

And the weirdest thing was, she seemed completely oblivious to the depths of trust necessary for what she had just handed him. He grabbed their coats off the ground and came inside before her brain could turn on.

CHAPTER FOUR

Never met a stranger, her mother always said, resigned, of her daughter. She wrote it as a caption under photos in their family albums, photos of Allegra on a beach with the kids she had picked up, back in the days when it had been cute. Once Allegra hit puberty, her willingness to talk to anyone had started freaking her mother out.

She had never met a stranger, but she didn't sleep with men she just met anymore. Not after the couple of tries in college and the shatteringly humiliating way they treated her the next morning. People weren't strangers when she met them, but they could *become* strangers with very little difficulty at all, apparently.

But he was so hot. He was so different. He hit her every sense, from his rough growl of a voice, to his scent of pine mingled with so many hints of other things, a wild roaming of scents, to the big body and shaggy pelt of rust and charcoal hair, to the taunting nearness of his texture. He smelled so familiar and exotic all at once, like she had known him a long time, like she could never know him enough. And all she had to do to satisfy the craving to know what he felt like was . . . give in to it. He made that so clear.

His body felt so hard under her hands it made her shiver and ache. He was so hot and so predatory, and *he stepped back,* throat muscles straining as he stared at the sky and breathed. He caught all that predatory instinct in an iron grip for her and let her go. Arousal wound into a crazy tension in her, like a guitar string about to snap.

She was old enough to let herself do something she knew better than to let herself do. Just this once. With a man who knew how to go after what he wanted, with full-on starving aggression—and still take no for an answer.

Hell, it had been six years since college. Maybe she was even old enough these days not to feel like shit in the morning.

Just let me get my hands on all those muscles, all right? Tomorrow morning can take care of itself.

She slipped her hands under his knit shirt as he shoved the door closed behind him, and he hissed, his head arching back. A momentary pang of guilt at how cold her fingers must be against his ribs, and then she just pressed them in anyway, running up his abs, over his chest, stretching the shirt out of her way.

He grabbed the hem of his shirt and ripped it over his head, pulling her into him as he rocked back against the door.

The curve of his biceps and his rock-hard body sent shivers of pleasure through her. He made a rough, low sound and hauled a handful of her hair up to his face, breathing deeply. She pressed her face into his chest and took her own breath. Such hot human skin, and yet the scent of pines and lonely winter prowls stayed with her.

She kissed his chest, and fingers flexed into her skull and, much harder, into her bottom. "Allegra," he muttered. "You have a perfect name."

She had to run her hands all over his torso again. When a woman got a chance to touch a body like that, she had to get as much of it as she could. He made such a hungry sound when she did. His fingers flexed again and again into her bottom, rocking her against his sex as she stroked him. A squirming built in her, hunger growing and growing, making her skin too flushed and hot as if it held too much pleasure. She nipped a little at his muscles to try to find some way to relieve it, wrapping her arms around his back and up over his shoulders, trying to press herself into him.

Their hips bumped and rubbed as he walked her to her couch, a crazy, hungry sensation. The cushions met her back, and her whole body arched in the delighted sense of no-return. She was doing this. She was really doing this.

And she was so smart. God, what a chance to seize. She would be crazy to pass him up. Maybe *this* was the reason she had felt so compelled to stay in Provence for Christmas. Because if she had gone home, she would have missed out on him.

His big hands stroked her thighs, up and down, from knee to crease, burning through her jeans, and his face nuzzled up her body, pushing the sweater away as he kissed her belly, her ribs, too close to her sex, too close to her breasts, touching neither. Tickling her with his jaw, making her flinch a little and relax into the hunger for more.

And when she was all relaxed, all hungry, shivering, yielding, his hands slid up under the sweater—callused, thorough hands—and pushed it off her, coming back to cup her breasts. He looked gorgeous over her, with the moonlight coming through the great window that gave a view onto the valley, silvering his big shoulders.

"So pretty," he murmured, slipping his thumbs under the edge of her bra to find her nipples, then easing them away to slide under her back, hunting for the catch while his jaw traced all along the edge of lace. Shivers of delight raced through her, until the bra fell away, and that prickle traced straight over one straining nipple, making her yelp and clutch at him.

He laughed a little, a rough hungry sound that fed her arousal, one hand slipping to cup her sex through her jeans, riding it, pressing it, as he kept twisting his face between her breasts, kissing, licking, rubbing with his jaw until she was frantic. "Please, R—" *What the hell was his name?* she thought, shocked at herself. *Oh, yeah.* "Raoul."

His face stilled just a second between her breasts. "That sounds good," he muttered to them, and his big palm rested against her belly. Hot and sure. Letting her know it was there and what it was going to do. "Say it again?"

His name? "Raoul."

"You can't say the R," he whispered in a queer, fierce, and very annoying delight—her French Rs were *quite good,* thank you. But his hand pressed more firmly into her belly, and the annoyance fell away, leaving her with no thought, only the sensations of him.

His hand slid south. Slowly. Under the jeans he must have gotten unbuttoned at some point. To the edge of her panties.

Under them.

Allegra twisted, making little whimpering sounds, so glad she did not know this man, he was not her friend. He was a stranger, and so she could make any sound she wanted. Be as frantic as he could make her. Let herself go entirely.

By the time his middle finger parted her folds, she was biting into his shoulder, making little begging sounds. He breathed harshly against her breasts, sliding his hand to cup her fully, and then another harsh breath as his hand shifted and savored exactly how wet and soft she was. She twisted, her head arching back, her body trying to drive into his.

He lifted his head and stared down at her. His thumb found just the right spot and deliberately, while he watched her face, made a slow tiny circle. She twisted her face away, throwing an arm over it, feeling too much even for a stranger to see.

"You're incredible," he said softly, his thumb circling again. And again. Testing the motion by the expression on her face, by the shivers of her body.

She whimpered, hips bucking into his hand. His face lowered until his breath blew into her neck. "Oh, I like that sound," he whispered. "Do it again for me?" His thumb circled.

She dragged her arm tighter against her face, moaning a little. This was taking her over too fast. She didn't understand herself. It was usually *hard* for her to make love, hard for her to slip out of that friendly world into eroticism and darkness. Hard for her to come, lovemaking an awkward, frustrating thing that never really fit right into her friendships.

He bit very gently at the arm that hid her face, licking, teasing down the exposed inner wrist, as his thumb played with her. Pleasure stretched her like a bowstring, between the textures playing against that ultrasensitive skin of her wrist and the even more sensitive spot between her thighs.

This was so *easy*. It was so fast. She was being sucked swirling into the delicious danger of him, pulled to some other place where she didn't know who she was.

She couldn't think for the pleasure. For the motion of his thumb, driving her somewhere she fought to avoid and wanted too desperately to go. She threw her hands up to grab the bars of her little metal bed, trying suddenly to hold on to something, as if a flood were sweeping over her.

He made a low, rough sound of approval that swept pleasure even higher through her. She was vibrating like a bow, little sounds low in her throat.

"Make that sound again," he whispered, a big finger slipping deep inside her.

She gasped and bucked against him. "R-Raoul."

His finger drove suddenly harder, making her writhe and clutch. "Or that one," he whispered fiercely. "I like that one even better."

"R-Raou—"

His thumb pressed down hard suddenly, his mouth biting his name off her lips, and pleasure speared up through her and wrenched her apart, wrenched his name in half, drove her into nowhere.

Just pleasure, pleasure, pleasure . . . and more of it . . . it wouldn't let her down, he wouldn't let her down. Until she threw both hands over her face and sobbed with it, a little, it was so shatteringly different from anything she had ever understood.

"You're beautiful," a harsh voice said wonderingly. "Oh, *bébé,* I want you so bad."

She was trembling, coming back into herself so slowly. "Too fast," she whispered through lips that felt untutored, as if they never had formed words before.

His head jerked up, his hands freezing. "*Putain, c'est pas vrai,*" he muttered. "You're changing your mind *now*?"

"No, me," she managed, although as the trembling eased, she felt so soft and pliant she could barely form words. "Too fast. I wanted to . . . take my time."

He inhaled sharply in relief, and his hand cupped her sex again, testing, making her shiver with little aftershocks. He made a little hot sound, reveling in her, in himself. "*Mon bonheur,* I really don't think you're done." His hand moved, and she twisted, wincing a little away from the sudden rise of pleasure again, the way her body was so ready to send her convulsing outside the world again. He laughed just a little, hungry, satisfied. "Maybe you'll be able to stretch it out your *third* time," he murmured.

Oh, Lord. His hand was—merciless. Sensation building again too soon, too intense. She couldn't do this again so soon. Not by herself.

She wrapped her arms around his shoulders and pulled herself up to him, bringing her mouth to his ear. "And I wouldn't change my mind," she whispered. "I want to feel you."

"Oh, *putain,*" he muttered helplessly. "Yes." His hands found her hips again. "Yes." He nudged her thighs around him, but she didn't need any encouragement, her breath tightening again, her whole body waiting for him. "*Yes.*" He drove into her, and she gasped once in time with his own gasp. Just for a second, he was too much, and she flinched a little away from him. He breathed heavily, holding still. "Too fast?"

Her muscles released in one great wash of pleasure. And clutched at him as he started to ease back. "Perfect. You're perfect." Her voice changed on the words, as she realized: *He really is.*

His head lifted again, focus shifting from the joining of their bodies to her face. He stared at her for a long moment, not moving. "*Mon bonheur,*" he finally breathed, driving slowly into her again. "So. Are. You."

And she had thought it was good before, but nothing compared to getting swept into that vortex of lost self with him in her body, him riding her, him holding her, as they got lost together.

CHAPTER FIVE

Allegra was drifting dreamily toward a doze, entirely content with the crazy choice she had made that evening, when arms slipped under her and carried her into her bedroom. A weird moment: She could whimper and beg a stranger, she could come for him, but could she turn her face into his chest and nuzzle?

He settled her under the cold comforter, and she winced more awake, her breath hissing as she scrambled for his heat.

He braced that big, beautiful body over her and grinned. He seemed very, very—happy. Ten years younger than he had just an hour ago. "Want me to warm you up?"

She still knew almost nothing about him. He still felt like a completely alien being. Not a friend, not someone who needed his problems solved with that bossy confidence that had always let her, an only child, insert herself into other people's lives so easily. She felt no confidence around him whatsoever. And yet he felt . . . exactly right. She placed a hand on his chest and gave him a little grin back. "Think you can last longer this time?"

He laughed, his smile quite wolfish, and let the weight of his hips settle onto hers. "Yes."

Well after midnight, he lay on his elbow, fingers idly tracing up and down her spine. Allegra was nearly asleep, her face turned away from him toward the window, her body having automatically slipped back into the position in which she always slept, facing that beautiful view of stars above and human stars falling away below. He had opened the shutters as one of the first things when he left the bed to go into the bathroom. The wind whined low in the tiles of the roof, but the window faced south, away from it.

"What a beautiful spot to be holed up in when the mistral blows," he murmured. "You must be able to see forever."

She grimaced a little and wiggled her body closer to his warmth. He probably gloried in the wind, this man. She could just see him climbing up onto the top of some north-exposed rise, his head tossed back, wind raking that rust-and-slate hair.

"So what are you doing tomorrow?" he asked very softly, and her heart gave a little hiccup and then just *melted*. He wanted to see her more? This had felt beautiful to him, too?

"If the mistral stops, I think I'm delivering *biscuits*." She used the closest French word for cookies, even though it was an inadequate translation. There was a whole Atlantic Ocean of difference between the dry, crisp French *biscuits* and her rich, buttery, melt-in-your-mouth chocolate chip cookies. When her French friends first bit into their soft, chewy goodness, they usually asked nervously if the cookie had been cooked enough, convinced she was feeding it to them half-raw. Allegra laughed. "I don't think it's in my best interests to have twelve dozen cookies sitting around here. But when the mistral blows, I can't seem to stop baking them. Fortunately, the neighbors and Madame Delatour like them."

A fractional pause of that hand on her back. "Madame Delatour? You know her?"

"Oh, you do, too? You're from around here?" Not necessarily a stranger passing through her night?

A little pause. "Not recently."

She smiled wistfully. "Coming home for Christmas?" She had gone home for Thanksgiving and come back to experience a true Provençal Christmas, but homesickness kept catching her, the closer they got to the actual day.

"That—would be nice," the low, rough voice behind her said. The energy coming from him was so much quieter and steadier now, compared to his all-out aggressive pursuit of her earlier. She liked that, too. The sense of peace. "To feel at home for Christmas."

His tone made her want to curl her hand over his, but she was enjoying the back stroke too much to roll off her stomach. "Well, anyway. If you used to live here, you know the Rosiers are the economic powerhouse of the region."

"I—was aware of that, yes."

"I'm doing my PhD on the scent trails, the role of perfume in immigration. Some of my own family ended up here, when they were getting out of Italy during the rise of Mussolini. They changed their name to Chaudron."

"The lavender growers?"

He knew more about flower production around here than he let on, didn't he? Or was that just standard knowledge for anyone growing up around Grasse? "Madame Delatour is one of the oldest people around here and grew up in the household of the head of the Rosier family, so she's been a good source of oral history and even artifacts and documents."

A tiny pressure from the fingertips resting on her back. "Artifacts and documents?"

Allegra shrugged. "Anyway, she kind of adopted me. I help her with her garden, she makes me soups and scents and soaps. It's crappy the way the Rosiers act as if she's not a real part of the family. She's ninety-six years old, and almost none of them ever go to see her."

Big fingers flexed once into her back. Her spine arched deliciously into the pressure. "They don't?" A thread of anger in that rough voice.

"*No.* Don't get me started. One of these days I'm going to tell the Rosiers exactly what I think of their idea of *real family,* and then good-bye to all this great access they let me have to their material."

"Be an interesting conversation to witness," he said and rolled her over to kiss her, a steady, insistent claiming of her mouth, until she was lost again in that hot, hard, wonderful body, her hands buried in the silk fur of his hair.

She slept profoundly afterward, and woke to the mistral, back at its worst.

She nuzzled her nose into the sheets, breathing an unfamiliar warm scent, and some little sneaky hope in her imagined someone *else* wanting to snuggle up inside while the wind blew, someone with a big body and huge metabolism who thought it was his dream come true to be stuck with a woman who liked to bake cookies against winter weather.

Soft movements through the room, muffled by the howl of the wind.

Soft like someone who wanted to escape unnoticed.

Oh.

That sneaky hope curled in on itself in shame. She kept her lashes against her cheeks, not sure what to do.

The sick memory of the only other two times she had tried sleeping with someone she had just met rose up in her, her happy belief she had found a friend, and a friend who was attractive, too, and then . . . the way she had been treated the next morning. Like she was dirt they couldn't wait to wash off their hands.

Oh, hell.

Her stranger was dressed, she saw through her lashes, and let her eyes flutter completely closed again, sick to her stomach. He even had his coat on. *Fine, then, leave. Don't you wake me up for an awkward nothing. Get out.*

He paused for a moment in front of her little collection of painted clay *santons,* the Provençal Nativity scene figures Allegra had started to collect, the bare bones of Mary, Joseph, baby, and donkey enriched by the quirky secondary character here or there that had charmed her: a little village baker, a truffle hunter with his pig, a woman carrying lavender. Raoul picked Mary up and looked at her a moment, then replaced her carefully, with a little sigh.

Allegra closed her eyes again as he turned but felt him come to her bedside table and pick something up. Hey— that was the little antique perfume box Madame Delatour had given to her.

His breath hissed through his teeth as he looked at it, tiny against his palm. The tarnish that caught in the filigree of silver was oddly suited to the wolf's head pattern, the wolf's teeth bare as it reached for the rose in the corner of the box. Raoul raised it to his nose to sniff the solid perfume inside that Madame Delatour had created for her.

His eyebrows rose. He took a photo of the perfume

box with his phone and hesitated a moment—then slipped the box into his coat pocket. The shock of the action nearly made her betray herself as awake.

He looked around, spotted her bra on the end of the bed, and draped that over the nightstand, covering up the perfume box's absence. The fact that it was her bra, removed last night by him from her breasts, burned her horribly, her stomach revolting. *He was a thief. He had stripped her naked, and now he was* stealing *from her.*

She wanted to protest, and then, for the first time, something hit her. He was over six feet tall. She was five-two. If she pitted herself against him, here in the small confines of her little house, what would happen?

She didn't know. The realization tore a wound across all that glorious, giddy night in which her body had been entrusted to his.

His hand closed around her shoulder, startling her so much she nearly hit him. Her eyes flew open, and she glared at him.

"It's just me." He crouched to make himself smaller, putting their faces on a level. "*Pardon.*" He gave her hostile expression, a curious, searching look, a cautious smile. "Not used to waking up with someone in your room?"

Not used to waking up with a thief. *A* big *thief. A man who could control her body effortlessly, a man she didn't have one chance in hell of fighting.* She felt so sick it was all she could do not to run to the bathroom, vomit him out of her, wash him off her. And she had thought the morning-afters of her two optimistic college-student hook-ups had been bad. Those guys hadn't *stolen* from her.

His eyebrows flexed as he studied her face. His smile faded, his eyes wary in a way that confused her. *He* didn't have to be afraid. "I've got to go," he said after a moment. His mouth twisted oddly. "You're probably going to want to call me in a little bit, so I wrote my number on your hand."

Oh, that bastard. Did he think she was so desperate she would call and beg him back, even after he stole from her?

She looked at her hand. Ten digits, starting with the 06 for cell phones, right there in the palm, with the black permanent marker he must have found in her desk drawer.

"Hard for anyone else to get rid of by stuffing it down a beer bottle," he said wryly, and then made her utterly sick by lifting that palm to his mouth and kissing it. "You know, you really shouldn't be so friendly with strangers."

Yes, tell me about it, you bastard.

He took a breath, watching her, and let it sigh out of him. "You're uncomfortable."

Oh, you think? Why would that be, exactly?

"Me, too," he admitted.

Why, is your conscience kicking you? Do you feel a little slimy picking up a woman in a bar so you can steal from her?

"No, I'm not," she said and rolled out of bed. He stood quickly, to steady her on her feet.

She smiled and leaned straight into him, past the revulsion, past the anger, going up on tiptoes, dragging her hands on his hips through his coat to scramble up a body too big to kiss without a ladder or help.

He helped. Pulling her up into him, kissing her hard. When she dropped back, his phone and her perfume box lay on the mess of sheets behind him. He was trying not to grin, his face lit in smug delight. *Look, I can screw a woman, steal from her, and still have her begging for more of me.*

"Well. Maybe I'll see you later," Allegra forced herself to say hopefully, like some pathetic *screwed* woman. She leaned against him for a long, clingy moment during which one hand left his back to wiggle the sheet behind him enough to hide the phone and perfume box. Then she picked up the permanent marker and wrote a number on his palm. She drew a heart around it for good measure and winked at him as she capped the pen. "There you go. Now you know where to find me."

"I knew where to find you anyway," he said with a little smile that looked so good on his unshaven face she wanted to hit him. "You showed me where you live." And then that grimace. "But I suspect you'll want to find me first."

Yeah, well, you are so wrong about that one. Bastard.

She smiled him out the door, locked it—and yanked on clothes, thrusting his phone and the perfume box into her coat pocket.

The wind bit at her as soon she stepped outside, fighting against the hooded cape that had seemed such a fashionable idea when she had seen it in Paris earlier that fall. Before she met the mistral, its force strong enough today to drive a car off an exposed road. A thermometer wouldn't show the day as that cold, but the wind stripped every bit of heat from human bodies as soon as it was generated.

Halfway down the path, wind driving at her back, something alerted her. She ducked into hiding just in time and watched him stride past. Grim, determined, heading straight back to her place, with a strong stride that cut through the wind as if it offered no resistance. *Put your hand in your pocket to check your spoils, did you?*

She waited long enough that he wouldn't hear her, and then took off at a flat-out run, heading straight for her car parked in the lower village below. It gave her only the tiniest smidgen of satisfaction to imagine him huffing and pounding and unable to get back in.

CHAPTER SIX

Never talk to strangers.

Allegra closed her hand tightly around the perfume box, in the inside pocket of her cape, stopping on the stairs. Madame Delatour's house clung to the walls of the old medieval town of Sainte-Mère, one of the many beautiful old hilltop towns that surrounded the flowering vales of the region. To reach the house, one climbed a street of stairs, winding up inside the wall, a great old bare vine growing the whole length of the stairs, thicker than a strong man's wrist. Not that she wanted to think about a strong man's wrist right now.

A stranger being, by definition, someone you don't know! she shouted at herself.

Even if he smells of fir trees and snow and a hunger to come in and eat cookies. And has a hard-muscled body and a ferocious, starved look.

Especially if. Especially if!

Of course, if it hadn't been for strangers, she would still be hiking along the road toward the nearest tow truck or at least some point with cell phone reception. Her body still felt achy from the slam into the ditch, or at least that was what she tried to tell herself all her aches came from. Even the inner thigh-muscle ones. What an awful day.

At least the curve of the stair-street sheltered her from the wind. No one answered the flower-shaped brass knocker, and her stomach clenched as it always did at that. Ninety-six years old. She tested the knob and found it unlocked, not unusual. Everyone in the old part of town knew Colette Delatour and often stopped by. The town's heroes, three-star chefs Gabriel and Raphael Delange, brought her tributes of fantastical pastries and luscious savory dishes on a regular basis. They gave her impossible gourmet extravagances, and she sat them down and fed them rustic soups the star chefs ate in blissful peace, as if they had finally found their way back to mama's kitchen.

A freshly washed bowl lay upside down by the sink in the empty kitchen. Allegra went on through to the garden, the old woman's favorite place, even in winter. Eerie to think that some of the plants in this garden had been re-seeding themselves since the days of fairytales, the garden as old as the medieval wall that sheltered it.

Winter put the garden into a deep slumber of roots and dormant plants, such as the *raiponce* or rampion that Madame Delatour turned into soups, to Allegra's profound delight. Nothing like eating *rapunzel* pulled from an old, old woman's walled garden. Wind swirled down into the sheltered space, carrying the unexpected scent of evergreen. Linens tossed wildly on a line.

Someone laden with dancing sheets was fighting a long, old nightgown that plastered his face and body as he freed it of its clothespins. Allegra took three steps toward him, half-expecting one of the Delange brothers or maybe some Rosier whose conscience had finally pricked him. They were all big like that.

Big . . . a sudden prickling dread rose up, pressing at her to run. But it was too late.

A strong hand pulled the nightgown down, and amber eyes glittered at her. "Surprise," Raoul growled.

Allegra jerked back. His hand caught her arm, a pile of hand-embroidered sheets crushing between them. "What are you doing here?" she spat. "What did you say to Madame Delatour to trick her into letting you in?"

He bared sharp canines. "I said, *Bonjour, Tante Colette, it's been a long time.*"

She gasped. Of course. Why hadn't she seen it before? His coloring was unusual for the dark-haired Rosiers, but the size, strong jaw, and arrogant cheekbones were classic Rosier. But if he was a Rosier, how was it that she hadn't met him yet? "So, what—you don't have time for your *ninety-six-year-old* great-aunt most days of the year, but God forbid you should see her giving away bits of your inheritance to the people who do care about her?"

"I've been in Africa," he snarled at her. "For most of the past twelve years. Since you're so familiar with us, maybe you can call to mind who the director of materials production in Africa for Rosier SA is?"

And yes, of course, there it was, a name without a face, waiting to be woken in her brain. Raoul Rosier.

The wind drove the sheets and nightgown into his face again. He released her arm and crushed them down. "And I come see her whenever I'm home," he said, almost sulkily, like a boy who had been caught being nice to the old lady next door.

"Especially when you're worried about your inheritance?"

He took a harsh breath and suddenly dumped the entire armful of linens onto her. She disappeared under the pile of them, and by the time her face had gotten free, he was unpinning the last of his great-aunt's nightgowns from the line in hard jerks. He pivoted when the line was empty and came back to her, a prowling excess of energy. "Actually, I was hoping to get my phone back," he told her, teeth bared again.

"I threw it out the car window. It wouldn't stop buzzing."

His teeth snapped. "Nice."

She smiled sweetly. "It's probably cheaper to replace than a silver perfume box from the Renaissance."

"Oh, definitely." His gaze raked her body through the sheets and whipping cloak, searching for hiding places. "But I bet you didn't throw that one out the window, did you?"

"I've got Mace," she said firmly, backing up a step.

His breath hissed between his teeth. He stared at her in incredulous rage. "Yes, and that would do you so much good right now. Within arm's reach of a man ten times stronger than you in high wind. *Bordel.*" He stalked past her into the house.

Allegra followed him to the laundry room, furious. "What did you do with Madame Delatour?"

"I ate her and was just looking for a nightgown that wasn't bloodstained so I could hide in wait for you in her bed," he said between his teeth, hauling out an iron and plugging it in. "Either that or she's up taking a nap. What the fuck took you so long to get here?"

"A gust of wind nearly drove me off a cliff on the drive up, and I ended up in the ditch on the other side instead when I overcompensated."

He froze in the middle of shaking out a sheet, white cloth billowing slowly down to reveal his rigid body.

"The roads around here are insane even without the wind, and I *might have been a little upset.*"

His eyes raked her body, up and down fast, and then again in a slow and excruciatingly thorough scan. "*Merde,*" he said very low. "Are you all right?"

She did her own raking sweep of him, putting all the scorn she could into it. "Oh, I'll be *just fine.*"

He weathered it, tried another step into the force of her scorn like a man battling for headway against the mistral. "Is your car all right? Do you need help?"

She curled her lip. "Not from you." *I can hold you in every bit as much contempt as you held me, this morning.*

The set of his mouth turned very grim. "Who got you out of the ditch?" he asked finally. "A passing stranger?"

"As a matter of fact, yes." She had made friends with a whole nice family.

The sharp edge of his teeth showed again. "You had an emergency number stamped right across your palm."

She curled her fingers over that permanent ink. "You mean the number to the phone at the bottom of that cliff?"

"*Putain,* Allegra, I had pictures on that phone." He swept the hot iron across the sheet, in a broad, aggressive move that was too fast to get all the wrinkles.

Still, it kind of confounded her that he was making the effort. "You, ah—iron?"

"For a ninety-six-year-old woman who thinks her world is falling apart if her sheets aren't ironed, yes. Don't get your hopes up."

Bastard. "Trust me, I don't have any hopes about you." She strode past him to the laundry sink, pitting Madame Delatour's handmade soaps against that permanent ink.

He watched her efforts grimly a moment, over the sweep of the iron. "At least mine was a real number."

Allegra gave him a sharp smile. "Sorry, my mother always told me not to give my number out to strangers."

"I bet that's not the only thing she told you not to do with strangers," he muttered, and her face flamed.

"So, what, I deserved the lesson?"

The iron stopped sweeping. He stared at her. "What lesson?"

"Your lesson." She tried to say it with sweet vindictiveness and was furious with herself when her eyes stung suddenly. "Last night and this morning."

He let go of the iron and took a step around the board toward her. "There weren't any *lessons.*"

"Well, I learned something, nevertheless," she told the running water sullenly. Her palm was growing raw from scrubbing, and the ink had barely faded.

He reached past her and shut the water off. "Allegra."

The scent of pine blended with the size of him, looming over her like safety. She stepped back, throat closing. "Don't burn that sheet. Her mother embroidered them." He cursed and turned back to grab the iron. "They might be part of your inheritance, too."

He stiffened, the iron poised just above the sheets. For a moment, he stood still, his muscles tight, and then finally spoke: "First of all, I don't have any expectations of receiving an inheritance from Tante Colette." But there was a little thrust to his jaw when he said it, like a boy saying he didn't expect his father to show up for his school play. A little hurt.

"Is that why you feel you need to steal it whenever you get the chance?"

The thrust grew harder. "Second of all, she would never give her mother's sheets to an unmarried nephew—"

"Oh, so at least you're not married," Allegra said snidely.

His fist clenched around the handle of the iron. She saw him swallow as he stared grimly down at the sheet.

"You change your mind about a man real fast, don't you?" His head lifted, and he locked those amber eyes with hers, his glittering. "Easy come, easy go?"

Her head jerked back. Her eyes narrowed. "You make me want to throw up just talking to you," she hissed at him and had the satisfaction of seeing *his* head jerk back in cold shock. "So no, not that easy."

She strode out.

CHAPTER SEVEN

Raoul focused on the ironing. He could see why Tante Colette said it was soothing. Long, steady sweeps with something heavy, flattening out a mess of wrinkles. Don't throw the heavy something through the wall. Just steady, steady, steady, until the sick clammy feeling goes away, and the anger becomes manageable, until all that's left is the fucking hurt.

Great. Just what he liked, to have the hurt brooding there, when all the protection of anger was gone.

He folded the sheet, pressing the folds exactly the way his aunt liked it, then spread the next one. Might as well do them all. She was ninety-six years old, and he knew damn well she would insist on doing it if no one else did.

Against the handle of the iron, the heart Allegra had drawn around her *fucking fake phone number* burned until he thought it would make a permanent brand. Every single time he had tried a different variant of that number—*maybe that was supposed to be an eight, not a nine, or was it a four, or . . . merde, allez, Allegra, answer*—that heart had scraped a little more salt into the wound.

He listened for the sound of Allegra's footsteps heading for the door, but apparently she didn't want to leave his aunt alone in his clutches, because the sound of her movements stayed in the kitchen. She could trust her little body in his hands for four fucking orgasms, but his ninety-six-year-old aunt might be in danger. Right.

Sheet number three. He used to take sheets like this for granted, handed down for generations, washed and ironed by one of the women in the family. His mom never let him leave the house with unironed underwear, either. But, of course, he had rejected all that when he'd fled the flower belt at nineteen in search of *life*. The universe. Everything. He had hired a local woman to iron his sheets and shirts for a while in Africa, but it just hadn't been the same as that painstaking love that went into it from his mother and aunts.

Because in the end, the sheets and shirts were a symbol and what mattered wasn't whether they were ironed but why they were. And after his mother died so unexpectedly—he hadn't even gotten back in time to say goodbye—he had stopped sending his ironing out, because lying on the crisp, clean sheets that did not smell of lavender had made it so hard to sleep. It was better not to even pretend he was home.

Like he had pretended last night. That warm, easy welcome of hers had made it so damn easy to delude himself. Those brown eyes tracing over him with excited wonder— a man could forget all kinds of things when a woman looked at him like that.

His jaw clenched sullenly as the wrinkles glided away under the sweep of his hand, leaving something pristine and perfect again.

It really was amazing how making that pristine freshness appear kept easing the tension in the nape of his neck. Something else was working its way through the lavender scent of the sheets and the steam of the iron, too.

Vanilla and butter and . . . chocolate? Something . . . warm and welcoming. It reminded him of Allegra, but a stronger, richer smell, something freshly baked, and his sensitive nose woke the rest of his body up until he was ready to howl with hunger.

He pressed the last fold into the last sheet and turned off the iron, tracking the smell to the kitchen.

Allegra's butt greeted him. A view he hadn't had a chance to appreciate before.

She straightened from the oven, with a sheet pan full of little round golden things, dotted with dark. The aroma nearly overwhelmed him. He could have leapt across the space, wrenched the pan out of her hand, and devoured both her and whatever she was baking.

All right, he could hardly beg for treats unless they were on speaking terms. So as much as it pissed him off to have her dismiss him so easily, *one* of them was going to have to be adult and talk. "The perfume box wasn't Tante Colette's to give you," he said, with an effort. "It belongs to the family."

Allegra whirled around. The rich air spun giddily at the movement, and his whole being howled with hunger. Brown eyes locked on him without one tiny degree of that open, welcoming friendliness at the bar.

Putain.

"Fuck you," she said.

All right, that was just . . . lovely.

That damn kiss before she got him out her door still burned in him, an acid he couldn't wash off. It had filled him with such relief, and guilt, and heat . . . and halfway down the trail, he had realized it was fake. A sick feeling still stirred in his stomach when he remembered slipping his hand into his pocket and discovering the perfume box was gone.

"And don't come near me. These pans are hot." Allegra

slid a spatula under the things on her pan, transferring them to a plate. His gaze tracked the little *biscuits* helplessly. And the hand that was holding the spatula. And the slim little body that hand belonged to. Up to the hard set of her jaw.

Putain.

His fists clenched slowly, in a memory of her crazy trust that whole long beautiful hike up through the pines. This morning, he had checked himself in her bathroom mirror to see if some fairy godmother had transformed him into someone who looked—safe. He'd stood there staring dumbfounded at the unshaven wild man he saw. Because he looked so unexpectedly familiar.

Allegra gazed back at him now for a long moment, as if he were . . . a stranger. Abruptly, she snatched up a cookie and took a big bite.

Goldenness yielded to her teeth in a way that seemed all soft and chewy and not at all like the crackly *biscuits* he was used to. He managed not to whimper. Allegra's eyes became fixed on his face, then narrowed ever so slightly. And then her face got a slightly sleepy look, and she took another bite, taking her time, making a soft little sound in her throat. "Chocolate chip cookies," she murmured. "I bet you've never tried them, have you?"

His teeth ground together as he realized what she was doing. Maybe he should try reasoning a little *harder*. "Allegra. I *need* that perfume box."

Her eyes flashed. "Thief," she said with disgust and turned her back on him.

Fury rode a wave of sickness, undoing all that ironing. She wasn't going to be *disgusted* by him. Not after she had welcomed him with such generous eager warmth. He wouldn't allow it.

"Allegra. That perfume box is part of a collection that has been in our family for five centuries. All of which disappeared during the war. It might help lead us to the rest of it."

"I'm not responsible for your family problems." The sharpness of her smile made the heart in his palm burn. "We're strangers."

That brought him a long hard step into that tiny kitchen. "Oh, no, we are not."

"Yes." Her smile pressed the heart into his palm like shards of glass. "We are."

His next stride brought him almost to her.

She lifted the now-empty tray. "Careful, Raoul. If that's your real name. This is hot."

"I don't give a fuck," he said, and yanked it away from her, dropping it on the counter—*fuck, that hurt*—and closing the last bit of space, his burnt hand lifting to cup her cheek.

Where it stung so much, he finally had to pull it away to see what damage he had done to himself. Lines of red showed from the fleeting hold.

Allegra's jaw was set so hard he thought she would break it. She dropped her oven mitt and grabbed his wrist, yanking his hand under the tap of the little kitchen sink.

The cold water felt so nice that he just stood there a moment, breathing in her gorgeous butter-vanilla-chocolate scent with that hint of something under it as if she was his. "And of course it's my real name," he said, finally realizing what she had implied. "What do you think, that I *lied* to you?"

"You draw an ethical line between screwing a woman to steal from her and lying?"

That one punched right into his gut. "I didn't—*screw you*." It burned his mouth even to say it. He grabbed her shoulder with his "good" hand, the one that had a lying heart drawn on it. "How *dare* you—"

"Call a thief a thief?" She gave him that same wide

smile she had given him over her beer, the one that had turned his initial predatory interest in her on its head. Left him too hungry to focus properly. Hadn't it been sincere either? "I don't know. I guess I have a nerve."

He took several hard breaths, staring down at her. She was really very tiny. Tiny enough to push back against the counter and kiss, with no possibility of resistance. It made him feel utterly protective.

Hard to protect a woman when she thought *you* were the disgusting threat. When you *were* the threat.

Bordel. She hadn't thought he was disgusting last night.

She had smiled up at him as he braced his body over hers, so much smaller, so much nicer than he was, and yet completely unafraid. And he had shattered that smile into ecstasy and then brought it back again.

Maybe he had gotten a little cocky this morning, about his ability to bring it back again. She turned his hard arrogance into something glorious, giddy, as if he were walking gold.

Until he had found himself pounding and pounding on her door, panic growing as silence greeted every plea to let him in.

"You do have a nerve," he said slowly. "You're not afraid of me at all, are you?" Not afraid to turn him into a beggar at her doorstep, certainly.

She left his hand under the running water and went back to the tray he had thrown, righting it and beginning to drop more *chocolate chip cookie* dough onto it. "Oh, I was afraid this morning," she said with that sharp smile. "When I woke up to find a man in my room stealing things."

She hooked up a big chunk of raw dough in her finger and ate it, just like that. Her eyes closed on it, as if she would far rather savor it than him.

Did it taste good raw? Had he? He had felt raw, last night. Raw and wild, only held together by her. It had felt so good, to lose himself with her arms wrapped around him, to lose himself and be home, all at once. As if he could never truly be lost. "You can't steal something that belongs to you. Or to your family."

Her brown eyes walled him away from her warmth. "You're pathetic."

He recoiled. He was *what*?

"If you thought you had a legitimate case, you could have discussed it with me. If you thought I was worth anything at all."

"I gave you my number," he said between his teeth. "My real number. So you could call me when you realized. I knew you wouldn't be happy." After he had given up his stupid, desperate attempts to make that lying-heart phone number of hers work, he had co-opted a cousin's phone and called his own number, over and over, restless, panicked, knowing she wouldn't answer but unable to keep himself from trying.

"Oh, because that shows respect? Stealing from me and leaving me a number so I can chase after you and yell about it? Maybe if I had yelled loud enough and long enough, you would have felt better, like I had gotten the shame out of your system."

That was the idea, yes. Better yet, he wanted her to crack and start pounding on his chest, like some old movie. He didn't think it would hurt much, and at this point any physical contact would be a relief. Then, after she calmed down, *she* could feel guilty for a while instead.

"Look, I just didn't want to talk about it this morning," he said tightly. There were some things you didn't want to ruin the first instant you woke from them. *Damn it.* "I'm not a morning person."

She gave him a scathing look. Anger surged up in him even higher, the desperate need to grab her and make her *stop looking at him like that.* His hand shot out, brushing her shoulder as he grabbed a cookie, biting into it hard.

She gasped in outrage, seething.

Deliciousness flooded his senses. Butter and sugar and yielding softness, and chocolate, and . . . her staring at him in pure fury. He snagged another one.

She smacked the back of his hand.

He smiled and snapped his teeth together over another bite.

"Those are not for you," she tried to growl.

For the pure pleasure of showing her pathetic effort up, he growled back. And saw her pupils dilate and goose bumps break out on her arms. *Good. Have you finally woken up to the fact that you have a predator after you, bébé?* "That's what you thought about *yourself* eighteen hours ago. It didn't take me long to change your mind."

She wanted to slap him so badly. He could see it in her eyes. He dipped a finger into her dough to see what it had tasted like raw.

Mmm. Who knew raw dough could be that good? He tried another bite, not sure which was more addictive, the hot, fresh-baked *cookie,* unlike any *biscuit* he had ever tasted, or the cold dough.

"Twice," she said with a curl of her lip in contempt. "It didn't take you long to change my mind twice."

She liked to sucker punch a man, didn't she? He leaned in on her. "Well, then, since it's so easy to change your mind about a man, let's see how long it takes me to change it again."

She twisted away just before his mouth closed on hers. An outraged part of his body pointed out, evilly, that she wouldn't have been able to escape if he had just grabbed her and—*shut up, merde.* He locked his hands against the counter on either side of her as the safest thing to do with them. Locking her in but *not* touching her. *See? Practically behaving well.*

And then he thought, *Fuck, if I want her to beat her anger out against my chest, why stop there?* And he slid his thigh right between her legs and lifted her up on it. Her eyes widened. Was that fury or did she maybe, just a little, still like it?

"Raoul," said a quiet voice behind him. "I think you need to take a walk."

He dropped his knee in a guilty heartbeat, turning. Tante Colette, hair neatly repinned, down from her nap. His great-aunt was a tall woman, and time had not much stooped her, but he still topped her by more than a head, of course. And Allegra didn't even reach the other woman's chin. His face flooded with shame.

He had just . . . just been trying to get *through* to her somehow. He so desperately would rather she hit him than call him pathetic. *Bordel.* He slunk back against the corner of the counter, a giant menace that had invaded this homey kitchen. That didn't belong here and should be kicked back out to deal with rebel warlords and get shot at and survive kidnapping attempts, just like his family kicked him out every time he tried to get accepted back here.

"I still can't get over how big you've gotten," his great-aunt said, her eyes traveling over his chest and arms brightly, which was the kind of thing she *always* did when he was a teenager: Read his mind and then rub in whatever guilt she found there. It was why those kind letters she had sent him from home had thrown him at first.

"I was this tall before I left," he said tightly.

Tante Colette spread her old hands wide enough to encompass an ogre. "You've filled out." Her little dog came out from behind her long wool skirt to sniff at his ankles.

"You don't have any trouble getting women to trust you, at that size?"

How could anyone who wrote such nice letters be in reality so *mean*? Raoul stepped farther away from Allegra before she could cringe from him in horror—and noticed, belatedly, that she was not in the least cringing. She was glaring at him and looking ready to go for his throat. *Merde,* if his aunt hadn't interfered, maybe she could have gotten this whole thing out of her system by now. He bet his throat could survive having hands that size wrapped around it.

He gave Tante Colette an accusing look.

"Raoul," she said calmly. "Would you go see if there are any turnips in the garden?"

There you go. Sent out into the cold to collect turnips. It really didn't compare to sending someone back to the tropics to negotiate with rebel warlords, but she was probably doing her best with what she had. Only he couldn't shake the upswelling of gratitude any time he was near his aunt, the memory of all those letters she had sent him, smelling of lavender and rose, when all he ever got from the rest of his family was a friendly sentence or two at the end of an e-mail asking if shipments were likely to continue uninterrupted. He hadn't been particularly close to his aunt before he'd left, a wild teenager while she was already over eighty and alienated from her stepfamily, and so he was surprised when the first letter arrived one day. And profoundly touched when they continued to arrive, regularly, for fourteen years.

So he slunk into the hallway at her request, hearing her say, "What's wrong, *pucette*?" before he even got five steps toward the garden. The answer was probably going to mean the end of his rose and lavender letters.

"I want to go home," Allegra said, and her voice didn't

sound angry at all, not like with him. It sounded shaky, as if she was trying not to cry.

He stilled in the dark hallway and half-turned.

"Raoul," his aunt called firmly. "This is a private conversation."

Putain. That was another reason he hadn't gotten along with his aunt as a teenager. She always knew when he was doing something wrong.

Merde, why? he thought viciously, as he yanked turnips. So easy, so warm, like curling up by a fire in the heart of winter. He had felt, for half the night, utterly right. It had seemed so perfect that right there on her bedside table, she would have a treasure that would confirm his place again in this world, please his grandfather, make the old patriarch look kindly on the grandson who didn't want to argue with rebel warlords anymore, who wanted to be back home. *I'm sorry I threw my home away. I'm sorry. All right? Let me come home for Christmas.*

He thought of the little collection of painted clay *santons* that Allegra had had in her place up in the old village. It was a first-year *santon* collection. The kind that could grow over generations of Christmases, into the giant collection it used to take him and all his cousins two days to help his grandmother put out.

His jaw twinged. He rubbed the muscle and came away with scraped fingers from the stubble.

He was so homesick he could barely stand it. But he needed her, to go home.

CHAPTER EIGHT

"It's Christmas," Madame Delatour said, as her little dog sniffed all over the floor for chocolate chip cookie crumbs. "If you have a home, it's a good time to go to it."

Allegra gazed uneasily at the perfume box on the table between them. If she were in Madame Delatour's shoes, she would hide it as far out of Raoul's sight as possible, but Madame Delatour only smiled at the whole story, with subtle satisfaction. Allegra pressed the little rose in the corner to open the box, then rubbed her finger over the solid perfume that blended roses and lavender and other scents that she couldn't recognize but that seemed, after months of using it, so familiar, and stroked her wrists with the perfume, like therapy. Madame Delatour smiled more deeply. "I still mean for you to have it, you know."

"Madame Delatour, if it's a family heirloom . . ."

"They've always had an unfortunate definition of family," the old woman said, a chill slipping into her voice. "Maybe they need to expand it."

Allegra closed the box again and looked down at the wolf's head on the lid, the waves of fur leaving slits to allow the scent of the perfume to escape. His teeth were so fiercely determined to catch that rose, always just out of his reach.

"I hope I don't have to force the present on you," Madame Delatour chided. "I think you'll be happy with it, in the end."

Allegra sighed, pushing the box farther away from her. "If I go home, I won't get to learn the thirteen desserts from you, Madame." According to Madame Delatour, thirteen desserts were a traditional part of the *Gros Souper* or big family Christmas Eve dinner. Madame Delatour seemed to make a habit out of collecting strays instead of actual family for hers.

The old woman smiled. "I can do that now, and you can teach them to your mother at home and think of me when you eat them Christmas Eve."

"But what would you do for Christmas Eve?" Allegra argued.

"What do you mean, what would she do?" Raoul said from the kitchen doorway, his arms full of turnips. Their eyes met, but she looked away from the jolt of him. "There's always a place for you at our family table, Tante Colette."

"You mean the place for the stranger?" Madame Delatour said dryly, referring to a long-established Provençal tradition of laying an extra place for whatever stranger might come to the door on Christmas Eve. "I thought that one was for you."

Raoul's face turned a little, as if he had just taken a slap. Allegra felt an absurd urge to put her body in front of his to protect him, which—*what?* Where had that come from?

"Only if you show up without warning," Raoul said finally. "If you warn us, we'll put you at the head of the table with Pépé."

"So he can interrogate me about where that perfume box came from?"

"Of course. Where did it come from, Tante Colette? It didn't once belong to a Renaissance perfumer named Niccolo Rosario by any chance? Who might have been attracted to a wolf pattern because his mother's maiden name was supposedly Lupo?"

The old woman bit into a cookie and smiled at Allegra. "Delicious. You are such a gem, *pucette*. I can see why you think a man shouldn't risk you for an old perfume box."

Raoul dumped the turnips in the sink with a clatter and smacked dirt off his sleeves so hard it had to hurt.

"I'm sorry I left it out where he could find it," Allegra said hopelessly. *Never talk to strangers. Not only do you betray yourself, but you get an old woman hurt, too.* "I just—what were the odds that the one Rosier I hadn't met would end up right where he could see it?"

"Oh, I think the odds were very high," Madame Delatour said with a thoughtful little smile, looking at Raoul.

It took Allegra a second, and then she pressed her forehead into her fingertips at the wave of sickness. *Yeah. What were the odds that Colette Delatour's little friend and possible confidante would find herself aggressively pursued in a bar by the one Rosier she hadn't met?*

Her fingers collapsed. She flattened her palm against her face. It hadn't even been spur-of-the-moment opportunism on his part, had it? The purpose of the whole night had been to use her.

Picking up a potato brush, Raoul attacked the turnips as if they were personal enemies.

"Madame Delatour, are you going to be all right with him?" Allegra asked the old woman.

His head jerked up, and he shot her a betrayed look. How dare he keep looking as if *he* was betrayed?

"Of course, *pucette.*"

"Then I think I'm going to go."

Raoul dropped the turnips. "I'll drive you."

"I don't have the perfume box anymore," Allegra told him coldly, gesturing to it on the table.

"Thank you," he said very tightly. "It would have been such a waste if I had cut your throat and buried you in the *garrigue* for nothing. Now you can consider yourself safe for the whole ride home." Accusation flared in those amber eyes.

I don't feel safe. I don't want to feel safe. Had she actually said those words to this man less than twenty-four hours ago? And felt—utterly safe?

"Is that too boring for you, compared to ending up over a cliff dead or in a ditch trusting strangers to help you out? I know how you like strangers," he added viciously.

Allegra flushed crimson. She wanted to throw something at him, but the only things on hand were the cookies, and he would probably snatch those out of the air with his teeth and swallow them whole. "I'll call you," she told Madame Delatour and grabbed her coat off the back of the chair, striding out the door.

Cold greeted her as soon as she stepped onto the stair-street, but no wind. The mistral had stopped. Just like that, the way everyone said it would. She stood blinking at air sparkling with cleanness. Movement was such a pleasure without the crazy wind to fight that she felt as if she were floating.

And then she remembered what she had left behind

her and yanked her coat on, striding through the winding streets.

Strong fingers pulled her hair out from under the drooping hood. She jerked away. "If I'd known you had so much trouble with the word *no,* I never would have talked to you in the first place."

"That's the trouble with strangers," Raoul said, his face tight. "You don't really know much about what they'll do, do you?"

"Evidently not."

"I don't remember hearing the word *no* from you last night."

She walked faster, a ridiculous effort. He still had to shorten his strides. Walking without the mistral to fight felt so surreally light that the physical release made it hard to hold on to her emotional opposition to Raoul. Her heart kept begging to find out what it would feel like to let go of that battle and just—float right back into him. Or even soar.

The street of stairs gave onto a great sweeping arch of a street near the top of town, down which curved colored houses, draped now with bedraggled Christmas lights looking wiry and confused after the mistral and extinguished by the brilliant sunlight. The slope dropped off so steeply afterward that the colored houses seemed to curve all the way to the distant sea. At night, the white Christmas lights arching down that street were gorgeous.

"What am I doing," Raoul asked finally, his voice chipped out of stone, "that you keep acting as if I'm a threat? I never hurt you, damn it. You put yourself completely in my hands, and I *never* abused that. I took *care* of you, Allegra. I tried."

"You stole from me." Allegra locked her arms around her aching chest. "That hurt."

"I didn't—" Raoul stopped and gave a hard shake to

his head that stirred the shaggy hair in the brilliant light. They had come out into the *place* where the town had set up its great Nativity display, in the half-circle of a wall and fountain turned off for the winter. The Nativity was an enormous creation of thousands of *santons,* hand-painted clay figures by a local artist who had won the right to do the Nativity this year. Behind plexiglass, shepherds hunched into an imagined mistral and a wolf brought his paws to the stable window, peering in wistfully.

Raoul stopped in front of the scene for a long time, then tilted his head back and squinted at the brilliant heaven-touched-earth sky. The air was swept so clean of dust by the seven-day mistral that he glittered, light striking shards off him like diamonds.

He extended his hand to her abruptly. "Can you at least let me talk to you, Allegra? You could have tried talking, this morning."

"So could you."

His jaw tightened. He bent his head a few centimeters and kept his hand out.

Allegra's chest tightened at the pose, the waiting persistent hand, the bent head, until she thought something in her *had* to snap, to relieve the pressure.

"I want to walk by myself," Allegra said flatly. "Are you going to respect that or are we playing survival of the strongest?"

Raoul's fingers curled into his palm. He shoved his hand into his pocket and just looked at her for a moment. His chest moved once in a long breath. "Go where you want," he said evenly, anger and something else compressed in his voice. "I was just asking."

He turned abruptly away and strode across the *place,* to a toy shop display window full of all kinds of treasures spilled from Papa Noël's sack.

Allegra turned the other way. She strode ten firm paces, eleven, her eyes stinging, and her lungs tightening until she could barely breathe. She looked back.

Raoul still stood in front of the toy store. His head had bent.

Her chest ached so much, she thought it would tear itself open. She turned abruptly and walked back to him. "The perfume box is with Madame Delatour," she said again, hard, her tone angry to punish him for the fact that she had come back. That betrayal this morning still hurt *so much.* And yet she could not stand to leave him there, looking betrayed. "I gave it back. It doesn't have anything to do with me anymore. You can leave me alone."

He said nothing for a moment, just breathing, staring at the retro toys, the planes and cars someone his age would have had as a child. "I'm sorry I took it without talking," he said finally. "But I would like to talk now."

CHAPTER NINE

It was too cold to sit still unless two people were willing to put their arms around each other, so they walked. The town's great *marché de Noël* extended along a wide pedestrian street to another *place* before Aux Anges, the Delange brothers' restaurant, and descended from there down a long street closed to traffic so that its slope could be filled with snow from one of the nearest ski resorts, farther up in the Alps. The slope had been lined with bales of hay and little Christmas trees covered with fake snow, and local children were riding down it in sleds provided by the town. No real snow ever fell here.

The silly charm of it made Allegra so homesick she could barely stand it. She didn't want to be here, among strangers with a stranger, watching someone else's kids have fun. She wanted to be home, safe. She wanted to be curled up by the fire with her mother, adding final touches to their own Christmas tree, full of the clothespin reindeer and paper-plate angels Allegra had made at school.

Raoul stepped into a side street, stopping against a great iron gate slightly set back from the street, a slumbering winter garden visible through it. He put himself on

the gate side, leaving her free to step away from him into
the public eye, his hands shoving even deeper in his pockets. His voice was very rough. "I had to start imposing
myself in strange cultures, where no one wanted to listen
to me or respect me or, sometimes, leave me alive, when
I was twenty-one. I've been doing it for twelve years
now. Fourteen, if you count from when I first went over. I
realize I—take what I want. If you don't take it, you
don't get it, damn it. And I must come across as—very
aggressive. Maybe that's why no one wants me back in
my own civilization. But you need to know that I would
never hurt you." His hand jerked out of his pocket suddenly and grabbed hers, lifting it so that her palm pressed
against his.

"Just—look," he said. The ink edge of the heart on his
palm peeked around her much smaller hand. "Really.
Never." He gazed at their hands for a long moment, and
then yanked his away as if hers stung and shoved it in his
pocket again. "And it meant a lot to me when you believed that."

She yanked her hand away, too, belatedly, wrapping
her arms around herself. "You *did* hurt me."

His eyes crinkled, searching her face, very intent. His
hand left his pocket again and cupped around her cheek.
She went very still, as if that touch warming half her head
was a butterfly's wing she could break with a wrong
movement. "I'm sorry," he said quietly. The quietest she
had ever heard him speak, quieter even than that soft moment at midnight, when he had stroked her back and they
had gazed out at the fall of nighttime hills below them to
the jewel-lit edge of the sea. "I don't think I realized that
I had touched anything but your body."

Her face flamed.

"I'm very sorry," he said, even more softly, eyes fixed
on her face. "I thought you would be mad, not hurt. I just

wanted to deal with that mad later, not first thing in the morning."

"You didn't think I would be hurt to realize I had just had my brains screwed out for the sake of someone's family?"

A harsh gasp, and then a rush of anger that tightened every line of his body, even to the fingertips pressed against her head. "*Putain,* stop saying that! I did not *screw*—damn you, Allegra!"

"Well, excuse me," she said stiffly. "I had run into the concept of being *used* before, but at least then sex was the use. It wasn't just a way to get to something else."

He pulled his hand away from her face and shoved that fist back into his pocket again. "You obviously can call last night whatever you choose to," he said, his voice so hard and . . . hurt? "*Screwing* or—" He broke off, the seams of his pockets straining under the pressure of his hands. The certainty rippled through her: *He was hurt, too.* "But I'm not nearly the multitasker you think I am, to have any other ideas in my head but one, after you told me I smelled like Christmas."

"But you don't, quite," she said involuntarily. His apology began to sink into her slowly, water filtering through hard rocks. "Christmas smells like baked things and cinnamon. You smell like pines and snow. Something far up in the hills looking down at Christmas." Wistfully. Looking down at it wistfully.

"Oh." He looked down with that hard set to his jaw. The set that *fought hurt,* she finally realized. After a moment, he said resentfully: "So vanilla and butter and chocolate? Is that Christmas to you?"

"That's more a year-round home smell." She tilted her head. "Where did you even get a taste for chocolate chip cookies? Most French people have never had them."

He just looked at her, a little hostile, a little defensive.

"I may have had some once before," he said finally, stiffly. "I didn't recognize them at first, because the other ones came in a Ziploc bag, all smashed up and dried out, after taking a month to get to me. Tante Colette sent them." His face—was that just the sunlight off the dusky rose paint of the house, or did it *flush* suddenly? He shut his mouth hard.

Allegra blinked. "I must have made those."

"Yes, she mentioned," he said, inexplicably hostile.

She stared at him for a long moment, that curiosity to know more about him pushing at her so much she could hardly stand it. "Can I buy you a drink?" she asked abruptly. Somewhere they could sit, with a table between them. Civilized and normal, two strangers meeting.

He blinked a couple of times. And looked just a little hopeful. "Are you picking me up again?"

"Last night, I was *initiating a conversation*," she said, driven. "Somehow, it works differently on you than every other man."

"Good," he said and reached out—and then caught himself and stuffed his hand back in his pocket before he actually took hers. Her hand felt disappointed. "Just so you're forewarned, I'm intending to keep it that way."

CHAPTER TEN

Raoul actually bought the drinks, the bartender ignoring her efforts as soon as Raoul reached for his wallet. Raoul gave her an amused glance, which somehow relaxed little muscles in her. The amusement felt—cozy. Intimate. Warm. She wanted to learn what else amused him, what made the smile deepen, what made him laugh out loud.

She felt like she was on a date, which confused her no end, since . . . well, surely dating was out of the picture at this point. One way or another. But if it was a date, flattered excitement licked through her to be on a date with him, a sense of pride she had never felt in the dating scene before.

Not that dating was her forte, not at all. Speed-dating, now that she could do. It took her about fifteen minutes to get to know a man, and up until now, that had been enough. The few times when she forced it, tried to develop it into something else against her own instincts, it hadn't worked out.

Then again, this time her instincts had told her to go all the way, and that hadn't worked out either.

She frowned as she slid into a booth across from him, wondering what he was doing there if he hadn't worked out, and his knees bumped hers as he slid in across from her. She crossed her legs quickly. That bumped them again.

She shifted to get at her pocket, and their legs rubbed, and every cell of her body flushed with heat. She got his phone out and shoved it across the table. "Here. I lied."

He picked it up and typed in his code, going to the photos immediately. His teeth clamped together when he saw the last one was of a man slicing bark off a cinnamon tree.

"If you want to show that perfume box to your family, talk to your aunt." She stuck out her chin.

"And the other one?" he asked grimly.

"You didn't have the right to take naked photos of me!"

"It wasn't naked! It was just your face." Profoundly re-laxed in sleep, her hair all mussed, a little smile on her face. "Damn it, Allegra." He shoved the phone into his pocket. He was angry again. All held in, but it burned in him, as if she had destroyed something precious.

"No trophy collecting." Those couple of mistakes in college had taught her a lot about how scummy men could be. A lesson anyone would have thought she would have *retained*. She had paged back through photo after photo, to see where the other sleeping, satisfied women were, but she had only found photos of flowers, and cin-namon bark, and vanilla beans, and occasionally of groups of playing children or a curious lemur or sunlight striking just right off a vast tropical river.

"It wasn't a—*trophy*. *Damn* you." His eyes raked over her face. "Damn you," he repeated, low, and turned his head away, brooding.

She scowled at him, feeling unreasonably guilty for

having erased a photo stolen of her while she was sleeping, and picked up her apricot juice.

He reached across immediately and took the bottle, pouring it into her glass for her, proving fourteen years on another continent hadn't knocked out any of those automatic little gallant gestures he had probably been trained in since birth. "Don't trust me with any alcohol in your system?" he said rather bitterly. "I did *ask* last night."

"Beer tastes disgusting," she said. "But you have to keep something alcoholic in front of you, or you're constantly fending off attempts to buy you some." Her mouth relaxed into involuntary ruefulness. "And cocktails taste good. I end up drinking them."

He just looked at her for a moment and then took a very long swallow of his beer. "And in all the time you've been doing this, I seriously turned out to be the worst man you ever picked up?"

"The last time I let a guy I met the same evening come back to my room with me, it was a dorm, I was twenty years old, and I hadn't yet learned my lesson about cocktails," she snapped, extremely pissed off. What the hell image did he have of her? Well, she guessed she knew now.

His eyebrows went up over his beer. And then his face split into the most wolfish self-satisfied grin. Which he wiped away as soon as her eyes narrowed on it. "So, ah—" He cleared his throat and twisted his beer glass. The triumphant grin flashed back and was squashed again. "The, ah—" It came back again, and this time he couldn't crush it out. "Really? And you're, what, twenty-five, twenty-six now? And you hadn't had anything to drink at all?" He looked so full of himself, it was a wonder he didn't burst.

She sighed and let her head sink back against the soft booth. Part of her was really tired, after three hours of sleep and a roller coaster of an emotional ride. But part of her zinged with energy at his proximity. "We're all idiots sometimes."

He frowned, the momentary flash of ebullience gone. And she wanted to kick herself for stomping it out. "So what made you such an—idiot?" he asked finally, reluctant on the last word, as if it hurt his mouth to say it.

Her gaze ran over him involuntarily. Uh . . . where to start. The snow-pine scent of him. The big, hard body. The gorgeous hair she wanted to sink her hands into. The way his eyes locked on her, and her brain shut down for any more thought than a giddy sense of luck: He *is going after* me? *All that drive and confidence and I'll-take-that-thank-you attitude—it's for* me?

Heat flushed through her, as it had before she slid off her bar stool and let him walk her home. Her body tingled in memory and . . . anticipation. *Hey, you. Stop anticipating. Nothing's happening again.*

Is it?

He did say he was sorry.

"A bad breakup?" he suggested. "You heard an ex was getting married? The last of your single friends just got engaged?"

She gazed at him blankly. What was he talking about? Oh. "No."

He frowned, confused. "What were you doing in that bar by yourself in the first place, then?"

"I just like meeting people." She shrugged. "As opposed to sitting up above the world, staring at all the lights below. It's a friendly bar, it's not like I'm going to get in trouble."

His lips parted in shock. Muscles tightened in the thigh brushing her knee under the table. "Are you telling me you *regularly* go to that bar by yourself, hang out long enough for every man present to start thinking about you, and then walk home after dark alone an isolated kilometer through the woods? So that every man in the area knows that's a habit of yours?"

"Everyone's very friendly," she said patiently.

His hand clenched on his beer, and he leaned forward abruptly. "Are you out of your fucking mind?"

She sat back, away from his aggression, scowling at him.

He took a hard breath and pressed himself back in his own seat. When he spoke again, it was clear he was trying to be calmer. "Allegra. Not to be overly possessive, but— no. Just—no. No. No. Fuck." He dragged his hand over his face, exhaling sharply. "*No.*"

"I wonder how I managed to survive to twenty-six without you," she said dryly, very angry. He made her sound like an idiot. Other than the cuss words, he sounded like her *dad.*

"I have no idea." He covered his eyes with one hand, squeezing them as if he was trying to get some vision out. "*Shit.*"

"You have a lot of testosterone," she said severely.

A ghost of a laugh shook out of him at that, and he dropped his hand from his eyes. Then he reached unexpectedly across the table and picked up her hand, cupping just her fingertips with his, running his thumb over her knuckles. "Allegra. I'm very sorry to be your idea of a macho asshole, but please don't do that anymore. It makes my hair stand on end."

He had pushed his sleeves back in the heat of the bar, and she saw with astonishment that he was telling the truth. The hairs on his forearm really were standing up.

She touched them, very curiously. Thought of harm to her literally gave him goose bumps? His thumb hitched in its stroke of her knuckles. Now that her fingertips were just barely brushing the risen hairs on his arms, the strength of that forearm was so very tempting. She wanted to curve her hand around it, savor it as being hers.

She had touched it last night. Grabbed it. Felt its strength as he held his weight off her, as he wrapped it around her body and pulled her back against him, as he pressed his fingers into her bottom and—

She swallowed, her hand settling cautiously over his forearm as if she were touching a stranger, for the first time.

The full contact between his muscles and her skin sent a shock of relief through her. A dissonance tuned into harmony.

His next breath was much softer. He covered her hand, holding it against his arm. Tension released slowly from the muscles under her hand. His thumb recommenced gliding over the knuckles of her other hand, callused and gentle. "So no bad breakup?" he checked, very softly.

She shook her head.

"No news that an ex was getting married?"

Another shake.

"No invitation to the wedding of your last single girlfriend from school?"

"My friends have been getting their degrees and starting their careers. No one's gotten married yet. One friend next summer."

"So," he said slowly, wonderingly, watching every flash of expression on her face, "there was no reason for you to end up with me, except . . . me?"

And that, she realized finally, was why it had hurt so much. It really had been only him—luring her into delighted folly. And for him, it never had been only her. "Hard for you to believe, isn't it?" she said very dryly, pulling her hands away.

"Yes." He couldn't seem to stop staring at her.

She shrugged, trying to pretend she could shrug the hurt off. "We don't all need more important motivations."

He frowned, for a second not following, and then he got it, and his eyes flashed. "Allegra, stop it. *Bordel.* I only had one motivation, and I think I was pretty damn obvious about it."

"So you didn't know who I was, when you came up to me in that bar? Didn't know I was a friend of Madame Delatour's?"

"Yes, I knew." The words were ground out of him.

She closed her eyes and sat back. *Oh, God, Mama, this is what you meant about not trusting strangers. You meant someone like this.*

"But you seriously underestimate at least one of us, if you think anything Tante Colette or my family might say would have any weight at all compared to you. And you don't seem like the type to underestimate *yourself,* Allegra."

"Tante Colette might say?" It was odd enough to catch her attention.

He shrugged impatiently. She could swear he was flushing again. "Just—stop it. I walked up to you in that bar because I thought if I saw one more man hit on you, I might have to hurt him, because I wanted you for me. I had no idea you weren't there to pick someone up, or that you didn't pick someone up at least once in a while, you seemed so at ease with it. But I could handle that. I'm quite comfortable cutting out the rest of the pack. I admit to being an arrogant, ruthless bastard this morning by pocketing that perfume box without talking to you about it first. I *am* an arrogant, ruthless bastard. Everyone agrees. But I—*putain.*" That rock-hard tension in his jaw appeared again. The one that meant hurt. "Was it not *good* for you, Allegra? Was I in some fucking dream world? How could you possibly think *that* came from a desire to get anything but . . . but you? And as much of you as I could."

"Then why did you get so angry when I got the perfume box away from you again?"

"Because you kissed me when you did it," he said between his teeth.

Her lips curled in on themselves, just a little ashamed.

"*Bordel.*" He pressed the beer glass against the inside of his own forearm, as if he needed to feel the shock of cold. His wolf eyes held hers, his smile very grim. "I thought you *liked* me, Allegra. I thought you were *happy,* to have me in your home. In your bed. In you, damn it. And you didn't even talk to me. You didn't even say, *What the hell are you doing?* And I know damn well you can talk to anybody about anything. But you just made up your mind about me faster than you made up your mind about every single other man who gave you his number at that bar the night before."

"You didn't talk to me either!"

"I made a *stupid* half-second decision because I didn't want to face a confrontation with the most gorgeous bit of good luck I have ever had in my life right then, first thing in the morning. But you made a judgment call, and I was *pathetic,* I was a *thief,* I was a *bastard* and a *threat. Merde,* Allegra. When you had made me feel *perfect.* Like the most incredible man in the world."

Something tightened in her chest until, suddenly, it snapped, and she took a trembling breath, shaken by the sudden expansion of her lungs. As if she really had thought she was going to die before she ever could breathe free again.

"Then I'm sorry, too," she said, very low, reaching out to cover his fist. Well, cover. Her hand didn't begin to cover his. "I never thought about it from your perspective."

That little twist of his mouth. His gaze was on her hand. "I know. I'm a stranger."

Yes. Still so deliciously different, as if she could sink into him forever and still be discovering things.

The fingers of his free hand began to trace her fingers over his fist, a light, callused stroke from knuckle to fingertip. "Perhaps you wanted to keep me that way."

"I kind of like it," she admitted, with a ghost of a feeling so alien to her that it took a long time to identify it. *Shyness.* Good Lord. "You being so much a stranger. It's fascinating."

His half-smile held a hint of wistfulness. "Funny, *I* felt as if I was coming home. But that's all right. I can live with fascination." He lifted his fist, catching her hand with his thumb when it started to slip off, and kissed her knuckles.

The touch of his lips shivered through her. She wanted suddenly, desperately, to crawl into his lap and wrap her arms around him, pressing her face against his chest, burying herself in him until the intimacy healed the wound. "I want to go home," she whispered, and didn't even realize she had said it until after she heard the words. What home had she been thinking of? It didn't even seem to have a place associated with it, just a big lap.

He drew a long breath and let it out with a sigh. "Why aren't you home already? Are there problems with your family?"

"No. I was there for Thanksgiving."

He got that vague look that meant the existence of Thanksgiving had percolated into his brain at some point via Hollywood but, like most French, he had never quite grasped it. His family probably got together for fifty-person dinners once a week. The Rosiers, for crying out loud.

"I thought it would be neat to see Christmas in Provence. But now . . . I miss my family."

"Yes." That little twist of his mouth that she didn't yet know how to read. And it fascinated her, the desire to learn how to read it. "I can understand that."

"Are you just visiting for Christmas?"

His thumb tightened its hold on her hand, and determination hardened his face suddenly. "No," he said with firm decision. "No, this time I'm coming home."

She searched his face. What was going on inside him? As her anger receded, it left her exhausted. That need to curl into him kept pressing at her.

But they weren't an old married couple who had had a bad fight. They were strangers who had had sex. *Oh, Mom. Why didn't I listen to you about strangers?*

He turned his hand over and let hers rest in his palm, gazing down at the contrast in size. Then he shot her a quick glance, almost tentative, which didn't seem possible for him any more than shyness was for her. "Do you want to come with me? Our Christmas is traditional, I promise you." His mouth curved wryly, but with a profound homesick hunger for exactly the thing he was amused by. "Very. And I'll make Tante Colette come."

Did she want to be in the middle of his enormous family, wrapped up in the heart of the tradition? Did she want to be there *with him?*

God, that was so much more flattering than imagining herself on a date. Scarily delicious, a top-of-the-roller-coaster adrenaline surging through her. "Really? With your family and everything? You wouldn't mind?"

He just looked at her a long moment. "You know, Allegra, when I walked up to you in that bar, it was because I wanted you."

Well, duh. "I know." *Her and what she knew about his family heirlooms,* a part of her thought traitorously.

"No, you don't. You think I just wanted to screw you." That bitter flash of his eyes.

She tried to pull her hand away, but he closed his around it. "I shouldn't have said that."

"But you did. Repeatedly. So you thought it and you believed it, while I was thinking and believing something entirely different. You don't know me. And I don't know you. But I still want to know you, Allegra. It's not as easy, and it's not as—painless, as you made me think it would be. Maybe we are still strangers. But I would like you to join me for Christmas."

CHAPTER ELEVEN

Children's laughter echoed from the sledding hill. Shoppers milled around the Christmas stalls, and she would have thought Raoul's size would help forge a way through the crowd, but in fact, he got stopped constantly. People called to him with one of his cousin's names, then realized who he was and were politely happy to see him back from Africa for the holidays. *How long are you staying?*

She looked up, that long way up into his face, trying to define the tension in him every time someone asked that question. If they had been something more than a very strange kind of strangers, she would have slipped her hand in his, against that tension. She kept thinking he needed a hand in his. Could people really not tell the difference between him and his cousins? Couldn't they see the gorgeous sienna tones in his hair, at least? All the other cousins were darker, or a brown with gold tints instead of copper. None of them had that lushness combined with the young touch of slate; none of the others had hair that made her fingers itch to sink into it.

None of them had that hint of wildness that pulled her insatiably.

He stopped in front of a stall selling *santons,* the little clay Nativity figures, nodding politely to a young woman who gave them both a wide smile and began talking about her father's work. The prize-winning artisan had done the town's Nativity scene, meaning the cost of even one hand-painted figure would have made quite a dent in Allegra's research fellowship. She tucked her hands firmly in her pockets, fighting the call of at least twenty different figures that begged to be added to her tiny collection.

Raoul picked up a shepherdess bent into the mistral, her blue hood blown off her blond hair, cape whipping behind her, a basket over one arm. He glanced at Allegra, a wariness she hadn't seen in him the night before. "Would you accept one from me? Or would it be a bad memory?"

Her eyebrows knit in an unfamiliar anxiousness. "It's too early to say what the memory will be like."

Raoul's mouth twisted. He turned the little windblown figure in his big hands and said something to the young woman behind the stall that made Allegra stiffen in indignation. He had just dropped into Provençal! What a rude, blunt way to shut her out of the conversation. Nobody the age of those two spoke Provençal. Unless they came from families that placed an extremely high value on their Provençal traditions . . .

Like the Rosiers and, say, a woman whose father was a famous artisan of one of the region's most traditional and best-known symbols. Raoul and the young woman had, in fact, a great deal in common. And Allegra knew how much he liked friendly, easy, welcoming women. . . .

Raoul spoke awkwardly, rusty, the young woman responding just as hesitantly, laughing with a mix of pleasure and embarrassment. Awkward because of a rarely used language neither spoke very well and that they were just using to *shut the American out?* Or awkward as in, *So, ah, are you doing anything tonight?* And, *Oh, umm, well, I don't know . . .*

Except Allegra could personally attest to the fact that when Raoul homed in on a woman and went after her, he showed about as much awkward hesitation as a wolf snatching a rabbit out of the snow.

The woman shook her head, apologetically. Raoul persisted, setting the blue shepherdess down, forgotten. Oh, yeah, *that* was more like him, the hard-headed pursuit of what he wanted. Now the woman was laughing and nodding. She handed Raoul a card, and Raoul pulled out one of his own cards and wrote a number on the back of it. Allegra scowled down at the permanent ink marking the same number on her palm.

Damn it, she really should have thrown his cell phone over a cliff.

She shoved her marked hand into her coat pocket and picked up a copy of the wolf she had noticed in the display in the square, the one with his paws raised to press against a stable window and look wistfully in.

"I hate that one," Raoul said, back in French.

Really? It spoke to her so strongly. She wanted to take that wolf home and put him in her little Nativity display where he could smell baking cookies—

"There." Raoul indicated a different wolf figurine, this one curled up in the stable at Mary's feet, like a dog let in by the fire. "It's Christmas, *merde.* Let the poor bastard in where he's warm."

Allegra picked up the second wolf, studying the head resting on paws, eyes watching with wary hopefulness, as if the wolf couldn't decide whether this was for real or someone was going to kick him out any minute. He was a sienna wolf. She looked up at Raoul again, the piece weighing in her hand, the choice of wolf growing enormous.

Raoul watched her, one fist curled by his side, saying nothing.

The young woman tucked his card into her pocket.

Allegra's eyebrows drew sharply together.

Raoul's mouth tightened.

Allegra gazed into those amber eyes and drew a slow, careful breath. *He just asked* you *to spend Christmas with his family. And surely not just so you can be interrogated about perfume boxes by his grandfather.*

Surely.

"We'll come back," he told the other young woman abruptly. "She hasn't made up her mind."

He uncurled Allegra's fingers from the wolf and set it back down on the table, putting a hand on her back to herd her away. "You have *no patience,*" she said indignantly. "Can't I think for five seconds?"

"I liked last night," he said grimly. "I liked when you didn't have to think about whether you wanted me or not. You just opened up and let me in."

Was that a crude sexual reference? Her face flushed.

Or was sex the metaphor here?

His hand fell away from her back and slipped into his pocket. He had led them down into the old *lavoir,* a stone structure that had been there since the Middle Ages, sheltering the women who gathered there to wash clothes. Once the bustling center of town gossip, the advent of washing machines had turned it into a place of quiet, the great worn stone a refuge against time. The market noise from the street above barely reached them, under the red-tiled roof that sheltered the spot. They were shut away, into their own little world.

So quiet. Water and stone.

She looked up at Raoul again. Hands in his pockets, he gazed at the dark stream, stilled here by a stone basin constructed eight hundred years ago.

The need for peace pushed at her again. She could not bear this wound between them. It felt wrong, a great gash through that beautiful, joyous night. She still thought herself justified in her reaction to a stranger she woke up to find stealing from her, even if it had been a long-lost family heirloom, and yet . . . she could not stand that angry hurt in him anymore. She didn't think she could stand to stay angry, herself. She wasn't an angry person.

She took a step toward him, drawn irresistibly by a need to be pressed up against that broad chest. Her heart began to beat very hard, afraid.

The thing about being an only child who calmly inserted herself into any life she saw around her rather than play alone was that, deep down, she didn't let herself *care* whether the other child thought she was weird, or rejected her, or took a little bossy persuading to let her help build the sandcastle. She just jumped past all that and asserted, to herself as well as to the world, that every normal person would be glad to know her, glad to have her friendship. She opened up to everyone—and protected her heart.

He shifted to face her as she stepped into him, chest rising and falling deeply. Her fingertips lifted, tentatively, to touch that chest.

The contact sent a little jolt of rightness through her. The nape of her neck wanted to unknot. *Keep going. Let me relax.*

Raoul stood very still.

She took the last step, her palm flattening on his chest, her face an inch from it, the scent of him warm and completely familiar. Not strange at all. Closing her eyes, she let her face sink forward onto his chest, and her nape released, the tension shivering out of her.

A sense of utter, physical safety enveloped her—his arms, sliding around her. Not too hard. Careful, gentle. Warm. Strong.

Her body safe, her heart panicked. A tight bud unfurling well before it was sure some great frost might not come and kill it. *I'm scared, I'm scared, I'm scared, I'm scared . . . he feels so good.*

Her weight sank more heavily against him. His arms took it, a little more snugly. Neither of them said a word, but she could hear the deep thud of his heart.

And still neither of them said a word.

And still. One of his hands slid up her back to curve around her head, gently rubbing her hair.

She never wanted to move again. She could have slept there, standing up. His heartbeat under her ear was slowing, a calmed, strong thing.

With a great sigh, he picked her up and sat suddenly, on the stone bench tucked into the wall of the *lavoir,* settling her into his lap.

Still without speaking, he leaned back against the wall, pulling his legs up on the length of the bench so that his body formed a V with her cradled in it. She could have been curled up in an armchair of him.

Allegra astonished herself by starting to cry. She was not a crier. And she was definitely not a slow, secret crier, tears sneaking out of her eyes like traitors onto someone's shirt. It was just that something that had felt so right had gone so wrong . . . and now, it felt . . . better. She began to cry harder. So much better.

A callused thumb rubbed under her eye, stroking away tears. "I'm sorry," he whispered. "I didn't mean to hurt you. I really—thought you were wonderful. I liked when you thought I was wonderful, too."

"You could have just asked." She was going to *smack* herself for crying, later, she knew it. But she couldn't stop. She felt so safe. "Just asked."

"I know," he said. "I know." He took a deep breath, as if to say something else, and then just sighed it out. "I know." His hand rubbed her back. "You could have said, 'Raoul, you bastard, what the hell do you think you're doing, that's mine.' That would have been okay, too. I would have liked that much, much, much better than realizing that kiss was a lie. I just wanted to show it to my grandfather. He's been convinced his stepsister made off with those heirlooms for so long, and there are some items that went missing that are far more precious even than a Renaissance perfume box. And . . ." A sigh under her body.

"And?" she mumbled finally.

"He's been looking for those things most of his life. Very possessive of his heritage, my grandfather."

"You love him." *More than you love me.* Not that she could say it out loud, because of course he loved his ninety-year-old grandfather, Resistance hero and honored patriarch, more than he loved a random woman he had picked up in a bar.

How could she have been so convinced, last night, that the pleasure was worth the risk, that nothing the morning brought would make her ashamed?

A long silence. "I want to come home." Something ferocious compressed in his voice, his chest vibrating under her ear. "I want to be back with my family. I want someone in it to—welcome me. I thought a long-lost family heirloom would make him happy."

He made himself sound like a great wolf bringing home a dead mouse in hopes of being let in through the door. For God's sake, at the end of the day, it was only a

Renaissance perfume box. He was a *person*. An amazing, larger than life, strong, aggressive, stubborn human being.

"They're your family," Allegra said, puzzled. A crazy, powerful, tightly bound, badly fragmented, intensely competitive family, but they hadn't struck her as *insane,* either. Who would turn him away? "I always thought the Rosiers put a lot of emphasis on family."

"Yes, but there are too many of us. There are only so many ambitious, aggressive people this world can hold. I gave up my place, and I lost the people who wanted to save it for me." Only because she was lying on him did she feel the tightness in his chest when he mentioned that loss.

"You chose to leave?" Allegra said, startled. Leave a heritage of flowers and scent and power? Who would reject *that?*

A wry grimace. "I was nineteen. I wanted to get away from roses and jasmine and being the big fish in a small pond."

"Small? Rosier SA has five thousand employees, worldwide."

"Provence. Trust me, when you're nineteen, the area around Grasse is a very small pond, and we fill it. Meaning, the generation before filled it, my father and uncles and aunts and grandfather. I wanted to see something *else,* be something else, travel the world, go on safari. And incidentally, not have to listen to them anymore. I was nineteen, so my ideas about what I wanted to do were pretty vague but they were *very* vivid. So I ended up going to the source of some of our raw materials in Central and East Africa, which was still a very crude and often broken supply chain, fourteen years ago, and by the time I was twenty-one, it was essentially all on my shoulders. The whole continent. Now, we provide more essences from some parts of that continent than any other company in the world," he added, triumphantly. "Everyone else gave up."

That last little bit was a brag, wasn't it? She smiled, deeply flattered by his desire to impress her.

"It might be different if"—a tiny faltering of his voice, dropping lower—"my mother were still alive, or if my father hadn't decided to abandon *his* heritage after she died and wasn't off in South America half the time these days. Or if my grandmother were still here. But she's not, and who knows, maybe I'm deluding myself about that, too."

Her hand petted his chest through his shirt, in an involuntary reflex to make him feel . . . wanted. Welcomed. His chest shifted under her in a long sigh.

"I made a stupid decision," Raoul repeated. "When I pocketed that perfume box. But I didn't mean to make you cry." He stroked both thumbs across her damp cheekbones, lifting her face off his chest so he could gaze at it. "*Allez, bonheur.* Forgive me," he coaxed. "Be happy again."

"I'm not upset anymore," she said, confused.

"Ah." His thumbs stroked the tears across her temples, into her hair.

"That's why I'm crying," she explained. "Because it feels so much better."

"It's a good thing you explained that to me." His hands, combing her damp hair back from her face, were very tender. Even in the midst of heated passion, this big, aggressive man had shown her tenderness, over and over, all night long. Maybe that was what had hurt him, that he had thought he could trust her with his tenderness, and she had forgotten it. She had believed in it exactly as little as anybody else did.

"Are you? Still upset?"

"Me?" He sounded startled, as if his own anger was so far away he had forgotten it had even existed. "No. No." His body shifted under hers, resettling her against him. "No." An arm wrapped heavily around her again, snuggling her down into the V of him. "Let's not move, all right?" whispered the man who had his butt and shoulders pressed against stone. "Let's not move ever again."

CHAPTER TWELVE

Of course, they did have to move again eventually. Allegra woke up, for one thing, profoundly startled, and an arm tightened around her when she jumped. "Shh. It's all right."

She pushed herself up on his chest, her dreams having had so little time to process the upheaval in her waking life, that for a moment she couldn't even remember she was in France much less what his name was.

"Raoul," he said to her bewildered eyes, his voice very dry.

She blinked a moment and then smiled suddenly, lowering her head to kiss him. His butt and shoulders must be in agony at this point, from that stone. How long had she been asleep?

"And I'm not a stranger," he whispered into her mouth, kissing her back, his hand curving against her jaw. "Not anymore."

She scrambled off him, feeling that weird feeling again, what was it? *Shyness.* And her much more familiar optimism. And considerable guilt for how uncomfortable he must be.

He started to stand immediately, but it took him a minute to complete the process, his face wincing and a hand going out to brace against the wall as he rolled his shoulders painfully and flexed his butt muscles. She tried to resist the urge to help that big body feel better—and then gave up and slid her arms around his waist to dig her fingers into his butt.

He inhaled sharply in pain, but those amber eyes lit with pleasure, tracking over her face. "You trust me a lot more than you realize you do," he said softly. "You wouldn't catch *me* falling asleep around someone twice my size I had just met the night before."

She wasn't sure she wanted to think about how completely she trusted him, so easily. He had failed that trust once . . . or maybe he hadn't. Maybe she had failed his trust in her. Or maybe neither of them had failed, in the end, because they had both kept fighting. "You meet people twice your size often?"

He smiled wryly. *Touché.* "Then again, people try to kidnap me enough that I don't really fall asleep around anybody, so I might not be the best judge."

Kidnap him? A powerful business head, whose family could afford millions in ransom, working in regions with all kinds of problems. Her heart seized her as she got a sudden terrifying glimpse of what that might be like. Her hands curled more firmly into his butt, holding on. "You know what I think? I think you need to quit that job and if your family doesn't like it, to hell with them. What kind of family lets you risk your life?"

"They don't want to have to send anyone else out to do it in my place," he said matter-of-factly.

It took a second for that to sink in, and then she gasped and threw her arms around him in a very hard hug. He was the one they were willing to *sacrifice*?

He picked her up by the waist and kissed her once

firmly before he set her back down on the ground. "I'll take it under advisement, *mon bonheur.*" He looped an arm around her waist and headed them out of the *lavoir*. "Do you still want a *santon?* They might have closed the stall by now."

Allegra frowned immediately. "Maybe from a different stall."

He smiled. "I'll get it for you. Don't worry about it. It's something you keep forever and pass on to your children; it's worth it to get the very best."

Allegra had never realized she had a part of her that could be deeply warmed by a man buying things for her, but there it was—she did. It felt like flattery and caretaking all wrapped into one. But he had misunderstood her primary objection to that particular artisan. "Why did you give her your number?" she asked sulkily. "And get hers?"

Raoul's eyebrows went up, and he searched her face. "You think I act like this all the time," he realized, in stunned enlightenment. "You have no idea how attracted I am to you, do you?" He pressed her against the stone post at the edge of the *lavoir* and stroked hair back from her face, to give him a clearer view. "That explains a lot."

"You had your clothes on this morning," she muttered. The hurt of *that* moment, before she ever saw him swipe the perfume box, swelled up, something that had been there festering even when she thought everything was healed. "Your coat. You were sneaking out."

His eyes flared in surprise and sudden comprehension. His hand curved around her cheek. "I had a meeting with my grandfather at nine. I wrote my number on your hand, which I think was a pretty clear message that I would be delighted if you called me. And I knew where you lived, so I could find you. Speaking of which, *please* don't ever lead another strange man right to your door like that again, Allegra. Please." His eyes winced shut, his hand flexing into her face.

Allegra lifted a hand to curve around *his* face. "You keep telling yourself I must act like this all the time, too. You don't have any idea how attracted I am to you, either, do you?" She blushed *shyly* again, oh, for crying out loud, but her heart felt too naked. Her hand petted the jaw he hadn't yet shaved today, and his body shifted even closer to hers, his eyes lighting with that hungry, happy look. "That explains a lot."

He crowded her in, lifting her up and into him until she was barely touching the ground with her toes. "I know how you like to make snap decisions about people, Allegra, but you know what I would like? A little bit more time to show you exactly how attracted I am to you." He touched the corner of her lips, cradled her head with one hand, and bent low to murmur in her ear. "Do you mind showing me, too?"

CHAPTER THIRTEEN

She didn't seem to mind.

It was the happiest Christmas he had spent since he was young enough to believe in Santa Claus. No, far happier than that. Believing in the Père Noël was nothing compared to learning to believe that this small, happy woman might not try to throw him right back out into the cold again the next time he misbehaved.

But *she* didn't seem to have any trouble, believing in him. Not now. He still couldn't fathom that. They would lie in front of her little fire, with the clementine peels she liked to set on the hearth to scent the room, playing cards, while he wondered if he could change the stakes from cookies to clothes. And he would look at their hands side by side, when they both reached for a card at the same time, and think, *How does she trust me like that? How does she welcome me in where everything is so warm, and she's so vulnerable, and smile at me? I hurt her.*

He finally asked her once, after he had won all the cookies a man could eat for the night and just wanted to lie on that rug with his head in her lap and let arousal uncurl, drowsy and fire-warmed and growing hungry.

She smiled down at him, petting his head, something he enjoyed so much he really wondered sometimes if he might be part dog. "You can learn a lot about a man by the way he says he's sorry."

Well, she had *cried,* damn it. He had *hurt* her. What the hell was he supposed to do, besides say he was sorry?

Her petting hand slid to curve around his jaw. He wanted to just curl his face into the embrace of her body and maybe . . . press his mouth right to the seam of her jeans. He wondered if she knew he could scent her arousal from here: clementines, and smoke, and her desire. If his family could ever bottle *that* perfume and all the happiness it contained, they would make another fortune.

Selling it to all those poor suckers who didn't have their head in the lap of the real thing.

In fact, if he had to start his own company as the only way to establish a place in the flower valleys again, that might be the scent he used to swipe the top luxury-house license away from Rosier SA. He could redirect all his supply lines and contacts in Africa right to his own new company, and headhunt some good noses from the family while he was at it. They would be livid, especially his grandfather, but . . . *It's either love or war, Pépé, and in the end, all's fair in both.*

"You can learn a lot about a man," Allegra said softly, "by the way he lets you sleep on him for hours, despite how hard the stone is under his butt."

Yeah, but she had dug her fingers into his butt later. Really hard. His butt was okay with that trade-off.

Besides, she had felt so soft and trusting in his arms, and he had just wanted to soak up as much of that as he could, in case she went back to hating him when she woke up.

"You can learn a lot about a man, by the way he goes

all out for you, no hint of stopping—and still takes no for an answer."

"I took no for an answer?" That didn't sound like him at all.

She smiled. "When you were trying to warn me against letting you in."

"But you didn't say no," he said, confused.

Her smile deepened. Sometimes she looked at him like . . . well, he didn't know if he wanted to risk articulating it, but . . . like she just *loved* him. Just the way he was. "But you tried so hard to let me have a chance to. So convinced you shouldn't be let in."

"I shouldn't have been let in," he pointed out involuntarily. "That was a crazy thing to do, Allegra. Don't do it again."

"Well, no, I can't now, can I?" she murmured, amused, while her hand caressed his hair, which had to be one of the three most perfect sensations in the world. "Only one wild wolf per household, I'm pretty sure."

Entirely guilt-free about leaving any other wolf out in the cold, he turned his head into the deeper embrace of her lap, letting his breath heat that seam of her jeans.

She made a little low sound of pleasure, her fingers flexing into his scalp. *Nice start,* he thought. *Let's see if I can make you love me a little more.*

But she said, "Do you think you'll ever be able to trust me?"

To—what? "To trust *you*? Me?"

"You could try to sound like it's remotely possible," she said, stiffly.

He rolled his head to look back up at her face. "Allegra. Have you looked at us?" He was lying with his head in her lap, and he still practically loomed over her. When she curled in *his* lap, her whole body fit. "I don't need to trust *you*."

"No?" she said softly.

He wasn't sure he wanted to let that little *no?* dig its way into his heart and find out all the trust issues inside it, but the fire was so warm, and the feel of her hand in his hair so beautiful. And that scent of her arousal so heady. He was damned sure not going to run away and end up back out in the cold.

"I think I hurt you," she said quietly. "Too. I think you're a lot more vulnerable and romantic than you think you are. The kid who ran off to Africa for the adventure rather than stick with the wealthy family that offered him all kinds of more practical opportunities to succeed."

"I'm not nineteen anymore, Allegra, and—"

She laid her fingertips over his mouth. He drew in a breath, silenced by the sensation of softness against his lips. No one *touched* him like that. Like . . . like he was hers to care about.

"And of course you are *very* ruthless and hardheaded," she said soothingly. "And that's why you iron your aunt's sheets and let a woman curl in your arms and cry."

Uh, well . . . he buried his head between her legs again, not at all sure how to defend himself from this kind of thing. Oh, wait, no, he bet he knew how to change this subject. He went with his instincts and bit her.

Not too hard, not too soft, right through the seam of her jeans.

She made a little gasping noise, and he grinned and put some more effort into it, and she didn't say another coherent word for the rest of the night.

Damn, he had spent almost all his adult life in the tropics, and it seemed like half that time, he had been dreaming of making love in front of a citrus-scented fire with a woman who thought he was wonderful. Which must be why he kept doing it so much, now that he got a chance.

                               *   *   *

The Rosiers' Christmas packed the patriarchal farmhouse so tightly that they burst its seams, light spilling
from the windows, people escaping the heavy old stone
walls to breathe outside under the stars, noise echoing
softly across the valley of roses, such a scraggly valley in
the winter, framed by hills of bare winter vineyards and,
higher up, rich green forests. And the stars glittered so
brilliant and low, here where the hills hid the bright lights
that lined the sea. The valley turned upside down in winter, Raoul said softly when they were walking up to the
house. Instead of picking roses, you wanted to reach up
and pluck all those stars.

Allegra liked people, but part of the reason she liked
them so much was that she was an only child, and the
sheer mass of Rosier humanity had her bouncing off big
male bodies everywhere she turned, until Raoul took exception to that and placed both hands on her hips, pulling
her back into the shelter of his body. And from then on he
held her to him, his fingers rubbing her hips minutely, like
a worry-stone. She reassured him, she realized suddenly.
His portable sense of belonging.

Practically pocket-size, she thought wryly, as he shifted
her body easily to allow someone to pass. She curled her
hand over his arm, and his mouth relaxed.

There were a *lot* of big men in his family. She had met
many of them before, while sitting on the floors of various
old farmhouses looking carefully through albums and
boxes of century-old photos, or while interviewing Jean-
Jacques Rosier and Colette Delatour and other grandfathers
and great-aunts who carried this region's memories. But all
of them together made for a lot of people and a lot of testosterone. Jean-Jacques had had sons, and those sons had had
sons, and even the presence of women from marriages and
second cousins could not quite set the balance right. Espe-

cially since neither Raoul nor his cousins had married and given this Christmas gathering the delight of children, something Jean-Jacques Rosier complained about severely.

The tree in the great living room, which was also serving as a dining room that evening, took up far too much space for the crowd they had, and it made her smile to think of one of the big Rosier men out in the field cutting it down, absolutely convinced it was smaller than it was. Ornaments of all shapes and descriptions crowded it, some such old, fragile glass that the family history on that tree filled Allegra with wonder. A Nativity scene covered the entire mantle above the huge fireplace and extended on down to tables set up at either side of it, and Allegra got lost in it for some time, tracing generations' worth of painted clay *santon* figures, some that must be a hundred years old or more, others by quirkier artists with younger paint, little kitten and puppy figurines that children must have given their grandmother as presents.

Although some members of the family seemed there for the night, others passed in and out, visiting before returning to their smaller family clusters at home. An unfamiliar couple arrived, the man tall and dark and with gorgeous clean lines to his face that probably photographed like a dream, the woman with straw-blond hair and an angular charm, like a student artist or an athlete. People gravitated toward her, while her smile lit up her face, and the brilliant-eyed, dark-haired man rested his hands on her hips, holding her back against him and watching the chatter with a kind of absorbed quiet, like someone who didn't relax very often.

"Léa and Daniel," Raoul said in response to her inquiring look. "Laurier," he added absently.

"The chef? I didn't know you were related to them!"

"Léa's a third cousin, on my grandmother's side. Plus,

they have that house in the hills." Raoul pointed to a precise point on a wall, as if he saw directly through it to where every single thing in this valley was. "So they're neighbors."

"Can we go *eat* there?"

He grinned down at her. "If I can talk Léa into fitting us in sooner than six months from now. She's tougher than she looks, when it comes to that restaurant. You sure you wouldn't rather spend the same amount of money on a luxury vacation to Costa Rica?"

Allegra blinked. Michelin three-star restaurants were so far out of her graduate-student budget that she had never really looked at the prices, but . . . *Costa Rica*? She needed to be a little more grateful for those tidbits from the Aux Anges kitchens that the Delange brothers were always sharing with her when they found her at Colette Delatour's.

"I'm kidding. We can do both if you want." Raoul bent down and pressed a kiss to her forehead. "I might be a tiny bit financially secure," he whispered, amber eyes alight with a very smug pleasure in the fact.

"I, on the other hand, am intellectually secure," Allegra informed him loftily, just to hold her own. Because her graduate stipend came to about five pennies a month.

He laughed. "Plus, you make really good cookies."

She grinned and rested back against him again. Warm. Snug. Entirely comfortable. Directly across the room, Daniel and Léa stood in very nearly the same position, Léa lit by a radiance from within and Daniel rarely speaking, completely secure in the hold on her waist that meant all that radiance belonged to him.

"I want that." Raoul's deep, low voice rumbled against the back of her skull and the nape of her neck.

She followed the direction of his gaze and frowned. "A luminescent blonde in your arms?"

He drew a lock of her dark, glossy hair through his fingers. "What they've got. They got married at the same age that I was running off to Africa, and every single Christmas I've come back, they've looked like that. I may be forty-three by the time I hit my own ten-year anniversary, but I want the same thing." His fingers flexed into her hips.

She was caught by his eyes, both of them locked into each other. *He's thirty-three,* she remembered. So to have a ten-year anniversary at the age of forty-three . . .

The moment stretched until she felt herself blushing softly and ducked her head. His hands slipped from her hips to circle completely around her waist, holding her snug against him. He had just laid himself right out there on the line for her, hadn't he? She curved her own arms over his, holding them to her.

Laughter was everywhere, kisses and hugs and glasses being raised in toasts, but after a little while of trying to fit into the place, she could see why Raoul felt so strongly that he didn't. Within the vast sense of family, everyone had their little nucleus of parents and children. And he was alone. Entirely alone and surrounded by fourteen years of jokes and references that did not include him. These things didn't bother her, because she had always been the only child who had to insert herself into friendships wherever she wanted them, and anyway, this wasn't her family, her one place to call home. But for him, the sense of isolation in a crowd was clearly a rawer, more wounding thing. Plus, his fourteen years in Africa must have left him a much warier and wilder person than when he had left, and far too conscious of his own roughness. How many times had he told her that she wasn't supposed to be letting him in?

Allegra slipped away from him—his fingers clutching for her hips a second too late—and went to the little armoire full of photos and family albums. While her research concentrated on the old albums of yellowing black-and-white photos, she had opened some of the others by accident, including some albums from the cousins' childhood. Now she found a spot on the arm of Madame Delatour's chair, smiling cheerfully at the old woman who was also self-isolated in a crowd.

"Oh, lord," Allegra said, deliberately letting a page fall open as Raoul came behind the chair to reclaim his hold on her. "Raoul, please tell me that's not you."

The photo showed five boys with various shades of russet to dark hair, naked but for their underwear, each body-painted entirely in a different color. Raoul, the tallest and the oldest, was green. She was pretty sure the blue boy was Damien Rosier. The purple one, the youngest, must be Tristan. Meaning the red and yellow were—

"*Merde,* not the alien photo!" Tristan cried, making a pretend grab for the album. He had to lean over the back of his Tante Colette's chair to reach, so that Colette Delatour was now embraced by people. His shoulders brushed Raoul's. "Who dragged that out? Can we not have *one* Christmas without that—"

Damien groaned, squeezing in between Raoul and Tristan to peer over Tante Colette's head. "*Merde,* Raoul, they're going to torture us with that photo the rest of our lives." In the photo of the naked boys, Raoul looked quite smug. "I hope it eats at your conscience. Do you know how many jokes I get about genies and bottles?"

"You're the one who picked blue, Damien. You said it was your favorite color." Raoul was grinning a little bit. Allegra could feel his hand relaxing on her shoulder, holding her less like his reassurance and more just like someone he loved to stroke. "You could have picked purple like Tristan."

"I did not *pick* that! You *made* me, because I was the youngest."

"We didn't have any pink," Damien informed his younger cousin kindly. His gray-green eyes glinted subtly.

"I like the underwear," Allegra commented. "The Lone Ranger suits you, Raoul. I'm not sure about Superman, though, Matt." Big, growly Matthieu, joining the group, gave the photo an utterly disgusted glare that he then transferred to Raoul. A middle cousin in age, Matt was the only son of Jean-Jacques's oldest son, which lined him up as the clan's future patriarch. It was an interesting role to have, among such intensely dominant only-son cousins.

"You know, it's your fault none of us will ever be able to get married," Matt informed Raoul.

"You sure you can't blame that on yourself?" Raoul retorted. The rough teasing was making him increasingly relaxed and happy, and Allegra hid a self-satisfied smile. "Not that I want to mention your damn grumpy temper again at Christmas, Matt."

Wait—"Why can't you get married because of this photo, exactly?" Not that this was a *pressing* concern of hers or anything, but—

"They'll show it at the wedding dinner if we do," Damien said. "I guarantee it."

"If you were the first one to get married, you might be able to outwit them and destroy the projector just in time, or something," Tristan said. "But the youngest wouldn't stand a chance. They would have figured out all the tricks, and it would be hopeless," he added glumly. "You'd end up doing the toasts with a giant banner of it right behind your head, probably. I can't believe you talked me into purple. I was only four!"

"Blame Raoul," Damien said. "I always do. Remember that time you burned the bottom of your shoes trying to jump over that bonfire?"

"I remember the time he got you all to climb over my garden wall and try to steal my *raiponce*," Tante Colette said, with a smile that relaxed her whole face. "I guess coming in through the unlocked door was too boring."

"Lucien broke his arm," Damien remembered and shook his head.

"It was Lucien's idea!" Raoul protested. "He just wanted to use my shoulders for a boost up." His hand slid so that his thumb could rest on the nape of Allegra's neck, rubbing it gently. She was pretty sure it was his way of saying thanks.

She smiled to herself as the argument over who had gotten whom into trouble grew to encompass more and more childhood memories, harking back to another unit this family used to have, not just the nuclear families but the solidarity of five male cousins who had once looked to Raoul as their ringleader.

It didn't bring his mother or grandmother back to life, and it didn't bring his father back from South America, and it most certainly didn't undo the effect of fourteen rough, isolated years. But she thought it helped a little.

CHAPTER FOURTEEN

"Still putting your family last in your life, I see," Raoul's grandfather said dryly later that night, when Raoul had escaped outside for a breath of fresh air. He wanted so badly to be comfortable in the uproar of family again, and yet he just couldn't, quite. "Don't show up, don't call. What, were you too sleepy to get out of bed and bother to see your grandfather?"

Raoul shoved his hands in his pockets, squinting at the stars, which shone with a heart-breaking brilliance tonight, in the sky swept clean by the mistral. Around them, hectares of roses stretched, stripped by the winter down to skinny branches and thorns. But still he breathed the scent of them in, a ghost perfume from every summer of his childhood, when he would come in coated with rose oils from a day's harvest. All the kids were expected to pitch in. "I lost my phone, Pépé. I apologized once already, didn't I?" He had stolen Damien's phone to keep calling Allegra, but the meeting with his grandfather had been completely forgotten by that point.

"When I was your age, we didn't even have phones, and I still managed to go see my grandfather when he asked for me. My father would have boxed my ears if I didn't."

"When you were thirty-three?" Raoul asked dryly.

"Are you thirty-three already?" his grandfather asked, offended. A tall man himself for his generation, he was only a few inches shorter than Raoul, even with age. He still stood amazingly straight for ninety, just as his step-sister did at ninety-six. "Why haven't you had kids yet, then? They won't even be able to know their own great-grandfather at this rate. What's the matter with you boys?"

"I've been trying to maintain our supply chains in the middle of conflicts and attempted kidnappings, Pépé. It's not conducive to family life."

"I met your grandmother when I was smuggling kids out of France in a wagon full of roses and she was their next guide over the Alps into Switzerland. You boys whine too much."

Raoul set his back teeth and wondered, reluctantly, if his grandfather had a point. The old man always did this to him. Raoul had once driven himself twelve miles to safety with a bullet hole in him, a ghastly experience that had taught him worlds about his ability to persist no matter how much it hurt. He had survived at least ten kidnapping attempts. He had kept Rosier money coming to small farmers whose kids might have starved to death if he let the unrest in their area convince him Rosier SA should turn to other sources. He had used sheer force of personality—aggressive personality—to get a crazy would-be warlord to release four drivers and not kill Raoul himself while he was at it. And yet whenever he determined that enough was enough, damn it, and he was going to come home, his grandfather somehow managed to make him feel like a big baby.

He remembered kids being jealous of him in school

when his grandfather would come share tales of his Resistance hero days, but frankly, it was hell having the man as a patriarch.

"Why don't you go talk to Tante Colette, and the two of you can reminisce one last time about smuggling those kids out?"

His grandfather's eyes flickered at that *one last time.* But . . . ninety-six and giving away family heirlooms . . . there weren't going to be many more chances to talk to Tante Colette about anything.

"Maybe if you're friendly to her, she'll tell you herself if she knows anything about Niccolo Rosario's things. It's her last chance, too."

His grandfather grunted. "I have a better chance of getting it out of that little American researcher. I knew you were the grandson to catch her for me."

Raoul tilted his head back and squinted at the stars. "I didn't catch her *for you,* Pépé."

"What do you mean by that? You told me you would go after her for me, didn't you?"

"I was in a sarcastic mood. Can we not bring this up again, Pépé? Fuck."

"Don't you talk to me that way, *jeune homme.*"

Raoul sighed. This was another way his grandfather got him to go back to Africa every damn year. Pure aggravation. But this time, rather than fantasize about freedom in the tropics, he thought about running away to Allegra's little house in the hills instead. And smiled.

His grandfather gave him a sharp, searching look. "She's a happy little thing, isn't she? I felt bad that time I made her cry."

Raoul pivoted, keeping his hands in his pockets because it was often a good precaution around his grandfather. The urge to strangle could come on so quickly. "*You* made her cry? What the hell did you do to her?"

"You made her cry, too? Already? I thought I raised you better than that."

"You didn't raise me." Raoul plunged his fists deeper into his pockets. Really, he would *never* be welcomed back into the bosom of his family if he strangled the old man. Unless his cousins elected him CEO in gratitude. "I had parents. What did you do to Allegra?"

"She got me talking. She gets everybody talking. That's why I think if Colette told anybody anything, it would be her."

No arguing with that.

"She was asking me questions for that immigration history thing of hers, and somehow she got me talking about smuggling those little kids out hidden in roses, and, I don't know, I guess she got a picture in her head. It hits people with hearts that way, you know, little kids curled up in rose petals, parents lost, being carried by strangers to the safety of strangers." His grandfather cleared his throat and squared his shoulders. "Kind of gets to you to see it, to tell the truth. That's why you keep doing it, even when you know you might be caught and tortured."

Damn, but his grandfather made him feel like a grain of dust in comparison sometimes. Of course he loved the old man. Who wouldn't? But it certainly was hard to fit in the same valley with him.

Raoul looked once again across the valley toward where Allegra's little house lay on the other side of the hills, and smiled a bit, his hands relaxing in his pockets. Maybe there was another place he fit just fine. God, she had made this Christmas dinner with his family so much more . . . whole. As if he belonged with someone or to someone at long last.

"How did you manage to get Tante Colette here?" Damien asked, coming out of the house. The women were inside preparing to serve the thirteen desserts, a sexist division of labor Allegra probably wouldn't put up with their whole lives, but she seemed to be enjoying herself tonight. Damien and Tristan had at least helped clear the table between courses, but Raoul had had to escape before he cracked at the pressure of so many people and so much noise and ran off to the hills. From which, of course, he would look back down longingly, wishing he could sneak back in and somehow *fit*.

Raoul shrugged. "Allegra, I think." It was hard to tell with Tante Colette. She might even have joined their Christmas for *his* sake, but his stomach swirled strangely when he tried to think that. Ever since he had failed to make it home before his own mother's sudden death, he had a really hard time believing he deserved to be loved. *Make sure you won't want it back again before you throw this family in the trash,* his grandfather had warned him, in one of their many fights before Raoul headed off to adventure at nineteen. If only he had listened.

"*Why* did you bring her, that's the other question," his grandfather said grumpily, as Tristan and Matt joined them, their shoulders rolling and settling, as if to savor how much more space there was outside the house than in it. Only Lucien was missing now, of the five first cousins, but Lucien had been missing for a long time. And unlike Raoul, he showed no inclination to come home, or even visit. He was another thing Raoul had wasted, maybe, when he ran off at nineteen in search of adventure. He and Lucien used to be so damn close. All their adventures were together.

"The last I checked, she was family," Raoul said. *Like me. We all want to fit.* "Speaking of which, maybe one of you can tell me why Allegra says Tante Colette sees more of Gabriel and Raphaël Delange than she does her own nephews."

"Their restaurant is only two streets away! I stop by at

least once a month," Matt protested, offended. "To make
sure she doesn't need any heavy lifting. *Nobody* can make
Tante Colette feel included enough, though. She's worse
than you."

What?

"It started way back when those two were kids."
Matthieu jerked his chin at their grandfather.

Pépé just lifted his chin and said nothing.

"I stop by every few weeks," Damien said indignantly.
"Gabe has to walk by her house on his way to his restaurant! I spend half my time in Paris right now, and do you
know how many family members I'm supposed to visit at
least once a month? I do my best. Besides, she always
looks at me as if she knows I left the house without ironing my underwear. And the next day, Maman always stops
by and irons it for me. It's enough to drive a man insane."

"Maybe you should try running the Africa division for
a year or so," Raoul suggested, not entirely ironically. "Instead of running around fulfilling everyone else's wishes
all the time."

Damien looked at him a moment and then looked away
across the winter-stripped rose field. He didn't say anything. Matt took a long breath at the thought of Africa and
sighed it out, gazing at the fields of roses that kept him
rooted there with vast pride and possessiveness . . . but
maybe a certain wistfulness.

The night made them resemble each other so much—
stripping the rust out of Raoul's hair so that it looked just
as dark as his cousins', turning Damien's gray-green eyes
and Raoul's amber to the same dark color as Matt's and
Tristan's. The night took their colors and left four tall men
with broad shoulders and proud bearing who could be
mistaken for each other in the dark. Lucien's absence
from that group left a hole almost as painful as his
mother's, although different. The absence of a shoulder

braced against a shoulder as they got into trouble, rather than a fond, proud maternal kiss.

He sighed. Lucien had come to visit him in the hospital in Central Africa, after he was shot, one of the very rare times anyone in the family had seen Lucien in the last decade, and even four years ago, Lucien had looked like a man who needed a home.

While the night made them all look the same to a stranger, it also subtly emphasized the differences that those close to them could see: the way Matt and Raoul were bigger, but Raoul always held himself alert, as if trouble might come out of the dark, while Matt held himself braced, as if trouble, when it came, would meet him head on and give full warning of the fact that he was going to have to bludgeon something. Damien, leaner, with an athletic intensity to him, had also a cool arrogance that somehow fed into his need to give people three times what they expected of him. Of them all, Tristan was by far the most relaxed in his skin, although Raoul didn't know how he did it; being the youngest of the five of them was not a task for the faint of heart.

Yes, they all had their differences, enough that someone who loved a man should be able to pick his form out in the dark. But Raoul didn't expect it, and when a hand slipped under his jacket and touched his spine, he whipped around and shoved Damien, the nearest, as hard as he could, adrenaline surging through him.

And then, one second too late, he caught himself.

Damien was knocked three steps before he managed to recover and keep his feet. "Damn it, Raoul! What's wrong with you? Don't tell me you're trying to start a fight on Christmas Eve."

"Sorry." Raoul's brain had overcome his reflexes now, and he pulled Allegra into a loop of his arm. "I just—startled." Now he really wanted to get away from people for a while, maybe drag Allegra off on a hike into the hills where they could be alone. Yes, he liked the idea of an alone that had Allegra in it with him. But he would be mad at himself, later, to have driven himself out of the Christmas gathering early, and wistful at having missed part of it.

"Sorry," Allegra murmured, too, pressing against him. "I just came out to tell you the thirteen desserts are ready."

He knew she was trying to distract everyone with the mention of the desserts, but unfortunately, they had been eating for three hours now, and none of them were nearly as motivated by the thought of thirteen desserts as they had been when they were kids. It was always nice to be reminded that he had found himself a thoughtful *sweetheart* of a woman, though.

"What were you trying to do, get me out of the line of fire?" Damien asked dryly, with something dark in the dryness, as he stepped back to the group.

Raoul didn't say anything, just looked at the stars for a while.

"Thanks," Damien said after a minute. "I appreciate the thought."

"*Croumpa un chut,*" Raoul murmured to Damien in Provençal so Allegra couldn't understand him.

"What does that mean?" Allegra asked promptly.

" 'Shut up,' " his grandfather *of course* told her. "You might want to learn a word or two of Provençal, if you're sticking with this one. Otherwise, how are you going to teach it to the kids?"

Raoul choked and didn't dare say anything. Smart predators were silent predators, and his damn grandfather was going to scare away his prey. And it *hurt* having to chase her down and talk her back around to liking him; he could stand not to have to do that again for at least another year. Was it at all reasonable to hope he could stay out of trouble with her for a year or two at a time?

"What?" Pépé protested into the crystalline silence that his grandsons left in the wake of his comment. "Somebody has to nudge you kids along. Although if you're thinking about producing heirs, Raoul, you had better quit traipsing all over Africa and make sure they're brought up in the family. No great-grandchild of mine is going to be raised where he doesn't know the smell of roses."

Oh, *pour l'amour de Dieu*. Instead of stealing family heirlooms he should have been getting somebody pregnant instead? Allegra was probably loving this.

"Yes, I'm home to stay," Raoul said flatly, to get the conversation off assumptions that might scare a woman who had just met a man into running to the other side of the Atlantic.

Dead silence. All the men stared at him, in the starlit night, and Allegra leaned her warm body against him, a shield that made all those stares not even bruise his skin.

"Did you tell my father?" Damien asked finally. Louis Rosier had headed Rosier SA for thirty years now and was responsible for directing a good deal of its astonishing global growth. The cousins' competitiveness had stood Louis in good stead, when it came to making them tools for the company's glory. Damien's own competitiveness had gotten to the point that if Uncle Louis regretted out loud that he hadn't made a different decision the day before, Damien would go out and fly around the planet fifty times to try to turn back time.

"No, but if there's no place for me with Rosier, I can always start my own company," Raoul said and let the edge of his teeth show just a little.

Everyone prickled to alert, Damien shifting to face him full on.

"You'll do *what*?" his grandfather asked incredulously.

"Well," Raoul said apologetically, "I like earning a lot of money. But if there's no room for me to do that with you here in Grasse these days, I'm pretty sure I can still do it against you. I've learned a lot in the past fourteen years. And I'm tired of working on the other end of the world, where people try to kidnap me and shoot at me. I want to come home."

"What is this, your crowbar approach to being let in?" Allegra murmured to him in English. Damien laughed wryly, catching it.

"Do you *always* have to start trouble?" Matt growled.

"If you don't go after what you want, you don't get it," Raoul said and Allegra tilted her head back, shaking her head ruefully. It had been a long time since someone laughed at him with that kind of warmth and affection, as if even his flaws were entirely welcome. His hand covered hers, pressing it between her stomach and his palm. "Let's go get our dessert," he told her. He was ready to be done with the Christmas dinner, so that he could go tuck himself up somewhere cozy and private with her for the night.

The men turned toward the house, Matthieu and Damien both brooding, and in the cool, clear night a bell rang out. Piercing and profound, as it had rung for eight hundred years. Once, twice, thrice . . . the little medieval church in their village at the far end of the valley was ringing people to Midnight Mass.

All the men paused, caught by the bells, their old, familiar call turned into something compelling by the midnight air, summoning up old ghosts of memories. Every single Christmas, all his life until his grandmother died, the whole family would go to Mass at Christmas. Mostly they walked; it was only three kilometers and they would rather drink good wine at Christmas dinner than stick with water and drive. All of them together, trooping down the road by the winter-bare rose fields, the boys chasing each other among the bushes and proudly taking their place beside the older men packing the walls against the back of the tiny, eight-hundred-year-old stone church to leave the pews for the women. Not that the women were thrilled with the seventeenth-century pews; his grandmother always brought cushions.

When she died, they lost the emotional power center, the force that moved them all from the house to the church on a cold Christmas night when people would rather sit at the table laughing and drinking. Damien's mother had tried, the next year, appealing to their memories of their grandmother and how important it would be to her. Raoul had started off all right in the back of the church, but as the familiar Latin rhythms echoed against stone—the priest always reverted to Latin for Midnight Mass—he found himself staring at his toes, as it grew harder and harder to swallow. Beside him, Matt folded his big arms and looked grim and enduring. Damien shoved his hands in his pockets and closed his eyes, the corners of his mouth pressed down. Tristan left them to go sit with his mother and put his arm around her. When Raoul finally slipped out, taking deep breaths, trying to shake the sting out of his nostrils, he spotted his grandfather, walking into the rose fields that started on the outskirts of the village. As he followed Pépé to catch him, the old man trailed his hand against the bare bushes as if they held flowers, stroking ghosts of petals even when the thorns tore at his skin. Raoul had fallen into step beside him, and neither of them spoke to each other, the whole walk back to the empty, empty farmhouse.

That was the last anyone tried to get them to go.

But as the bells rang out, twelve times, they all tilted their heads in the direction of that Christmas call, wistful not for the Mass itself but for that time in their lives, when their grandmother was their heart. When they all held together around that solid center of confident, warm love.

When his own mother was still alive. He would have kept going for his own mother, if she had wanted it.

Raoul rested his hands on Allegra's shoulders, so glad for her warmth it almost squeezed his heart out. His cousins' glances flickered just briefly to that intimacy and then away, as if shying from a hurt.

And it occurred to him that of all the men there, he might be the only one who, right at that moment, had a person to call home.

CHAPTER FIFTEEN

Rough, exposed stone formed the walls of the room in which Allegra and Raoul slept, since Tante Félicie never allowed anyone to drive home after all that Christmas wine. The stone breathed roses out of its very pores, the room having once been used for extracting oils, long ago, before the Rosiers' role in the world of perfume production grew and grew and grew. Lavender snuck in a whisper of an embrace from the crisp white sheets embroidered with white-on-white jasmine and green leaves. Ginger and spices overwhelmed all, a great big hug sent across the sea and spilled across Allegra's lap in the form of cookies.

"I can't believe you sent an express pickup to get my stocking from my mother, when I agreed to join you for Christmas." Allegra tried hard not to sniffle.

Raoul shrugged, clearly embarrassed and pleased at the success of the gesture. "I knew you were missing home."

She bent and kissed him.

His smile deepened. He lay with the heavy comforter spilling off his shoulders, the chill farmhouse morning very quiet, the walls of their room too thick to let in the sound of a creature stirring, even if one was. "She sent you two. I wasn't sure which one was your favorite."

One, somewhat worn with use, had a little girl made out of felt on it, with a red hood and brown yarn braids. The other was a rich midnight blue, with pristine white fur trim. "I think this one was for you." Allegra smiled as she passed the blue one across.

He blinked. "Your mother—sent me a Christmas stocking?"

"It's blue," she said. "And very masculine, see? Like she made for my father. You must have made a really good impression, over the phone." Sending an express mail pickup for her only daughter's Christmas stocking so that Allegra would have a little bit of her own home for Christmas would have won her mother over quite fast. Plus, he had an awesome voice. If you threw in that sexy-as-hell accent he had when he spoke in English, her mother must have been about as bowled over as her daughter had been.

Raoul blinked again, much harder, and then kept his lashes lowered, his face flushing as he struggled with some wave of emotion. "That was—nice of her," he said low.

Allegra curled her hand over his shoulder and squeezed gently, not saying anything, and then pulled another little package out of the stocking, leaving him time to deal with whatever feelings had surged in him at thoughts of mothers and Christmas and being welcomed by a stranger across the sea who had never even met him.

His lashes lifted again, and he watched her face as she unwrapped the gift he'd put inside to reveal a jeweler's box, her eyes widening, and then widening further when it opened to reveal a delicate platinum Y-necklace, at its tip a star . . . no. She looked closer. A tiny, exquisite rose, with a little ruby for the center. A rose for his family symbol, his name. A stamp of possession so filigreed and delicate that she could pretend not to realize it if she wanted more time.

"Raoul," she said softly. "It's beautiful."

He watched her fasten the necklace so that the rose draped in the V of her flannel pajamas, a deep contentment radiating out of him. "The next one is my favorite, though," he said, and she dug into her stocking again for an object carefully taped in bubble wrap.

A *santon,* the one from the Christmas market that day, a young shepherd woman fighting the mistral on her way home, but instead of the original's blue cape, this one had been painted with a red that matched Allegra's coat that first night, and the blond hair had been changed to deep brown. In the basket over her arm, the little round *galettes* of the original had been dotted with specks of brown to suggest a chocolate chip cookie.

She clapped her hands—and therefore, accidentally, the *santon* itself—to her mouth in delight, gazing at Raoul over it with stinging eyes.

"I had him make a special version for me," he explained. "That's what I was doing when you got all jealous because I was talking to his daughter in Provençal." He looked rather smug about that moment of jealousy. "Although I don't really want to give it away now," he admitted, eyeing the little red-cloaked, cookie-carrying shepherdess in her hands hungrily. "Maybe we could share?"

Share their Nativity scene. Nativity scenes like this were built for generations. Allegra's smile trembled. She stroked a finger over the girl in red.

"We'll take turns," Raoul said. "We can go to your family's for Christmas next year, so you're not always the one who has to feel homesick. Or I'll fly them over here, and we'll show them a Provençal Christmas."

She was going to cry. She was definitely going to cry. She thrust a package into his hands. "I got you this one," she said softly.

His big fingers ripped apart that bubble-wrap to reveal—

The curled-up blissful wolf, the one who was welcomed into the stable.

"But I don't really want to give it up, either," she said. "Maybe we could share?"

He curled his hand around her arm and pulled her down to him, kissing her, and it was a long time before they got back to the few presents at the bottom of the stocking.

One of which was a small, wrapped rectangle. "Oh," Allegra said cautiously, before she even opened it. Scent slipped through the porous tissue paper to tease Raoul's sensitive nose.

Both their names were on the card of handmade paper, and she handed it to him to rip open. He gazed at the lid of the perfume box a long moment, the rose the wolf strained forever to reach with its sharp teeth.

"What do you want me to do?" he asked finally.

Allegra shook her head. "I think you can do whatever you want at this point. She's clearly up to something."

He ran a thumb over the lid.

"At a guess," Allegra said low, "she wants to change her world before she leaves it. And her world is this family that she never quite got to be a full part of."

"You know, it's partly her own *fault* that she never felt part of this family," Raoul said, and then tilted his head suddenly, hearing his own words. Allegra held his eyes with a wry, encouraging smile.

Fine, then. Message to himself received. He opened

the lid and rubbed his thumb over the solid perfume Tante Colette had filled it with, breathing deeply.

"She very clearly wants you to have a home," Allegra said quietly, laying a hand over his arm. "That's one thing she wants to change."

He nodded, touched suddenly more deeply than he could say. It was all a bit much, for his wary heart: Allegra here, wearing his necklace, and her mother sending cookies for him, and Tante Colette. . . . He felt as if he were blooming outward, his heart one of their own roses unfurling in deepest winter, which scared him because . . . well, roses that bloomed in the winter got frozen in the cold. As Allegra had proven to him once already. Better to be the wolf than the rose, no? No? Even if that frost of Allegra's, once melted, had flooded him with so much warmth and forgiveness and willingness to try again, it was amazing a man could still stay wary under it. "She started writing me stories about you about a month after you met her, you know," he said quietly. "She sent a picture once, too, of you laughing. And a bag of crumbs that were probably cookies when they were put in the package."

Allegra's eyebrows went up. "*I* was the lure your Tante Colette was using to bring you home?" Her eyes rounded as she absorbed that, and a delicate flush colored her cheeks. "She must really like me," she said wonderingly.

Raoul had been thinking that Tante Colette must really like *him,* which was scrambling his insides badly enough, but at Allegra's interpretation, his heart squeezed so hard, he thought the thing might just crush itself. "Allegra." He closed his hand over hers. A little too hard, but when you saw something you wanted, you had to grab it, just not so hard you mashed its petals. Yeah, no—his original reading of that box was right. *He* was the wolf. *She* was the rose. Right. Much more masculine and safer that way.

"She never said anything to me about *you*." Allegra sounded a little offended.

"Maybe she knew you needed a stranger, and that I . . . really didn't."

She wiggled her hand around enough to try to close her fingers around his bigger palm, and he focused as hard as he could on the perfume box. "It's, ah, it's me, you know," he said after a moment. He had to clear his throat. Force his voice to sound strong instead of choked.

Allegra's finger slipped in between his and touched the tarnished silver lid, tracing the rose and then the wolf that wanted it. He still could not quite believe she let that small hand play so trustingly between his larger ones. It still shivered pleasure through him, just to feel the brush of her skin. "Yes, I recognized you."

"No, I mean—the scent. She tried to blend in all the things from my life. Roses, jasmine, lavender . . . then all those scents from Africa she was always asking me to send her." He had to shut up then. He couldn't keep his voice even.

Allegra's finger ran over the solid perfume and she brought the scent to her nose to breathe in. A realization crossed her face, and she stiffened abruptly, indignantly. "She gave this to me *months* ago. Has she had me marking myself with your scent all this time?"

Raoul's eyebrows shot up. And then he laughed out loud and rolled onto his back, a flash of pure delight releasing all the tangled emotions. "I *love* Tante Colette."

Allegra gave him a very stern look that made him want to kiss her in the worst way. "Yes, well—just be aware then that if this is you, she also *gave you to me*. As in, you know, to *own*."

She had such a funny minatory tone as she said that, as if she expected him to object. He shifted over to nestle his head in her lap, and, sure enough, she immediately sank her fingers into his hair. It was official, he thought, as his whole body hummed into the feel of her petting and into the scent of her so close: He was definitely part dog. Or something related. "On a silver platter, almost," he told her, proffering her the silver perfume box.

"You don't want to show it to your grandfather to soften his hard heart?"

The idea of great-grandkids already seemed to be softening his grandfather's hard heart, but Raoul didn't want to terrify her, so he only shook his head. "You know what? They're ninety and ninety-six. Let them try talking to each other like adults—" His voice tripped as the oddest thought crossed his brain. Tante Colette had filled her letters with stories of Allegra, and Pépé had sent him into that bar after her. What if they *were* talking to each other?

Conspiring to make him feel at home?

No, that didn't even make sense. The idea of those two communicating like reasonable people—because they *wanted* him—was too much for his brain to process. He reached up to touch one finger to the tiny rose against her breastbone, precious metal and more precious skin. "You know I fell in love with you when you told me I smelled like Christmas, don't you?"

Her eyes lit. But she said, "Raoul. You hadn't even met me yet. You shouldn't rush into things with strangers like that, you know."

He laughed, almost sleepily. "Not like you?"

"I was just excited by how sexy you were, to be honest," she said. "I didn't fall in love with you until I woke up on you in an old stone *lavoir.*"

Hunh. It hadn't been the great sex the night before? But then again, that *lavoir had* been a nice moment. It had melted his heart out and helped compensate for his aching butt and shoulders. The trust and forgiveness when she fell asleep in his arms that way had been what convinced him that maybe . . . she was his. His to keep. To be kept by. They were home. "It kind of—grows," he said, shifting his hands awkwardly to try to illustrate. Because they were his hands, and he was a Rosier, and that was how Rosiers illustrated growing things, the awkward gesture resembled a rosebud opening.

She bent and kissed his fingertips. "Yes, it does, doesn't it?" she said and snuggled up into his arms for Christmas morning.

THE 24 DAYS OF CHRISTMAS

Linda Lael Miller

CHAPTER ONE

The snow, as much a Thanksgiving leftover as the cold turkey in the sandwich Frank Raynor had packed for lunch, lay in tattered, dirty patches on the frozen ground. Surveying the leaden sky through the window of the apartment over his garage, Frank sighed and wondered if he'd done the right thing, renting the place to Addie Hutton. She'd grown up in the big house, on the other side of the lawn. How would she feel about taking up residence in what, in her mind, probably amounted to the servants' quarters?

"Daddy?"

He turned to see his seven-year-old daughter, Lissie, framed in the doorway. She was wearing a golden halo of her own design, constructed from a coat hanger and an old tinsel garland filched from the boxes of Christmas decorations downstairs.

"Does this make me look like an angel?"

Frank felt a squeeze in his chest as he made a show of assessing the rest of the outfit—jeans, snow boots, and a pink T-shirt that said "Brat Princess" on the front. "Yeah, Lisser," he said. "You've got it going on."

Lissie was the picture of her late mother, with her short, dark and impossibly thick hair, bright hazel eyes, and all those pesky freckles. Frank loved those freckles, just as he'd loved Maggie's, though she'd hated them, and so did Lissie. "So you think I have a shot at the part, right?"

The kid had her heart set on playing an angel in the annual Christmas pageant at St. Mary's Episcopal School. Privately, Frank didn't hold out much hope, since he'd just given the school's drama teacher, Miss Pidgett, a speeding ticket two weeks before, and she was still steamed about it. She'd gone so far as to complain to the city council, claiming police harassment, but Frank had stood up and said she'd been doing fifty-five in a thirty, and the citation had stuck. The old biddy had barely spoken to him before that; now she was crossing the street to avoid saying hello.

He would have liked to think Almira Pidgett wasn't the type to take a grown-up grudge out on a seven-year-old, but, unfortunately, he knew from experience that she was. She'd been *his* teacher, when he first arrived in Pine Crossing, and she'd disliked him from day one.

"What's so bad about playing a shepherd?" he hedged, and took a sip from his favorite coffee mug. Maggie had made it for him, in the ceramics class she'd taken to keep her mind off the chemo, and he carried it most everywhere he went. Folks probably thought he had one hell of an addiction to caffeine; in truth, he kept the cup within reach because it was the last gift Maggie ever gave him. It was a talisman; he felt closer to her when he could touch it.

Lissie folded her arms and set her jaw, Maggie-style. "It's dumb for a girl to be a shepherd. Girls are supposed to be angels."

He hid a grin behind the rim of the mug. "Your mother would have said girls could herd sheep as well as boys," he replied. "And I've known more than one female who wouldn't qualify as an angel, no matter what kind of getup she was wearing."

A wistful expression crossed Lissie's face. "I miss Mommy so much," she said, very softly. Maggie had been gone two years, come June, and Frank kept expecting to get used to it, but it hadn't happened, for him *or* for Lissie.

I want you to mourn me for a while, Maggie had told him, toward the end, *but when it's time to let go, I'll find a way to tell you.*

"I know," he said gruffly. "Me, too."

"Mommy's an angel now, isn't she?"

Frank couldn't speak. He managed a nod.

"Miss Pidgett says people don't turn into angels when they die. She says they're still just people."

"Miss Pidgett," Frank said, "is a—stickler for detail."

"A what?"

Frank looked pointedly at his watch. "You're going to be late for school if we don't get a move on," he said.

"Angels," Lissie said importantly, straightening her halo, "are always on time."

Frank grinned. "Did you feed Floyd?"

Floyd was the overweight beagle he and Lissie had rescued from the pound a month after Maggie died. In retrospect, it seemed to Frank that *Floyd* had been the one doing the rescuing—he'd made a man and a little girl laugh, when they'd both thought nothing would ever be funny again.

"Of course I did," Lissie said. "Angels always feed their dogs."

Frank chuckled, but that hollow place was still there, huddled in a corner of his ticker. "Get your coat," he said.

"It's in the car," Lissie replied, and her gaze strayed to the Advent calendar taped across the bottom of the cupboards. Fashioned of matchboxes, artfully painted and glued to a length of red velvet ribbon, now as scruffy as the snow outside, the thing was an institution in the Raynor family. Had been since Frank was seven himself. "How come you put that up here?" she asked, with good reason. Every Christmas of her short life, her great-aunt Eliza's calendar had hung in the living room of the main house, fixed to the mantelpiece. It was a family tradition to open one box each day and admire the small treasure glued inside.

Frank crossed the worn linoleum floor, intending to steer his quizzical daughter in the direction of the front door, but she didn't budge. She was like Maggie that way, too—stubborn as a mule up to its belly in molasses.

"I thought it might make Miss Hutton feel welcome," he said.

"The lady who lived in our house when she was a kid?"

Frank nodded. Addie, the daughter of a widowed judge, had been a lonely little girl. She'd made a point of being around every single morning, from the first of December to the twenty-fourth, for the opening of that day's match-box. This old kitchen had been a warm, joyous place in those days—Aunt Eliza, the Huttons' housekeeper, had made sure of that. Putting up the Advent calendar was Frank's way of offering Addie a pleasant memory. "You don't mind, do you?"

Lissie considered the question. "I guess not," she said. "You think she'll let me stop by before school, so I can look inside, too?"

That Frank couldn't promise. He hadn't seen Addie in more than ten years, and he had no idea what kind of woman she'd turned into. She'd come back for Aunt Eliza's funeral, and sent a card when Maggie died, but she'd left Pine Crossing, Colorado, behind when she went off to college, and, as far as he knew, she'd never looked back.

He ruffled Lissie's curls, careful not to displace the halo. "Don't know, Beans," he said. The leather of his service belt creaked as he crouched to look into the child's small, earnest face, balancing the coffee mug deftly as he did so. "It's almost Christmas. The lady's had a rough time over the last little while. Maybe this will bring back some happy memories."

Lissie beamed. "Okay," she chimed. She was missing one of her front teeth, and her smile touched a bruised place in Frank, though it was a sweet ache. Not much scared him, but the depth and breadth of the love he bore this little girl cut a chasm in his very soul.

Frank straightened. "School," he said with mock sternness.

Lissie fairly skipped out of the apartment and down the stairs to the side of the garage. "I know what's in the first box anyway," she sang. "A teeny, tiny teddy bear."

"Yup," Frank agreed, following at a more sedate pace, lifting his collar against the cold. Thirty years ago, on his first night in town, he and his aunt Eliza had selected that bear from a shoebox full of dime-store geegaws she'd collected, and he'd personally glued it in place. That was when he'd begun to think his life might turn out all right after all.

Addie Hutton slowed her secondhand Buick as she turned onto Fifth Street. Her most important possessions, a computer and printer, four boxes of books, a few photo albums, and a couple of suitcases full of clothes, were in the backseat—and her heart was in her throat.

Her father's house loomed just ahead, a two-story saltbox, white with green shutters. The ornate mailbox, once labeled "Hutton," now read "Raynor," but the big maple tree was still in the front yard, and the tire swing, now old and weather-worn, dangled from the sturdiest branch.

She smiled, albeit a little sadly. Her father hadn't wanted that swing—said it would be an eyesore, more suited to the other side of the tracks than to their neighborhood—but Eliza, the housekeeper and the only mother Addie had ever really known, since her own had died when she was three, had stood firm on the matter. Finally defeated, the judge had sent his secretary's husband, Charlie, over to hang the tire.

She pulled into the driveway and looked up at the apartment over the garage. A month before, when the last pillar of her life had finally collapsed, she'd called Frank Raynor and asked if the place was rented. She'd known it was available, having maintained her subscription to the hometown newspaper and seen the ad in the classifieds, but the truth was, she hadn't been sure Frank would want her living in such close proximity. He'd seemed surprised by the inquiry, and, after some throat clearing, he'd said the last tenant had just given notice, and if she wanted it, she could move in any time.

She'd asked about the rent, since that little detail wasn't listed—for the first time in her life, money was an issue—and he'd said they could talk about that later.

Now she put the car into park and turned off the engine with a resolute motion of her right hand. She pushed open the door, jumped out, and marched toward the outside stairs. During their telephone conversation, Frank had offered to leave the key under the doormat, and Addie had asked if it was still safe to leave doors unlocked in Pine Crossing. He'd chuckled and said it was. All right, then, she'd said. It was decided. No need for a key.

A little breathless from dashing up the steps, Addie stopped on the familiar welcome mat and drew a deep breath, bracing herself for the flood of memories that were bound to wash over her the moment she stepped over that worn threshold.

A brisk winter wind bit through her lightweight winter coat, bought for southern California, and she turned the knob.

Eliza's furniture was still there, at least in the living room. Every stick of it.

Tears burned Addie's eyes as she took it all in—the old blue sofa, the secondhand coffee table, the ancient piano, always out of tune. She almost expected to hear Eliza call out the old familiar greeting. "Adelaide Hutton, is that you? You get yourself into this kitchen and have a glass of milk and a cookie or two."

Frank's high school graduation picture still occupied the place of honor on top of the piano, and next to it was Addie's own.

Addie crossed the room, touched Frank's square-jawed face, and smiled. He wasn't handsome, in the classic sense of the word—his features were too rough cut for that, his brown eyes too earnest, and too wary. She wondered if, at thirty-seven, he still had all that dark, unruly hair.

She turned her head, by force of will, to face her younger self. Brown hair, not as thick as she would have liked, blue eyes, good skin. Lord, she looked so innocent in that photograph, so painfully hopeful. By the time she graduated, two years after Frank, he was already working his way through college in Boulder, with a major in criminal justice. They were engaged, and he'd intended to come back to Pine Crossing, as soon as he'd completed his studies, and join the three-man police force. With Chief Potter about to retire, and Ben Mead ready to step into the top job, there would be a place waiting for Frank the day he got his degree.

Addie had loved Frank, but she'd dreamed of going to

a university and majoring in journalism; Frank, older, and with his career already mapped out, had wanted her to stay in Pine Crossing and study at the local junior college. He'd reluctantly agreed to delay the marriage, and she'd gone off to Denver to study. There had been no terrible crisis, no confrontation—they had simply grown apart.

Midway through her sophomore year, when he'd just pinned on his shiny new badge, she'd sent his ring back, by Federal Express, with a brief letter.

Though it was painful, Addie had kept up on Frank's life, through the pages of the Pine Crossing *Statesman.* In the intervening years, he'd married, fathered a child, and been tragically widowed. He'd worked his way up through the ranks, and now he was head man.

Addie tore herself away from the pictures and checked out the kitchen. Same ancient oak table, chairs with hand-sewn cushions, and avocado green appliances. Even Eliza's antique percolator was in its customary place on the counter. It was almost as if the apartment had been preserved as a sort of memorial, yet the effect was heart-warming.

Suspended above the counter was Eliza's matchbox Advent calendar, the fraying ends and middle of the supporting ribbon carefully taped into place.

A powerful yearning swept through Addie. She approached the calendar, ran her fingers lightly from one box to another. Her throat closed, and the tears she'd blinked away earlier came back with a vengeance.

"Oh, Eliza," she whispered, "I'd give anything to see you again."

Pulling on the tiny ribbon tab at the top, she tugged open the first box, labeled, like the others, with a brass numeral. The miniature teddy bear was still inside.

She'd been five the night Frank came to live with his aunt, a somber, quiet little boy, arriving on the four o'clock bus from Denver, clutching a threadbare panda in one hand and a beat-up suitcase in the other.

Needing a distraction, Addie opened the cupboard where Eliza had kept her coffee in a square glass jar with a red lid. Bless Frank, he'd replenished the supply.

Addie started a pot brewing, and while the percolator was chortling and chugging away, she went downstairs to bring in her things. By the time she'd lugged up the various computer components and the books, the coffee was ready.

She set the computer up in the smaller of the two bedrooms, the one that had been Frank's. Other memories awaited her there, but she managed to hold them at bay while she hooked everything up and plugged into the telephone line.

In her old life, she'd been a reporter. She had done a lot of her research online, and kept up with her various sources via e-mail. Now, the Internet was her primary way of staying in touch with her six-year-old stepson, Henry.

The system booted up and—bless Frank again—she heard the rhythmic blipping sound of a dial tone. Evidently, he hadn't had the phone service shut off after the last renter moved out.

She was into her e-mail within seconds, and her first reaction was disappointment. Nothing from Henry.

Perched on the chair at the secondhand desk where Frank had worked so diligently at his homework, when they were both kids, she scrolled through the usual forwards and spam.

At the very end was a message with the subject line, THIS IS FROM TOBY.

Addie's fingers froze over the keyboard. Toby was her ex-husband. They'd been divorced for two years, but they'd stayed in contact because of Henry. She'd had no legal claim to the child—in the darkest hours of the night she still kicked herself for not adopting him while she and Toby were still married—but Toby had a busy social life, and she'd been a free baby-sitter. Until the debacle that brought her career down around her ears, that was. After that, Toby's live-in girlfriend, Elle, had decided Addie was a bad influence, and the visits had all but stopped.

Trembling slightly, she opened the e-mail.

MEET THE FOUR O'CLOCK BUS, Toby had written. That was all. No explanations, no smart remarks, no signature.

"Damn you, Toby," she muttered, and scrabbled in the depths of her purse for her cell phone. His number was on speed dial, from the old days, before she'd become a *persona non grata*.

His voice mail picked up. "This is Toby Springer," he said. "Elle and I are on our honeymoon. Be home around the end of January. Leave a message, and we'll get back to you then."

Addie jammed the disconnect button with her thumb, checked her watch.

Three-ten.

She fired back an e-mail, just in case Toby, true to form, was shallow enough to take a laptop on his honeymoon. He was irresponsible in just about every area of his life, but when it came to his loan-brokering business, he kept up.

WHERE IS HENRY? Addie typed furiously, and hit Send.

After that, she drank coffee and paced, watching the screen for an answer that never came.

At five minutes to four, she was waiting at the Texaco station, in the center of town. The bus rolled in right on time and stopped with a squeak of air brakes.

The hydraulic door whooshed open.

A middle-aged woman descended the steps, then an

old man in corduroy pants, a plaid flannel shirt and a quilted vest, then a teenage girl with pink hair and a silver ring at the base of her right eyebrow.

Addie crammed her hands into the pockets of her coat and paced some more.

At last, she saw him. A bespectacled little boy, standing tentatively in the doorway of the bus, clutching a teddy bear under one arm.

Henry.

She'd been afraid to hope. Now, overjoyed, Addie ran past the gas pumps to gather him close.

CHAPTER TWO

Henry sat at Eliza's table, huddled in his favorite pajamas, his brown hair rumpled, his horn-rimmed glasses slightly askew. "So anyway," he explained, sounding mildly congested, "Elle said I was incrudgible and Dad had better deal with me or she'd be out of there."

Addie seethed. She hadn't pressed for details the afternoon before, after his arrival, and Henry hadn't volunteered any. They'd stopped at the supermarket on the way home from the Texaco station, stocked up on fish sticks and French fries, and come back to the apartment for supper. After the meal, Henry had submitted sturdily to a bath, a dose of children's aspirin, and the smearing on of mentholated rub. Then, exhausted, he'd donned his pajamas and fallen asleep in Frank's childhood bed.

Addie had spent half the night trying to track Toby down, but he might as well have moved to Argentina and taken on a new identity. It seemed he'd dropped off the face of the earth.

Now, in the chilly glare of a winter morning, Henry was more forthcoming with details. "Dad and me flew to

Denver together; then he put me on the bus and said he'd call you when he'd worked things out with Elle."

Addie gritted her teeth and turned her back, fiddling with the cord on the percolator. The Advent calendar dangled in front of her, a tattered, colorful reminder that there was joy in the world, and that it was often simple and homemade.

"Hey," she said brightly, turning around again, "it's the second of December. Want to see what's in the box?"

Henry adjusted his glasses and examined the length of ribbon, with its twenty-four colorful matchboxes. Before he could reply, a firm knock sounded at the front door.

"Come in!" Addie called, because you could do that in Pine Crossing, without fear of admitting an ax murderer.

A little girl dashed into the kitchen, wearing everyday clothes and a tinsel halo. Addie was struck dumb, momentarily at least. *Frank's child,* she thought, amazed to find herself shaken. *This is Frank's child.*

Addie had barely had time to recover from that realization when Frank himself loomed in the doorway. His badge twinkled on the front of his brown uniform jacket.

One of her questions was put to rest, at least. Frank still had all his hair.

He smiled that slow, sparing smile of his. "Hello, Addie," he said.

"Frank," she managed to croak, with a nod.

He put a hand on the girl's shoulder. "This is my daughter, Lissie," he said. "She's impersonating an angel."

The brief, strange tension was broken, and Addie laughed. Approaching Lissie, she put out a hand. "How do you do?" she said. "My name is Addie. I don't believe I've ever had the pleasure of meeting an angel before." She peered over Lissie's small shoulders, pretending to be puzzled. "Where are your wings?"

The child sighed, a little deflated. "You don't get those unless you're actually in the play," she said. "Shepherds aren't allowed to have wings."

Addie gave Frank a quizzical look. He responded with a half smile and a you've-got-me shake of his head.

"I made the halo myself," Lissie said, squaring her shoulders. She'd been sneaking looks at Henry the whole time; now she addressed him directly. "Who are you?"

"Henry," he replied solemnly, and pushed at the nose-piece of his glasses.

"My dad got married, and his wife says I'm incrudgi-ble."

"Oh," Lissie said with a knowing air.

Frank and Addie exchanged glances.

"Sorry to bother you," Frank said, nodding toward the Advent calendar. A smile lit his eyes. "Lissie was hoping she could be around for the opening of Box Number 2."

Addie's throat tightened. Those memories again, all of them sweet. "You do the honors, Miss Lissie," she said with a grand gesture of one arm.

Lissie started toward the calendar, and once again Frank's hand came to rest on her small shoulder. Although they didn't look at each other, some silent message trav-eled between father and daughter.

"I think Henry should open the box," Lissie said. "Un-less being incrudgible means he'll mess it up."

Henry hesitated, probably wondering if incrudgibility was, indeed, a factor in the enterprise. Then, very care-fully, he dragged his chair over to the counter, climbed up on it, and pulled open the second box. Lissie looked on eagerly.

Henry turned his head, his nose wrinkled. "It's a balle-rina," he said with little-boy disdain.

Addie had known what was inside, of course, knew what was tucked into all the boxes. She'd been through the ritual every Christmas of her childhood, from the time she was five. Eliza had let her choose that tiny doll from a shoebox full of small toys, the very first year, dab glue onto its back, and press it into place.

She looked at Frank, looked away again, quickly. She'd been so jealous of him, those first few weeks after his arrival, afraid he'd take her place in Eliza's affections. Instead, Eliza had made room in her heart for both children, each lost and unwanted in their own way, and let Addie take part in the tradition, right from the first.

"We'd better be on our way," Frank said, somewhat gruffly. "Lissie's got school."

Addie touched Henry's forehead reflexively, before helping him down from the chair. Despite the aspirin and other stock remedies, he still had a slight fever, and that worried her.

"Are you going to go to my school?" Lissie asked Henry. "Or are you just here for a vacation?"

"I don't know," Henry said, and he sounded so bereft that the insides of Addie's sinuses burned. Damn Toby, she thought bitterly. Damn him for being selfish and shallow enough to put a small boy on a bus and leave him to his fate. Did the man have so much as a clue how many things could have gone horribly wrong along the way?

Frank caught her eye. "Everything all right, Addie?" he asked quietly.

She bit her lower lip. Nodded. Frank didn't keep up with gossip; he never had. It followed, then, that he didn't know what she'd been accused of, that she'd staked her whole career on a big story, that she'd almost gone to jail for protecting her source, that that source, as it turned out, had been lying through his capped and gleaming teeth.

Frank looked good-naturedly skeptical of her answer. He shrugged and raised a coffee mug to his lips. It was white, chipped here and there, with an oversized handle and Frank's name emblazoned in gold letters across the front, inside a large red heart.

"Thanks," he said.

Addie had lost track of the conversation, and it must have shown in her face, because Frank grinned, inclined his head toward the Advent calendar, and said, "It means a lot to Lissie, to open those boxes."

"Maybe you should take it back to your place," she said. Henry and Lissie were in the living room by then; one of them was plunking out a single-finger version of "Jingle Bells" on Eliza's ancient piano. "After all, it's a family heirloom."

"It seems fitting to me, having it here," Frank reasoned, watching her intently, "but if you'd rather we didn't come stomping into your kitchen every morning, I'd understand. So would Lissie."

"It isn't that," Addie protested, laying a hand to her heart. "Honestly. It was so sweet of you to remember, but—" Her voice fell away, and she struggled to get hold of it again. "Frank, about the rent—you didn't say how much—"

"Let's not worry about that right now," Frank interrupted. "It's almost Christmas, and, besides, this is your home."

Addie opened her mouth, closed it again. Her father, the judge, had quietly waited out her ill-fated engagement to Frank, but he'd been unhappy with her decision to go into journalism instead of law. When she refused to change her major, he'd changed his will, leaving the main house and property to Eliza. A year later, he'd died of a heart attack.

Addie had never been close to her father, but she'd grieved all right. She hadn't needed the inheritance. She'd buckled down, gotten her degree, and landed a promising job with a California newspaper. She'd been the golden girl—until she'd trusted the wrong people, and written a story that nearly brought down an entire chain of newspapers.

Frank raised his free hand, as though he might touch the tip of her nose, the way he'd done when they were young, and thought they were in love. Then, apparently having second thoughts, he let it fall back to his side.

"See you tomorrow," he said.

CHAPTER THREE

Addie awoke to silvery light and the sort of muffled sounds that always meant snow. She lay perfectly still, for a long time, hands cupped behind her head, grinning like a delighted fool. Snow. Oh, how she had missed the snow, in the land of palm trees and almost constant sunshine.

Henry was trying to make a phone call when she got to the kitchen. After a moment's pause, she started the coffee.

"I hate my dad," he said, hanging up the receiver with a slight slam. "I hate Elle, too."

Addie wanted to wrap the child in her arms and hold him close, but she sensed that he wouldn't welcome the gesture at this delicate point. He was barely keeping himself together as it was. "No, sweetie," she said softly. "You don't hate either of them. You're just angry, and that's understandable. And for the record, you're not incorrigible, either. You are a *very* good boy."

He stared at her in that owlish way of his. "I don't want to go back there. Not ever. I want to stay here, with you."

Addie's heart ached. *You have no rights,* she reminded

herself. *Not where this child is concerned.* "You know I'd love to have you live with me for always," she said carefully, "but that might not be possible. Your dad—"

Suddenly, Henry hurled himself at her. She dropped to her knees and pulled him into her arms.

There was a rap at the front door.

"Addie?" Frank called.

Henry pulled back and rubbed furiously at his eyes, then straightened his glasses.

"Come in," Addie said.

Frank appeared in the doorway, carrying his coffee cup and a bakery box. He paused on the threshold, watching as Addie got to her feet.

"Do you sleep in that stupid halo?" Henry asked, gazing balefully at Lissie, who pressed past her father to bounce into the kitchen.

"Henry," Addie said in soft reprimand. He wasn't usually a difficult child, but under the present circumstances . . .

"You're just jealous," Lissie said with cheerful confidence, striking a pose.

Frank set his coffee mug on the counter with an authoritative thump. "Lissandra," he said. "Be nice."

"Well, he is," Lissie countered.

"Am not," Henry insisted, digging in his heels and folding his arms. "And your hair is poofy."

"Somebody open the box," Frank put in.

"My turn," Lissie announced, and dragged over the same chair Henry had used the day before. With appropriate ceremony, she tugged at the little ribbon-pull at the top of the matchbox and revealed the cotton-ball snowman inside. He still had his black top hat and bead eyes.

"We could build a snowman, after school," Lissie told Henry, inspired. "And my hair is not *either* poofy." She paused. "You *are* going to school, aren't you?"

Henry looked up at Addie. "Do I have to?"

She ruffled his hair, resisted an impulse to adjust his glasses. He hated it when she did that, and, anyway, it might call attention to the fact that he'd been crying. "I think you should," she said. She'd had him checked out at the Main Street Clinic the day before, and physically, he was fine. She had explained his situation to the doctor, and they'd agreed that the best thing to do was keep his life as normal as possible.

Henry sighed heavily. "Okay, I'll go. As long as I get to help build the snow-dude afterwards."

Frank refilled his coffee mug at the percolator and helped himself to a pastry. "Sounds like a fair deal to me," he said, munching. He looked at Addie over the top of Lissie's head. "You going to help? With the snowman, I mean?"

Addie flushed and rubbed her hands down the thighs of her jeans. "I really should look for a job."

"School doesn't get out until three," Lissie reasoned, climbing down from the chair. "That gives you plenty of time."

"I'll take a late lunch hour," Frank put in, offering Addie a bear claw. Her all-time favorite. Had he remembered that, or was it just coincidence? "I heard there was an opening over at the *Wooden Nickel*. Receptionist and classified ad sales."

Addie lowered the bear claw.

"Kind of a comedown from big-city journalism," Frank said. "But other than waitressing at the Lumberjack Diner, that's about all Pine Crossing has to offer in the way of employment."

She studied his face. So he did know, then—about what had happened in California. She wished she dared ask him how *much* he knew, but she didn't. Not with Lissie there, and Henry already so upset.

THE 24 DAYS OF CHRISTMAS   271

"I'll take the kids to school," Frank went on, raising
Addie's hand, pastry and all, back to her mouth even as he
turned to the kids. "Hey, Hank," he said. "How'd you like
a ride in a squad car?"

The snow was still drifting down, in big, fat, pristine
flakes, when Addie set out for the *Wooden Nickel,* armed
with a truthful résumé and high hopes. The *Nickel* wasn't
really a newspaper, just a supermarket giveaway, but that
didn't mean the editor wouldn't have heard about her ex-
ploits in California. Even though the job probably didn't
involve writing anything but copy for classified ads, she
might be considered a bad risk.

The wheels of the Buick crunched in the mounting
snow as she pulled up in front of the small storefront
where the *Wooden Nickel* was published. Like most of the
businesses in town, it faced the square, where a large,
bare evergreen tree had been erected.

She smiled. The lighting of the tree was a big deal in
Pine Crossing, right up there with the pageant at St.
Mary's. Henry would probably enjoy it, and the festivities
might even take his mind off his father's disinterest, if
only for an evening.

Her smile faded. *Call him, Toby,* she pleaded silently.
Please call him.

Mr. Renfrew was the editor of the *Wooden Nickel,* just
as he had been when Addie was a child. He beamed as she
stepped into the office, brushing snow from the sleeves of
her coat.

"Addie Hutton!" he cried, looking like Santa, even in
his flannel shirt and woolen trousers, as he came out from
behind the counter. "It's wonderful to see you again!"

He hugged her, and she hugged him back. "Thanks,"
she said after swallowing.

"Frank was by a little while ago. Said you might be in the market for a job."

It was just like Frank to try and pave the way. Addie didn't know whether to be annoyed or appreciative, and decided she was both. "I brought a résumé," she said. She had only a few hundred dollars in her checking account, until the money from the sale of her furniture and other personal belongings came through from the auction house in California, and now there was Henry to think about.

She needed work.

"No need for anything like that," Mr. Renfrew said with a wave of his plump, age-spotted hand. "I've known you all your life, Addie. Knew your father for most of his." He paused, frowned. "I can't pay you much, though. You realize that, don't you?"

Addie smiled, nodded. Her eyes were burning again.

"Then it's settled. You can start tomorrow. Nine o'clock sharp."

"Thank you," Addie said, almost overcome. Her salary at the *Wooden Nickel* probably wouldn't have covered her gym membership back home, but she blessed every penny of it.

Mr. Renfrew gave her a tour of the small operation and showed her which of the three desks was hers.

When she stepped back out into the cold, Frank just happened to be loitering on the sidewalk, watching as members of the volunteer fire department strung lights on the community tree from various rungs of the truck ladder.

Addie poked him good-naturedly in the back. "You put in a good word for me, didn't you?" she accused. "With Mr. Renfrew, I mean."

Frank grinned down at her. "Maybe I did," he admitted. "Truth is, he didn't need much persuading. How about a cup of coffee over at the Lumberjack?"

She looked pointedly at the mug in his right hand. "Looks as if you carry your own," she teased.

Something changed in his face, something so subtle that she might have missed it if she hadn't been looking so closely, trying to read him. Then his grin broadened, and he upended the cup, dumping the dregs of his coffee into a snowbank. "I guess I need a refill," he said.

They walked to the diner, on the opposite side of the square, Frank exchanging gruff male greetings with the light-stringing firemen as they passed.

Inside the diner, they took seats in a booth, and the waitress filled Frank's mug automatically, before turning over the clean cup in front of Addie and pouring a serving for her.

"What happened in California?" Frank asked bluntly, when they were alone.

Addie looked out into the square, watching the firemen and the passersby, and her hand trembled a little as she raised the cup to her mouth. "I made a mistake," she said, after a long time, when she could meet his eyes again. "A really stupid one."

"You've never done anything stupid in your life," Frank said.

Except when I gave back your engagement ring, Addie thought, and immediately backed away from that memory. "That's debatable." She sighed. "I got a tip on a big scandal brewing in the city attorney's office," she said miserably. "I checked and rechecked the facts, but I should have *triple*-checked them. I wrote an article that shook the courthouse from top to bottom. I was nearly jailed when I wouldn't reveal my source—and then that source turned out to be a master liar. People's reputations and careers were damaged. My newspaper was sued, and I was fired."

Frank shook his head. "Must have been rough."

Addie bit her lower lip, then squared her shoulders. "It was," she admitted solemnly. "Thanks to you, I have a job and a place to live." She leaned forward. "We have to talk about rent, Frank."

He leaned forward, too. "That whole place should have been yours. I'm not going to charge you rent."

"It should have been Eliza's, and she left it to you," Addie insisted. "And I *am* going to pay rent. If you refuse, I'll move."

He grinned. "Good luck finding anything in Pine Crossing," he said.

She slumped back in her seat. "I'm paying. You need the money. You can't possibly be making very much."

He lifted his cup to his mouth, chuckled. "Still stubborn as hell, I see," he observed. "And it just so happens that I do all right, from a financial standpoint anyway." He set the mug down again, regarded her thoughtfully. "Tell me about the boy," he said.

She smiled at the mention of Henry. For all the problems, it was a blessing having him with her, a gift. She loved him desperately—he was the child she might never have. She was thirty-five, after all, and her life was a train wreck. "Henry is my stepson. His father and I were badly matched, and the marriage came crashing down under its own weight a couple of years ago. I fell out of love with Toby, but Henry is still my man."

"He seems troubled," Frank remarked. The diner's overhead lights shimmered in his dark hair and on the broad shoulders of his jacket. Danced along the upper half of his badge.

"My ex-husband isn't the most responsible father in the world. He remarried recently, and evidently, the new

Mrs. Springer is not inclined to raise another woman's child. Toby brought him as far as Denver by plane, then put him on a bus, like so much freight. Henry came all that way alone. He must have been so scared."

Frank's jawline tightened, and a flush climbed his neck. "Tell your ex-husband," he muttered, "never to break the speed limit in my town."

While Floyd the beagle galloped around the snowman in ever-widening circles, barking joyously at falling flakes, Henry and Lissie pressed small stones into Frosty's chest, and Addie added the finishing touch: one of Frank's old baseball caps.

The moment was so perfect that it worried Frank a little.

He was telling himself not to be a fool when Almira Pidgett's vintage Desoto ground up to the curb. She leaned across the seat, rolled down the passenger window, and glowered through the snowfall.

"Well," she called, raising her voice several decibels above shrill to be heard over the happy beagle, "it's nice to see our chief of police hard at work, making our community safe from crime."

Lissie and Henry went still, and some of the delight drained from Addie's face. Out of the corner of his eye, Frank saw Lissie straighten her halo.

You old bat, Frank thought, but he smiled as he strolled toward the Desoto, his hands in the pockets of his uniform jacket. "Hello, Miss Pidgett," he said affably, bending to look through the open window. "Care to help us finish our snowman?"

"Hmmph," she said. "Is that Addie Hutton over there? I must say, she doesn't look much the worse for wear, for someone who almost went to prison."

Frank's smile didn't waver, even though he would have liked to reach across that seat and close both hands around Almira's neck. "You ought to work up a little Christmas spirit, Miss Pidgett," he said. "If you don't, you might just be visited by three spirits one of these nights, like old Ebenezer Scrooge."

CHAPTER FOUR

"It's a Christmas tree," Henry announced importantly, the following morning, after opening the fourth box. Frank had lifted him onto the counter for the unveiling. "Are *we* going to get a Christmas tree, Addie?"

"Sure," Addie said, a little too quickly. Her smile felt wobbly on her face. There had still been no call from Toby, no response to her barrage of e-mails and phone messages. And every day that Henry stayed with her would make it that much more difficult, when the time came, to give him up.

"It's too early for a tree," Lissie said practically, watching as Henry scrambled down off the counter with no help from Frank. She looked especially festive that day, having replaced the snow-soaked gold tinsel in her halo with bright silver. "The needles will fall off."

"We had a fake one in California," Henry said. "It was made of the same stuff as that thing on your head, so the needles *never* fell off. We could have left it up till the Fourth of July."

"That's stupid," Lissie responded. "Who wants a Christmas tree on the Fourth of July?"

"Liss," Frank said. "Throwing the word 'stupid' around is conduct unbecoming to an angel."

The little girl sighed hugely. "It's useless trying to be an angel anyway," she said. "I guess I'm going to be a shepherd for the rest of my life."

Addie straightened Lissie's halo. "Nonsense," she said, suppressing a smile. "I think it's safe to say that you most certainly will not be a shepherd three weeks from now."

Outside, in the driveway, a horn bleated out one cheery little honk.

"Car pool," Frank explained when Addie lifted her eyebrows in question.

She hastened to zip Henry into his coat. He endured this fussing with characteristic stoicism, and when he and Lissie had gone, Frank lingered to refill his cup at the percolator.

"No word from Wonder Dad, huh?" he asked.

Addie shook her head. "How can he do this, Frank?" she muttered miserably. "How can he just *not call*? For all he knows, Henry never arrived, or I wasn't here when he did."

"He knows," Frank said easily. "You've been calling and e-mailing, haven't you?"

Addie nodded, pulling on her coat and reaching for her purse. She wanted to get to work early, show Mr. Renfrew she was dependable. "But he hasn't answered."

"And you think that means he didn't get the messages?"

Addie paused in the act of unplugging the coffeepot. Frank had a point. Toby was a master at avoiding confrontation, not to mention personal responsibility. He wouldn't call, or even respond to her e-mails, until he was sure she'd had time enough to cool off.

She sighed. "You're right," she said.

Frank gave her a crooked grin and spread his hands.

"Are we still on for the tree-lighting ceremony tonight?" he asked.

Addie nodded, glanced at the Advent calendar, with its four open boxes. Twenty to go. "Have you noticed a pattern?" she asked. "I mean, maybe I'm being fanciful here, but the first day, there was a teddy bear. Henry was carrying a bear when he got off the bus. Then—okay, the ballerina doesn't fit the theory—but yesterday was the snowman. We built one. And today, it's the Christmas tree, and the shindig at the square just happens to be tonight."

Frank put a hand to the small of her back and gently propelled her toward the doorway. "The bear," he said, "was pure coincidence. The snowman gave the kids the idea to build one. And the fire department always lights the tree three weeks before Christmas."

They'd crossed the living room, and Frank opened the front door to a gust of dry, biting wind. Addie pulled her coat more tightly around her. "All very practical," she said with a tentative smile, "but I heard you tell Miss Pidgett she might be visited by three spirits some night soon. If that's not fanciful, I don't know what is."

They descended the steps, and Frank didn't smile at her remark. He seemed distracted. "Lissie really wants that part," he fretted. "The one in the pageant at St. Mary's, I mean. And Almira isn't going to give it to her, not because the kid couldn't pull it off, but because she doesn't like me."

Addie thought of Lissie's tinsel halo and felt a pinch of sorrow in the deepest region of her heart. "Maybe if you talked to Miss Pidgett, explained—"

Frank stopped beside his squad car, which was parked in the driveway, beside Addie's station wagon. "I can't do that, Addie," he said quietly. "I'm the chief of police. I can't ask the woman to do my kid a favor."

She touched his arm. Started to say that *she* could

speak to Miss Pidgett, and promptly closed her mouth. She knew how Frank would react to that suggestion; he'd say she was over the line, and he'd be right.

Frank surprised her. He leaned forward and kissed her lightly on the forehead. "Thanks, Addie," he said.

"For what?"

"For coming home."

CHAPTER FIVE

Addie stopped on the sidewalk outside the *Wooden Nickel,* at eight forty-five A.M. precisely, to admire the glowing tree in the center of the square. She hoped she would never forget the reflection of those colored lights shining on Henry and Lissie's upturned faces the night before. After the celebration, they'd all gone back to Frank's place for spaghetti and hot cocoa, and Addie had been amazed that she didn't so much as hesitate on the threshold.

When she and her father had lived there, the very walls had seemed to echo with loneliness, except when Eliza or Frank were around.

Now another father and daughter occupied the space. The furniture was different, of course, but so was the atmosphere. Sorrow had visited those rooms, leaving its mark, but despite that, the house seemed to exude warmth, stability—love.

A rush of cold wind brought Addie abruptly back to the present moment. She shivered and pushed open the front door of the *Wooden Nickel,* and very nearly sent Mr. Renfrew sprawling.

He was teetering on top of a foot ladder, affixing a silver bell above the door.

Addie gasped and reached out to steady her employer. "I'm sorry!" she cried.

Mr. Renfrew grinned down at her. "What do you think of the bell?" he asked proudly. "It belonged to my grandmother."

Addie put a hand to her heart. The bell was silver, with a loop of red ribbon attached to the top.

"What's the matter?" Mr. Renfrew asked, getting down from the ladder.

In her mind's eye, Addie was seeing the little bell in the Christmas box Lissie had opened that morning. Silver, with red thread.

She smiled. "Nothing at all," she said happily, unbuttoning her coat. "It looks wonderful."

"There's a phone message for you, Addie," put in Stella Dorrity, who worked part-time helping Mr. Renfrew with the ad layouts. "He left a number."

Addie felt her smile fade. "Thank you," she said, reaching out for the sticky note Stella offered.

Toby. Where on earth had he gotten her work number? She'd only been hired the day before.

Shakily, she hung up her coat and fished her cell phone out of her purse. "Do you mind if I return the call before I start work?" she asked Mr. Renfrew.

"You go right ahead," he said, still admiring his bell.

"You'd better move that ladder," Stella told him, arms folded, "before somebody breaks their neck."

Addie slipped into the cramped little room behind the reception desk, where the copy machine, lunch table, and a small refrigerator stood shoulder to shoulder.

She punched in the number Stella had taken down, not recognizing the area code.

Toby answered on the third ring. "Yo," he said.

"It's about time you bothered to check up on your son!" Addie whispered.

A sigh. "I knew you'd take care of him."

"He's scared to death," Addie sputtered. "When I saw him get off that bus, all alone—"

"You were there," Toby broke in. "That's what matters."

"What if I hadn't been, Toby? Did you ever think of that?"

"Listen to me, Addie. I know you're furious, and I guess you have a right to be. But I had to do something. The blended-family thing isn't working for Elle."

Addie closed her eyes, counted to ten, then to fifteen, for good measure. Even then, she wanted to take Toby's head off at the shoulders. "Isn't *that* a pity? Tell me, Tobe, did you think about any of this before you decided to tie the knot?"

"It's love, babe," Toby said lightly. "Will you keep him—just until Elle and I get settled in?"

"He's a little boy, not a goldfish!"

"I know, I know. He wants to be with you, anyway. Do this for me, Addie—please. I'm out of options, here. I'll straighten everything out with him when we get back from—when we get back."

"What am I supposed to tell Henry in the meantime? He needs to talk to you. Damn it, *you're his father.*"

"I'll send him a postcard."

"A postcard? Well, that's generous of you. It's almost Christmas, you've just shipped him almost two hundred miles on a Greyhound, all by himself, and you're going to *send a postcard*?"

Another sigh. Toby, the martyred saint. "Add, what do you want me to do?"

"I want you to call him. *Tonight,* Toby. Not when you get back from your stupid honeymoon. I want you to tell Henry you love him, and that everything will be all right."

"I do love him."

"Your idea of love differs significantly from mine," Addie snapped.

"Don't I know it," Toby replied. "All right. Let's have the number. I'll give the kid a ring around six, your time."

"You'd better, Toby."

She knew he wanted to ask what she would do about it if he didn't. She also knew he wouldn't dare.

"Six o'clock," he said with resignation, and hung up in her ear.

"I think Lissie sleeps in that dumb halo," Henry observed that night as he sat coloring at the kitchen table. Addie was at the stove, whipping up a stir-fry, and even though she had one ear tuned to the phone, she was startled when it actually rang. She glanced at the clock on the opposite wall.

Six o'clock, straight up.

"Could you get that, please?" she asked.

Henry gave her a curious look and stalwartly complied.

"Hello?"

Watching the boy out of the corner of her eye, Addie saw him stiffen.

"Hi, Dad."

Addie bit her lip and concentrated on the stir-fry, but she couldn't help listening to Henry's end of the conversation. Toby, she could tell, was making his stock excuses. Henry, playing his own customary role, made it easy.

"Sure," he finished. "I'll tell her. See you."

"Everything cool?" she asked carefully.

Henry adjusted his glasses. "I might get to stay till February. Maybe even until school lets out for the summer."

Addie dealt with a tangle of feelings—exhilaration, annoyance, dread and more annoyance—before assembling a smile and turning to face the little boy. "Is that okay with you?"

Henry grinned, nodded. "Yeah," he said. "Maybe he'll forget where he put me, and I'll get to stay forever."

Although she wanted to keep Henry for good, Addie felt a stab at his words. He was so young, and the concept that his own father might misplace him, like a set of keys or a store receipt, was already a part of his thought system.

She dished up two platefuls of stir-fry and set them on the table. "We have to take this one step at a time," she warned. Toby was a creature of moods, changeable and impulsive. If things went badly with Elle, or if the new wife was struck by a sudden maternal desire, Toby might swoop down at any moment and whisk Henry away, once and for all.

"Do you think she sleeps in it?" Henry asked, settling himself at the table.

Addie was a few beats behind. "What?"

"Lissie," Henry said patiently, reaching for his fork. "Do you think she sleeps in that halo?"

CHAPTER SIX

Seated at her desk, the telephone receiver propped between her left shoulder and her ear, Addie doodled as she waited for her sales prospect, Jackie McCall, of Mc-Call Real Estate, to come back on the line. A holly wreath, like the one in that morning's matchbox, took shape at the point of her pencil.

The bell over the front door jingled, and Almira Pidgett blew into the *Wooden Nickel,* red-cheeked and rushed. Her hat, with its fur earflaps, made her look as though she should have arrived in a motorcycle sidecar or a Model T—all she lacked was goggles.

Alone in the office, Addie put down her pencil, cupped a hand over the receiver, and summoned up a smile. "Good morning," she said. "May I help you?"

"Where," demanded Miss Pidgett, "is Arthur?"

Addie held on to the smile with deliberation. "Mr. Renfrew had a Rotary meeting this morning. He's in the banquet room at the Lumberjack."

Miss Pidgett, plump and white-haired, had been an institution in Pine Crossing for as long as Addie could remember. She had been Addie's teacher, in both the first and second grades, but, unlike Lissie, and Frank, for that matter, Addie had always enjoyed the woman's favor. She'd played an angel three years in a row, at the Christmas pageant, and graduated to the starring role, that of Mary, before going on to high school.

Now Miss Pidgett sighed and tugged off her knit gloves. "I wish to place an advertisement," she announced.

Jackie McCall came back on the line. "Sorry to keep you waiting, Addie," she said. "It's crazy over here. Would you mind if I called you back?"

"That would be convenient," Addie replied.

Miss Pidgett waited, none too patiently, at the counter, while Addie and Jackie exchanged good-byes and hung up.

"I don't think it's proper for you to spend so much time with Frank Raynor," the older woman blurted out, her expression grim.

Addie took a deep breath. Smiled harder. "Frank is an old friend of mine," she said. "Now, about that advertisement—"

"He's an outsider," Miss Pidgett insisted.

"He's lived in Pine Crossing for thirty years," Addie pointed out.

"His mother was the town tramp," Miss Pidgett went on, lowering her voice to a stage whisper. "God knows who his father was. Anybody but Eliza Raynor would have refused to take him in, after all that happened."

Addie felt a flush climb her neck. She couldn't afford to tell Miss Pidgett off, but she wanted to. "I don't know what you're talking about," she said, approaching the counter. "Were you interested in a classified ad, or something larger?"

"Full page," Miss Pidgett said, almost as an aside. "Don't tell me you didn't know that Janet Raynor ran away with Eliza's husband. That's why they have the same last name."

"I *didn't* know," Addie said carefully, feeling bereft. "And I don't think—"

Miss Pidgett cut her off. "Your father hired Eliza out of the goodness of his heart. She was destitute, after her Jim and that trollop ran off to Mexico together. They got a quickie divorce, and Jim actually *married* the woman, if you can believe it. A few years later, he ditched her, and Janet had the nerve to send that boy to live with Eliza."

Addie's face warmed. Oh, well, she thought. She could always apply for a waitress job at the Lumberjack. "I didn't know any of those things," she reiterated quietly, "but it doesn't surprise me to learn that Eliza took in a lonely, frightened little boy and loved him like her own. After all, none of what happened was Frank's fault, was it?"

Miss Pidgett reddened. "Eliza was a fool."

"Eliza," Addie corrected, "was the kindest and most generous woman I have ever known. You, on the other hand, are an insufferable gossip." She paused, drew another deep breath. "If I were you, I'd keep a sharp eye out for the ghosts of Christmas past, present, and future!"

"Well!" Miss Pidgett cried, and turned on the heel of one snow boot to stomp out the door.

The bell over the door jangled frantically at her indignant departure.

Mr. Renfrew, just returning from his Rotary breakfast, nearly collided with Miss Pidgett on the sidewalk. Through the glass, Addie saw the old woman shake a finger under his nose, her breath coming in visible puffs as she ranted, then stormed off.

"I'll be darned if I could make heads or tails of what *that* was all about," Mr. Renfrew observed when he came inside. He looked affably baffled, and his ears were crimson from the cold. "Something about taking her business to the *Statesman*."

"I'm afraid I told her off," Addie confessed. "I'll understand if you fire me."

"The old bat," Frank said at six o'clock that evening as he hung a fragrant evergreen wreath on Addie's front door, after listening to her account of Miss Pidgett's visit to the *Wooden Nickel*. The children were in the yard below, running in wild, noisy, arm-waving circles around the snowman, joyously pursued by Floyd the beagle.

Addie hugged herself against the chill of a winter night and gazed up at Frank, perplexed. "No one ever told me," she said. "About your mother and Eliza's husband, I mean."

Frank gave her a sidelong glance. "Old news, kid," he said. "Not the kind of experience Aunt Eliza would have shared with her employer's little girl."

"There must have been so much gossip. How could I have missed hearing it?"

He touched the tip of her nose, and Addie felt a jolt of sensation, right down to her heels. "You were Judge Hutton's daughter. That shielded you from a lot."

Addie bit her lower lip. "I'm so sorry, Frank."

He frowned, taking an unlikely interest in the wreath. "About what?"

"About all you must have gone through. When you were little, I mean."

He turned to face her, spread his hands, and spared her a crooked grin. "Do I look traumatized?" he asked. "Believe me, after five years of sitting outside bars, waiting for my mother, the gossips of Pine Crossing were nothing. Aunt Eliza loved me. She made sure I had three square meals a day, sent me to school with decent clothes on my back, and taught me to believe in myself. I'd say I was pretty lucky."

Addie looked away, blinked, and looked back. "I was so jealous of you," she said.

He touched her again, laying his hand to the side of her face, and the same shock went through her. The wheels and gears of time itself seemed to grind to a halt, and he bent his head toward hers.

"Daddy!"

They froze.

"Damn," Frank said, his breath tingling against Addie's mouth.

She laughed, and they both looked down to see Lissie gazing up at them from the yard, hands on her hips, tinsel halo picking up the last glimmers of daylight. Henry was beside Lissie, the lenses of his glasses opaque with steam.

"You can't kiss unless there's mistletoe!" Lissie called.

"Says who?" Frank called back. Then, to everyone's surprise, he took Addie's face in his hands, tilted her head back, and kissed her soundly.

Afterward, she stared up at him, speechless.

CHAPTER SEVEN

"A shepherd," Henry said when the matchbox was opened the next morning. Lissie peered in, as if doubting his word. Frank had brought the child to Addie's door before dawn that morning, haloed, still in her pajamas and wrapped in a blanket. There had been an automobile accident out on the state highway, and he had to go.

"Hurry up, both of you," Addie replied with an anxious glance at the clock. "I don't want to be late for work." To her way of thinking, she was lucky she still had a job, after the scene with Miss Pidgett the day before.

An hour later, Frank showed up at the *Wooden Nickel,* looking tired and gaunt. He filled his coffee mug from the pot in the small break room. "Where is everybody?" he asked, scanning the office, which was empty except for him and Addie.

"Mr. Renfrew had a doctor's appointment, and Stella went to Denver with her sister to shop for Christmas presents," Addie said. The office, never spacious to begin with, seemed to shrink to the size of a broom closet, with Frank taking up more than his share of space.

Frank rubbed the back of his neck with one hand and

sighed before taking a sip of his coffee. "Hope she's careful," he said. "The roads are covered with black ice."

Addie waited.

"The accident was bad," he told her grimly. "Four people airlifted to Denver. One of them died on the way."

"Oh, Frank." Addie wanted to round the counter and put her arms around him, but she hesitated. Sure, he'd kissed her the evening before, but now he had the look of a man who didn't want to be touched. "Was it anyone you know?"

He shook his head. "Thanks for taking care of Lissie," he said after a long silence. He was staring into his coffee cup now, as though seeing an uncertain future take shape there.

"Anytime," Addie replied gently. "You okay?"

He made an attempt at a smile. "I will be," he said gruffly. "It just takes a while to get the images out of my head."

Addie nodded.

"Have supper with us tonight?" Frank asked. He sounded shy, the way he had when he asked her to his senior prom, all those eventful years ago. "Miss Pidgett is casting the play today. I figure Lissie is going to need some diversion."

Addie ached for the little girl, and for the good man who loved her so much. "My turn to cook," she said softly. "I'll stop by St. Mary's and pick up the kids on my way home." There was no daycare center in Pine Crossing, so the children of working parents gathered in either the library or the gym until someone came to collect them.

"Thanks," Frank said. He was on the verge of saying something else when Mr. Renfrew came in.

The two men exchanged greetings, and the telephone

rang. Addie took down an order for a classified ad, and when she looked up from her notes, Frank was gone.

"Nice guy, that Frank," Mr. Renfrew said, shrugging off his overcoat.

"Yes," Addie agreed, hoping she sounded more casual than she felt.

"Miss Pidgett been back to place her ad?"

Addie felt a rush of guilt. "No," she said. "Mr. Renfrew, I'm—"

He held up a hand to silence her. "Don't say you're sorry, Addie. It was about time somebody put that old grump in her place."

With that, the subject of Almira Pidgett was dropped.

Henry raced toward the car when Addie pulled up outside the elementary school that afternoon, waving what looked like a brown bathrobe over his head. Lissie followed at a slower pace, head down, scuffing her feet in the dried snow. Even her tinsel halo seemed to sag a little.

Addie's heart went out to the child. She pushed open the car door and stood in the road.

"I'm a shepherd!" Henry shouted jubilantly.

Addie ruffled his hair. "Good job," she said, pleased because he was so excited. She watched Lissie's slow approach.

"I'm the innkeeper's wife," the little girl said, looking wretched. "I don't even get to say anything. My *whole part* is to stand there and look mean and shake my head 'no' when Mary and Joseph ask for a room."

Addie crouched, took Lissie's cold little hands in hers. "I'm so sorry, sweetie. You would have made a perfect angel."

A tear slipped down Lissie's right cheek, quivered on

the shoulder of her pink nylon jacket. It was all Addie could do in that moment not to storm into the school and give Miss Pidgett a piece of her mind.

"Tiffany Baker gets to be the most important angel," Lissie said. "She has a whole bunch of lines about good tidings and stuff, and her mother is making her wings out of *real* feathers."

Addie stood up, steered the children toward the car.

"That sucks," Henry said. "Tiffany Baker sucks."

"Henry," Addie said.

"Last year she got to go to Denver and be in a TV commercial," Lissie said as she and Henry got into the backseat and fastened their seat belts. In the rearview mirror, Addie saw Lissie's lower lip wobble.

"There are six other angels," the little girl whispered. "I wouldn't have minded being one of them."

Addie had to fight hard not to cry herself. The child had been wearing a tinsel halo for days. Didn't Almira Pidgett have a heart?

"Maybe we could rent some Christmas movies," she suggested in deliberately cheerful tones.

Lissie pulled off her halo, held it for a moment, then set it aside. "Okay," she said with a complete lack of spirit.

CHAPTER EIGHT

Frank shoved a hand through his hair. "It's been nine days," he whispered to Addie in her kitchen that snowy Saturday morning. "I thought Lissie would be over this play thing by now. Is it really such a bad thing to play the innkeeper's wife?"

Addie glanced sadly at the Advent calendar, still taped to the bottom of the cupboard. Lissie hadn't shown much interest in the daily ritual of opening a new matchbox since the angel disappointment, and that morning was no exception. The tiny sleigh glued inside looked oddly forlorn. "It is if you wanted to be an angel," she said.

"I haven't seen her like this since Maggie died."

Addie sank into a chair at the table. Frank, leaning one shoulder against the refrigerator and sipping coffee, sighed.

"I wish there was something I could do," Addie said.

"Join the club," Frank replied, glancing toward the living room. Henry and Lissie were there, with the ever-faithful Floyd, watching Saturday morning cartoons.

"Sit down, Frank," Addie urged quietly.

He didn't seem to hear her. He was staring out the window at the fat, drifting flakes of snow that had been falling since the night before. "This isn't about Lissie," he said. "That's what makes it so hard. It's about me, and all the times I've butted heads with Almira Pidgett over the years."

Addie's mouth tightened at the mention of the woman, and she consciously relaxed it. "It's not your fault, Frank," she said, and closed her hands around her own coffee cup, grown cold since the pancake breakfast the four of them had shared half an hour before. "Miss Pidgett is a Grinch, plain and simple."

Just then, Addie thought she heard sleigh bells, and she was just shaking her head when a whoop of delight sounded from the living room. Henry. Henry, who was wary of joy, already knowing, young as he was, how easily it could be taken away.

"There's a man down there, driving a sleigh!" Henry shouted, almost breathless with glee. "He's got horses pulling it, instead of reindeer, but he sure looks like Santa!"

"Who?" Frank asked, pleasantly bemused.

Addie was already on her way to investigate. Henry was bounding down the outside stairs, followed by Floyd, and, at a more sedate pace, Lissie. Frank brought up the rear.

Mr. Renfrew, bundled in a stocking cap, ski jacket, and quilted trousers, all the same shade of red, waved cheerfully from the seat of a horse-drawn sleigh.

"Merry Christmas!" he called. "Anybody want a ride?"

Henry was jumping up and down. "I do!" he shouted. "I do!"

"Can Floyd come, too?" Lissie asked cautiously.

Mr. Renfrew's eyes twinkled as he looked over the children's heads to Frank and Addie. "Of course," he answered. Then, in a booming voice, he added, "Don't just stand there! Go put on your cold-weather gear and jump in!"

CHAPTER NINE

There were two bench seats in the back of that old-fashioned sleigh, upholstered in patched leather and facing each other.

"Want to ride up here with me, boy?" Mr. Renfrew asked Henry, his eyes twinkling.

Henry needed no persuading. He scrambled onto the high seat, fairly quivering with excitement. "Can Lissie have a turn, too?" he asked, his breath forming a thin, shifting aura of white around his head.

A sweet, almost painful, warmth settled over Addie's heart. She glanced at Frank, who hoisted the overweight beagle into the sleigh to join Lissie, who was already seated, facing backward.

"Sure, Lissie can have a turn," Mr. Renfrew said, turning to smile down at the child.

Lissie, who had been subdued since putting away her tinsel halo, perked up a little, grinning back at him. Floyd, perched beside her, gave her an exuberant lick on the cheek.

Frank helped Addie up into the sleigh, then sat down

beside her, stretching his arm out along the back of the seat, the way a shy teenage boy might do on a movie date. He wasn't quite touching her, but she felt the strength and substance and warmth of him just the same, a powerful tingle along her nape and the length of her shoulders. The energy danced down her spine and arched between her pelvic bones.

It was all she could do not to squirm.

Mr. Renfrew set the sleigh in motion, bells jingling. There was a jerk, but then they glided, as though the whole earth had suddenly turned smooth as a skating rink. Addie bit down on her lower lip and tried to focus on the ride, wincing a little as Lissie turned to kneel in the seat, her back to them, ready to climb up front when she got the nod.

"Addie." Frank's voice. Very close to her ear. Fat snowflakes drifted down, making silent music.

She made herself look at him, not in spite of her reluctance, but *because* of it. The decision was a ripple on the surface of something much deeper, churning far down in the whorls and currents of her mind.

"Relax," he said. "You think too much."

Some reckless sprite rose up out of that emotional sea to put words in Addie's mouth. "You might not say that if you knew what I was thinking *about*."

Frank lowered his arm, let it rest lightly around her shoulders. "Who says I don't?" he countered, with a half grin and laughter in his eyes. But there was sadness there, too, and something that might have been caution. Perhaps, like Henry, Frank was a little afraid to trust in good things.

Addie blushed and looked away.

They rode over side streets and back roads, and finally left Pine Crossing behind, entering the open countryside. After getting permission from both Addie and Frank, Mr.

Renfrew let Henry drive the team, then Lissie. The snow came down harder, and the wind grew colder, and Floyd alternately barked and howled in canine celebration.

Addie had a wonderful time. Something had changed between her and Frank, a subtle, indefinable shift that gave her an odd thrill, a feeling both festive and frightening. She decided to think about it later, when Frank and Lissie weren't around, and Henry had gone to bed.

After an hour or so, they returned to Pine Crossing, traveling down the middle of the main street, between parked cars. Frank sat up very straight, looking imperious and waving in the stiff-handed way of royalty as various friends called amused greetings from the sidewalks.

Lissie climbed back down into the seat beside Floyd as they passed the school, and Addie noticed the deflation in the child's mood. Her small shoulders sagged as she looked at the reader board in front of St. Mary's.

PLAY REHEARSAL TONIGHT, 6 PM
MARY, JOSEPH AND ANGELS ONLY.

Addie bristled inwardly. The sign was obviously Almira's handiwork, and it might as well have said, *Innkeeper's wife will be turned away at the door.*

"No room at the inn," she murmured angrily.

Frank squeezed her hand, so she knew he'd heard, but he was watching Lissie, who sat with her head down, obviously fighting tears, while Floyd nibbled tentatively at the pom-pom on top of her pink knitted cap.

"Life is hard sometimes, Liss," Frank said quietly. "It's okay to feel bad for a while, but sooner or later, you've got to let go and move on."

Addie's throat tightened. She wanted to take the child in her arms, hold her, tell her everything would be all right, but it wasn't her place. Frank was Lissie's father.

She, on the other hand, was little more than an acquaintance.

They passed Pine Crossing General Hospital, then the Sweet Haven Nursing Home. An idea rapped at the backdoor of Addie's brain; she let it in and looked it over.

She barely noticed when they pulled up in front of the house.

Frank got out of the sleigh first, helped Addie, Lissie, and the dog down, then reached up to claim Henry from the driver's seat. Everyone thanked Mr. Renfrew profusely, and Frank invited him in for coffee, but he declined, saying he had things to do at home. Almost Christmas, you know.

"Better get Floyd inside and give him some kibble," Frank told his daughter, laying a hand on her shoulder. "All those snowflakes he ate probably won't hold him long."

Lissie smiled a little, nodded, and grabbed Henry by the arm. "Come on and help me," she said. "I'll show you where we're going to put up the Christmas tree."

Addie thrust her hands into the pockets of her coat and waited until the children were out of earshot. "What if there were more than one way to be an angel?" she asked.

Frank pulled his jacket collar up a little higher, squinted at her. "Huh?"

"You kept so many of Eliza's things," Addie said, looking up at him. If they'd had any sense, they'd have gone in out of the cold. "Do you still have her sewing machine?"

"Maggie used it for mending," Frank answered with a slight nod, and then looked as though he regretted mentioning his late wife's name. "Why?"

"I'd like to borrow it, please."

Frank looked at his watch. "Okay," he said. "What's this about?"

Having noted the time-checking, Addie answered with a question. "Do you have to work tonight, Frank?"

"Town council meeting," he said. "That's why I didn't suggest dinner."

"I'll be happy to look after Lissie and Floyd until you get home," she told him, so he wouldn't have to ask. But she was already on her way to the steps leading up to her over-the-garage apartment.

Frank caught up with her, looking benignly curious. "Wait a second," he said. "There's something brewing, and I'd like to know what it is."

"Maybe you'll just have to be surprised," Addie responded, watching as snowflakes landed in Frank's dark hair and on his long eyelashes. "Right along with Miss Almira Pidgett."

Frank searched her face, looking cautiously amused. "Tell me you're not planning to whip up a trio of spirit costumes and pay her a midnight visit," he said. "Much as I love the idea, it would be trespassing, and breaking and entering, too. Not to mention harassment, stalking, and maybe even reckless endangerment."

Addie laughed, starting up the steps. "You have quite an imagination," she said. "Drop off the sewing machine before you leave for the meeting if you have time, okay?"

He spread his hands and then let them flop against his sides. "So much for my investigative skills," he said. "You're not going to tell me anything, are you?"

Addie paused, smiled, and batted her lashes. "No," she said. "I'm not."

CHAPTER TEN

"Why are we going to a thrift store?" Henry asked reasonably. He blinked behind his glasses, in that owlish way he had. He and Lissie were buckled in, in the back of Addie's station wagon, with Floyd panting between them, delighted to be included in the outing. Lissie was still very quiet; in the rearview mirror, Addie saw her staring forlornly out the window.

She flipped on the windshield wipers and peered through the increasing snowfall. The storm had been picking up speed since they got home from the sleigh ride with Mr. Renfrew, and now that dusk had fallen, visibility wasn't the best. "I plan to do some sewing, and I need material," Addie answered belatedly, wondering if they shouldn't just stay home.

Lissie showed some interest, at last. "Mom used to make my Halloween costumes out of stuff from the Goodwill," she said.

"I was Harry Potter Halloween before last," Henry said sadly, as Addie drew a deep breath, offered a silent prayer, and pulled out onto the road. "This year, Dad and Elle went to a costume party, but I didn't get to dress up."

Addie felt a pang of guilt, bit her lower lip. She'd thought of calling, inviting Henry to come trick-or-treating in her apartment complex, but she'd overruled the urge. After all, Toby and Elle had made it pretty clear, following all the publicity, that they didn't want her around Henry.

"With those glasses," Lissie remarked, perking up, "you wouldn't even need a costume to look like Harry Potter."

"I had a cape, too," Henry told her in a lofty tone. "Didn't I, Addie?"

Addie gazed intently over the top of the steering wheel. "Yes," she answered. Toby had dropped him off at her apartment that Halloween afternoon, a few months after their divorce became final, without calling first, flustered over some emergency at work. She'd fashioned the cape from an old shower curtain and taken him around the neighborhood with high hopes and a paper sack. They'd both had a great time.

"I was a hobo once," Lissie said. "When Mom was still alive, I mean. She bought an old suit and sewed patches on it and stuff. I had a broom handle with a bundle tied to the end, and I won a prize."

"Big deal," Henry said.

Addie pulled up to a stop sign intersecting the main street through town, and sighed with relief. The blacktop, though dusted with a thin coating of snow, had recently been plowed. She signaled and made a cautious left turn toward the center of Pine Crossing.

The lights of St. Mary's shimmered golden through the falling snow. Addie would have preferred not to pass the school, with the rehearsal going on and Lissie in the car, but it didn't make sense to risk the children's safety by taking unplowed side streets.

When they rolled up in front of the thrift store, at the opposite end of town, Lissie hooked a leash to Floyd's collar. She and Henry walked him in the parking lot while Addie hurried inside.

An artificial Christmas tree stood just inside the door, offering a cheerful if somewhat bedraggled welcome. Chipped ornaments hung from its crooked boughs, and a plastic star glowed with dim determination at its top.

I know just how you feel, Addie thought, as she passed the tree, scanning the store and zeroing in on the women's dresses.

She selected an old formal, a musty relic of some long-forgotten prom. The voluminous, floor-length underskirt was satin or taffeta, with the blue iridescence of a peacock feather.

"I don't think that will fit you," said a voice beside Addie, startling her a little. "It's a fourteen-sixteen, and you can't be bigger than an eight. But you can try it on if you want to."

Addie turned and smiled at the young girl standing beside her. Her name tag read, "Barbara," and she was chubby, with bad skin and stringy hair. "I just want the fabric," Addie said. "Is there anything here with pearl buttons? Or crystal beads?"

Barbara brightened a little. "Jessie Corcoran donated her wedding gown last week," she said. "It's real pretty. Her mom told my mom she ordered it special off the Internet." She paused, blushed. "I guess things didn't work out with that guy from Denver. For Jessie, I mean. Since she came back home to Pine Crossing one day and chucked the dress the next—"

"She might want it back," Addie mused.

Barbara shook her head, and her eyes widened behind the smudged lenses of her glasses. "She stuffed it right into the donation box, out there by the highway—my friend Becky saw her do it. Didn't even care if it got dirty, I guess. People dumped other stuff right in on top of it, too. A pair of old boots and a couple of puzzles with a lot of pieces missing."

"My goodness," Addie said.

Barbara produced the dress, ran a plump, reverent hand over the skirt. The bodice gleamed bravely with pearls and tiny glass beads. In its own way, the discarded wedding gown looked as forlorn as the Christmas tree at the front of the store.

"How much?" Addie asked.

Barbara didn't even have to look at the tag. "Twenty-five dollars," she said. "Are you getting married?"

Addie was taken aback, as much by the price as by the question. "Ordered special" or not, the dress was hardly haute couture.

Barbara smiled. "It's a small town," she said. "I guess you used to live in Frank Raynor's house. Now you're staying in the apartment over his garage and working at the *Wooden Nickel*. Down at the bowling alley—my mom plays on a league—they're saying Frank's been alone long enough. He needs a wife, and Lissie needs a mother."

Addie opened her mouth, closed it again. Shook her head. "No," she said.

"You don't want the dress?"

"No—I mean, yes. I *do* want the dress. I'll give you ten dollars for it. But there isn't going to be a wedding." She wanted to make sure this news got to the bowling league, from whence it would spread all over the county.

Barbara looked disappointed. "That's too bad," she said. "Everybody got their hopes up, for a while there. Fifteen dollars, and the dress is yours."

"I'm sorry," Addie said. She glanced toward the front windows bedecked in wilting garland, and thought of Lissie's halo, now a castoff, like Jessie Corcoran's wedding gown and the peacock-blue prom dress. "Fifteen dollars it is," she told Barbara. "I'd better hurry—the roads are probably getting worse by the moment."

Five minutes later, she was out the door, her purchases carefully folded and wrapped in a salvaged dry cleaner's bag. Henry, Lissie, and Floyd were already in the backseat of the station wagon.

"Buckle up," she told them, starting the engine.

"What did you buy in there?" Henry wanted to know.

"Secondhand dreams," Addie said. "With a little creativity, they can be good as new."

"How can dreams be secondhand?" Lissie asked, sounding both skeptical and intrigued.

Addie flipped on the headlights, watched the snowflakes dancing in the beams. "Sometimes people give up on them, because they don't fit anymore. Or they just leave them behind, for one reason or another. Then someone else comes along, finds them, and believes they might be worth something after all."

"That's really confusing," Henry said. "Can we stop for pizza?"

"No," Addie replied. "We've got beans and weenies at home."

"I wanted to be an angel," Lissie said, very softly. "That was my dream."

"I know," Addie answered.

It was after ten when Frank climbed the stairs to Addie's front door, listened for a moment to the faint whirring of his aunt's old sewing machine inside, and knocked lightly. Floyd let out a welcoming yelp, the machine stopped humming, and Frank heard Addie shushing the dog good-naturedly as she crossed the living room and peered out at him through the side window.

Her smile, blurred by the steamy glass, tugged at his heart.

"Shhh," she said, putting a finger to her lips as she opened the door. He wasn't sure if she was addressing him or Floyd. "Lissie's asleep in my room."

Frank stepped over the threshold, settled the dog with a few pats on the head and some ear ruffling, and eyed the sewing setup in the middle of the living room. Bright blue cloth billowed over the top of an old card table like a trapped cloud, the light from Eliza's machine shimmering along its folds.

He set Maggie's coffee mug aside, on the plant stand next to the door, and stuffed his hands into the pockets of his jacket. "Are you going to tell me what you're making, or is it still a secret?"

"It's still a secret," Addie answered with a grin. Her gaze flicked to the cup, then back to his face. "Do you want some coffee? I just brewed a pot of decaf a few minutes ago."

He hesitated. "Sure," he said.

"How did the meeting go?" Addie started toward the mug, then stopped. Frank handed it to her.

"Fine," he said.

"You look tired." Carrying the mug, she headed for the kitchen. "Long night?"

He stood on the threshold between the living room and the kitchen, gripping the doorframe, watching her pour the coffee. For an instant, he flashed back to that afternoon's sleigh ride, and the way it felt to put his arm around her shoulders. He shook off the memory, reached for the cup as she approached, holding it out. "Yeah," he said.

Hot coffee sloshed over his hand, and the mug slipped, tumbling end over end, shattering on the floor. The whole thing was over in seconds, but Frank would always remember it in slow motion.

Addie gasped, put one hand over her mouth.

Frank stared at the shards of Maggie's last gift, disbelieving.

"I'm sorry," Addie said. She grabbed a roll of paper towels.

He was already crouching, gathering the pieces. "It wasn't your fault, Addie." He couldn't look at her.

She squatted, a wad of towels in her hand, blotting up the flow of coffee. He stopped her gently, took over the job. When he stole a glance at her face, there were tears standing in her eyes.

"Maggie's cup," she whispered. He didn't remember telling her his wife had made the mug; maybe Lissie had.

"Don't," he said.

She nodded.

Floyd tried to lick up some of the spilled coffee, and Frank nudged him away with a slight motion of his elbow. He put the pieces of the cup into his pocket, straightened, and disposed of the paper towels in the trash can under the sink.

"Shall I wake Lissie up?" Addie asked tentatively, from somewhere at the periphery of Frank's vision.

He shook his head. "I'll do it," he said.

Lissie didn't awaken when he lifted her off Addie's bed, or even when he eased her into her coat.

"Thanks for taking care of her," he told Addie as he carried his sleeping daughter across the living room, Floyd scampering at his heels.

Addie nodded and opened the door for him, and a rush of cold air struck his face. Lissie shifted, opened her eyes, and yawned, and the fragments of Maggie's cup tinkled faintly in his pocket, like the sound of faraway bells.

An hour later, with Lissie settled in her own bed and Floyd curled up at her feet, Frank went into the kitchen and laid the shards of broken china out on the counter, in a jagged row. There was no hope of gluing the cup back together, but most of the bright red heart was there, chipped and cracked.

"Maggie," he whispered.

There was no answer, of course. She was gone.

He took the wastebasket from the cupboard under the sink, held it to the edge of the counter, and slowly swept the pieces into it. A crazy urge possessed him, an unreasonable desire to fish the bits out of the garbage, try to reassemble them after all. He shook his head, put the bin away, and left the kitchen, turning out the lights as he passed the switch next to the door.

The house was dark as he climbed the stairs. For the first six months after Maggie died, he hadn't been able to sleep in their room, in their bed. He'd camped out in the den, downstairs, on the fold-out couch, until the night Lissie had a walking nightmare. Hearing his daughter's screams, he'd rushed upstairs to find her in the master bedroom, clawing at the covers, as if searching, wildly, desperately, for something she'd lost.

"I can't find my mommy!" she'd sobbed. "I can't find my daddy!"

"I'm here," he'd said, taking her into his arms, holding her tightly as she struggled awake. "Daddy's here."

Now Frank paused at the door of his and Maggie's room. *Daddy's here,* he thought, *but Mommy's gone. She's really, truly gone.*

He went inside, closed the door, stripped off his jacket, shoes and uniform, and stretched out on the bed, staring up at the ceiling. His throat felt tight, and his eyes burned.

Maggie's words came back to him, echoing in his

mind. *I want you to mourn me for a while, but when it's time to let go, I'll find a way to tell you.*

A single tear slipped from the corner of his right eye and trickled over his temple. "It's time, isn't it?" he asked in a hoarse whisper.

Once again, he heard the cup smashing on Addie's kitchen floor.

It was answer enough.

CHAPTER ELEVEN

Addie didn't even try to go to sleep that night. She brewed another pot of coffee—no decaf this time—and sewed like a madwoman until the sun came up.

It was still snowing, and she was glad it was Sunday as she stared blearily out the front window at a white-blanketed, sound-muffled world.

"Can I open the calendar box," Henry asked from behind her, "or do we have to wait for Lissie?"

Addie took a moment to steel herself, then turned to smile at her stepson. Still in his pajamas, he wasn't wearing his glasses, and his dark hair was sleep-rumpled. Blinking at her, he rubbed his eyes with the backs of his hands.

"We'd better wait," she said. Lissie might show up for the ritual, but she wondered about Frank. The look on his face, when that cup tumbled to the floor and splintered into bits, was still all too fresh in her mind.

Of course it had been an accident. Addie understood that, and she knew Frank did, too. Just the same, she'd glimpsed the expression of startled sorrow in his eyes, seen the slow, almost reverent way he'd gathered up the pieces. . . .

Something a lot more important than a ceramic coffee mug had been broken.

"Couldn't I peek?" Henry persisted, still focused on the matchbox calendar. In a way, Addie was pleased; he was feeling more secure with the new living arrangement, letting down his guard a little. In another way, she was unsettled. For all his promises that Henry could stay until February, or even until school was out for the summer, Toby might appear at any moment, filled with sudden fatherly concern, and whisk the child away.

"I guess," she said, just as a firm rap sounded at the front door.

"They're here!" Henry shouted, bounding across the linoleum kitchen floor and into the living room.

Frank stepped over the threshold, looking grimly pleasant, and Addie knew by the shadows in and beneath his eyes that he hadn't had much more sleep than she had, if any. There was no sign of Lissie.

"Where's Halo Woman?" Henry asked, taking his glasses from the pocket of his pajama top and jamming them onto his face.

Frank smiled at the new nickname. "Lissie's got a fever this morning," he said. "The doctor's been by. Said she needs to stay in bed, keep warm, and take plenty of fluids."

"And you have to work," Addie guessed aloud, folding her arms and leaning against the framework of the kitchen door because she wanted to cross the room and embrace Frank. She sensed that he wouldn't welcome a show of sympathy just then.

He nodded. "The roads are wicked, thanks to all this new snow. I've got every man I could call in out there patrolling, but we're still shorthanded."

"We could baby-sit her," Henry announced. He grinned. "And dog-sit Floyd."

Addie watched Frank's face closely. He didn't like asking for help, she could see that. "Mrs. Jarvis usually watches her when there's a crisis," he said, "but her sister just moved into the nursing home, and she's been spending a lot of time there, trying to help her adjust."

"What's easier, Frank?" Addie said gently. "For Henry and me to come down to your place, or for you to bring Lissie and Floyd up here?"

He thrust a hand through his snow-sprinkled hair, glanced at the sewing machine and billows of blue fabric. "You've got a project going here," he reflected. "And Lissie would probably enjoy a visit. I'll wrap her up in a quilt and bring her up." He was quiet for a long moment. "If it's really all right with you."

"Frank," Addie told him, feeling affectionately impatient, "of *course* it is."

"I better get dressed!" Henry decided, and dashed off to his room.

"About the cup," Frank began, looking miserable. He'd closed the door against the cold and the blowing snow, but he didn't move any closer. The gap between them, though only a matter of a dozen feet, felt unaccountably wide. "I guess I overreacted. I'm sorry, Addie."

She still wanted to touch him, still wouldn't let herself do it. "It meant a lot to you," she said gently.

He nodded. "Just the same," he reasoned in a gruff voice, "it was only a coffee mug."

Addie knew it was much more, but it wasn't her place to say so. "Go and get Lissie," she told him. "I'll bring out some pillows and a blanket, make up the couch." She paused, then went on, very carefully, "Have you eaten? I'm going to make breakfast in a few minutes."

"No time," he said with a shake of his head. "I'll hit the

drive-through or something." He hesitated, as if he wanted to say something else, opened the door again, and went out.

Because she felt a need to move and be busy, exhausted as she was, Addie went into her room and grabbed the pillows off the bed. She was plumping them on one end of the couch when Frank returned, carrying Lissie. Floyd trailed after them, snowflakes melting on his floppy ears, wagging not just his tail, but his whole substantial hind end. Addie would have sworn that dog was grinning.

Henry, dressed and hastily groomed, waited impatiently until Lissie was settled. "What about the calendar box?" he blurted. "Can we look now?"

"I know what it is, anyway," Lissie said with a congested sniff. She was still in her flannel nightgown and smelled pleasantly of mentholated rub.

Henry looked imploringly up at Addie.

"Go ahead." She smiled.

Frank wrote down his cell phone number, handed it to Addie, kissed his daughter on top of the head, and left the apartment. The place seemed to deflate a little when he was gone.

"It's a dog!" Henry announced, returning to the living room. He'd dragged a chair over to the cupboards to peer inside that day's matchbox. "Brown and white, like Floyd. But a lot littler."

"It's snowing really hard," Lissie fretted, turning to look out the front window. "Dad said the roads are slick. Do you think he'll be okay?"

Addie sat down on the edge of the couch, giving Lissie as much room as she could, and touched the child's forehead with the back of her hand. "Sure he will," she said quietly. "What would you like for breakfast? Scrambled eggs, or oatmeal?"

"Oatmeal," Lissie answered.

"Scrambled eggs," Henry chimed in at the same moment.

Addie laughed. "I'll make both," she said.

The kids ate in the living room, watching a holiday movie marathon on television, while Addie washed the dishes. The phone rang just as she was putting the last of the silverware away.

"Hello?" she said cheerfully, expecting the caller to be Frank checking up on his daughter.

"I'm in Denver," Toby said.

Addie stretched the phone cord to its limits, hooked one foot around a chair leg, and dragged it close enough to collapse onto. *"What?"*

"I can't believe this snow."

Addie closed her eyes. Waited.

Toby spoke into the silence. "How's Henry? Can I talk to him?"

She couldn't very well refuse, but stalling was another matter. Her stomach felt like a clenched fist, and her heart skittered with dread. "What are you doing in Denver?"

"Put Henry on, will you?"

Addie turned to call the boy, and was startled to find him standing only a few feet away, watching. She held out the receiver. "It's your dad," she said.

Henry didn't move. She couldn't see his eyes, because of the way the light hit the lenses of his glasses, but his chin quivered a little, and his freckles seemed to stand out.

"I can't leave," he said. "I'm a shepherd."

Addie blinked back tears. "You've got to talk to him, buddy," she said very gently.

He crossed to her, took the phone.

"I can't leave, Dad," he said. "I'm a shepherd."

Addie started to rise out of her chair, meaning to leave

the room, but Henry laid a small hand on her arm and looked at her pleadingly.

"In the play at school," he went on, after listening to whatever Toby said in the interim. "Yeah, I like it here. I like it a lot."

Addie rubbed her temples with the fingertips of both hands.

"No, it didn't come yet." Henry put a hand over the receiver. "Dad sent a box," he said to Addie. "Christmas presents."

Addie's spirits rose a little. If Toby had mailed Henry's gifts, he probably intended to leave the boy with her at least through the holidays. On the other hand, Toby was nothing if not a creature of quicksilver moods. And he was in Denver, after all, which might mean he'd changed his mind. . . .

"I understand," Henry said. "You're stuck because of the snow. You shouldn't try to drive here. The roads are really bad—Lissie's dad says so, and he's the chief of police."

More verbiage from Toby's end. Addie didn't catch the words, but the tone was upbeat, thrumming with good cheer.

"Right." Henry nodded somberly. "Sure, Dad." He swallowed visibly, then thrust the phone at Addie. "He wants to talk to you again."

Addie bit her lower lip, nodded for no particular reason, and took the receiver.

"Addie?" Toby prompted, when she was silent too long. "Are you there?"

"Yes," she said, sitting up very straight on her chair, which seemed to be teetering on the edge of some invisible abyss. One false move and she'd never stop falling.

"Look, I was planning to rent a car, drive down there, and surprise Henry with a visit. But it looks like that won't be possible, because of the weather. I'll be lucky to get out of here between storm fronts, according to the airline people."

Addie let out her breath, but inaudibly. She didn't want Toby to guess how scared she'd been when she'd thought he was coming to take Henry away, or how relieved she was now that she knew he wasn't. "Okay," she said.

Toby chuckled uncomfortably. "You know, I remember you as being more communicative, Addie. Cat got your tongue?"

She glanced sideways, saw that Henry was still standing close by, listening intently. Floyd had joined him, leaning heavily against the boy's side as if to offer forlorn support. "I guess I'm just surprised. I thought you were on your honeymoon."

"Elle got bored with the tropics. She's in Manhattan, doing some Christmas shopping. Her folks live in Connecticut, so we're spending the holidays with them. I decided I wanted to see the kid, and picked up a standby seat out of LaGuardia—"

The trip was a whim, to Toby. *Henry* was a whim.

Don't say it, Addie told herself. *Don't make him angry, because then he'll come here, if he has to hitch a ride on a snowplow, and when he leaves, Henry will go with him.* "I'm sorry it didn't work out," she said instead. It wasn't a complete lie. As much as Henry wanted to stay in Pine Crossing with her, he was a normal little boy. He loved his father and craved his attention. A visit would have delighted him.

"Tell Dad you'll take a picture of me being a shepherd," Henry prompted.

Addie dutifully repeated the information.

"A what?" Toby asked, sounding distracted. Maybe they were announcing his flight back to New York, and maybe he had simply lost interest.

"Henry's playing a shepherd in the Christmas play," Addie said moderately and, for her stepson's sake, with a note of perky enthusiasm. "I'll take some pictures."

"Oh, right," Toby answered. "Okay. Look, Addie—I appreciate this. My dad sent you a check." He lowered his voice. "You know, for the kid's expenses."

Henry and Floyd returned to the living room, summoned by Lissie, who called out that they were about to miss the part where Chevy Chase got tangled in the Christmas lights and fell off the roof.

"Your dad?" Addie asked, very carefully.

Toby thrust out a sigh. "Look, we're kind of living on Elle's money right now. The mortgage business isn't so great at this time of year. And since Henry isn't hers—"

Chevy Chase must have taken his header into the shrubbery, because Henry and Lissie hooted with delighted laughter.

"Henry can stay with me as long as necessary," Addie said, again with great care, framing it as a favor Toby was doing for her, and not the reverse. "Try not to worry, okay? I'll take very good care of him."

Toby was quiet for so long that Addie got nervous. "Thanks, Add," he said. "Listen, it's time to board."

"Where can I get in touch with you, Toby? In case there's an emergency, I mean?"

"Send me an e-mail," Toby said hurriedly. "I check every few days." With that, he rang off.

They were all asleep when Frank let himself into the apartment at six-fifteen that evening, even the dog. Lissie snoozed at one end of the couch, Henry at the other. Addie had curled up in the easy chair, her brown hair tumbling over her face.

Frank felt a bittersweet squeeze behind his heart as he

switched on a lamp, turned off the TV, and put the pizza boxes he was carrying down on the coffee table.

Floyd woke up first, beagle nose in overdrive, and yelped happily at the prospect of pepperoni and cheese. The sound stirred Lissie and Henry awake, and, finally, Addie opened her eyes.

"Pizza!" Henry whooped.

Frank laughed, though his gaze seemed stuck on Addie. The situation was innocent, but there was something intimate about watching this particular woman wake up. Her tentative, sleepy smile made him ache, and if she asked how his day had gone, he didn't know what he'd do.

"How was your day?" she inquired, standing up and stretching both arms above her head. Making those perfect breasts rise.

"Good," he managed, figuring he sounded like a caveman, barely past the grunt stage. He averted his gaze to Lissie, who was off the couch and lifting one of the pizza box lids to peer inside. "Feeling better?" he asked.

Lissie nodded, somewhat reluctantly. "I'll probably have to go to school tomorrow and listen to Tiffany Baker bragging about being an angel in the Christmas play," she said, but with some spirit.

"Probably," Frank agreed.

Floyd put both paws up on the edge of the coffee table and all but stuck his nose into the pizza. Grinning, Frank took him gently by the collar and pulled him back.

"I'll get some plates," Addie said, heading for the kitchen.

"Bring one for Floyd," Henry suggested.

Addie laughed, and Frank unzipped his uniform jacket and shrugged it off, thinking how good it was to be home.

CHAPTER TWELVE

Much to Lissie's annoyance, and Frank's relief, the child was well enough to go to school the next morning. The snow had stopped, and though the ground was covered in glittering white, there was a springlike energy in the air.

Addie was in a cheerful mood, humming along with the kitchen radio while she supervised the opening—with a suitable flourish on Lissie's part—of that day's calendar box. Inside was a miniature gift, wrapped in shiny paper and tied in a bow.

Henry scrunched up his face, intrigued. "Is there anything inside it?"

"No, silly," Lissie responded. "It's supposed to represent a Christmas present."

"I'm getting presents," Henry said. "From my dad. He sent a box."

"You need a Christmas tree if you're going to get presents," Lissie reasoned. "Dad's getting ours tonight, after work."

Henry looked questioningly at Addie. "Are we getting one, too?"

"Sure are," Frank put in, before Addie could answer.

"A real one?" Henry asked hopefully.

"The genuine article," Frank promised, hoping he wasn't stepping on Addie's toes in some way. Maybe she wanted buying the tree to be a family thing, just her and Henry. It took some nerve, but he made himself meet her eyes.

She looked uncertain.

"You two put on your coats and head for the car," Frank told the kids. "I'll drop you off at school on my way to work."

They dashed off.

"Everything okay, Addie?" Frank asked quietly, when the two of them were alone in the apartment kitchen. She was dressed for another day at the *Wooden Nickel*.

She hugged herself. "I wasn't really planning on Christmas," she said. "And I've been so busy since Henry got here, I haven't really thought about it."

He wanted to cross the room, maybe touch her hair, but things were still a little awkward between them. Had been since Maggie's mug had struck the floor. "I shouldn't have said anything about the tree."

"It's okay," she said. "I don't have ornaments, though, or lights."

"A lot of your father's stuff is still in the storeroom," he reminded her. "I'm pretty sure there are some decorations." He paused, shoved a hand through his hair. "Damn, Addie, I'm sorry. I wish I'd kept my mouth shut."

Her smile faltered a little. "I vaguely remember strings and strings of those old-fashioned bubble lights," she said wistfully. "And lots of shiny ornaments. They must have been packed away when Mom died—Dad didn't care much about Christmas. Said it was a lot of sentimental slop, and way too commercial. He used to give me money and tell me to buy what I wanted."

Frank's spirits plunged like an elevator after the cable

breaks. *Way to go, Raynor,* he thought. *First, you put Addie on the spot in front of the kids, and now you remind her that her childhood Christmases wouldn't exactly inspire nostalgia.*

He found his voice. "Look, you helped me out yesterday when I needed somebody to look after Lissie. I'll spring for an extra evergreen. We could make a night of it—hit the tree lot, then have supper at the Lumberjack, afterward. The kids would like that."

She grabbed her coat off the back of a chair and shrugged into it. "Sure," she said, but she sounded sad. "Thanks, Frank."

He spent the rest of the day kicking himself.

The box from Toby was waiting on the doorstep when Addie arrived home from work late that afternoon. She'd picked Henry and Lissie up at school, and Henry was beside himself with excitement.

"Can I open it?" he asked, peeling off his coat. Lissie had gone to let Floyd out, but she'd be joining them in a few minutes for hot cocoa.

Addie's mood, bordering on glum ever since morning, lifted a little. She smiled as she hung up her own coat. "Let me peek inside first," she suggested. "Just in case the stuff isn't wrapped."

"Okay," Henry said. The two of them had wrestled the large box over the threshold, and it was sitting on the living room floor, looking mysterious. "I didn't think he'd really send it," he confided. "Sometimes Dad says he's going to do stuff, and he forgets."

Addie ruffled his hair. "Well, he didn't forget this time," she said. She got a knife from the silverware drawer and advanced on the box. Henry was fairly jumping up and down while she carefully cut the packing tape.

"I know about Santa Claus," Henry announced, out of the blue. "So you don't have to worry about filling my stocking or anything like that."

Addie stiffened slightly and busied herself with the box. She didn't want Henry to see her face. She pulled back the flaps and looked inside, relieved to find packages wrapped in shiny, festive paper and tied with curling ribbon. "It's okay to look," she said.

Henry let out a whoop of glee and started hauling out the loot. He had the packages piled around the living room in an impressive circle when Lissie and Floyd came in. Lissie was carrying her tinsel halo in one hand.

"Whoa," she said, beaming. "You really cleaned up!"

Floyd made the rounds, sniffing every box.

"I wish today was Christmas," Henry said.

Lissie sagged a little. "Me, too," she confessed. "Then that stupid play would be over, and I wouldn't have to feel bad about not being an angel."

Addie brought out the cocoa she'd been brewing in the kitchen, the old-fashioned kind, like Eliza used to make for her and Frank on cold winter afternoons. "Feeling bad is a choice, Lissie," she said. She'd made a few calls that day, when things were slow at the *Wooden Nickel;* her plan was coming together. "You could just as easily choose to feel good."

Lissie frowned. "About what?"

"About the fact that there are other ways to be an angel," Addie said.

The kids zeroed in on the hot chocolate and looked up at her curiously, with brown foamy mustaches.

"What other way is there," Lissie inquired, "besides getting hit by a truck or something?"

"That would be a radical method," Addie allowed, eyeing the sewing machine and her thrift-store creation of peacock blue taffeta. "I spoke to someone at the hospital today. At the nursing home, too. There are some people there who would really like a visit from an angel, especially at Christmas."

Lissie's gaze strayed to the sewing project, and the light dawned in her eyes. "You made me an angel dress?"

Addie nodded. "It's pretty fancy, too, if I do say so myself."

Lissie crossed to the card table, where the sewing machine was set up, and laid a tentative hand on the small, shimmering gown. Except for the hem, a few nips and tucks to make it fit perfectly, and some beads and sequins rescued from the scorned wedding dress, it was complete.

"Would I have to sing?" Lissie asked in a voice small with wonder.

Addie laughed. "No," she said. "Not if you didn't want to."

"There aren't any wings," Henry pointed out, ever practical. "You can't be an angel without wings."

"I think I could rig something up," Addie said. The wings wouldn't be as fancy as Tiffany Baker's feathered flying apparatus, but the skirt of Jessie's wedding dress would serve if she bent some coat hangers into the proper shape.

"Do they need a shepherd, too?" Henry asked hopefully.

"A shepherd would be the perfect touch," Addie decided.

Lissie was standing on the coffee table, halo askew but on, looking resplendent in her blue angel duds, when Frank rapped at the door, let himself in, and whistled in exclamation. Addie, with a mouthful of pins, offered a careful smile.

"I get to be an angel after all," Lissie told her father.

Frank looked confused. "Don't tell me. Tiffany Baker has been abducted by space aliens. Shall I put out an all-points bulletin?"

Lissie giggled, though whether it was Frank's expression or the concept of her rival being carried off to another planet that amused her was anybody's guess. "I'm going to visit people in the hospital, and the nursing home. Addie's making my wings out of coat hangers."

Frank smiled. "Great idea," he said, looking at Addie. He took in the array of Christmas presents lying all over the room. "Looks like Santa crashed his sleigh in here."

Addie, who had been kneeling to pin up Lissie's hem, finished the job and got to her feet. "Want some coffee?" she asked Frank, and then wished she hadn't. Now he'd be thinking about the broken mug again, missing Maggie. She blushed and looked away.

He made a show of consulting his watch, shook his head. "We'd better get to the tree lot," he said. "Everybody ready?"

Floyd yelped with excitement.

Addie's gaze flew to Frank's face. So did Henry's and Lissie's.

"Can Floyd go, too?" Lissie asked.

Frank sighed. "Sure," he said, after a few moments of deliberation. "He can sniff out the perfect tree and wait in the car while we're in the Lumberjack having supper. We'll bring him a doggy bag."

How many men would include a beagle on such an expedition? Unexpected tears burned in Addie's eyes. That was the moment she realized the awful, wonderful truth. She'd fallen in love with Frank Raynor—assuming that she'd ever fallen out in the first place. The downside was, he still cared deeply for his late wife. She'd seen his stricken expression when the cup was broken.

The children, naturally oblivious to the nuances, shouted with joy, and Floyd barked all the harder. Addie's hands trembled a little as she helped Lissie out of the gown.

"You're an amazing woman," Frank said quietly, standing very close to Addie, while the kids scrambled to get into their coats. "Thank you."

Addie didn't dare look at him. The revelation she'd just undergone was too fresh—she was afraid he'd see it in her eyes. "We'd better take my station wagon," she said. "It probably wouldn't be kosher to tie a couple of Christmas trees to the top of your squad car."

He didn't answer.

A light snow began as they drove to the lot, Frank at the wheel. From the backseat, the kids sang "Jingle Bells," with Floyd howling an accompaniment.

Within half an hour, they'd selected two lusciously fragrant evergreen trees, and Frank had secured them in the back of the station wagon. When they pulled up in front of the Lumberjack Diner, Floyd sighed with patient resignation, settled his bulk on the seat, and went to sleep.

"This feels almost like being a family," Frank said quietly, as the four of them trooped into the restaurant. "I like it."

The waitresses were all wearing felt reindeer antlers bedecked in tiny blinking lights. "Blue Christmas" wailed from the jukebox, and various customers called out cheerful greetings to the newcomers. There were a couple of low-key whistles, too, and when Addie stole a look at Frank, she was amazed to see that he was blushing.

"About time you hooked up with a woman, Chief," an old man said, patting Frank on the shoulder as he passed the booth where they were seated. "Good to see you back in Pine Crossing, Addie."

She felt warm inside, but it was a bruised and wary warmth. *Don't get your hopes up,* Addie warned herself in

the silence of her mind. When she sneaked a look at
Frank, unable to resist, she saw that he was blushing
again. And grinning a little.

The meal was delicious, and when it was over, there
were plenty of scraps for Floyd. He gobbled cheerfully
while they drove home, the car full of merriment and the
distinctive scents of fresh pine and leftover meatloaf.

Frank sent Lissie and Floyd into the house when they
arrived, and Henry plodded up the apartment stairs, worn
out by a jolly evening. He didn't even protest when Addie
called after him to start his bath.

She hesitated, watching as Frank unloaded the trees.
The snow was falling faster, stinging her cheeks.

"It'll need to settle, and dry out a little," Frank said,
setting the tree Addie had chosen upright on the sidewalk,
stirring that lovely fragrance again.

Addie laid a hand on his arm. "Thank you, Frank," she
said very softly. "For the tree, for the meal at the Lumberjack, and for caring about a dog's feelings."

He looked surprised. "I'm the one who should be
doing the thanking around here," he said, and when she
started to protest, he raised a hand to silence her. "Lissie's
wearing her halo again. For one night, she gets to be an
angel. I can't begin to tell you what that means to me,
Addie."

Addie's throat tightened. If she stayed one moment
longer, she'd tell Frank Raynor straight out that she loved
him, and ruin everything. "I'd better make sure Henry
doesn't get to looking at his presents, forget to turn off the
tap, and flood the bathroom," she said, and hurried away.

She felt Frank watching her and would have given anything for the courage to look straight at him and see what
was in his face, but she couldn't take the risk.

The stakes were suddenly too high.

CHAPTER THIRTEEN

"It's an angel," Lissie said dismally, before Henry got that day's matchbox open. The day of the pageant had come, and while the little girl was ready to play the innkeeper's wife to the best of her ability, Addie knew it wouldn't be any fun for her.

She glanced at Frank, then laid a hand on Lissie's shoulder. "We're booked at the hospital and the Sweet Haven Nursing Home," she reminded the child. She'd found an old white boa, on a second trip to the Goodwill, and planned to glue the feathers onto the clothes-hanger wings on her breaks and during her lunch hour. Lissie's wings wouldn't be as glorious as Tiffany's, but they would be pretty and, Addie hoped, a nice surprise. "Tomorrow night, six o'clock. The patients are looking forward to it."

Lissie nodded.

Frank took the kids to school that morning. Addie had an extra cup of coffee, then set out for work in the station wagon.

At three-ten that afternoon, Lissie burst into the

Wooden Nickel, setting the silver bell jingling above the door. Addie, taking her break at her desk, quickly shoved the half-feathered wing she'd been working on out of sight.

"Is everything all right?" she asked.

Lissie beamed. "Tiffany got another commercial," she blurted. "She had to be in Denver *today,* and there's no way she can get back in time for the pageant. Miss Pidgett got so upset, she had to go lie down in the principal's office, and Mr. Walker, the teacher's aide, said *I* could take Tiffany's place!"

Stella and Mr. Renfrew applauded, and Addie rounded the counter to hug Lissie. "It's a miracle," she said.

"How come your fingers are sticky?" Lissie wanted to know.

Addie ignored the question. "Do you know the angel's lines?"

" 'Be not afraid,' " Lissie spouted proudly, " 'for behold, I bring you tidings of great joy!' "

"Guess you've got it," Addie said, her arm around Lissie's shoulders. "Have you told your dad?"

Lissie shook her head. "He's on patrol," she replied, and suddenly, her brow furrowed with worry. "Tiffany took her costume with her. I've got my dress—the one you made—but the wings—"

"There will be wings," Addie promised, though she didn't know how she was going to pull that off. There were still two hours left in the workday, and the pageant was due to start at six-thirty.

"Great!" Lissie cried. "Henry's over at the library. Are you going to pick us up, or is Dad?"

"Whoever gets there first," Addie said, her mind going into overdrive.

Lissie nodded and went out, setting the bell over the door to ringing again.

"Another angel gets its wings," Stella said with a smile.

"We'd better get to gluing," Mr. Renfrew added, eyes sparkling.

"Do you suppose there's anything seriously wrong with Miss Pidgett?" Addie fretted, gratefully parceling out feathers stripped from the thrift-store boa and handing Arthur Renfrew the second wing, which was made from the skirt of Jessie Corcoran's wedding gown.

"She's run every pageant since 1962," Stella put in. "Maybe she's just worn out."

"More likely, it's a case of the 'means,' " Mr. Renfrew said, opening a pot of rubber cement and gingerly gluing a feather onto an angel's wing.

Frank arrived at St. Mary's at six-thirty sharp, fresh from the office, where he'd filled out a lengthy report on a no-injury accident out on the state highway, and scanned the crowd. Miss Pidgett, sitting in a folding chair toward the front of the small auditorium, fanned herself with a program and favored him with a poisonous look.

He smiled and nodded, just as though they were on cordial terms, and she blushed and fanned harder.

A small hand tugged at his jacket sleeve, and he looked down to see Lissie standing beside him, resplendent in her peacock blue angel gown and a pair of feathered wings.

"I thought you were the innkeeper's wife," he said stupidly. The fact was, he couldn't quite believe his eyes, and he was afraid to hope she'd landed the coveted role of lead angel. He checked his watch, wondering if he'd somehow missed the pageant, and Lissie had already changed clothes to make an unscheduled visit to Sweet Haven.

"Tiffany's in a toilet paper commercial, up in Denver,"

Lissie said, glowing. "She took her wings with her, but Addie made me these, so I'm good to go."

Addie. Frank felt as though the breath had just been knocked out of his lungs. He crouched, so he could look straight into his daughter's eyes. "Honey, that's great," he said, and the words came out sounding husky.

"Did you bring a camera? Henry promised his dad some pictures."

Just then, Addie arrived, looking pretty angelic herself in a kelly green suit. Her hair was pinned up, with a sprig of mistletoe for pizzazz. "I've got one," she said, waving one of those yellow throwaway numbers. "Hi, Frank."

"I'd better go," Lissie told them. "Maybe angels are like brides. Maybe people aren't supposed to see them before it's time!"

"Maybe not," Addie told her.

Lissie put up her hand, and the two of them did a high five.

The audience, mostly consisting of parents, grandparents, aunts, uncles and siblings, shifted and murmured in their folding chairs, smiling holiday smiles.

Frank made a point of looking at Addie's back.

"What?" she asked, fumbling to see if her label was sticking out.

"I was looking for wings," Frank said. "It seems some angels don't have them."

Her eyes glistened, and the junior high school band struck up the first strains of "Silent Night." "We'd better sit down," she whispered, and they took chairs next to Mr. Renfrew and Stella.

The lights went down, and the volume of the music went up. The stage curtains creaked and shivered apart. A small door stood on stage right, with a stable opposite. A kid in a donkey suit brayed, raising a communal chuckle from the audience.

Mary and Joseph shuffled on stage, looking suitably weary. Joseph knocked at the door, and it nearly toppled over backward. Henry peered out of the opening, blinking behind his glasses, and started shaking his head before Joseph could ask for a room. Addie took a picture with the throwaway, and the flash almost blinded Frank.

Henry, taking the innkeeper thing to heart, shook his head again. "No!" he shouted. "I said *no!*"

"Oh, dear," Addie whispered. "He's ad-libbing."

Frank laughed, which earned him a glower from Miss Pidgett, who turned in her seat and homed in on him like a heat-seeking missile.

"You can have the barn!" Henry went on. He was a born actor.

Joseph and Mary drooped and consigned themselves to the stable. Henry slammed the door so hard that the whole thing teetered. Addie gripped Frank's arm, and they both held their breaths, but the efforts of the eighth-grade shop class held.

The donkey brayed again, but he'd already been up-staged by the innkeeper.

Shepherds meandered onto the stage, in brown robes, each with a staff in hand. One carried a stuffed lamb under one arm. They all searched the sky, looking baffled. Henry, bringing up the rear, shoved at the middle of his glasses and wrote himself another line.

"What are all those things in the sky? Angels?"

The other shepherds gave him quelling looks, but Henry was undaunted.

"It's not every night you see a bunch of angels hanging around," he said.

In what he hoped was a subtle move, Frank took Addie's hand.

Miss Pidgett rose out of her seat, then sat down again.

There was a cranking sound, and Lissie descended

from the rigging on a rope, wings spread almost as wide as her grin. Less splendid angels inched in from either side of the stage, gazing up at her in bemusement.

"Now *there's* an angel!" Henry boomed, looking up, too.

A ripple of laughter moved through the crowd, and Addie covered her face with her free hand, but only for a moment. She was smiling.

Lissie shouted out her lines, and the unseen stage-hands cranked her down. Somebody made a sound like a baby crying, and attention shifted to Mary and Joseph. Darned if there hadn't been a blessed event.

After the pageant, refreshments were served in the cafeteria, and Addie took at least twenty pictures of Henry and Lissie. Practically everybody in town, with the noticeable exception of Miss Pidgett, stopped to compliment both kids on their innovative performances.

They glowed with pride, but the angel and the shepherd were soon yawning, like the rest of the cast.

"I'll take them home in the station wagon," Addie said.

"Meet you there in a couple of minutes," Frank replied, feeling oddly tender. "I just want to say hello to the mayor."

Addie nodded, gathered up the kids and their gear, and left.

Frank completed his social obligation and was just turning to go when there was a scuffle in a far corner of the room. Instinctively, he headed in that direction.

Miss Almira Pidgett lay unconscious on the floor.

CHAPTER FOURTEEN

It was after ten when Addie saw the lights of Frank's squad car sweep into the driveway. Lissie was asleep on the couch, still wearing her costume and covered in a quilt, and Henry had long since fallen into bed. Neither of them had wanted to leave the twinkling Christmas tree, standing fragrant in front of the window.

Addie pulled on her coat and went out onto the stairs. Frank had called her from the hospital earlier, where Almira Pidgett was admitted for observation, and she'd been waiting for news ever since. It had been difficult, pretending nothing was wrong while Lissie and Henry celebrated their theatrical debuts, but she hadn't wanted to ruin their evening, so she'd kept the old woman's illness to herself.

Frank appeared at the bottom of the stairs, paused, rested one hand on the railing, and looked up.

"Is she all right?" Addie asked.

Frank's shoulders moved in a weary sigh, but he nodded. "Looks like Miss Pidgett will be in the hospital for a few days. The doctor said it was diabetic shock. Good thing she wasn't home alone."

Addie sagged with relief. She might not have been Miss Pidgett's greatest fan, but she'd been desperately worried, just the same.

"Come upstairs and have some coffee," she said.

Frank grinned, started the climb. "You looked pretty good in that green outfit tonight," he told her.

She'd exchanged her good suit for jeans, sneakers, and a flannel shirt. "Lissie stole the whole show," she said with a laugh. The wind was cold, and it was snowing a little, but the closer Frank got, the warmer she felt. Go figure, she thought.

He ushered her inside, paused to admire the Christmas tree. They'd decorated it together, and it had been a sentimental journey for Addie. She'd been surprised to realize how many memories those old ornaments stirred in her. They hadn't been able to use the bubble lights—they were ancient, and the wires were frayed—but Frank had anted up some spares, and the whole thing looked spectacular, especially with Henry's much-handled presents wedged underneath.

Floyd, lying in the kitchen doorway, got up to waddle across the linoleum and greet his master. Frank closed the door, ruffled the dog's ears, and then went to stand next to the couch, looking down at his sleeping daughter.

"They were something, weren't they?" he asked quietly.

Addie smiled. "Oh, yeah," she said. "What a pair of hams."

They went into the kitchen, and Addie put on the coffee. Frank sat down at the table and rubbed his face with both hands. It was a weary gesture that made Addie want to stand behind him and squeeze his shoulders, maybe even let her chin rest on top of his head for a moment or two, but she refrained.

"The last thing I need," Frank muttered, "is a shot of caffeine."

"I've got decaf," Addie said.

"Perish the thought," Frank replied.

She laughed. "You're a hard man to please, Frank Raynor." She moved toward cupboards next to the stove, meaning to get out a bag of cookies, but Frank caught her hand as she passed.

"No, actually," he said, "I'm not." And he pulled her onto his lap.

She should have resisted him, but she didn't. Her heart shimmied up into her throat.

For a moment, it seemed he might kiss her, but he frowned, and touched the tip of her nose instead. "How come you gave back my engagement ring, Addie Hutton?" he asked, very quietly.

Tears burned behind her eyes. "I was young and stupid."

He moved his finger and planted a kiss where it had been. "Young, yes. Stupid, never. I should have waited for you, Addie. I should have known you needed an education of your own."

She touched his mouth very lightly. "You wouldn't have met Maggie," she reminded him. "And you wouldn't have had Lissie."

He sighed. "You're right," he said. "But you wouldn't have met Bozo the Mortgage Broker, either. And you wouldn't have gotten into all that trouble in California."

She couldn't speak.

"What are you going to do now?" Frank asked, his arms still tight around her. "You can't work at the *Wooden Nickel* for the rest of your life, selling classified ads. You're a journalist. You'll go crazy."

"I've been thinking about writing a book," Addie admitted.

Frank's eyes lit up. "Well, now," he said. "Fiction or nonfiction?"

"A romance novel," Addie said, and blushed.

He raised one eyebrow, still grinning. "Is that so?"

Just then, the phone rang.

Because it was late, which might mean the call was important, and maybe because the atmosphere was getting intense in that kitchen, Addie jumped off Frank's lap and rushed to answer it with a breathless, "Hello?"

"Addie," Toby said. "I hope you weren't in bed."

Addie blushed again. "No—no, I was up. Is everything okay? Where are you?"

"Connecticut," Toby answered. "Addie, I have news. Really big news."

Addie closed her eyes, tried to brace herself. He was coming to get Henry. She'd known it was going to happen. "What?" she croaked.

"Elle and I are going to have a baby," Toby blurted. "Isn't that great?"

Addie's eyes flew open. Frank was setting the cups on the counter.

"Great," she said.

"I guess you're wondering why I'd call you to make the announcement," Toby said, sounding more circumspect.

Actually, she hadn't gotten that far. She was still trying to work out what this meant to Henry, and to her. "Right," she said.

Frank raised his eyebrows, thrumming the fingers of one hand on the countertop while he waited for the coffee to finish brewing.

"The pregnancy will be stressful," Toby went on. "For Elle, I mean. That's why I was wondering—"

Addie held her breath.

"That's why *we* were wondering if you'd keep Henry for a while longer."

Addie straightened. "You'll have to grant me temporary custody, Toby," she said. "I won't have you jerking Henry back and forth across the country every time it strikes your fancy."

"Is that what you think of me? That I'd do something like that?"

What *was* the man's home planet? "Yes," she said. "That's what I think."

Toby got defensive. "I could send Henry to stay with my dad and stepmother, you know."

"But you won't," Addie said. She'd received a check from Toby's father in that day's mail. It would pay some bills, and provide a Christmas for Henry, and she was very grateful. According to the enclosed note, Mr. Springer and his third trophy wife were spending what remained of the winter in Tahiti.

"All right," Toby admitted. "I won't."

"Ground rules, Toby," Addie said, as Frank gave her a chipper salute. "I want legal custody, signed, sealed and delivered. And you will call this child once a week, without fail."

"You got it," Toby agreed with a sigh.

"One more thing," Addie said.

"What?" Toby asked sheepishly.

"Congratulations," Addie told him.

Frank poured the coffee, carried the cups to the table. He'd taken off his uniform jacket, hung it over the back of a chair. His shoulders strained at the fabric of his crisply pressed shirt.

"Thanks," Toby said, and the conversation was over.

"I take it a celebration is in order?" Frank asked.

Addie jumped, kicked her heels together, and punched one fist in the air.

"Not much gets past a Sherlock Holmes like me," Frank said.

CHAPTER FIFTEEN

Frank's tree glittered, and a Christmas Eve fire flickered merrily in the hearth. Three stockings hung from the mantelpiece—Lissie's, Henry's, and Floyd's. Nat King Cole crooned about merry little Christmases.

"They're asleep," Frank said from the stairway. "I guess that second gig at the hospital and the nursing home did them in. Who'd have thought Almira Pidgett would turn out to be a fan of the angel-and-shepherd road show?"

Addie smiled, cup of eggnog in hand, and turned to watch him approach. Miss Pidgett had warmed to Lissie and Henry's impromptu performance when they shyly entered her hospital room the night after the pageant, and tonight, she'd welcomed them with a twinkly smile. "Christmas is a time for miracles," she said.

Frank took the cup out of her hand, set it aside, and pulled her close. "You think it's too soon?" he asked.

"Too soon for what?" she countered, but she knew. A smile quirked at the corner of her mouth.

"You and me to take up where we left off, back in the

day," Frank prompted, kissing her lightly. "I love you, Addie."

She traced the outline of his lips. "And I love you, Frank Raynor."

"But you still haven't answered my question."

She smiled. "I don't think it's too soon," she said. "I think it's *about time.*"

"Do I get to be in your romance novel?"

"You already are."

He gave a wicked chuckle. "Maybe we'd better do a little research," he teased, and tasted her mouth again. Then, suddenly, he straightened, squinted at the Christmas tree behind her. "But wait. What's that?"

Addie turned to look, confused.

Eliza's Advent calendar was draped, garland-style, across the front of the tree.

"Why, it's Aunt Eliza's Advent calendar!" Frank said, and twiddled at a nonexistent mustache.

"You might make it in a romance novel," Addie said, "but if you're thinking of going into acting, don't give up your day job."

"We forgot to check the twenty-fourth box," Frank said, recovering quickly from the loss of a career behind the footlights.

"We did not forget," Addie said. "It was a little crèche. The kids looked this morning, before breakfast."

"I think we should look again," Frank insisted. "Specifically, I think *you* should look again."

She moved slowly toward the tree, confused. They'd agreed not to give each other gifts this year, though she'd bought a present for Lissie, and he'd gotten one for Henry.

The twenty-fourth box, unlike the other twenty-three, was closed. Addie slid it open slowly, and gasped.

"My engagement ring," she said. The modest diamond

was wedged in between the crèche and the side of the matchbox. "You kept it?"

Frank stood beside her, slipped an arm around her waist. "Eliza kept it," he said. "Will you marry me, Addie?"

She turned to look up into his eyes. "Oh, Frank."

"I'll get you a better ring, if you want one."

She shook her head. "No," she said. "I want this one."

"Then, you will? Marry me, I mean?"

"Yes."

He pulled her into his arms, kissed her. "When?" he breathed when it was over.

Addie was breathless. "Next summer?"

"Good enough." He laughed, then kissed her again. "In the meantime, we can work on that research."

CHRISTMAS ANGEL

Kat Martin

CHAPTER ONE

December, 1865

Yankees. More damn blue-belly Yanks. Angel Summers's lips went thin just to look at them. She swept back her skirts to let one of them pass, then glared at his blue-coated back with all the venom that had built inside her these four long years.

Just thinking of the Federal troops who had occupied Savannah for almost twelve months made a bad taste surface in her mouth. She swallowed to chase it away, but the bitter taste of defeat remained. She wondered if it would ever completely fade.

Lifting her chin, determined to ignore the soldiers making their way along the boardwalk, a new batch that had arrived three days ago on the military train from Atlanta, Angel stepped into the open door of Whistler's Dry Goods store.

"Mornin', Miz Summers." The balding merchant stood behind the counter, a green leather apron tied around his ample girth.

"Good mornin', Mr. Whistler." She asked about his

wife and daughter's health, and he asked about her little brother, the only member of her family left since the war. "Willie's just fine. Growin' like a weed. He's gonna be even taller than our daddy."

She didn't like to think of their father, killed in the fighting at Shiloh, or her mother, who had taken to her bed not long after and died of a broken heart. Instead she thanked God for sparing little Willie. William Summers, Jr., blond and blue-eyed, just as she was. Seven-year-old Willie, who was now her whole world.

"The boy is surely full of mischief," she said with a smile, "but he's smart as a whip. He loves to read, and already he can cipher faster than I can." She didn't say he was also desperately lonely, that he ached for his parents, for the loving home they'd all shared before the war.

She didn't say that she ached for them, too. That she missed the days of grandeur when she was the belle of Summers End, her family's cotton plantation, and every young man in Savannah was out to capture her hand.

She tried not to think of those days anymore. It hurt too much when she looked down at her threadbare clothes, at the white pique cuffs on her blue wool dress that were frayed but finely mended, at the worn, pill-sized balls in the palms of her white cotton gloves, the mended holes in her stockings.

Four years ago, wearing such clothing would have been unheard of. She had dressed in silks and satins then, worn hoops so large they barely fit through the huge, carved front door. Now her hoops were discarded for more practical clothes, like the ones she had on.

And she was lucky to have those.

"What can I get you, Miz Summers?" The merchant scratched his balding head. "Whatever it is, it's likely we'll be out of it." The shelves of the store were nearly stripped bare. Only remnants remained, mostly bags of dried fruit, a few kegs of salt pork, some salted cod, a crate of sugar cones, and a few meager sacks of flour. A half-empty barrel of pickles sat in the corner. The cracker barrel was empty and covered with dust.

Supplies were a luxury, the shortages even worse since the Yankees had occupied the city.

"I just need a can of baking powder, Mr. Whistler. Christmas is coming. I was hoping to do some special cooking for the holidays, but it looks like it won't be much. I'm afraid the cow's gone dry."

The merchant simply nodded. Nothing was easy these days.

She paid for the baking powder and Mr. Whistler put it into her basket.

"There was one new shipment that come in," he said. "Yard goods from down to the mill near Charleston. Some of it's real purty." His glance ran over her mended dress. "You might want to have a look."

Ignoring the wash of color that rose into her cheeks, Angel headed toward the wall where he pointed, then stood staring at the beautiful lengths of cloth. A green plaid tartan wool, a calico cotton, some plain black bombazine for mourning. She hadn't dressed in mourning for over a year. She vowed that in the streets of Savannah, she had seen so much black she would never wear the hideous color again.

She ran a finger lovingly over a length of rich plum velvet. The cloth was so fine it made her ache inside just to touch it. It had been years since she'd worn anything so lovely—not since her girlhood, not since the days before the war when the future had stretched so shiny bright in front of her. When her life had been filled with joy and she had been so very much in love.

She eyed the fabrics a little while longer, enjoying the starchy smells and luxurious feel, escaping from thoughts that only brought pain. Then heavy footfalls caught her attention, swinging her mind in a different direction. She felt his presence even before he spoke and for an instant she wondered if her thoughts had somehow conjured him.

"Good morning . . . Angel. . . ."

The words whispered past her ear and her breath caught inside her. She didn't need to turn to recognize the man who stood so near. The man she hadn't seen in over four years.

She pivoted slowly to face him, her heart thumping a maddening tattoo. He was taller than she remembered, his skin a burnished, suntanned hue nearly as dark as his thick chestnut hair. His shoulders were wider, layered with muscle, his eyes a darker brown than she recalled.

"Joshua . . ." With his winsome smile, dark eyes, and finely arched brows, he'd been the handsomest boy in Chatham County. Now Josh Coltrane was a man, and the creases beside his eyes and the hard line of his jaw only made him more attractive.

"I saw you walk in," he said. "It's good to see you, Angel."

Dear God, Josh was here. A flesh-and-blood man standing right in front of her. Memories rushed in. The first time they had danced, the first time he had kissed her beneath the mistletoe at Christmas just this time of year. The ache returned, stronger than before, a pain she had dealt with, she thought. Josh was alive. She hadn't known for sure, hadn't allowed herself to care one way or the other. She took a deep breath, forcing a stiffness into her spine and courage into her suddenly weakened limbs.

"My name is Angela. I wish I could say it was good to see you, Josh, but it isn't. I can't believe you would have the nerve to come back here."

The smile on his beautiful mouth slid away. "The war's over—in case you haven't noticed. I'm still in the army, which means I go wherever they send me. I'm assigned to the hospital at Fort James Jackson."

His dark blue uniform fit him perfectly, stretching across his broad shoulders, tapering to a narrow waist, the color a glaring reminder of why they had parted. A stripe ran the length of his long, lean legs, and high black boots rose to his knees. She pulled her gaze back to his face, tried to ignore the shivery feeling inside her.

"That's right," she said. "How could I have forgotten? It's Dr. Coltrane now." She studied the gold bars on his shoulders—he was a captain, but also a Union doctor.

"Funny . . ." His eyes ran over her from head to foot, unreadable as they assessed her. "I haven't forgotten a single thing about you, Angel."

Her pulse went faster. She forced her chin up a notch. "I told you my name is—"

"Sorry, sweeting, I don't take orders from you. I never did, if you recall." A corner of his mouth curved faintly. "There was a time that was something you liked about me."

"There was a time you weren't a traitor—a dirty, blue-belly Yank."

His jaw went tight. "My mother was born in Pennsylvania. I went to medical school there. I was as much a Northerner as I was from the South. I had to follow my conscience. I told you that the day I left."

"Yes, you did. And I told you that if you joined the Union, as far as I was concerned you were dead. I meant what I said. Now if you'll excuse me, Captain Coltrane, I have better things to do than waste my time talking to a good for nothin' Yank."

She started toward the door, her heart still thudding in a way she wished it wouldn't, when the bell above the church at the end of the street began to clang. This time of day, the frantic ringing of iron could only mean trouble, and an unwelcome shiver ran down her spine.

"What's going on?" Josh asked, coming up beside her just as she opened the door.

"I—I don't know. Everybody's running toward the train station."

He glanced off toward the tracks that had been repaired and put back into service since the end of the war. They disappeared into the forest—and so did a goodly portion of Savannah's townspeople.

Angel stopped Eliza Barkley, her closest neighbor, as the heavyset woman ran out the door of the feed store next to the mercantile. "Mrs. Barkley—what in the name of heaven is going on?"

"Yankee supply train comin' in from Atlanta's been derailed. Union goods is strewn all over the forest." The laugh she loosed was so shrill it sounded more like a cackle. "You best get a move on. Stuff's just lyin' there— free for the pickin's." Lifting her skirt up out of the way, she waddled off toward the disappearing tracks.

"Sonofabitch," Josh said, "that train was carrying medical supplies for the hospital out at Fort Jackson. We've run out of nearly everything." He started walking with the rest of the people, his long-legged strides eating up the distance. Although she wasn't short, Angel had to hurry to keep up.

After all these years, it felt odd to be walking at Josh Coltrane's side, though once she thought she'd be facing life beside him every day. Just as they neared the forest, she stumbled. Josh caught her arm, and a strong hand wrapped around her waist to steady her.

"All right?" he asked.

Her cheeks flamed and her mouth went dry. She'd forgotten what it had felt like when he touched her, the way her stomach went all buttery and soft. "I'm fine," she snapped, jerking away, undone and embarrassed by her reaction. "I don't need any help from you."

He looked at her hard. "Sorry. Yankee or not, I guess I'm still too much of a gentleman to stand by and let a lady take a fall." He stepped away from her then, touched the brim of his cockaded hat in farewell. "Have a good day, Miss Summers." He didn't look back as he headed toward a group of approaching soldiers.

He hadn't seemed surprised to see her. She wondered if he knew that her parents were dead and that she and Willie were barely subsisting at Summers End, once one of Savannah's most successful plantations. She glanced down at her threadbare clothes and it galled her that he should see her brought so low.

A group of giggling matrons walked past, but Angel's eyes remained locked on Josh Coltrane's tall, broad-shouldered form as he walked away. Warm, sweet memories of the happy times they'd shared mixed with the anger she felt at his betrayal, the hatred of the Yankees who'd destroyed her world, and the ache she felt at seeing him again.

How long would he stay? she wondered. How many times would she run into him? How would she be able to avoid him?

Feeling the hard knot of misery unraveling in her stomach, she only knew that somehow she would have to make certain she did.

"Cap'n Coltrane?"

"Yes, Lieutenant?"

"We've formed a perimeter around the wrecked train, just like you said, but, sir, by the time we got there, most of the goods were already gone."

"That's right, sir," a gangly corporal named Baker put in. "This wasn't no accident. They were waiting when the train ran off the tracks. They must've done something to cause it."

"Just because the war is over, Corporal Baker, doesn't mean people forget. Unfortunately, that takes time." Josh knew that firsthand—after the way Angel had greeted him today. Then again, he wasn't surprised by her reaction. He had known, the day he headed north, that it was over between them. He had sacrificed his love for Angela Summers for the cause that he believed in.

Seeing her today he wondered, as he had a thousand times these past four years, if the sacrifice had been worth it.

"Damn—we really need those supplies," the bearded lieutenant was saying.

Josh's face went hard. "I know." God, did they. The men at Fort Jackson were some of the last casualties of the war—men injured in one of the final battles, too sick to make the long journey home, or never would.

They needed morphine to ease their pain and quinine to fight the malaria. Gauze and bandages were aboard that train, along with laudanum, chloroform, blue pill, Spirit of Nitre, calomel, and a dozen other medicines—and he needed all of them badly. "I'll speak to Colonel Wilson. He's probably already got men out there searching. Maybe he'll be able to find the people who took it and bring the stuff back."

"Odds aren't good, sir. Half the folks in Savannah went away with an armload of goods. They'll be eatin' and drinkin' high off the hog tonight."

"If they do, it'll be the first time in a very long time. At any rate, most of the foodstuffs were headed for the officers' tables. The men can get along without them. It's the medical supplies we need, and the townfolks don't need them the way we do. If we're lucky, they'll give them back."

The bearded man snorted. "Not likely, sir. Damned Johnny Rebs got the notion they're entitled."

Josh said nothing. Lieutenant Ainsley was right. Hatred against the Union forces ran high in Savannah, especially with Christmas approaching. It had been almost a year—December 20, 1864—since Sherman had stormed into Savannah on his march to the sea. Fort Jackson had fallen, along with the city, leaving a devastated populace in its wake.

They wouldn't give up the supplies unless they were forced to, and no one even knew who had them.

"It's gonna be a helluva rotten Christmas for those men," the lieutenant said.

Josh simply nodded. And an equally bad one for him, he added silently as he walked back toward town, his thoughts returning to Angel, remembering how he'd felt the moment he'd seen her.

He had told himself it was over between them, that he could come to Savannah as he had been ordered, that he could see her and not feel a thing. He was in love with Sarah Wingate, a woman he had met in Pennsylvania. Well, maybe not in love, but they had a lot in common and they were good together. There were no scars between them, no past to haunt them. He cared about Sarah and though he hadn't asked her to marry him, he planned to as soon as he returned.

Now all he could think of was Angel. How much she had changed in the last four years, that she had grown from a girl into a woman. A beautiful, sensuous woman. She was just seventeen when he had left. Now she would be twenty-one.

Though she was older, her face looked much the same, the smooth, wide forehead with its widow's peak in front, the high cheekbones, the small cleft in her chin. He knew she hadn't married. He'd checked on her when he'd first arrived in Savannah—just as a friend, of course. She had never had a husband or children, yet her figure was riper, her breasts fuller, even more seductive than he remembered. Four years ago, every time they'd been together, he had ached to touch them, counted the days till they'd be married and she would be his.

He had told himself he was over her, but the moment he had seen her, he'd been nearly overcome with the same hot lust he had felt so long ago. It was followed by a powerful urge to pull her into his arms.

Damnation! Angel Summers was a ghost from his past, nothing more. He wanted her, yes. Now he knew he probably always would. But any chance for happiness they'd ever had had been lost with the war.

Angel would never forgive him for fighting for the Union, and with her parents both dead, her hatred was even greater.

It was hopeless even to think of her.

Yet Josh Coltrane discovered in the days to come that as hard as he tried, he could not stop.

A great big, juicy Virginia ham. Angel hadn't seen the likes of it in years. At least not on the Summerses' usually very sparse table.

"Boy, that ham sure looks good." Slender seven-year-old Willie knelt on the seat of a high-backed chair in the dining room, staring at the bounty in front of him.

"Yes, suh, Master William," said Serge, once the Summerses' Negro butler, "it shorely do. We gots ham an' corn cakes an' yo' Aunt Ida done made some o' dat redeye gravy."

Angel smiled at the gray-haired black man who was now a member of the odd little foursome that had made up her family since the war. "I guess we can finally thank the Yankees for somethin'," she said with a glance at the ham.

"Oughts to be thankin' 'ol Pete Thompson an' his boys," Serge countered. "Way I hear it, him an' Harley Lewis is the ones what took out dat train."

Angel frowned at the stoop-shouldered old man. "Well, for heaven's sake, if they are, they had better keep quiet about it. Those Yanks have been runnin' all over the countryside tryin' to catch whoever did it and looking for the stolen supplies."

"Liberated," corrected Angel's aunt, Ida Summers-Dixon, a beefy woman with coarse, iron-gray hair. "That's what our neighbor, Mrs. Barkley, says." Ida had come to Summers End just after the war, her husband dead, her house burned to the ground, another lost soul looking for solace in a world gone mad.

"Dat's right," Serge said. "Miz Barkley says all them goods was bein' held prisoner by the Yanks an' them boys just come along an' set it free." He grinned, exposing a flash of white against his shiny black skin. He had turned sixty-seven just last week, had been with the family for as long as Angel could remember. When the war ended and the slaves on the plantation were freed, Serge remained. Summers End was his home, he'd said. As long as he was welcome, he would stay.

Angel thought that perhaps that was another thing they could thank the Yankees for. Until the war, it had never occurred to her there was anything wrong with slavery. She had been raised to believe it was just part of living in the South. Now, after working side by side with Serge, Miles, Betty, and others of her father's former slaves, she couldn't imagine treating them as anything but equals.

"Liber . . . liber . . ." Willie struggled with the word as they finished saying grace and began to pass around the steaming bowls of food.

"Liberated," Angel supplied. She smiled as she handed her plate to Serge, who filled it with a thick slab of the luscious sugar-cured ham. "Mrs. Barkley can be very convincing. When she sent over the ham, she reminded me of all the foodstuffs the Yankees plundered when they came through here last year."

"Mrs. Barkley had quite a bit to say, as a matter of fact," Ida said, passing the platter of corn cakes to Serge. "She told me Josh Coltrane was back in Savannah. She said she saw you talking to him the day of the train wreck. Is Josh back, Angel?"

The gravy ladle she held tilted precariously, nearly spilling the rich, dark liquid onto the frayed but spotless white tablecloth. "Yes . . . yes, he is."

"Why didn't you tell me?"

Angel took extra care as she poured the gravy over the ham and set the ladle back in the chipped china gravyboat, the last of a broken set that was once her family's pride and joy. "Because it doesn't matter whether he's here or not. Josh Coltrane is a Yankee traitor. Whatever was between us is over and done."

Ida's round face looked skeptical. "What did the two of you talk about? Did you ask him if he was married?"

"M-married?" The thought had never occurred to her. She couldn't imagine Josh Coltrane married to anyone but her. It was insane to feel that way, yet the notion of Josh with a wife and children made her suddenly sick to her stomach.

"That's what I asked," her aunt repeated as if Angel were a little slow-witted. "Did you find out if Josh has a wife?"

"I don't know if he's got a wife—I didn't ask him. Why would I? I don't give a damn if he's married or not!"

The table fell silent. Even little Willie stopped wolfing down his food.

"Wh-what I mean is, it's none of my business what Josh Coltrane is or isn't. What he does is none of my concern." She frowned at her aunt. "And I'm surprised at you, Aunt Ida. The Yanks killed your husband and your brother. I'd think you'd hate Josh Coltrane and everything he stands for."

Ida lifted her china cup and took a sip of the chicory they pretended was coffee. "A lot of good men believed in the Union. My husband's cousin was a Yank. So was Josh Coltrane's mama. She and I were best friends once. I know the way you felt about Josh. I just thought that maybe . . . now that the war is over . . ."

Angel tried to swallow a bite of ham, but the meat stuck in her throat. She tossed her napkin down on the table and stood up. "The Yanks destroyed my family. They destroyed Summers End and left Willie and me all by ourselves. You may be able to forgive Josh Coltrane, but the war will never be over for me!"

Angel left the table and fled the dining room, her eyes suddenly wet with tears. It hadn't happened since her mother died. Josh Coltrane had done what no amount of hardship had done for the past two years. It was just one more strike against him.

Fort James Jackson overlooked the Savannah River just a few miles east of the city. It was started in the early 1800's, a huge brick fortress built much like a castle that even had a moat and a drawbridge. In December a year ago, William T. "Cump" Sherman had captured the fort when his troops overran the city on his infamous march to the sea.

The fort was used as a hospital now, the place Josh had recently been stationed. It was hardly a spot he would have chosen, since the structure was in such bad repair. With the Confederacy gone broke, there hadn't been money to spend on the neglected buildings, and the

Union had done little better. Water dripped through holes in the barracks' ceilings, bricks crumbled at the rear of the magazine, and the cisterns clogged up and often wouldn't run.

Josh had set men to work making the needed repairs, but the government had no long-range plans for the fort, and money for construction was sparse. With the war so recently ended, materials were sparse as well.

As he stood at the entrance to the makeshift hospital in one of the drafty converted barracks, Josh stared down the long row of wooden cots. Forty-five sick and injured men huddled beneath their threadbare blankets, some of them sweating with fever, others shaking with cold. A moan rose from somewhere down the line, and off in the distance he could hear a soldier weeping.

As he started through the line of injured men, Josh thought of the military train that had been derailed and the valuable supplies they had lost. The government was still chaotic. The requisition for supplies had taken weeks and now those supplies were lost. How many more weeks could these men hang on?

Cursing beneath his breath, he strode along the row of cots, stopping to check on a patient here and there or offer a moment of comfort, then finally reached the young blond soldier who was crying.

"Pain that bad, Bennie?" he asked, squatting at the young man's bedside.

The boy sniffed a little, then wiped his eyes with the cuff of his nightshirt. Bennie was only sixteen. "Sorry, Doc. I don't know what got into me. . . ." He tried to smile, but it came out crooked and forlorn. "Pain's no worse than it has been. Guess maybe it's just that . . . well, it's almost Christmas. I was hopin' I'd be home."

Josh squeezed the young soldier's hand. "You'll get home, Ben. Maybe not in time for Christmas, but you'll get there. You've got to believe that." The boy had taken a lead ball in the leg at Citronelle in Alabama last May, a battle fought after the war was officially ended. Complications set in. Benjamin Weatherby lost a leg, and he still wasn't healed enough to make the long journey back to South Carolina. Only time would tell if he ever would be.

"Can I get you anything?" Josh asked.

"You already did, Doc. Thanks for the encouragement. I'm gonna get home, Doc, just like you said."

Josh squeezed the young man's shoulder. "Good boy." They talked for a little while longer, then Josh moved up the aisle once more.

He paused at the door to the barracks, turning to speak to his assistant. "Dr. Medford?"

The tall, gaunt man looked up from the patient he worked over. "Yes, Doctor?" He was two years younger than Josh but the war had made him look older, his sandy brown hair already thinning, his eyes sunken into a weathered face.

"I'm going into town to see Colonel Wilson. I want to find out if he has any leads on who might have taken those medical supplies. I've got to convince him how badly we need them. He's got to do whatever it takes to get them back."

"The men are suffering terribly," Silas Medford said.

Josh nodded. "It may take me a while. Can you handle things here while I'm gone?"

"Of course."

"If you need me, you know where to find me. If I'm not there, I'll leave word where I've gone."

Si Medford smiled. "Yes, sir."

Josh knew they were counting on him. He had seen it in each man's eyes as he'd walked down the aisle. He wouldn't let them down, he vowed. They'd been let down too many times already.

CHAPTER TWO

Josh leaned over the wide mahogany desk in the study of the Davenport house on State Street across from Columbia Square. Colonel Wilson was using the beautiful old home as his headquarters until more permanent quarters could be built.

"We need those medical supplies, Colonel Wilson," Josh said. "The men are in terrible shape. Surely there is something you can do."

The stout, barrel-chested colonel leaned back in his brown leather chair. "We know the stuff wasn't destroyed in the wreck. The car containing the medical supplies was one of the few that came through the derailment undamaged. Unfortunately, by the time our men got there, it was totally cleaned out. Somebody's got your supplies, but any tracks they might have left were erased by the hordes of people who came to pick through the wreckage."

"What about a reward?" Josh suggested. "Most of these people need money pretty badly."

"We've already done that. Posters will be up all over town by the end of the day." The colonel riffled through a stack of paperwork in front of him. "A reward might work, but I doubt it. In their own way, these people are still fighting the war. Giving back supplies is tantamount to aiding the enemy. They simply won't help us."

Josh ran a hand through his thick, dark-brown hair. "Surely there's some way to convince them."

"Perhaps there is."

Josh leaned closer. "Sir?"

"The best hope we have, Captain Coltrane, is you."

"Me!"

"That's right. You grew up here in Savannah. You know these people better than anyone else in the regiment. I'd suggest you talk to them, convince them to give back those supplies you need so badly."

Josh scoffed. "If I may say so, sir, I'm the last person they'd be willing to listen to."

"That may be so. But it appears to me it's the only option you have. In the meantime, I've already sent in another requisition order. Eventually the stuff you need will get here."

Eventually, Josh thought. In the meantime, his patients were dying . . . or lying there in pain.

The colonel shoved back his chair and came to his feet. "Good luck, Captain Coltrane."

Josh quietly saluted. He'd need a lot more than luck if he was going to get back those badly needed medicines.

Closing the study door behind him, he walked through the lovely old home beneath molded plaster ceilings, past the beautiful elliptical stairway, and made his way out the front door. Calling on his former friends, people who felt he'd betrayed them by joining the North, wasn't something he looked forward to doing, but with every step he took, he thought of young Ben Weatherby and his determination strengthened.

Perhaps he could convince them. He had to give it a try.

* * *

It was warm this December, even for the South. Clouds floated overhead and late afternoon rays dampened his back beneath his blue wool coat as another door slammed behind him. The day had passed in a nightmare of disappointment and rejection. It didn't take long to discover most of the young men he had known had been killed in the war; others were still scattered across the country, trying to make their way home.

Kirby Fields, once his neighbor to the east, met him on the porch with a shotgun. Red Donnelley stood on crutches, one arm gone above the elbow, his surly manner speaking more eloquently than his brief, pointed "Go to hell" words.

By late afternoon, he'd exhausted most of his list of former acquaintances and found himself just below the road leading into what had once been Coltrane Farms. He'd been there only once since his return. His parents were no longer living and the place was so rundown and overgrown it made his chest hurt just to look at it. He'd walked through the cold, empty house, overwhelmed with bitter memories. He'd locked the door, hung a "For Sale" sign on the gate, and ridden away.

As a boy, he'd loved the farm, couldn't wait till he grew up and could help his father run it. But the South was no longer his home. Once his enlistment was up, he'd be returning to Philadelphia to set up his medical practice. His mother's family owned a number of northern factories. During the war, their profits had soared. His mother's share had gone to him. He was a rich man now, one of few men from the South who had come out of the war ahead.

Philadelphia and Sarah Wingate—that was his destiny now. With luck, he would make a home there and finally settle down.

Josh glanced ahead, a feeling of familiarity running

through him as he passed over the old bridge and continued up the lane. He was riding toward the farm again today, on his way to Summers End. The huge plantation bordered Coltrane Farms to the south, just a quarter-mile off the road leading to Fort Jackson.

Angel Summers was his last chance to make people listen. He had to convince her to help him.

Or maybe he just wanted an excuse to see her again.

Whatever the truth, a few minutes later he had crossed the bridge, turned off the road, and ridden up behind the big white house. Dismounting, he led his bay horse beneath the branches of a huge magnolia tree, then stood watching the slender blonde woman working on her hands and knees in the vegetable garden.

It was a sight almost hard to believe. The lovely Miss Summers, once the belle of Savannah, up to her elbows in dirt. And yet she looked as beautiful as she had in peach moire silk. Maybe even more so. The sun had tinted her cheeks a rosy pink and freckled her nose. Strands of her golden hair nestled against her throat, loose from the simple snood that rested on her shoulders.

Her breasts heaved with exertion, ripe and straining against her dress. Unhindered by stays or hoops, her simple brown skirt clung to her hips, outlining the rounded curves. Desire slid through him. He wanted to reach out and touch her, to cup the fullness of her breasts, to stroke them until they hardened against his hand. Even after four long years, he could still recall the berry taste of her lips, the span of her narrow waist.

His body hardened, his blood going thick and heavy, pounding as if he were still twenty-three and she just seventeen.

As though he had never been with a woman.

Josh Coltrane had been with a number of women in the past four years. At first he had done it to forget her, to wash Angel from his mind and heart. Then, as the war progressed, because he needed the solace, the few short hours to forget the blood and gore of the battlefield.

Now, looking at Angel, he realized he felt more just watching her work in the garden than he'd felt with the most practiced whore.

Angel gripped the trowel and jammed it into the dirt, unseating another stubborn weed. She was working along a row planted with cabbage and kale, hoping the winter wouldn't be too hard on them. They needed fresh vegetables desperately, and they couldn't afford to reseed. And Christmas was coming. She tried to make the holidays special for Willie, to keep their family traditions alive, even though their parents were gone. A big Christmas dinner was one of them.

The trowel slammed down and she dug out a weed, then winced as something thorny bit into her hand. "Ouch!" A soft curse escaped, followed by the rumble of a man's deep voice.

"You all right, Angel?"

Her head snapped up, whipped toward the sound. Her body went as stiff as the hoe on the ground beside her. She took a deep breath and released it slowly, collecting herself, forcing away the pain, burying the hurt beneath her anger. "Well, if it isn't the infamous Captain Coltrane."

"Dr. Coltrane at present, since it appears you're in need of one." His voice still carried a trace of the South, she noticed, a soft drawl that whispered over her like the gentlest wind.

"I-I'm fine," she said, wiping away the dirt as he knelt beside her, then sucking at a single drop of blood. When she looked up, Josh was staring at her mouth.

"I'd be happy to do that for you," he said softly.

Her stomach contracted; moist heat unfurled. He was kneeling so close she could feel the warmth of his body, hear the rustle of fabric when the muscles moved beneath his sky blue shirt.

"I told you I was fine." She came to her feet, dusting off her hands, brushing the dirt off her brown woolen skirt, trying to ignore the too-rapid patter of her heart. She looked up and Josh was smiling, his brown eyes full of mirth. "What's so funny?"

"Hold still." His hand came up to her cheek. "You've got a smudge of dirt on your nose." He cradled her face as he brushed it off and his gentle touch made her tremble.

Angel quickly stepped away. "Wh-what do you want? Why did you come here?"

He assessed her a moment, as if he sized her up. "I need your help, Angel. I hate to ask you. If there was any-one else I could turn to, I would. I was hoping . . . for old times' sake . . . you might agree."

Angel eyed him warily, trying not to notice the way his shirt stretched over his powerful shoulders, the way his breeches hugged his hard-muscled thighs. His face was tanned and lean, his features harder than she remem-bered. She wanted to reach out and touch him, assure her-self he was really there. "You want me to help you do what?"

"That train your friends derailed was loaded with medical supplies. The hospital's been waiting for them for weeks. Without them, the men are suffering badly. I was hoping you would help me get them back."

Angel said nothing for the longest time, her mind clouding with thoughts of betrayal. "I can't believe it. You actually came here to ask me for help? You must be out of your mind."

Josh's mouth went thin. "Maybe I am. Maybe I was fool enough to remember the compassionate young woman I once fell in love with. A woman who couldn't stand to see anyone suffer, not even an animal. Remember the fawn you found with the broken leg? You cried for hours when your daddy had to shoot it. You remember that, Angel?"

She sniffed and glanced away. "I remember."

"There are forty-five men in that hospital. Some of them are young, some are old, some are dying, some are fighting desperately to live. All of them need comfort, Angel. You can help me give it to them."

Her chest squeezed, tightened a hard knot inside her. He was painting a terrible picture. She didn't like to think of Union soldiers as men. They were simply blue-belly Yanks. The enemy. She only shook her head. "I can't help you."

Josh gripped her arms. "You could if you wanted to. The townspeople have always respected the Summers family. They respect you, Angel. They've got no real use for that much medicine and we'll pay them to give it back. They'll do it if you ask them to."

Angel jerked away. "Well, I won't ask them. Not for a bunch of blue-belly Yanks." She whirled, pointing toward the house with its peeling paint and broken shutters, to the withered fields, empty ramshackle barn, and beyond.

"Take a look around, Josh. Summers End is gone. Mama and Daddy are dead. Everything I once loved is gone. The North did that. Your precious Union. If you think I'm going to help even one Union soldier, you are sorely mistaken."

"The war is over, Angel."

"Not around here, it isn't."

"For God's sake, Angel, it's Christmas. Doesn't that count for something?"

"It didn't count for much last year when Sherman

rolled over us like so much flour under a millstone. Savannah was a Christmas gift for Lincoln—that's what he said."

He looked at her and his eyes grew dark with disappointment. It made her heart twist inside her. Dear God, how could she still care what Josh Coltrane thought of her?

"You've changed, Angel," he said softly.

Hurt rippled through her, yet she knew it was the truth. "And you haven't?"

His mouth thinned faintly. "You're right. Both of us have changed. I wish I could say it was for the better." He backed up a few paces, his eyes still on her face. Then he touched the brim of his hat in farewell. "Good-bye, Miss Summers. I hope you have a very merry Christmas."

He turned away from her then and set off toward his horse. Just watching him walk away made her stomach tighten inside her. Her heart was pounding, hammering against her ribs. Dear God, she didn't want him to leave. She damned him to hell for making her feel that way, damned him for the power to still make her care when she'd believed that power was gone.

Anger rose like a tidal wave inside her. Josh Coltrane had betrayed her. He had chosen his precious cause over a lifetime together. He hadn't loved her enough to stay.

Now he needed her help and he actually expected her to give it. Well, Josh Coltrane could just go straight to hell!

Josh and his assistant, Silas Medford, worked through most of the night. Without the drugs he needed, his patients weren't sleeping, either. Still, by nine o'clock that morning, he was mounted and on the road, riding beneath

a wintry blue sky. He had thought of a couple more people who might help him, then he was headed back to
Summers End for another talk with Angel.

Strangely, considering how badly his first attempt to
convince her had gone, he'd decided to try again.

He had thought about it all of last night, running the
minutes they'd shared, the words she had spoken, back
through his mind. There was something he had seen in
her eyes, something that didn't match the harsh words she
had spoken, something of pain and regret.

The war had done that to her. It had taken her mama
and daddy, destroyed her home, her way of life. And he
had done it when he'd left her. He knew he had hurt her.
Until he had seen her, he hadn't known how much.

The war had forced her to grow up, had taught her to
be tough to survive, to protect her little brother.

But strength did not preclude compassion. It was
buried, perhaps, but Josh believed that it was still there.
Compassion had been a deeply rooted part of the woman
he had loved. Though she had done her best to convince
him it was gone, he believed he had seen it; behind the
pain, behind the anger, it flickered in those clear blue
eyes.

And there was something else that might work in his
favor. Ida Dixon lived with Angel. He'd discovered that
when he'd arrived in Savannah, and Ida was once his
mother's friend.

Riding to the front of the house this time, he reined up,
tied the horse to the hitching post out in front, and
climbed the wide porch stairs. The house was built in the
Federal style with huge white Doric columns. Once it was
a showplace. Now broken green shutters hung at the windows and the ornate front door needed a fresh coat of
paint. He stood in front of it, thinking of the last time he
had come here before the war, the time he'd said good-

bye to Angel, the pain that had lashed through them both as he'd ridden away. Steeling himself, he knocked on the door, then waited with his plumed hat in his hand.

The door creaked open. "Yes, suh?" The Summerses' aging butler stood framed in the opening. Only his clothing had changed. Worn canvas breeches and a faded gingham shirt replaced the immaculate white linen jacket and tailored black trousers he had always worn.

"Hello . . . Serge." He had to stretch for the name, then he smiled as he recalled it.

Serge smiled, too. "Mista Josh. I hardly recognized you."

"Four years of war can do that to a man."

Serge nodded, knowing the words were true.

Josh noticed the old man's hair had turned completely gray. "I came to see Mrs. Dixon and Miss Summers. Do you know if they happen to be in?"

"Who is it, Serge?" a woman's husky voice called out. He could hear her heavy footsteps as she walked into the entry.

"It's Mista Josh, ma'am. He come to see you an' Miz Angel."

The older woman swept past the butler, stopped to give Josh an assessing glance, then surprised him with a wide, welcoming smile, the first he'd received since his return to Savannah.

"Good Lord, Josh Coltrane, you surely are a sight for sore eyes. Come in, come in."

The hug the big woman delivered felt good. Damn good. It made him feel like he was home. He wasn't, of course. Savannah would never be his home again.

"I brought this for you." He held out a small brown paper sack and Ida took it, opened the sack, and stared at the contents.

"Coffee! Real fresh-ground coffee!" She took a long,

lingering sniff. "Landsakes, it's been ages since we had any of that 'round here." She smiled. "All I got is chicory on the stove. I can make some of this if you—"

"What you've got is fine, Mrs. Dixon."

"Aunt Ida," she corrected. "I was always Aunt Ida to you before. The war hasn't changed that, has it?"

Josh smiled. "Not for me. It's good to see you, Aunt Ida."

"It's good to see you, too, Josh. Angel's gone across the way to fetch Willie home for supper, but she'll be back shortly. You can wait for her in the parlor."

"Actually, I came to see you, too." He passed the door to the parlor and followed the beefy woman into the steamy kitchen. There was a separate kitchen outside, he recalled, for use in the summer and to help prevent fires, but the household was so small now, apparently they cooked inside. And the old black cookstove would help to heat the house.

"Angel told me you came by," Ida said, pouring him a cup of the chicory they used for coffee, then one for herself. "I guess she wasn't much pleased to see you."

"I don't suppose she was."

"What about you?" Ida asked, as direct as he remembered. "Were you glad to see her?"

Too glad, he thought. Too damned glad. "She's still as pretty as ever. Maybe even prettier."

"That's not what I asked you, Josh."

"The war ended whatever we might have had, Aunt Ida. Surely you know that."

"You married?" she asked and he smiled.

"No."

"Got a girl somewheres?"

His mouth curved. "Kind of."

"Where?"

"Philadelphia."

"You goin' back there when you get out?"

"I plan to set up my medical practice there."

"Gonna marry the girl?"

"I'm not sure." Where had that come from? He'd been pretty damned sure two weeks ago. But two weeks ago he hadn't seen Angel Summers again. "I imagine, sooner or later, we'll marry. I haven't asked her yet."

Ida took a sip of her coffee, set the blue enamel cup back down on the kitchen table. "Angel told me why you came by."

"I need her help, Aunt Ida. I need both of you to help me." He told the buxom woman about the men in the hospital at the fort. About the medicines that had been stolen and how badly he needed them back.

"If you're set on convincing Angel, you've set yourself a sizable task, Josh Coltrane."

A movement sounded in the doorway. "Too sizable, I'm afraid—even for you, Josh."

He came up from his chair and turned to face her, felt his breath lodge just to see her standing so close after all these years. How many times had he seen her like that in his dreams, her cheeks rosy, her golden hair beginning to come undone? How many times had he imagined kissing her, making love to her?

He shook his head, forcing the images away, trying to make the blood stop thundering in his ears.

"I'm not going to help you, Josh." There was turbulence in her eyes, and the pain was there. He recognized it now for what it was. He had done that to her. Hurt her far more deeply than he had imagined. It made a knot of regret ball in his stomach.

The screen door slammed. A little boy rushed past her, hurling himself into the room. He stopped dead still when he saw Josh, took a step backward into Angel's skirts. She wrapped an arm protectively around his shoulders.

"You're a Yank," the boy said. "What are you doin' here?"

Josh smiled. "I'm a friend of your sister's. You were pretty small when I left. I guess you don't remember."

"Angel doesn't have no Billy Yanks for friends."

"This is Josh Coltrane, Willie," Angel said gently. "He used to live at Coltrane Farms." All the love and compassion he remembered in the past surfaced as Angel hugged the boy. "He isn't going to hurt us."

Willie's small body trembled, and for the first time Josh realized the boy was afraid. "The war is over, Willie. No one's going to hurt anyone now."

Willie said nothing, just eased farther back against Angel. "Josh is a doctor, not a soldier," she said.

The boy said nothing.

"Why don't you go outside and play for a little while longer," Angel said. "Rusty's still out there, isn't he?"

Willie nodded, his golden hair, lighter than Angel's, shimmering in the light coming in through the window. "I still need more pine branches if we're going to finish decorating for Christmas. Maybe you and Rusty could gather some more and bring them in."

"Can we string holly berries tonight?" the child asked.

"If you two will go pick some." Willie's face lit up. "Go on then. Supper isn't far off. I'll call you when it's ready."

Willie surveyed Josh for a final moment more, turned, and raced back out the door.

"He's a good-looking boy," Josh said.

"He's the spitting image of our father." Angel's spine went stiff. "But he'll never know that because our father is dead. I'm not going to help you, Josh."

His gaze swung away from the tight lines of Angel's face. "Then perhaps Ida will." He turned to the older woman, praying that in Ida he had finally found someone who could see beyond the past.

Ida's glance traveled from Josh to Angel and back again. "I'm from Macon, Josh, not Savannah. I've only been here since the end of the war. But I'll speak to the folks I know, tell them about the sick men in the fort. Maybe I can get them to listen."

"Aunt Ida!" Angel's face went pale. "You can't mean to help the Yankees!"

"They're men, Angel, and they're sick. I got to do what I think is right."

Angel said nothing, just stood there staring at her aunt. Then she turned and walked back through the screen door she had come in.

"Thank you, Ida," Josh said, dragging his attention back to the woman on the opposite side of the table. "You can't know how much I appreciate what you're doing."

"Don't count on it doin' much good, Josh. The rest of these folks are even more stubborn than Angel."

Josh just nodded. Angel was stubborn, all right. She always had been. But it was anger and pain she was fighting. It was hurt and betrayal that was keeping her from doing what was right.

For the ten thousandth time, he wished he could change the past, that the war had never come.

Unfortunately, it had—and nothing could ever change that.

CHAPTER THREE

Standing at the side of the house, Angel watched Josh Coltrane ride away. In the past, Coltrane Farms had raised beautiful blooded horses. Angel had never seen a man who could sit a horse as gracefully as Josh.

She watched him until his tall frame crested the rise and disappeared over the hill, but she couldn't stop thinking about him. He was a harder man now, rugged in a way he wasn't before, yet the tenderness inside him remained, the warmth in his expression. Where had that tenderness gone in her? When had she lost it?

It hadn't happened all at once, she was sure. It had begun to slip away the day Josh rode off to join the Union Army. More of it died with the news that her father had been killed at Shiloh, the final bits and pieces destroyed when her mother took to her bed and slowly ebbed away, joining Daniel Summers in an early grave.

Now Josh was back but he wouldn't be here long. She'd been standing at the kitchen door far longer than he knew. She had heard him say he was returning to Pennsylvania, marrying a girl who lived there. Just thinking about it made Angel's insides tighten into a hard knot of pain. Why did he have to come back? Why couldn't he have left her alone?

She thought of the way Josh had looked sitting there in the kitchen, his mouth curved into a smile, his dark eyes glowing with warmth. He looked like he belonged there, as if he had finally come home. It had taken every ounce of her will not to cross the room and throw her arms around him.

Dear God, how could she hate him so much when part of her still loved him? How could she ache for him when part of her wanted him to ride away and never return?

It was that part she had to hang on to. That was the part that would protect her from being hurt again.

Angel brushed at a tear, weary deep down in her bones. Lifting her skirts to avoid the muddy earth, she made her way to the rear of the house, climbed the stairs, and stepped inside the steamy kitchen. She needed to start making supper. Willie would be hungry and when he came in there was no doubt he'd be full of questions about the Yank who had come to Summers End.

Questions about Josh. Questions she didn't know how to answer.

Dragging a big iron frying pan out from under the dry sink, she set to work beside Aunt Ida, trying to drive thoughts of Josh Coltrane out of her head.

Willie Summers ducked beneath the branches of an overhanging willow and watched the uniformed soldier ride away. Blue-belly Yank. What was he doing at Summers End? Why was he talking to Angel? And why was she so upset?

He would probably never know, he figured. Grown-ups never told him anything. They always said he was too young, or that he'd figure it out when he got older.

Willie motioned to his friend as the soldier rode away, and Rusty Lewis raced from his own hiding place into the umbrella of darkness under the willow.

"What'd *he* want?" Rusty asked.

Willie shrugged his thin shoulders. "I don' know. Whatever it was, you can bet my sis didn't give it to 'im."

Rusty laughed. He was a year older than Willie, taller and more filled out. Willie was small for his age, his chest narrow and bony, his short legs rooster-thin.

"I bet she didn't," Rusty said. "Your sis don't like them bluecoats much."

"Me neither," Willie said.

"Me neither," said Rusty, "and that makes three."

Willie laughed and the two of them raced out from under the tree. By the time they got to the top of the hill at the end of the pasture on their way to pick holly berries, they were running flat out, not looking where they were going, paying not the least bit of attention. Neither boy noticed the half-buried barrel of a cannon. They had seen it there some months back, but there was so much abandoned army equipment around that they didn't give it much notice anymore.

As Willie whizzed up the hill and leaped into the air at the top, it was too late to avoid the heavy, rusted-out length of iron. He landed hard on the barrel and his foot gave way beneath him, the bone crunching as it splintered, then gouging him with pain as it knifed its way through the thin skin on his calf.

"Aieee!" he screamed as another wave of pain seared through him, then another and another, until all he felt was a single burning spasm. It sucked his will and his eyes rolled back, dragging him into the darkened tunnel of unconsciousness.

*   *   *

"Miss Summers! Miss Summers, come quick! It's Willie! It's Willie, Miss Summers—he's hurt real bad!"

"Oh, dear God!" Angel ran toward the commotion out back—the patter of small running feet and the shout of her brother's name. The child was nearly hysterical and talons of fear cut into her.

"Willie!" Racing out on the porch, she nearly collided with Rusty, whose face was red, his breath coming out in a series of wheezes.

"Where's Willie? Rusty, please, you have to tell me where he is."

Serge ran up before he could answer. "What's happened, Miz Angel?"

"Willie's been hurt," Rusty said. "We was racin' across the old cow pasture to the top of the hill. Willie got there first, only he didn't stop. He jumped off that little ledge up there—you know the one, Miss Summers?"

"Yes . . . I-I know the one." She started hurrying in that direction, forcing herself to stay calm, but her knees were shaking beneath her skirt.

"There's an old cannon up there, buried in the dirt. Willie didn't see it when he jumped and he landed right on the barrel. He broke his leg real bad and he was yellin'. Then he stopped movin'. We gotta hurry, Miss Summers."

But Angel was already running, old Serge right beside her. The ancient man was breathing hard trying to keep up, but Angel didn't dare slow.

When she topped the rise and saw Willie's crumpled figure lying at the bottom, she nearly blacked out herself. "Oh, God." Avoiding the ledge, she rounded the hill and ran straight to her brother's unconscious figure.

"Willie! Willie, can you hear me?" He moaned a little and his eyes fluttered open as she shifted his head onto her lap. Serge knelt beside her, surveying the bone that protruded through his pant leg.

"It's broke real bad, Miz Angel, gone clean through the skin." He jerked off the scarf around his neck and tied it around the leg above the break to stop the bleeding. "I'll go get the wagon so's we can get him back to the house, then I'll go fetch Dr. Gordon."

Angel nodded weakly. She couldn't seem to think. "Oh, Willie." She stroked the small blond head, then Serge's words began to penetrate her cold haze of fear. Dr. Gordon was the only doctor left in Savannah, a drunk who was usually nowhere to be found. Their neighbor, Mrs. Barkley, was good at doctoring, but she couldn't set a bone as badly broken as Willie's.

Her mind veered to tall, capable Josh Coltrane. Josh would know what to do but there was no way she could ask him for help—not when she'd just refused to help *him*.

She would find Doc Gordon and make sure he was sober. He had set plenty of broken bones in his day, but the thought of the drunken doctor working over her little brother made her stomach knot with worry. She would figure out something, she vowed. She couldn't stand to see Willie suffer.

By the time Serge arrived with the wagon, she had fashioned a splint from an old piece of wood and secured the leg to it with strips of her petticoat, making the limb immobile. Willie had regained consciousness, which eased her fear, but pain contorted his small features, making her feel even worse. He was trying not to cry as she held him in her lap for the short ride back to the house, but tears kept rolling down his cheeks.

"It's all right, honey," she said, but her own eyes glistened with tears. "Everything's going to be fine."

When they reached the house, Aunt Ida waited on the

porch. "Get him upstairs and out of those clothes," she commanded. "Serge, you go after Josh Coltrane. He was headed back to the fort."

Angel bristled. "I'm not asking Josh for help." She glanced down at the child's bloody pant leg. "Doc Gordon can set the leg."

Ida frowned. "He can, long as he's sober. Guess we'll just have to wait and see."

Angel chewed her bottom lip. She ought to go to Josh, ask him to help Willie. She would, she vowed, but only if she had to.

"I'll be back quick as a wink," Serge said, creaking his way back up to the seat of the wagon. "Willie's gonna be jes' fine. Old Serge says so." With a flick of his long, wrinkled fingers, the reins slapped hard on the bony horse's rump and the wagon rolled away.

Doc Gordon was sober, thank God. The leg was set with what appeared to be competence and efficiency, and Angel breathed a sigh of relief as she followed the doctor back down the stairs from Willie's room.

"The laudanum will help him sleep. Give him a drop or two in a glass of warm milk whenever he needs it." She thought of the drugs she had seen in his bag—each of them marked with Union Army labels—and knew they had come from the train wreck. She didn't feel one bit guilty, since Willie had need of them, but she couldn't help wondering if Doc Gordon had the rest of the medical supplies.

"Keep him warm," Doc said. "Make certain there are no drafts in the room. There is always the possibility of putrefaction with an injury like this, but William is young and healthy. He should heal just fine as long as he stays off the leg."

He pulled his stethoscope from around his fleshy neck and stuffed it into his black leather bag. He was a man in his late fifties, ruddy complected with a round, veined, drinker's nose. "I'll be back tomorrow to see how he's doing."

"Thank you, Dr. Gordon." She walked him to the door determined not to ask, but the words seemed to come of their own volition. "I was wondering . . . I noticed the laudanum you left upstairs has a Union label on it."

He nodded. "The train wreck, you know. Can't say as I'm sorry."

"D-did you wind up with all the medicine out of the supply car?"

"Good heavens, no. I couldn't use that much stuff in the next three years. There was a box of medicine and bandages and blankets on my door when I came into the office. I have no idea where it came from, but it was surely appreciated."

Angel's glance strayed upstairs. "It surely is, Dr. Gordon." She bit down on her lip. "About your fee . . . I'll pay you the rest of what we owe just as soon as the laundry money comes in." She had given him all of her egg money. She prayed the hens kept laying.

The doctor left and Angel went back upstairs. Willie was sleeping, his small form huddled beneath the quilt Aunt Ida had made for him on his seventh birthday. She gently brushed the blond hair out of his face, then ran her fingers over his name where it was embroidered with loving care on the edge of the quilt.

She bent and kissed his forehead. "Sleep tight, sweetheart," she said into the stillness of the room. Tomorrow he would feel better. In the meantime, he would need hot, nourishing food, and to see that he got it, there was a mountain of work to do.

* * *

Angel bent over the steaming tub of laundry that boiled next to the outside kitchen. It galled her to wash the Union officers' dirty clothes, but they needed the money and there wasn't much else she could do. Except maybe sell Summers End, and she wasn't yet ready to do that. Just the thought of leaving her beloved home made an aching knot ball inside her chest. Besides, with money so tight, there probably wouldn't be any buyers.

Angel blotted her forehead with an elbow, stirred the huge iron cauldron, and glanced up at the sun. It was growing late in the afternoon and the doctor still hadn't returned. Willie was restless and only the laudanum helped ease his pain. He looked pale and sunken, and she was worried about him.

Evening came but the doctor didn't. Angel spent a restless night beside Willie, who fretted and tossed and fought the covers, complaining he was too warm. By morning, she was exhausted.

She sent Serge back into town for the doctor, but no one knew where he was. Someone said he had gone out in the country to deliver a baby. Perhaps he had. Perhaps he'd gone off on another of his benders.

By the morning of the third day, Angel was flat-out scared.

"He isn't any better, Aunt Ida," she said, as she walked into the kitchen. "His leg is all swollen and red and now he has a fever."

"Did he drink all of Mrs. Barkley's fever medicine?"

Remembering the face her brother had made, Angel almost smiled. "He said it tasted like pig slop, but he got the last of it down."

Ida shook her head. "I don't know . . . maybe by to-morrow . . ."

But Angel kept on walking. "I'm not waiting until tomorrow. I'm not going to let Willie suffer because of my pride. I'm going after Josh."

Ida's broad face lit up. "Now you're talkin'. Josh will know what to do."

"I should have gone to him in the first place. I should have—"

"There's not a darn thing wrong with Doc Gordon—leastwise not when he's off the bottle—and he was good and sober the day he worked on Willie. You don't worry none about what you did or didn't do. You just go get Josh and everything will be all right."

"I hope so, Aunt Ida. I'd never forgive myself if something happened to Willie." The back door slammed behind her as she hurried out to the stable. The old sorrel gelding, the only horse they had left, usually pulled the wagon. She could go faster riding across the fields, taking the shortcut through Coltrane Farms, so she dragged out a worn old saddle and lifted it up on the horse's bony back.

Jamming her sturdy brown shoe into the stirrup, she pulled herself up on the hard leather seat and tried not to think of the picture she made with her skirts rucked up and her stockings exposed nearly to her knees. She tried not to remember her lovely padded sidesaddle or her royal blue velvet riding habit with the jaunty little hat cocked over her forehead.

Instead, she dug her heels into the old horse's ribs and set off toward Fort Jackson.

Half an hour later, she was riding up in front, staring up at the imposing brick fortress, shading her eyes against the sun so she could see.

"Hold it there, miss," one of the soldiers called out as she rode across the moat, which these days looked more like a giant mud sump. "I'm afraid you'll have to state your business before I can let you in."

Her chin went up. "I-I'm a friend of Dr. Coltrane's.

I'm here on a matter of urgency. Please . . . you must let me see him."

"Of course, miss," the soldier said. "If you'll just follow me, I'll see if I can find out where he is."

She rode the horse behind the lanky soldier, then dismounted and waited while he went into the barracks that served as a hospital, but apparently Josh wasn't there. They found him in the back of the quartermaster's office, rummaging through boxes, rounding up supplies. At the sound of her voice, he came up from where he knelt and his hard features softened when he realized who it was.

"I-I'm sorry to bother you, Captain Coltrane, but I was hoping I might speak to you for a moment."

"Of course." Long strides carried him to her side. He caught her arm and led her into a small, barren office, where he seated her on a rickety wooden chair and closed the door.

"What's wrong, Angel? You're as pale as a sheet."

"It's Willie." Tears burned her eyes. She tried to blink them away, but several spilled down her cheek. "He's sick, Josh. He broke his leg clear through the skin. The doctor set it, but he isn't any better. If anything, he's worse. I-I know I have no right to ask, but could you—"

"Of course I'll come." He reached for her hand and gave it a squeeze, and her body went weak with relief. "And you have every right to ask me. Whether you believe it or not, I'm still your friend."

Angel glanced away, unable to look into those warm brown eyes a moment more. He wasn't her friend. He was the enemy. She had to remember that. But in moments like these, it was hard to convince herself.

"When did this happen?" Josh asked.

"Three days ago. Dr. Gordon was supposed to come back and see him, but he never showed up."

Josh frowned. "Yes, I remember Doc Gordon. He's the best you've got left in Savannah?"

"He's the only doctor we have, Josh."

"As I recall, he's good when he's sober."

"He was sober when he worked on Willie. Otherwise, I never would have let him."

A corner of his mouth kicked up. "No, I don't imagine you would have." He took her arm again, urging her toward the door, and as worried as she was, she noticed the heat of his hand through her clothes. There was strength there, too, and some of it began seeping into her.

"Let me get my bag and we'll go," he said.

Angel merely nodded. Josh was coming. She had told herself he would, but she hadn't really been certain. Josh would help Willie. That was all that mattered now.

CHAPTER FOUR

Josh rose from the little boy's bedside. Willie was sleeping again, his face flushed with fever.

"Doc Gordon did a fine job setting the leg. It's properly aligned. The bone should mend without a problem. Unfortunately, the tear in the skin where the bone protruded doesn't look good. I'm afraid there may be some infection."

"You—you mean it's putrefied?" Angel asked, her big blue eyes wide with horror.

His jaw clamped. He had seen so much of that during the war, and too many cases of amputation. "Not yet. There's a lot of inflammation, though. That's what's causing his fever." He looked down at the boy's thin leg where it sat propped on a pillow. He had changed the dressing, but beneath the splint the flesh was red and swollen, warm to the touch. Willie's fever was rising and his pulse was too fast.

"I've cleaned the wound again and given him some more of the laudanum." His gaze flicked to the bottle stamped "Union Army" that sat on the dresser, and he had to clamp hard on his jaw not to ask her where it had come from. "I have to go back to the fort for a while. I'll return as soon as I can."

"Tomorrow?" she asked, hope mixed with fear in her voice.

He thought how much she had suffered these past four years. In her own way as much as the men on the battlefield. He smiled. "Tonight—if you can manage a place for me to sleep."

Angel's smile held relief, a soft smile that made her look like the young girl she had been. "We've got plenty of room. Nothing so grand as the old days, but at least your bed will be clean and warm." She walked with him out the bedroom door and down the stairs, then paused a moment in the entry.

"About the laudanum," she said, as he opened the door, "I asked Doc Gordon about it. He said he found a box of supplies on his doorstep. That's all he has from the wreck and he doesn't know where those came from."

His gaze ran over her, came back to her face. Lines of fatigue marred her forehead. Worry darkened her bright blue eyes. "Thanks for asking, Angel." He wanted to hold her, to take her in his arms and comfort her, to erase the past and every bitter word that had ever passed between them. He wanted things to be like they were, but he knew they never could be.

"As I said, I'll be back as soon as I can. In the meantime, Willie's going to need a number of different medicines, supplies that were lost in the train wreck. If you can't find Doc Gordon or he doesn't have them, maybe you can find a way to get them."

Her jaw firmed up. "I'll get them. I'll do whatever it takes to see that they're here."

He smiled. If she had been a handful before—and she surely had—he could only imagine the man it would take to deal with her stubborn will now. "Try to get some

Dover's powder. I'll need blue pill, quinine, some ipecacuanha powder, barley water, Spirit of Nitre, and some cream of tartar. Can you remember all that?"

She repeated the items aloud. "I'll write them down as soon as you're gone."

"Then I'll see you tonight."

"Yes . . ." she said. "Tonight," and the word and her smile washed over him.

Forcing his gaze from her face, he crossed the porch, still seeing her features, her pretty blue eyes, and the cleft in her chin. Untying his horse, he swung up on its back, then reined off toward the shortcut through Coltrane Farms. Knowing how worried she was, he hated to leave her, but there were patients who needed him more. He hated to make the trip across land that had once been his home—the memories were always too painful. He hated to come back to Summers End, knowing he still wanted Angel, knowing he couldn't have her, knowing that each moment he spent with her would make his need for her even more fierce.

So much hate. No wonder there wasn't the slightest chance that things could be mended between them.

The moon was up, nearly full tonight, but the wind had shifted and blown a cloud cover in. Angel waited anxiously by the window watching for Josh to ride up, then hurried out on the porch to greet him.

"Are you still planning to stay?" she asked with a glance toward the saddlebags slung over the back of his horse.

"I told you I would. How's the boy?"

Walking toward him, she watched his easy movements as he swung down from the saddle. "Unfortunately, he looks about the same. You go on in. I'll take care of your horse."

He started to protest, snapped his mouth closed and

nodded. It wasn't like Josh to let a woman do a man's work and undoubtedly he remembered the pampered young lady she had been. But Willie came first. There really was no choice.

"Go on," she urged with a smile that came close to amusement. "Believe me, I've done this before. I won't be gone long."

He went inside and she led his horse out to the stable for water and a forkful of hay. When she returned to the house, she found Josh with Ida, upstairs in Willie's bedroom.

He glanced from her brother to her as she walked in, and the tension in his jaw sent a spiral of fear shooting through her. "It's not good, Angel. I need those medicines badly."

She had gone to her neighbor, Mrs. Barkley, as soon as Josh had left the house. Rumor had it that one of the Barkley boys had been involved in the train wreck. If anyone could get what they needed, it was Eliza Barkley.

"We should have them first thing in the morning," Angel said. "I still don't know who has your supplies, but I have friends who know. They said they could get what we need."

"Good enough," Josh said, turning back to the boy.

"He's been real fitful," Ida said, rocking in a chair across from where Willie was sleeping. He lay tossing and turning on the bed, his hair damp with perspiration and sticking to his temples. Josh sat beside him, pressing cold, wet cloths against his forehead.

"He took some broth a little earlier," Ida said, "but he seems awful weak to me."

"We'll keep an eye on him tonight. If those medicines arrive in the morning, there's a chance they'll do the trick."

They took turns sitting with Willie. At two in the morning, Ida walked in to relieve her, but Angel was too worried to sleep.

"I'm all right, Ida. I'll stay with him. You go on back to bed."

But her aunt simply pulled her to her feet. "Go on now. At least go out and stretch your legs for a while. Fix yourself a glass of warm milk or somethin'."

Her muscles did need stretching. Her back ached from sitting in one place for so long, and a slight headache banged at her temple. Making her way out the door, she went downstairs, but she didn't head for the kitchen. Instead, she pulled her blue woolen wrapper more closely around her and made her way outside, onto the wide covered porch.

The wind was still blowing, whistling through the trees, ruffling the pale hair that hung down her back and fluttering the hem of her robe. Leaning against a tall white column, she stared out into the darkness, thinking of Willie, worrying about him, thinking of the dark-haired man upstairs.

At least she thought he was in the house till his tall figure stepped out of the shadows on the porch.

"You should be sleeping, Angel. Worrying about Willie won't make him get well any faster."

She turned in his direction, watched his long graceful strides as he approached her, tried to control the gnawing ache that rose in her chest just to look at him. "You aren't sleeping, either."

He stopped next to her, smiled down into her face. "What I do doesn't matter. I'm bigger, I'm older, and I'm a doctor. That means you're supposed to do what I say."

The breeze mussed his hair. A strand tipped forward above his dark eyes, and she fought an urge to brush it into place. "I never did what you said before. I don't suppose I'm going to start now."

His smile grew broader, a gleam of white in a strong, hard jaw. "No, you didn't, and no, I don't suppose you will." His hand came up to her cheek, lifted a windblown curl away, and tucked it behind an ear. "What would you have done if we had gotten married? The vows say a wife is supposed to love, honor, and obey."

Her heart clenched, tightening painfully inside her. She stared into those compelling brown eyes and memories threatened to overwhelm her. "I'd have done my best to be a good wife to you, Josh. I would have done everything I could to make you happy."

His gaze slid down to her mouth. She could feel it as if he touched her, and her bottom lip began to tremble. Josh reached out and stilled it with the pad of his thumb. His eyes grew more intense and she thought she heard him groan. Then he was tilting her head back, bending forward, settling his mouth over hers.

Dear God, it was the sweetest, most devastating kiss she had ever known. The softest caress, a moment of aching tenderness, then his lips crushed down, and heat swept through her.

She was in his arms before she realized what was happening. By then she didn't care. She only knew it was Josh, that in an instant, four long, agonizing years had been washed away, that for these few bittersweet moments the past did not exist. She was the girl who loved Josh Coltrane and he was the man who loved her.

She gave in to the sweetness, the yearning, kissing him back, parting her lips as he urged her to do, allowing his tongue to sweep in. He smelled faintly of leather and horses, and a man's scent that was Josh's alone. Warmth slid through her; sweet, damp heat seeped into her core. She wound her fingers in his hair, let the strands slip through, felt the muscles bunch in his neck and shoulders.

His chest pressed into her breasts and her nipples tightened beneath her cotton night rail. His hands roamed her back and everywhere he touched her she burned. He cupped her face and deepened the kiss, drinking in more of her, allowing her to take more of him. He had kissed her before, but never like this. This was a man's kiss. And now she was a woman.

A lonely woman who had loved this man and never thought to feel his touch again. His mouth moved to her ear. He pressed kisses there, then trailed a line of kisses along the column of her throat. Warmth spiraled through her, waves of building heat that crested and peaked and scorched even hotter.

"Joshua. . . ."

"Angel. . . . God, how I've missed you." The robe fell open. His fingers tugged at the tie on her nightgown, allowing it to fall off one shoulder. His lips pressed there, firm and warm, softer than she would have expected, hotter, more determined. She gripped his shoulders as he bared a breast, stared at it with reverence, then took her nipple into his mouth.

Scorching pleasure. Hot ripples of flame. Dear God, she had never imagined . . .

"Angel. . . ." His hand cupped her breast as he kissed her again, urging her back against the big white pillar. His arousal pressed against her, a rock-hard ridge she finally recognized for what it was, a man's rampant desire for her. Little by little, it burned through her haze of pleasure and began to shout a warning. Josh had been gone four years. Men changed in four years. The war changed them. Josh was a Yank. Yankees took what they wanted. They had raped women all over the South—she had heard the terrible stories.

She broke free of the kiss, breathing hard, her senses spinning, the warning growing louder, a buzzing that filled her ears. "Josh, please . . . we can't . . . we can't do this." She thought of the woman Josh would marry, a Northerner, someone more like him. He was in love with the woman, not with her. She wondered if he simply meant to use her, if he had become that kind of man since the war.

He kissed her again, pulled her back into his arms, found her mouth, and captured her lips. Heat roared, made her dizzy, but still she pushed him away. "Josh! Y-you have to stop. We—we can't do this!"

His breathing came fast and rough, his eyes were as dark as the night around them. She had never seen him look that way. Hard. Ruthless. Determined. A man used to command, used to getting what he wanted.

A shiver of fear slid through her.

Josh must have felt it, for his head fell back and he sucked in a great breath of air. "I'm sorry, Angel. I never meant for that to happen. You don't have to be afraid."

"I-I'm not afraid." But she was. And not just of Josh. Thinking of what she'd let happen, Angel was afraid of herself. She took a step backward, pulling the robe closed around her with a shaky hand.

"I'm sorry," Josh repeated. "I promise it won't happen again." His fists were clenched, she saw, and his jaw looked tight. He worked to force himself under control.

"It was my fault as well," she admitted softly, hoping he couldn't see the rose in her cheeks as she thought of the way he had touched her. "We loved each other once. Your coming back just made us remember."

He raked a hand through his thick chestnut hair. "I suppose that's it." He glanced up and fixed his eyes on her face. "I won't lie about it, Angel. I wanted you then. I want you now. I know it wouldn't work, that there's too much grief between us, but it doesn't make me want you any less."

Angel said nothing. Her breast still ached from the way he had touched her. Her mouth still tingled from his kiss.

"I won't hurt you, Angel. Not again. I give you my

word." No, she thought. He wouldn't hurt her again. She wasn't going to let him. "We had better go back in."

Josh simply nodded. Willie was all that mattered. At least they both felt the same about that.

Josh tossed and turned, but he couldn't fall asleep. He wasn't even certain he wanted to. Every time he closed his eyes, he saw Angel. Angel with her golden hair sliding through his hands like silk, Angel with her head thrown back, her pale skin flushed with passion. Angel with her breasts bare, more sensuous than he had imagined. He could still taste her mouth on his lips. Her scent still clung to his clothes.

He fisted his hands, recalling the softness of her skin, the tightness of her nipples. He was hard as he lay on the bed, his body throbbing with a bittersweet fire. He had known it would be like this, the wanting. Known it, but it was far worse.

Now as he lay beneath a quilt she had fashioned, trying to ignore the soft ache in his groin, he told himself again that he wanted her but he didn't love her.

Part of him believed it. Just as he had abandoned her, Angel had abandoned him. If she had loved him, she would have understood why he'd had to leave. If she had cared enough, she would have accepted his decision, hoped and prayed he would return.

Get out, Josh Coltrane! she had shouted instead. *You're dead to me—do you hear? Dead to me and everyone here who ever loved you. Don't come back, Josh. If you do—if Confederate soldiers don't kill you first—I swear to you I will!*

She couldn't have loved him, not the way he thought she did. At least that's what he had believed. But the years had eased the pain and he'd had time to think. Eventually, he had come to understand how young she was. How young they both were. Young and naive.

Now she was a woman. Different from the one he remembered. Different and far more attractive than she had ever been as a flighty, pampered young girl.

Josh rolled over on the bed, wishing the morning would come, wishing he could stop thinking of Angel, hoping the boy in the room next door wouldn't be another casualty in a war that never seemed to end.

Eventually, he gave up, dragged his shirt and breeches on, and hauled himself downstairs for a cup of coffee. By the time the first gray light of dawn broke over the horizon, the supplies he needed sat on the porch. Old Serge found them and came creaking up the stairs, carrying them in his arms, hauling them into the room where Josh sat next to Willie.

"They here, Mista Josh. Dat medicine you needed— it's done showed up on the porch!"

"Thank God." He took the box from Serge's wrinkled hands and immediately began to take inventory. Everything he'd asked for and more, along with cotton pads and bandages. He'd been using home remedies so far, a concoction of whatever medicinals he could conjure: chamomile out of the garden, root of sweet weed Serge had dug from a swampy spot in the river, milkweed from the thicket. They all had their value and he wasn't completely convinced that their use, on occasion, wasn't more successful than the latest modern drugs.

Still, he was relieved the supplies had come. He only wished he had more for his patients at the fort.

"Is dey anythin' I can do?" Serge asked, still standing in the doorway.

"You can get me some more hot water. I'd like to change the dressing on Willie's leg before I leave."

The little boy stirred. He blinked when he saw Josh's

uniform, and sat up in the bed. "What—what're *you* doin' here? You get away from me! I don't want no dirty Yank touchin' me." It was the first time the child had been awake enough to realize he was there. Josh might have smiled if that had been a good sign, but the fever dulling the boy's light blue eyes was hardly good news.

"It's all right, Willie, I'm a doctor. Doctors aren't the same as regular soldiers. It doesn't really matter what color their uniform is."

A rustle of skirts drew his attention. Angel stood not two feet away, one eyebrow cocked as if neither she nor Willie believed what he said.

"Make him go away, Angel," the boy said. "I don't want no Billy Yank—"

"Hush, sweetheart." Angel knelt beside him, reached out and took his hand. Watching her, Josh ignored the tightness binding his chest. "Dr. Coltrane is a very old friend. He used to be our neighbor. He's come to help you get better."

"It hurts," Willie said, his eyes tearing up. "It hurts so bad."

"I know, sweetheart. Pretty soon you'll feel better."

Willie just looked at her. When? his blue gaze silently asked. Then his eyelids slowly closed and he drifted back to sleep. Josh applied the salves he had made, gave Angel instructions on what medicines Josh should have, when, and how much. Then the dressings were changed and he was finally ready to leave.

"When—when will you be back?" she asked and there was that look of fear again.

"Tonight. Let's hope there's some change for the better." But he wasn't sure there would be and he wasn't sure what he would do if there wasn't.

CHAPTER FIVE

Angel paced in front of the hearth in the downstairs parlor. The room had once been grand—Persian carpets on the inlaid parquet floors, expensive Chinese vases, heavy brocade silk draperies. Now the carpets and vases had been sold, the floors were scuffed, and the draperies were faded.

Funny how much the loss had mattered before. Now, with Willie so terribly sick upstairs, it didn't seem to matter anymore.

For the tenth time that afternoon she walked to the window. Long pine boughs had been linked together to form evergreen garlands that hung from the top of the windows. They'd cut snowflakes from white paper squares and pasted them on the glass, and a wreath of holly decorated the wall above the mantel. They had started getting ready for Christmas, but Willie's accident had put an end to what little holiday spirit they had been able to muster.

The only present she wanted now was for her little brother's leg to get well.

Angel stared out the window as she had done before, but it was too early for Josh's return. She should be taking the soldiers' clean laundry back to town, or collecting eggs from the hen house, since Willie wasn't able. Instead, she stood there staring, worrying about her brother, waiting for Josh and hoping he would come early.

But none of the four mounted men she spotted riding up the lane to Summers End was Joshua Coltrane. Since the end of the war, it was common for Confederate soldiers to stop by on their journey back home, and the butternut color of the men's jackets, ragged and dirty as they were, said that's what these men were.

Angel pushed open the door as the soldiers drew near, then suddenly wished that she hadn't. The war had taken the cream of Southern men. Those still living had returned to their families as swiftly as they could. Those who hadn't yet gone home were often wanderers, outcasts with no family to return to.

Still, it was the Yankees she feared, not war-torn Confederate troops, no matter how hardened they might appear.

"Afternoon, gentlemen." Angel smiled up at their beefy leader, a sergeant according to the yellow stripes on his jacket sleeve. "Welcome to Summers End."

"Thank you, ma'am." He tipped his hat. "Your man around?"

"My father died at Shiloh. What can I do for you, sergeant?"

"Sorry to bother you, ma'am, but me and the boys is headin' home. We've traveled a goodly distance. Thought maybe you might find us a bite of food or at least let us water our horses."

She pointed toward the rear of the house. "The watering trough is out back. We haven't got much to eat around here, but I imagine I can rustle up something."

"That'd be mighty obligin'," a bearded soldier said.

"You go on and tend your horses," Angel said. "I'll bring the food out as soon as it's ready."

The sergeant touched the brim of his wide-brimmed gray hat. "Thank you, ma'am."

As the men rode away, Angel returned inside the house. Ida was already at work in the kitchen. Apparently, she had seen the men from upstairs.

"Those poor boys sure look the worse for wear, don't they?"

"They're going home," Angel said. "I feel sorry for them." She walked to the dry sink. "How's Willie?"

" 'Bout the same, I'm afraid. Serge is with him. I'll be glad when Josh gets back."

So would she, Angel thought. At least part of her would be. The other part tried not to remember the way she had felt when he had kissed her. Instead, she set to work beside Ida, heating a kettle of beans, carving thick chunks of bread and several slabs of cheese.

"I'll take it out to them," Ida said, but Angel shook her head.

"I'll do it. You've been working all day. You've got to be dead on your feet. Why don't you go back up and sit with Willie? Let Serge catch a nap if he can."

Ida smiled with a hint of relief. She was a heavy woman. Since morning, she'd been making mincemeat from the last of the dried fruit and a haunch of venison. Standing as she had for so many hours made her thick legs ache unbearably.

"I won't be long."

"Take your time," Ida said. "Those boys look like they could use a little friendly conversation."

Slinging a towel over one shoulder, Angel picked up the tray and started for the door. The youngest soldier saw her and came to help her carry it. He couldn't have been more than eighteen. On a second trip, she brought out the beans, setting the kettle on a tree stump near the watering trough.

It was brisk but not cold. A milky sun kept the temperature from falling. Still, something about the men made her uneasy and she decided not to stay, turning instead back toward the house.

"Where you goin', pretty girl?" the sergeant asked, setting his tin plate of food on the ground and coming quickly to his feet. "Why don't you stay and keep us company for a while?"

Unconsciously, she backed up as he drew near, caught herself and stood her ground. "I-I have to go in."

His hand came out, his skin rough, the fingernails long and dirty as he caught her chin. "Not yet, you don't. Right, boys?"

Two of them laughed. "That's right, Sarge." In minutes, the four of them stood around her.

"We don't mean to hurt ya, ma'am," the bearded soldier said, "but me and the boys, we ain't been with a woman in more'n two years. We done talked it over, and well, we just gotta have ya."

"What—what are you talking about?" She started backing away, praying she had misunderstood his words.

"I'll take her first," the sergeant said, blocking her retreat, "seein' as it was my idea to come here." Before she could run, he caught her arm, clamped a hand over her mouth, and jerked her against him. Fear shot through her, pinpricks of alarm that sent shivers along her spine. She tried to twist free, tried to pry his hand away, but his hold was relentless and he dragged her down on the ground.

"It won't do ya no good to fight, ma'am. Just be easy and ya won't get hurt."

"I'm next," the bearded man said, and Angel began to fight in earnest. Already he was unbuttoning his breeches and so was the sergeant. She felt the bigger man's hands on her leg, shoving up her skirt. Her struggles increased and so did her fear. Oh, dear God! She glanced toward the house. Willie's room faced the front, not the rear, and Serge was probably sleeping. She kicked out with her foot, but her shoe slammed into the soldier's thick leather boot. Sinking her teeth into the fleshy hand that covered her mouth, she heard him curse, then felt the burning sting of a slap across her face.

"Dammit, I said to lay still."

"Hurry up!" the bearded soldier hissed. "We ain't got all day." Then the sharp click of a gun being cocked echoed just a few feet away. The rustle of clothing ceased. The sergeant seemed frozen in place, one hand still clutching a button on his trousers.

"Very slowly," a familiar voice said, "let the lady go and back away." The sergeant's hand crept down toward his weapon but Josh's hard voice stopped him. "I wouldn't do that if I were you." He motioned to the others. "You men—keep your hands out in front of you, well away from those guns, and back away."

Cold air seeped through her thin pantalets as the sergeant lifted his heavy bulk off her. Angel's hands were trembling so badly she could barely pull her skirt back into place.

"You all right, Angel?"

"Y-yes." Josh was here! He had come just like he said. But her teeth were chattering and it wasn't from the cold.

"You men throw down your weapons. Take it nice and easy. Angel, you get over here behind me."

For once, she did as he told her, moving to stand so close to Josh's back she could feel the heat pouring off his hard-muscled body.

"Get me some rope," he told her, his Spencer rifle pointing straight at the sergeant's heart. "You men weren't happy just getting through this war alive. Now you'll be spending the next few years in a Federal prison."

Angel started shaking even harder. Oh, dear God, she

knew about those places. Kirby Fields had been in one. He still couldn't talk about it without crying. A grown man like Kirby. He wasn't afraid of anything, but he cried when he talked about Elmira.

"Go on, Angel," Josh said firmly. "Go get the rope."

She still didn't move. They deserved to be in prison for what they'd tried to do, and yet . . . "Let them go, Josh."

He turned a little, till he could see her from the corner of his eye. "Are you insane? These men may be Confederates, but they would have raped you just the same."

"I-I know what they meant to do. I don't think they've done it before. The war did it—it's made them half crazy. It did things to all of us. Let them go, Josh, please. Do it for me."

He cursed long and fluently, words a younger Josh Coltrane wouldn't have said. "You men hear that? Miss Summers wants me to let you go. Unfortunately, the lady is a helluva lot more forgiving than I am." The smile he flashed was wolfish and cold. "I'll make you a deal. I'll give you a head start. You get on those horses and ride out of here. By the time I get back to Fort Jackson and turn you in, you can be a good ways down the road."

The men glanced from one to another. There wasn't one that didn't look a little bit ashamed. "You got a deal, Yank." The sergeant motioned toward Angel. "We didn't come here to hurt her. She was just so damned pretty. . . ."

"Get out," Josh said coldly.

Angel didn't realize she was gripping his arm until the men rode out of sight and she felt his fingers curl over her hand. He turned and eased her into his arms, holding tightly against his chest.

"I would have killed them," he said. "I'm a doctor and I swear I would have murdered every last one."

Angel slid her arms around his neck and clung to him, her body still trembling with the remnants of fear. Confederate soldiers would have raped her. A Yankee soldier had saved her. The world had turned upside down, had gone completely insane. Dear God, she was so confused!

"Angel . . ." Josh whispered, stroking a hand through her hair. "Sweeting, are you all right?"

She eased herself away, wanting to escape him. Wanting to stay right where she was. "I'm all right . . . now."

He turned her face to study the red mark on her cheek. "Bastards."

Ignoring the warmth of his hand, she eased herself farther away, smoothing the front of her skirt. She didn't want to think about Josh, the way he had come to her defense. She didn't want to hear her heart thrum the way it was, just being near him.

"We'd better get back to the house," she said. "Willie isn't getting any better. In fact, I think he's worse."

Josh went tense. "Come on." Taking her hand, he led her toward the back door.

Angel paused as he pulled it open. "I'm frightened, Josh. I can't stand to see him hurting. What are we going to do?"

Josh didn't answer. Not until he reached the little boy's bedside. One look at Willie and the lines of his face went grim.

"We've got to take him back to the fort. I need to watch him around the clock. If you want to come with him, I can arrange a place for you to sleep."

"You can't take a little boy to an army post! For heaven's sake, the place is full of Yankee soldiers!"

"Fort Jackson is a hospital, Angel. Willie's fever's got to be stopped. If it isn't, he'll go into convulsions. Since I can't stay here all the time, Willie's got to go there."

Angel bit her lip. Yankees. Would there ever be an end to them? "Are you sure there's no other way?"

"Willie needs constant medical attention. This is his best chance to get it."

Angel looked at little Willie, saw the way his thin chest rose and fell, the way he tossed on the bed. Her brother needed Josh just as she had needed him today. What did it matter where the child was as long as she was with him? "All right, we'll take him to the fort."

"I'll tell Ida to get his things," Josh said. "Tell Serge to hook up the wagon, then pack what you need."

Angel nodded. One look at Willie and her chest went tight. He had to be all right—he had to be!

Twenty minutes later they were packed and ready and loaded aboard the wagon. Before night had fallen they had passed through the heavy stone porticos of Fort Jackson.

"We'll get Willie settled in the hospital," Josh said. "Then I'll find a room for you."

"All right."

He led her toward a wooden barracks, Willie cradled against his broad chest. Pulling open the heavy wooden door, Josh led her into the dimly lit interior. The smell hit her first, as sharp and painful as a blow to the head, sending the bile up in her throat.

"I should have warned you," he said, catching a glimpse of her pale face. "You aren't going to be sick?"

Her chin hiked up but she had to wet her lips. "I'm fine."

"You get used to it after a while. I should have said something. We're not used to civilians out here."

She fought down another wave of nausea. "It's all right. I told you, I'm fine." But of course she wasn't. Neither was she prepared for the rows of suffering men she found inside the barracks. Two long lines of white-draped bodies, the bed linens clean but some of the wounds weeping blood, forming dark red patches on the sheets.

The place was clean and neat, meticulously so. Which wasn't surprising. Josh's own home had always been spotlessly cared for. But the stench of ammonia, putrefied wounds, sweat-soaked male bodies, and vomit made drawing a breath nearly impossible.

The building itself contributed to the gloominess. The white-painted walls were yellowed and peeling. The damp smell of mildew rose up from the floors. Whale oil lanterns cast an eerie glow into the open rafters, and the hazy, flickering shadows of the men moved ominously over the walls.

"We'll put Willie on a cot up in the front. Dr. Medford and I will take turns watching him."

"Dr. Medford?"

The sandy-haired man walked up just then. "Did I hear someone mention my name?"

Josh smiled. "Silas, this is Miss Summers. Her brother has a compound fracture. Fever's set in. We'll be keeping an eye on him for a while."

The thin doctor glanced toward the boy on the cot. A sandy brow arched up. "I doubt Colonel Wilson would approve your treating a civilian in an army hospital."

"Colonel Wilson doesn't need to know everything that goes on out here. Miss Summers and I are old friends. Her brother needs help and we're going to help him. Do you have a problem with that, Doctor?"

Silas Medford's thin lips curved upward. "Not in the least." He turned to Angel. "A pleasure meeting you, Miss Summers. I'll do my best for your brother."

Angel simply nodded. It was difficult to concentrate with the unfamiliar sounds in the room. Several men were snoring, others were whispering, one played a soulful harmonica tune. She found herself turning toward the poignant notes and realized a number of the soldiers were staring, their sunken, hollow gazes focused on her.

"They don't mean to be disrespectful," Josh said. "Most of them aren't much more than boys. The others are family men. They miss their wives and daughters. All of them just want to go home."

She studied the men's disheartened faces. "They all look so sad."

Josh's dark gaze moved to her eyes. "They are. Low morale is part of the reason these men haven't gotten well as fast as they should have. It's not an easy thing for the army to treat."

Angel said nothing, just kept staring at the sea of lonely faces staring back at her. Wearing hospital gowns instead of their blue uniforms, they didn't look like Yankee soldiers. They just looked like lonely, suffering men.

"Come on," Josh said. "Silas will watch after Willie while I get you settled in."

Angel let him lead her away, but in her mind's eye, all she could see was the dismal hospital room with its endless rows of beds, and the faces of those poor sick men.

Josh arranged quarters for Angel in a room that had once been occupied by the fort commander's wife. All that remained was an old iron bed, a scarred wooden dresser, a table, and two chairs, but there was a fireplace in one corner to keep the place warm, and it wasn't far from his own quarters, so he could keep an eye on her.

It probably wasn't necessary, he thought as he returned to his own room and readied himself for bed. There weren't that many men at the fort. The officers were all first rate and discipline had never been a problem. Still, since he'd stumbled onto the Confederates who had tried to rape her, he couldn't stand the thought of her being too far away.

He had always been protective of women. As a man

raised in the South, it was simply his way. Still, his concern for Angel went beyond Southern manners. He hadn't realized how possessive—how wildly protective—he felt toward Angel until he had seen her with those men.

He hadn't lied to her. He could have strangled every man-jack sonofabitch with his own bare hands.

He understood their wanting her. He wanted her that same way, had since the moment he had seen her in Whistler's Dry Goods. But now he realized his feelings went way beyond that. He didn't want another man touching her. He would kill to keep anyone from hurting her.

The thought was unsettling, particularly since his plans for the future did not include Angel Summers. Sarah Wingate was the woman he would marry. He had abandoned the South, given up his birthright when he had joined the Union Army. He was no longer welcome here. He had no choice but to make the North his home. Josh sighed as he pulled back the covers and climbed naked into bed. Just thinking of Angel made him hard, and he only had a few hours to sleep before he had to spell Silas Medford in the ward. He tried to fall asleep, but tossed and turned instead. Finally he got up, dressed, and went back to the hospital. What he didn't expect to find in the barracks this time of the night was Angel Summers.

Angel pressed the tin cup to the young soldier's trembling lips. With his thin frame propped against her shoulder, she helped him steady himself enough to drink.

"Thank you, ma'am," said the dark-haired youth who was sick with a bowel disorder. "That was mighty kind of you." There was such a smile of gratitude on the young corporal's face, Angel's throat went tight.

"Get some sleep," she said to him. "You need your rest if you're going to get well."

"Yes, ma'am. And thank you again." He settled back on the cot and his eyes slid closed. Instead of the restless tossing that had drawn her reluctantly to his bedside, he drifted into a peaceful slumber.

She hadn't meant to get involved with the soldiers. They were Yankees, after all—she wasn't about to help them. But they were also men, and sitting for so long in the darkness beside Willie's bed, her attention had reluctantly been drawn to the groans of pain, the sleepless thrashing, the sounds of weeping in the darkness. She couldn't just sit there, knowing the men were hurting.

Footsteps coming down the aisle distracted her. Josh appeared like a specter out of the darkness. "You're supposed to be in bed, Angel."

"I couldn't sleep. I thought I might as well be here." She glanced back at the soldier on the bed. "Corporal Miller was thirsty. I brought him some water."

His eyes touched hers and there was so much tenderness in his expression, Angel felt a tightness in her chest.

"Thank you," Josh said. "With the war over and most of the men gone home, we're short-handed here. I'm sure the men appreciate any help you can give them." He didn't say more, just walked her back to the chair beside Willie's bed, then went off to check on his patients.

Angel leaned over, ran her fingers through her brother's tousled blond hair. His breathing was shallow and his face looked flushed, but at least the medicine Josh had given him kept the pain at bay. The men on the cots had little to keep them from hurting.

Her gaze locked with a dark-eyed soldier just a few feet away. He had lost the use of his legs, one of the men had told her, and with them, his dull gaze said, he had also lost the will to live. Her feet moved toward him of their own accord. Try as she might, she couldn't seem to stop them.

"Can I get you something . . . ?" She glanced at the name penned on the paper above the cot. ". . . Lieutenant Langley?"

The man said nothing, but the anguish in his expression seemed to grow worse.

"My name is Angel Summers. Dr. Coltrane is taking care of my little brother."

He was younger than he'd looked from a distance. No more than twenty-four or -five, yet his face was lined and his skin rough, scarred in several places.

"Are you sure there is nothing I can get you?" He shook his head, but his eyes welled with tears. Angel's stomach knotted. "Are you in pain?"

Another shake of his head. He turned his face away from her into the pillow, but a tear rolled down his cheek.

"Lieutenant Langley, please . . . won't you let me help you?"

The dark eyes were back, and a spark of anger flashed there. "I don't want your help. I don't want to be treated like a helpless cripple . . . even if that's what I am." Absently, he rubbed his lifeless legs. "I want to be the man I was before."

She smoothed the hair back from his forehead. "You are the man you were before. Nothing can change that. You've just lost the use of your limbs."

He only shook his head. "You don't understand."

"Then why don't you explain it to me?"

He turned away, then dragged in a slow, shaky breath. "Seeing you tonight, watching the way you moved, listening to the sound of your voice . . . it reminded me of Laura. She was blond like you . . . beautiful like you. We were going to be married. I've lost her now. I can't ask her to marry me. I couldn't take care of her. I can hardly take care of myself."

Angel's heart turned over. She knew the pain of losing

someone you loved. "Does she know you've been injured?"

"You mean does she know I'm a cripple? No, and I'm not going to tell her."

"But you must, Lieutenant. If she loves you, she won't care what's happened to you. She'll just be grateful to God that you're still alive."

But the soldier shook his head. He turned away from her again and the light she had sparked seemed to fade. She left him staring into space, his jaw tight, his features grim, and made her way back to Willie. But she couldn't help thinking about the soldier, wondering if the girl he loved would still want him. She knew if the man had been Josh, if he had been crippled as he fought for the Southern cause, she would still have wanted him.

She glanced toward his tall frame, watched him working over one of his patients. Josh hadn't been crippled in the war, he had simply been a traitor. Still the words she had spoken to the soldier rang in her head. *If she loves you, she won't care what has happened to you.* True love meant accepting a man the way he was, without strings, without reservation. She couldn't help wondering if, in a way, she hadn't failed Josh just as much as he had failed her.

CHAPTER SIX

Josh reined his saddle horse toward the knoll overlooking Coltrane Farms. He'd had to get away from the hospital, from the suffering in his patients' eyes that he could do nothing about. Mostly he had to get away from Angel—and the turmoil just looking at her was doing to his insides.

Josh lifted his hat, letting the cold wind ruffle his dark hair, then settled the brim low across his forehead. Urging the bay to a faster pace, he dropped off the hill toward the house that had once been his home. It wasn't as fancy as the white-columned mansion at Summers End, but it had a sturdy, two-story wood frame, a porch all around, and a well-furnished parlor. There were five bedrooms upstairs—plenty of room for children, his mother had said. But there'd only been him and his sister, and Janie hadn't lived to be ten years old.

It was one of the reasons he had wanted to be a doctor. Perhaps he could have saved her, he used to think.

Josh reined up in front of the empty yellow house. He had always loved the old place. After he'd met Angel, he had dreamed of building one just like it for the two of them and the children they would raise on a piece of this good Coltrane land.

He eyed the "For Sale" sign he had placed in the window. Just looking at the bold black letters made the inside of his mouth feel dry. He didn't want to sell it, not really. Not deep down in his gut. Since his return to Savannah, he had come to realize just how much he had missed the South. How much he longed for the warm spring evenings, the sweet smell of summer grasses, the taste of Southern home cooking.

Josh swung down from the bay, looped the reins over the hitching post out in front of the house, and stepped up on the porch. It felt so right being here, so good deep down inside. In the past few days, even memories of the parents he had lost weren't enough to dull that sense of belonging.

Gazing off toward the fallow fields, for the first time since his return, Josh admitted how much he wanted to come back home.

A rooster crowed somewhere in the distance, gone wild, he supposed, since the place had been abandoned. He glanced around the yard, pulled open the door that was never locked, and stepped inside the parlor. Much of the furniture was gone, but an amazing amount still remained: petit point pictures his grandmother had stitched, a pair of cut crystal whale oil lamps, a portrait of his parents above the cloth-draped horsehair sofa. In the old days, this time of year the house would have been decorated for Christmas, candles glowing, holly wreaths above the hearth.

The place seemed oddly empty without the holiday cheer, and strangely silent now. He wanted to see it sparkling with light again, filled with the love and laughter he had known in the house as a boy.

Standing in front of the empty hearth, he ran his hand

along the mantel, stirring up a small cloud of dust, but his thoughts remained on the farmhouse and the land he had loved. They needed a doctor in Savannah. True, they resented him now, but with time and hard work that resentment could eventually be overcome. He wanted to come home, to rebuild his life here at Coltrane Farms.

As he walked back out on the porch, he admitted something else.

He wanted Angel Summers to be part of that life.

An image of her sitting beside Lieutenant Langley came to mind. She had tried to resist the soldiers she thought of as her enemy, but her compassionate nature just wouldn't let her. He recalled the way she treated old Serge, the tender care she gave her little brother. She was more of a woman than she ever had been before, and the truth was he still loved her.

Time hadn't changed that, as he had once believed. The war hadn't done it. He loved her, and deep down he believed she might still love him.

For the first time in days, Josh really smiled. He had won Angel's hand against half the men in Chatham County. She'd be just as big a challenge now—more so, as much as she hated Yankees—yet if the way she had kissed him was any indication, he believed he had a chance.

Still, with the war and all that had happened, it wouldn't be easy to mend the rift between them and make a life together. And it wasn't just Angel—the whole damned town was against him. It was a perilous undertaking, definitely fraught with risk. It was even more risky to gamble his heart again.

Josh flashed another smile, this one determined. Angel Summers was worth the risk.

* * *

Angel paced the floor of Mrs. Barkley's parlor. She hated leaving Willie, but she couldn't stand to sit in the barracks a moment more.

"Please, Mrs. Barkley, you've got to tell me how you got that medicine. I have to speak to the men who took it and convince them to give it back. I heard Harley Lewis was involved and maybe Pete Thompson. I thought perhaps your sons—"

"I'd like to help ya, child, I truly would, but my boys ain't budgin' an inch on this. As far as Harley and Pete is concerned, they ain't got the stuff no more, leastwise not all of it."

"Then where is it?"

"Way I heard tell, it's sorta scattered hereabouts. Some went to Doc Gordon, you got some, other folks took what they wanted. Ain't no one person's got the lot of it."

Angel sank down on the small settee in front of the fire. "Josh needs that medicine. If you could see those men, Mrs. Barkley, I know you'd want to help them. Tell me what I can do."

The older woman sighed. Setting aside her knitting, she came heavily to her feet and walked over to Angel. "You're that bound and determined, there is one thing you might do."

"What's that?"

"There's a big town meetin' in the mornin'. Business is off real bad this year. Everybody's worried about it. 'Course, money's real tight, and they ain't much in the stores for sale, but it's more than that. Streets don't have no decorations this year. Stores ain't done up like they usually are for the holidays. Nobody round here seems to have the spirit of Christmas."

"It's the Yankees," Angel said. "They came bustin' in here last year—Sherman and his soldiers. Everybody still remembers how bad it was."

"I suppose that's it. Whatever it is, Mayor Donaldson is gonna do some speechifyin', try to brighten everybody's mood."

"I heard about the meeting. You're suggesting I talk to folks there?"

"Probably won't do no good, but if I was set on tryin', that's what I'd do."

Angel smiled. She stood up from the sofa, then leaned over and hugged her neighbor. "You're a jewel, Mrs. Barkley, you truly are."

The older woman waived her words away. "I don't like to see men hurtin' any more than you do, not if there's somethin' I can do to stop it."

Angel smiled again. "Thank you, Mrs. Barkley."

"And give that little brother of yours a hug for me. Tell him I'll whip him up a batch of them molasses cookies he likes just as soon as he gets home."

"I'll tell him," she said, seeing Willie's image, one of the prized cookies clutched in each of his small hands. A hard ache rose in Angel's throat. Eliza Barkley was a good friend. The best. Eliza would stand by her, she knew. Now if she could only manage to convince the rest of the people in Savannah.

Josh strode into the barracks, heading straight for little Willie's bed. An orderly sat beside him while Silas Medford tended one of the patients on the ward. He gave the child a dose of calomel and rhubarb, checked the medicinal plaster he had placed on the boy's narrow chest, but saw that his fever still hovered well above normal.

With a sigh of regret, he turned to the orderly. "Have you seen Angel . . . Miss Summers, that is?" He had already tried her quarters as soon as he'd returned from the farm, but she wasn't in.

The bone-thin orderly, a former patient now recovered but still twenty pounds underweight, moved to the foot of the bed. "She was here all mornin', Doc. Then she said she had an errand to run. Said she'd be back just as quick as she could."

Josh nodded, but his gaze remained on Willie. The boy's appetite had waned, leaving him weak and emaciated. Even the icy water they kept him bathed in hadn't been able to break the fever's raging grip. Josh worked over the child for a little while longer, checking the leg and changing the dressing. As he had said, the bone was well-set and on the mend, but the skin around the tear was purple and swollen, puffy and warm to the touch. If they couldn't stop the infection, the injury would putrefy. Gangrene would mean the boy would lose the leg—or worse.

"We'll have to change those cold compresses more often. Bathe his neck and shoulders as well as his stomach and legs. We've got to get that fever down."

"Yes, sir," the orderly said.

Satisfied he had done all he could, Josh turned away, his thoughts shifting once more to Angel. Where had she gone? he wondered. Whatever she was doing had to be important or she wouldn't have left her brother. More worried than he should have been, it took him several more seconds to realize there was something different about the barracks.

Partly it was the smell. The scent of evergreen drifted up from branches heaped in piles beside the soldiers' beds, helping to mask the nauseous hospital fumes, and mounds of red berry holly were scattered across the rough wooden floors.

"What's all this?" Josh asked the orderly.

"It's Miss Angel. She said the place was depressing. She said it was Christmas and we ought to do somethin' about it. She got some of the off-duty soldiers to go out and scavenge up what they could. Now the patients that are well enough are makin' Christmas garlands and stringin' holly berries. Lieutenant Ainsley volunteered to cut us a big pine tree. Miss Angel says she's gonna help us decorate the tree for Christmas."

Josh glanced around the room. At least half of his patients were involved some way or other in making Christmas decorations. The sight raised an ache in his chest.

Damn, why hadn't he thought of this? Healing was mental as well as physical. He didn't have the medicines his patients needed, but something like this could have helped to lift their spirits.

He looked over at young Ben Weatherly. He hadn't seen the boy smile like that in weeks. He was working a needle and thread—the kind of supplies they had plenty of—pushing it through long green pine stems, sewing the branches together to form a garland for the walls. Other men were making holly wreaths, using pine cones for decoration. Several wreaths were finished and sitting on tables along the walls, a few white candles blazing in the center.

Josh started forward, his smile nearly as big as the men's. Angel had done this. She'd been able to put her prejudice aside and help these men so desperately in need. The hope he had felt at the farm rose up, stronger now than it was before.

Angel, he thought. *You're mine, dammit. You always have been.* Now all he had to do was find some way to convince her.

It was dark when Angel returned to the fort. Leaving her horse with one of the men, she hurried into the barracks, making her way straight to her brother. His eyes were open, as dull and glazed as they were the last time he'd been awake, but he smiled when he saw her and that gave her hope.

"Willie, sweetheart. How are you feeling?" She reached out and captured his hand. Feeling how hot it was, her hope turned to despair.

"The soldiers are making Christmas stuff. They're gonna put it up on the walls as soon as they get finished."

Tears burned Angel's eyes. This wasn't the Christmas she had wanted for Willie. "That's right, honey. Pretty soon this place will look just like home." Of course, even home wasn't decorated this year. Not with Willie so sick.

"You know what I want for Christmas?" Willie said.

"What, sweetheart?"

"I want to get well so I can go home."

Her heart hurt. "That's what I want, too." It was the truth. It was the only gift she cared about, and she prayed for it every day.

Willie's lackluster gaze moved over the room, watching the soldiers work. "Can I make some decorations, too?" he asked weakly.

Angel forced a smile. "Of course you can. Why don't we string some berries?"

He nodded, but by the time she returned with a bowl of the tiny red berries, he had already drifted back to sleep.

"Where the hell have you been?" Josh's voice slammed into her with the force of a blow, arriving well before the sound of his heavy boots. "It's getting dark out there. After what happened with those Confederates, I thought you'd know better than to—"

"I had something important to do." Her chin came up. "Besides, it's none of your business where I go—not any more."

"You're wrong, Angel. As long as you're here at the fort, you're my responsibility. That makes it my business."

Angel set her jaw. Josh might have changed in some ways, but he was still the domineering, overprotective male he had always been. "I went to see Mrs. Barkley. You were right— these men need those supplies. I was hoping I could get them."

His anger drained away. Josh sighed wearily. "I'm sorry. I was worried, is all." He raked a hand through his heavy chestnut hair, lifting the dark strands that hung just below his collar. "I shouldn't have yelled at you."

Something warm unfurled inside her. Josh was worried about her. Never mind that it shouldn't matter, that she shouldn't care one whit that a Yankee captain had been concerned. "How's Willie?" she asked, trying not to notice the fatigue in Josh's dark eyes. "He was awake when I got back. I thought maybe his fever had broken, but I don't . . . I don't think it has."

"I wish I could tell you he was better. He's holding his own. That's about it. We're doing the best we can."

Angel glanced away. "I know that, Josh."

"He'll sleep now. The orderly will stay with him. Why don't we go for a walk?"

She glanced at her brother, saw that Josh was right and Willie was deeply asleep. As tired as she was, looking at Josh's handsome features, her fatigue seemed to fade. "I'd like that."

They left the barracks and prowled the mostly empty fort, strolling across the yard, ending up beneath the ramparts where a few battered cannon still protruded from the walls above them.

"I want to thank you, Angel, for what you're doing for the men. I haven't seen that much life in them since I came to the fort."

Angel shook her head. "I never meant to help them. As far as I was concerned, they were Yankees. I never meant to lift a finger."

They stopped in the shadows behind an empty barracks. "Then why did you?" Darkness threw his face into harsh relief, outlining the hard planes and valleys. Lines of fatigue dug creases beside his deep brown eyes. He looked older, more rugged. He was still the handsomest man she had ever seen.

"You were right about that, too," she said. "They're men, just like any others. No one should have to suffer that way."

"You spoke to Mrs. Barkley. You tried to help them. You'll never know how much I appreciate that."

"I haven't given up, Josh. I'm going to try again." She told him about the town meeting she planned to attend in the morning, and the pride in his eyes made the breath catch in her throat.

His hand came up to her cheek. "Angel . . ." Then he was bending his head, slanting his mouth over hers and capturing her lips.

Pleasure speared through her, blocking the deepening chill. Josh pulled her closer, wrapped her in his arms, and Angel gave in to the incredible sensation, savoring the closeness, feeling the old familiar rush of love. Josh deepened the kiss, probing with his tongue, teasing the corners of her mouth till she parted her lips, making her tremble. She clutched his shoulders and he drew her closer, kissing her more thoroughly, sending little shivers along her spine.

Oh, dear God, it felt so good to kiss him. A tiny voice whispered that it was wrong, that what she and Josh had was over, that he belonged to someone else. She tried to ignore the voice, but the voice would not be still.

"Josh," she whispered, ending the kiss, pulling herself away. "Please don't do this."

"You wanted me to kiss you, Angel. Don't try to deny it."

She only shook her head. "It's over, Josh. You know it and so do I."

"Are you sure?"

"You're a Yankee, Josh. This is Georgia. What else is there to say?"

Josh didn't answer. Instead his eyes searched her face—dark eyes, knowing eyes, trying to read her thoughts, assessing her, it seemed.

"It's getting cold out here," he said. "We had better be getting back in."

She nodded, but didn't say more. She almost wished he had argued, tried to convince her it might still work. She should have felt relieved that he hadn't; instead, she felt suddenly sad.

"I ordered a fire made in your quarters," Josh said. "I figured you'd be chilled when you got back."

She gave him a half-hearted smile. He had always been thoughtful that way. "Thank you."

"I suppose you'd think it was scandalous if I came in for a cup of tea." He flashed her a disarming smile and her dismal mood lifted a bit.

"What about Willie?"

"I've given him some laudanum. He won't wake up before morning."

"All right then, Captain Coltrane, you may come in. There's no one around. Besides, I've suffered things far worse than a bit of scandal."

Far worse, Josh thought, recalling the war, the loss, and grief she had known in the last four years. Taking Angel's arm, he led her through the shadows back to her room, guided her inside, and closed the door. All the way there, he was thinking of the way she had kissed him, that he could feel her hunger, nearly as strong as his own.

What he was about to do was rash, and dangerous for both of them. But his time with Angel was limited. Either the boy's fever would break—which he fervently hoped—and Angel would return to Summers End, or the colonel would arrive and demand the child be removed to the care of civilians. Once she was gone, the odds would be against him.

Angel was his—he knew that now. What he needed was a way to make her see. Words wouldn't work—not with Angel. But there was something he could do that might just convince her.

Josh meant to seduce her.

CHAPTER SEVEN

Josh watched Angel's movements as she hung the tea kettle from the long iron arm suspended above the fire. As she bent toward the hearth, her simple brown wool skirt draped over her rounded hips. Her breasts strained forward, pressing against the front of her white cotton blouse.

Seated in a chair beside the table, his body grew hard just looking at her, his blood heating up, pulsing thickly into his groin. God, he had wanted her for so long.

"Almost ready," Angel said, but her eyes didn't quite meet his. There was something intimate about being in such close quarters, about the simple act of her serving him tea.

Her glance caught his and her cheeks went pink. A stray glance touched the old iron bed in the corner, then slid back to the hearth. She was thinking of their kiss, he knew, perhaps recalling the way he had touched her that night at Summers End. He was thinking of it, too, and he ached to touch her that way again.

"Come here, Angel." She looked up at the tone of his

voice, softly commanding yet gently persuasive, and another warm flush lit her cheeks. She turned away from the fire and started toward him, and Josh rose to his feet, blowing out the lamp as he stood up, leaving the glow of the fire to light the room, painting the small space in shades of orange and gold.

"What—what do you want?"

"I want to kiss you, Angel. It's what you want, too. It's why I'm here and both of us know it."

She swallowed and slowly shook her head, but she didn't back away. Josh cupped her face with his hands, leaned forward and brushed her lips with a kiss. They were as soft as petals, sweet as sugar, and so very warm. He deepened the kiss, molding his mouth over hers, parting her lips with his tongue and stroking deeply inside. He drew her closer, into the circle of his arms, and his fingers found the pins in her long golden hair. He pulled them one by one, setting the heavy mass free, letting it fall past her shoulders, then sifting his fingers through it. It felt like silk against his hand.

"Angel," he whispered, kissing her again—soft, slow kisses, drugging kisses that made her pulse speed up, made it throb, he saw, at the base of her throat. He tasted her there, trailing his mouth along her neck, his hands massaging her back, drifting lower, cupping her bottom and drawing her against his arousal. She sucked in a breath when she felt it and began to pull away. Josh eased his hold and simply kissed her again.

In moments, he felt her relax, trusting him once more— wrongly so, for he meant to take advantage. He had to. He wanted to. It was the right thing for both of them.

Angel returned Josh's kiss, letting the fierce heat roll over her, giving in to the terrible hunger she felt each time she saw him. It's only a kiss, she told herself as his tongue swept in, delving deeply, as his hands roamed down her back, then moved lower, cradling her once more against his sex.

He was hard there, thick and heavy, bigger than she would have imagined. Yet this time she wasn't frightened. She wanted him to kiss her, to touch her. For these few moments, she wanted to forget the past, forget the fear she felt for her brother. She ached to lose herself in the sweetness of his lips, the warmth of his hands moving over her body. She barely noticed when her blouse fell open, the buttons parting as if by magic, the fabric easing from the waistband of her skirt then sliding off her shoulders.

Instead she closed her eyes and slid her fingers into the hair at the nape of his neck, felt his hand at her waist, felt his palm moving upward, gliding over her thin chemise. He eased one of the straps away, lowering the fabric and baring one of her breasts. As the heat of his hand cupped the fullness, it occurred to her that she should stop him, end this growing madness before it went any further. Then the unwelcome thought slid away.

She didn't want to stop him, not now. She loved Josh Coltrane, had ached for him for the last four years. And the last of her will had entirely slipped away. No matter what the future held, for these few precious moments, Josh belonged to her as he had before, and nothing was going to take those moments away.

"You're so beautiful," Josh whispered, his eyes on her breasts, his long dark fingers caressing them, making the nipples peak. "I want you, Angel. I want you so damned much."

He kissed her again, rained kisses along her bare shoulders, bent his head and took a nipple into his mouth. Angel sucked in a breath at the white-hot fire racing through her, the scorching waves of heat that made it impossible to think. Arching her back, she gave herself up to his touch, reveled in it, unconsciously pleaded for more.

"That's right, sweeting, let yourself go. Let me taste you, Angel."

She gave in to his coaxing, her head falling back as he laved her nipple, then gently bit the end. Waves of pleasure washed through her, ripples of heat and wanting, and suddenly she was desperate to touch him, to caress his hard male flesh as he was caressing her. Frantic fingers worked the buttons on his sky blue shirt, pulled it open, then slid into the softly curling hair across his chest. It was ridged with muscle, thick slabs that tightened wherever she touched. She ringed a flat male nipple and heard Josh groan.

"Angel . . ." Then he was lifting her up, carrying her the few short paces to the old iron bed. She should stop him, she knew. One day he would leave her as he had done before, return to the North and the woman he would marry. He couldn't stay in the South, not anymore. Instead she let him strip away her clothes and settle her in the middle of the old iron bed, then watched as he stripped away his breeches and boots.

Standing naked beside the bed, he looked hard and male, his shaft thrusting forward, firelight playing over the thick bands of muscles on his shoulders, the sinews across his chest.

"I want you," he said, leaning over her, every inch of him sleekly male, dark and masculine and aroused. "I need you, Angel."

She touched his face, felt the firmness of his jaw and the roughness of his day's growth of beard. "I need you, too, Josh." He was a Yankee. It would never work between them, but tonight that didn't matter. She loved him, she needed him, and for now that was enough.

Settling himself beside her on the bed, Josh took her in

his arms and captured her lips, fitting them perfectly together. His big hands kneaded her breasts, teasing her nipples, making them ache and distend, then he took the stiff tip into his mouth. Tasting her with his tongue, he laved and suckled until her whole body tingled with pleasure, and fire scorched through her blood.

Damp heat slid through her; an aching warmth settled into her core. He must have sensed it, for his hand moved lower, laced through the soft curls above her sex, and a finger eased inside her. She was hot and wet, throbbing with need, aching for him to touch her, wanting even more.

"You're ready for me, love. Don't be frightened."

"I'm not frightened."

His finger dipped deeply, stretching the soft, plump folds, preparing her. He kissed her as he came up over her, a hot, deep, scorching kiss that had her moaning, her body writhing beneath him.

"You're mine," he whispered as he parted her legs with his knee and eased himself inside. "You've always been mine. Say it, Angel. Tell me you know it's the truth."

"I'm yours, Josh."

His hard body shuddered at her words. When he reached the wall of her innocence, he paused and a soft look stole over his features. Then he took her mouth in another fiery kiss, thrusting deeply with his tongue the same instant he thrust with his body.

Her sharp cry of pain was muffled by his lips. He held himself still, propped on his forearms, the muscles in his shoulders stiff with tension. "I'm sorry, love. I tried not to hurt you."

She reached a shaky hand up to his cheek, rested her palm against it. "It's all right. The pain is fading already." Josh smiled with such tenderness it made her heart turn over. Then he started to move, sliding even deeper, filling her with his hardness and a piercing pleasure that seemed to have no end. When his thick length could go no further, he began to ease himself out, then slowly he sank back in. With each of his movements, the pleasure increased, multiplied tenfold, and in minutes, his slow, deep strokes had her arching beneath him.

Heat roared through her, a lush, glittering fire that beckoned her to far-off places. Out and then in, the rhythm increasing, the flames and the fever, the heavy thrust and drag of his shaft and his slick, hot, burning kisses. A trembling began in her stomach and an odd sort of tightening gripped her muscles lower down.

"Josh . . . ?" she whispered, barely aware she had spoken, feeling the deep, pounding thrusts, lost in passion.

"Let it come, Angel, let it happen. Do it for me."

She relaxed then, letting her uncertainty slide away, and the moment she did, a sweeping wave of pleasure washed over her. Pinpricks of light and pulsing heat mingled with a sweetness she could taste on her tongue. Her body arched upward, taking him deeper, and above her Josh's hard frame went tense. His head fell back as he reached his release, his body tightening, shuddering, and finally going still.

For a moment he seemed frozen, then he sagged against her, his long, lean frame covered with a sheen of perspiration.

She wasn't certain of the words he whispered as he pulled her into his arms. She wanted to believe he had said that he loved her, but she wasn't sure. Her eyelids felt heavy, her body languid as fatigue settled in. They were both so very tired.

They made love once more in the middle of the night, and he held her with aching tenderness.

She didn't awaken till just before dawn.

* * *

Angel blinked then blinked again, trying to remember where she was. She noticed a heavy, musky-sweet smell, then felt the warm presence of the man still sleeping beside her. She sat up with a start as images of their hot night of passion came rushing in. Color flooded her cheeks to think that Josh had seduced her.

Or perhaps, she thought, it was she who had seduced him.

Dear God, she had slept with a Yankee! But another part of her remembered the beautiful night they had shared, said that the Yankee was Josh, and that it didn't matter.

Angel leaned closer, hearing the sound of his breathing, knowing she should wake him before dawn lightened the sky. Seeing how deeply he slept, she didn't have the heart.

For most of the three days before, he'd been up around the clock with Willie and he still looked exhausted. Her cheeks grew warm to think their hours of lovemaking had only added to his fatigue, and in truth she wasn't yet ready to face him. She wasn't sure what he would say to her, or what she might say to him. Better to simply avoid him.

She would check on Willie, sit with him for a while, then be on her way to town before Josh ever awakened.

As she dressed in her simple navy blue dress with the white pique cuffs, she couldn't resist a glance to where he lay sleeping. He had tossed off the covers, leaving him bare to the navel and exposing a long, masculine leg. She could still recall the power of his hard-muscled body moving above her, the way it had felt to be joined with him. The love she had felt in his arms.

An ache rose in her throat to think of losing him, yet she had known from the start that he could not stay. He had left the South for good when he had joined the Union Army. There was no place here for him now.

And he had a woman in the North.

A sharp pain knifed through her. Perhaps last night should never have happened. Perhaps she had been a fool.

She didn't care, she thought as she pulled her woolen cloak from the hook beside the door, slipped outside, and closed it behind her. No matter what happened, she would never regret the night they had shared.

It was a memory she would cherish through the long, lonely, bitter years without him.

"Mornin', Miss Angel." The men all called her that now, ever since she had organized the Christmas decorations. "I was just comin' to fetch you." The orderly, Private Vogel, met her at the barracks' door.

"Oh, dear God—Willie!" She started into the barracks, then turned back. "What's happened? He hasn't gotten worse? He's not . . . ?" Her chest constricted with terror. She would never forgive herself if Willie had needed her and she had been making love to Josh instead of being with him.

The red-haired orderly grinned, exposing the gap between his two front teeth. "You got your Christmas wish, ma'am. Your brother's fever broke 'bout an hour ago. The swellin's gone down in his leg. It looks like he's gonna be fine."

Tears rushed into her eyes. "Oh, thank God." Hurrying past him, she raced into the barracks and found Dr. Medford standing beside Willie's cot.

"Good news, Miss Summers. Your brother's fever has gone down. He's definitely on the mend."

She nodded, brushing a tear from her cheek. "Private Vogel told me. I can't thank you enough, Dr. Medford."

"Mostly it was Josh. I think he willed that boy to get

well. I've never seen him more determined. Of course, he feels that way about all of his patients."

She sat down next to Willie and took his small hand. "I know he does. Willie had the medicine he needed to help him get well. If your other patients had it, their chances would be far greater." She smiled down at her brother.

"Hello, sweetheart."

Willie fidgeted and she plumped his pillow. "The doctor says I'm better. Can we go home?"

Angel squeezed his hand. "We'll have to see what Dr. Coltrane says. He might want you to stay another day." Willie's mouth curled down in disappointment. He still looked sunken and thin, but his light blue eyes were alert and a hint of color brightened his pale cheeks.

She pulled the covers up to his chin. "That wouldn't be so bad, would it? If you stayed you could help the men decorate their Christmas tree."

A spark lit his eyes. "Did they get one?"

"Lieutenant Ainsley brought in a great big one. It's sitting just outside."

"I guess it'd be all right if we stayed till the tree was done."

Angel smiled. "In the meantime, would you like me to read to you for a while?"

He surprised her with a shake of his head. "Private Vogel was telling me stories about the war."

She flashed the orderly an uncertain glance and he looked a little sheepish. She wasn't sure war stories were a good idea, but it was obvious Willie was feeling better. She pulled the watch fob from the pocket of her skirt and flipped open the lid to her daddy's gold watch.

"Well, then, if Private Vogel has time for a few more stories and you don't need me for a while, there's something important I need to do in town. I'll be back just as soon as I'm finished, all right?"

Willie nodded. He was looking at the red-haired orderly with undisguised hero worship. She bent over and kissed him on the forehead. "I won't be long, I promise."

Only long enough to attend the town meeting in Savannah. One of her Christmas prayers had been answered. With any luck at all, perhaps the second one would be as well.

Josh awoke with a start. He had kicked off the covers and the cold in the room had finally seeped into his sleep-deadened senses. He reached for Angel, felt nothing but the empty bed, glanced around the small room, and realized she had gone.

Sonofabitch! He had planned to talk to her last night after they had made love, while her body was still soft and pliant from his touch. He meant to tell her how much he loved her, explain that he meant to stay in Savannah, to make a place for himself here again. He'd meant to convince her to marry him.

Damnation! What the hell must she be thinking? That he meant to seduce her, then leave her? That all he wanted was to bed her?

Sonofabitch!

The sun was well up when he got to the hospital. He hadn't slept that late in as long as he could remember. He paused at Willie's bedside, his eyes going wide to see the boy propped up on his pillow.

A big grin broke over Josh's lips. "Morning, Willie. How are you feeling?"

"Pretty good, Doc. Private Vogel says you helped me get better. I guess you're not too bad for a Yankee."

Josh smoothed a hand over the boy's rumpled blond hair. "And you're not too bad for a Reb." They talked as Josh checked the leg. "Your sister been in?" he asked with careful nonchalance, certain she had been there as soon as she had awakened.

"She was here first thing," Willie said with a yawn. "She went into town, I think. She said she'd be back as quick as she could."

The town meeting. How the devil could he have forgotten? Then he thought of the night he had spent in her bed and knew exactly how he could forget. Josh smiled. "Get some rest, Willie. Tomorrow's Christmas Eve. Looks like you'll be home in time for Christmas, after all."

The boy beamed at his words. Josh left him with the orderly who seemed to have become his friend, made a quick round of his patients, then headed out to the stable.

The most important thing he could do for the men was get back those medical supplies. If Angel was willing to try, he wanted to be there to help her.

CHAPTER EIGHT

The meeting at city hall was nearly over by the time Angel dragged open the heavy wooden door. Merchants sat next to housewives on roughhewn benches, men just back from the war sat next to widows whose husbands had been killed. Angel recognized most of the faces, and, of course, Mayor Donaldson, the short, balding man at the podium.

At present, he was speaking to the merchants on their final piece of business—that they should all be friendlier to the Blue Coats—since the town was in need of Yankee dollars.

"It's a sad thing to say, friends and neighbors, but the Yanks are responsible for the hardships we're all suffering. The best revenge we can have is to get our hands on some of that Northern coin."

"Here, here!" Mr. Whistler of the dry goods store put in, followed by a mumble of agreement from the crowd. It wasn't exactly the note she would have chosen to present her case, but a glance at the clock said time was running out.

"Excuse me, Mayor Donaldson. Would it be possible

for me to speak to the group for a moment? There's a topic I'd like to discuss."

He tipped his head back and stared at her through his pince-nez spectacles. "Is that you, Miss Summers?"

"Yes, Mr. Mayor." She started up the aisle. Before he could deny her the chance to speak, she'd reached the podium.

"What is it, Miss Summers?" he said with a tone of impatience.

Angel took a deep, calming breath and turned to the people on the benches. "I'd like to talk to you all about the train wreck." She went on to recount the day of the derailment and the goods that were taken. "The Yankees haven't pressed us to give back the food we've all been enjoying, but they need those medical supplies. They were intended for the wounded men at Fort Jackson. I didn't realize how badly they were needed until I went to the hospital and saw the injured soldiers for myself."

"What the devil was you doin' out there, girl?" Kirby Fields' look was accusing. "An army post ain't no place for a decent Southern girl." The others nodded mutely.

Ignoring the disapproval stamped across the sea of faces, Angel explained about Willie and how Josh Coltrane had taken him to the fort to tend his badly broken leg. "Before I went there, I felt just the way you do. I lost my mother and father. Union forces left Summers End in ruins. I hated the Yankees for everything they'd done. But watching those soldiers . . . seeing how much they were suffering, I realized they were men just the same as any others, just like those of you here. They're lonely and they're hurting. All they want to do is get well so they can go home."

"You're just sweet on Coltrane!" someone shouted. "You always were."

"I loved Josh once," she said. *I still do.* "But that's not what this is about. It's about letting go of the past. About seeing things the way they really are. The truth is there are good men and bad men on both sides of a war." She told them about the Confederate soldiers who had come to Summers End, about what they had tried to do. "People were hurt and killed in the North as well as the South. Terrible things were done by men in both armies. The important thing is, the war is over. It's time to forget the past and try to build ourselves a decent future."

A few men mumbled, then a big man shouted from the crowd, "You can forget the past if you want to. I lost both my brothers at Manassas. I ain't about to forget!"

The air squeezed tight in Angel's chest. She knew what it felt like to lose the people you loved. Still, it was the suffering men who were important now. Surely there was something she could say that would make them see.

"You're right, Hank Larkin. I can't forget what happened, either. I doubt anyone in this room ever will. But it's Christmas. Above the pulpit in the church down the street there's a banner. It reads Peace on Earth, Good Will Toward Men. In the last four years, most of us have forgotten what that means. Now is our chance to remember."

She studied the faces in the crowd. "Those men at Fort Jackson . . . I've come to know a number of them. They're good men. They're sick men who need your help. This meeting today was supposed to be about Christmas, about finding the Christmas spirit Savannah seems to have lost.

"I'm asking you to search your hearts. If you do, you'll see the joy of Christmas is still there. It's always been there, deep down inside you. You've just forgotten how to reach it. If you want to find that joy, if you want to get back the spirit of Christmas, you can do it very simply. You can help those men at the fort."

For long, weighty moments, no one spoke. The crowd just stared at her and didn't say a word. Her heart sank like a stone inside her. She hadn't reached them. They were as stubborn and unbending as she had been. Nothing she had said had done an ounce of good. Fighting the sting of tears, Angel walked back up the aisle, her head held high, glancing neither right nor left. She shoved open the door to the foyer, closed it behind her, and sagged against it.

For a moment she closed her eyes, swamped by feelings of failure. When she opened them again, she saw Josh Coltrane push away from the wall, and her heart starting pounding against her ribs.

"What—what are you doing here?"

He smiled at her softly. "I heard what you said in there. No matter what happens, I'm proud of you for having the courage to say it." His expression was unreadable, yet his dark brown eyes were full of warmth.

Thinking of the night they had shared, Angel glanced away, hoping to hide the color that washed her cheeks. "It didn't do a lick of good."

"You tried. That's all one person can ask of another. It's more than anyone else did." He held open the door and she walked past him out onto the street.

"Willie's better," she said, still unwilling to meet that penetrating gaze. Was he thinking of the night they'd spent together? Was he remembering, as she was trying so very hard not to?

"Your brother's going to be fine. I sent a message to your aunt telling her you and Willie would be home in the morning." His eyes were fastened on her mouth. He looked like he wanted to kiss her.

Her color heightened again as a sliver of heat shimmered through her. Dear God, what the man could do with a single glance. She tried to smile, but all she could think of was Josh. Josh kissing her, Josh touching her.

"Th-thank you for helping Willie . . . and everything else you've done."

"Everything else I've done?" he repeated, taking her arm, urging her forward, pulling her off the boardwalk around a corner out of sight. "Are you thanking me for taking your innocence last night?"

Her face went even hotter. "I—I was thinking about those Confederate soldiers. Last night, I was—"

"What you were last night, my love, was wonderful. We were wonderful, Angel—together. Just the way we were always meant to be."

"What—what are you talking about?"

"I'm telling you that what happened between us proves that we're meant to be together. I love you, Angel. I always have. I'm asking you to marry me."

"M-marry you?"

"That's right. I asked you once before, remember?"

A tight ache rose in her throat. She loved Josh Coltrane. After last night, she realized just how much. "Savannah is my home, Josh. Your home is in the North. I could never be happy there."

He tipped her chin with a long dark finger. "Coltrane Farms is my home. I'm not letting the war drive me away."

"You can't possibly mean to stay—you know the way you'd be treated!"

"In the meeting you said it was time to forget the past, to start thinking about the future. That's what I'm going to do, Angel. I want that future to be with you. I want you to marry me."

Oh, dear God, was it possible? Her heart thrummed crazily to think of it. "You have a fiancée, Josh. What would she have to say about that?"

Amusement crinkled the corners of his dark eyes. "If you mean Sarah Wingate, she isn't my fiancée."

"You told Aunt Ida you were going to marry her."

"I told your aunt I was thinking about marrying her. And what were you doing eavesdropping? I figured you'd finally outgrown that."

"I wasn't eavesdropping. I just happened to overhear what you said."

He grinned. "The truth is I hadn't made up my mind about Sarah, not until I saw you. Then I knew that as much as I cared for her, I didn't love her. I was in love with a fiery-tempered little baggage with long blond hair and freckles on her nose. I've loved her for as long as I can remember."

"Oh, Josh!" Angel went into his arms and he held her tightly against him. Tears burned her eyes and clogged her throat. She loved him so very much.

"Marry me, Angel." A corner of his mouth tipped up. "Let me make you an honest woman."

Angel pulled away, one blond brow arching up. "That's why you made love to me, isn't it? You seduced me on purpose. You thought that once we made love, I—"

"I figured that once we made love, once you knew how good we were together, you wouldn't be able to refuse me."

"Josh Coltrane, you are—" He pulled her back into his arms and kissed her until she was breathless.

"What am I, Angel?"

A warm smile curved her lips. "You're the most wonderful man I've ever known."

"And?" he prodded.

"And I'd be proud to marry you—even if you are a good for nothin' Yankee."

Josh laughed out loud, a richly male, incredibly happy sound. Then he kissed her, long and deep. "We've waited four years," he said. "Let's get married as soon as we can."

A bright smile curved her lips. "How does tomorrow sound?"

Josh hugged her tight against him. "Perfect." As they walked down the street toward the wagon she had driven into town, only thoughts of the men at the fort, the sick men they had failed to help, kept both of them from grinning.

Tonight was her last night at the fort. Angel couldn't say she was sorry to be leaving, but she couldn't deny there was something poignant in spending Christmas Eve at the hospital with the wounded men.

As soon as she and Josh had returned to Fort Jackson, they had helped the patients finish decorating their towering Christmas tree. Before they'd left town, Josh had stopped at the dry goods store. He had bought her the beautiful length of plum velvet she had been admiring the first day he had seen her and a dozen miniature carved wooden soldiers as a Christmas gift for Willie. He had also purchased every candle Mr. Whistler had in stock.

The huge pine tree glowed with them now, and so did the wreaths on the tables. He'd also bought yards of red ribbon and the men had made big red bows, which hung on the walls and brightened the mantel. Small red bows were tied to the branches of the tree.

"Isn't it beautiful?" Willie said, staring at the imposing tree with his big, bright blue eyes.

"It's wonderful," Angel said.

Josh smiled. "For the first time, it really feels like Christmas."

There was a lighter atmosphere on the ward tonight, yet it didn't stop the dull moans of pain that occasionally rose from the beds, or the fever and chills that tortured a patient in the grips of malaria.

It didn't ease the hurting, but it soothed the men's weary spirits. Angel guessed it would have to be enough.

"Miss Angel?" Private Vogel approached her as she sat by Willie's bed. "Ben Weatherby asked if he could speak to you a moment."

"Of course." The red-haired orderly led her to Corporal Weatherby's cot and she sat down beside him.

"Hello, Benjamin."

"Hello, Miss Angel." He smiled at her shyly. "Me and the boys . . . well, we just wanted to wish you a Merry Christmas. Dr. Coltrane told us what you done, standin' up for us and all."

"It wasn't anything, Ben. I didn't get the medicine you need."

"It might not be anythin' to you, ma'am, but it was somethin' special to us. We wanted you to have this . . . somethin' for you to remember us by." He handed her a small, carved, wooden angel. The face looked remarkably similar to her own. "You're our Christmas Angel, ma'am. Ain't none of us ever gonna forget you."

She blinked to hold back tears, but they burned her eyes just the same, and a hard lump clogged her throat. She glanced around the room and saw that the soldiers were watching. "Thank you, Ben." She smiled at the men and brushed a tear from her cheek. "Thank you all. I hope next year you'll all be home for Christmas."

No one said a word, but there were tears in more than one man's eyes.

"Dr. Coltrane!" someone shouted. "Hey, Doc, you gotta come see this!"

Wondering what the commotion could be, Angel joined Josh at the door. They went outside and across the yard, then stopped dead still at the gate leading into the fort.

Dozens of candles lit the night. Men and women in

wagons rolled down the road and men carried boxes tied to the backs of their horses. It seemed half the people in Savannah had come to the fort this night.

Kirby Fields rode at the front. As the wagons drew near, he left the rest of the group and rode ahead, stopping his horse just a few feet away from where they stood. He tossed down the box he carried, which landed in the dirt at Josh's feet.

"We brought the stuff you wanted. Angel was right in what she said. It's Christmas. God meant for men to share their blessings with those in need of them. There's peace again in this land and we should be grateful." He pointed toward the box he had thrown on the ground. "Those medicines you needed . . . we brung 'em all back, leastwise all we still had. Use 'em to help your sick men."

Josh looked up at the man who had once been his friend. The muscles contracted in his throat; he had to swallow before he could speak. "Thank you, Kirby. You'll never know how much this means." He turned as the others approached, watched in silence as each man rode up and dropped off his load of supplies. "Thank you for what you're doing. God bless you. God bless all of you."

When all the supplies were unloaded, Kirby tipped his hat to Angel and extended a hand to Josh. "Merry Christmas," he said.

Angel smiled, feeling an ache in her throat. "Merry Christmas, Kirby."

By the end of the hour, the supplies had all been carried inside and put away—or put to use where they were needed. Only one mysterious box remained.

"What's in that?" Angel asked.

Josh just smiled. "Come on, I'll show you." Carrying the box over to Lieutenant Langley's bedside, Josh bent down next to the man with the paralyzed legs and lifted the lid.

"This is for you, Lieutenant Langley. It still has to be assembled but once it is, you can get up out of that bed. I didn't want to mention it until it actually got here, just in case it never made it."

The brooding, dark-eyed soldier looked up. "What the devil is it?"

"A chair on wheels. A wheelchair," Josh said. "You can get around on your own, once we get it put together."

Lieutenant Langley stared at the pieces in the box, then looked up at Angel. "I got a letter from my girl. Someone wrote to her, told her I'd been shot. She knows I can't walk. She says she doesn't care, says she wants me just the same." His eyes held hers, hope and fear mingled in his expression. "Doc says I can probably still have children. Do you think, ma'am . . . do you think a woman could still love a man who had to sit in one of these?"

Oh, dear Lord. Angel imagined how she would feel if the man were Josh. "I'd love him," she said. "I wouldn't baby him, mind you. I'd make him carry his own weight, but I'd love him. I'd marry him and I'd give him dozens of babies."

Lieutenant Langley gave her a smile, the first she had seen. It was amazing how handsome he was. "Thank you, ma'am. Thank you, Doc, and . . . Merry Christmas."

"Merry Christmas, Lieutenant," Josh said softly, leading Angel away before the lieutenant could see the tears shimmering in her eyes. He guided her to the door, pointed to the mistletoe hanging above it, took her in his arms, and kissed her so thoroughly her knees went weak.

"Merry Christmas, Angel," he said.

Angel grinned. "Merry Christmas, Yank," she said, and a cheer went up from the men.